A  ORIGINAL

ADVENTURE TIME

SUGARY SHORTS
VOLUME 4

ROSS RICHIE CEO & Founder • MATT GAGNON Editor-in-Chief • FILIP SABLIK President of Publishing & Marketing • STEPHEN CHRISTY President of Development • LANCE KREITER VP of Licensing & Merchandising • PHIL BARBARO VP of Finance
ARUNE SINGH VP of Marketing • BRYCE CARLSON Managing Editor • MEL CAYLO Marketing Manager • SCOTT NEWMAN Production Design Manager • KATE HENNING Operations Manager • SIERRA HAHN Senior Editor • DAFNA PLEBAN Editor, Talent Development
SHANNON WATTERS Editor • ERIC HARBURN Editor • WHITNEY LEOPARD Editor • CAMERON CHITTOCK Editor • CHRIS ROSA Associate Editor • MATTHEW LEVINE Associate Editor • SOPHIE PHILIPS-ROBERTS Assistant Editor
AMANDA LaFRANCO Executive Assistant • KATALINA HOLLAND Editorial Administrative Assistant • JILLIAN CRAB Production Designer • MICHELLE ANKLEY Production Designer • KARA LEOPARD Production Designer • MARIE KRUPINA Production Designer
GRACE PARK Production Design Assistant • CHELSEA ROBERTS Production Design Assistant • ELIZABETH LOUGHRIDGE Accounting Coordinator • STEPHANIE HOCUTT Social Media Coordinator • JOSÉ MEZA Event Coordinator • HOLLY AITCHISON Operations Coordinator
MEGAN CHRISTOPHER Operations Assistant • RODRIGO HERNANDEZ Mailroom Assistant • MORGAN PERRY Direct Market Representative • CAT O'GRADY Marketing Assistant • LIZ ALMENDAREZ Accounting Administrative Assistant • CORNELIA TZANA Administrative Assistant

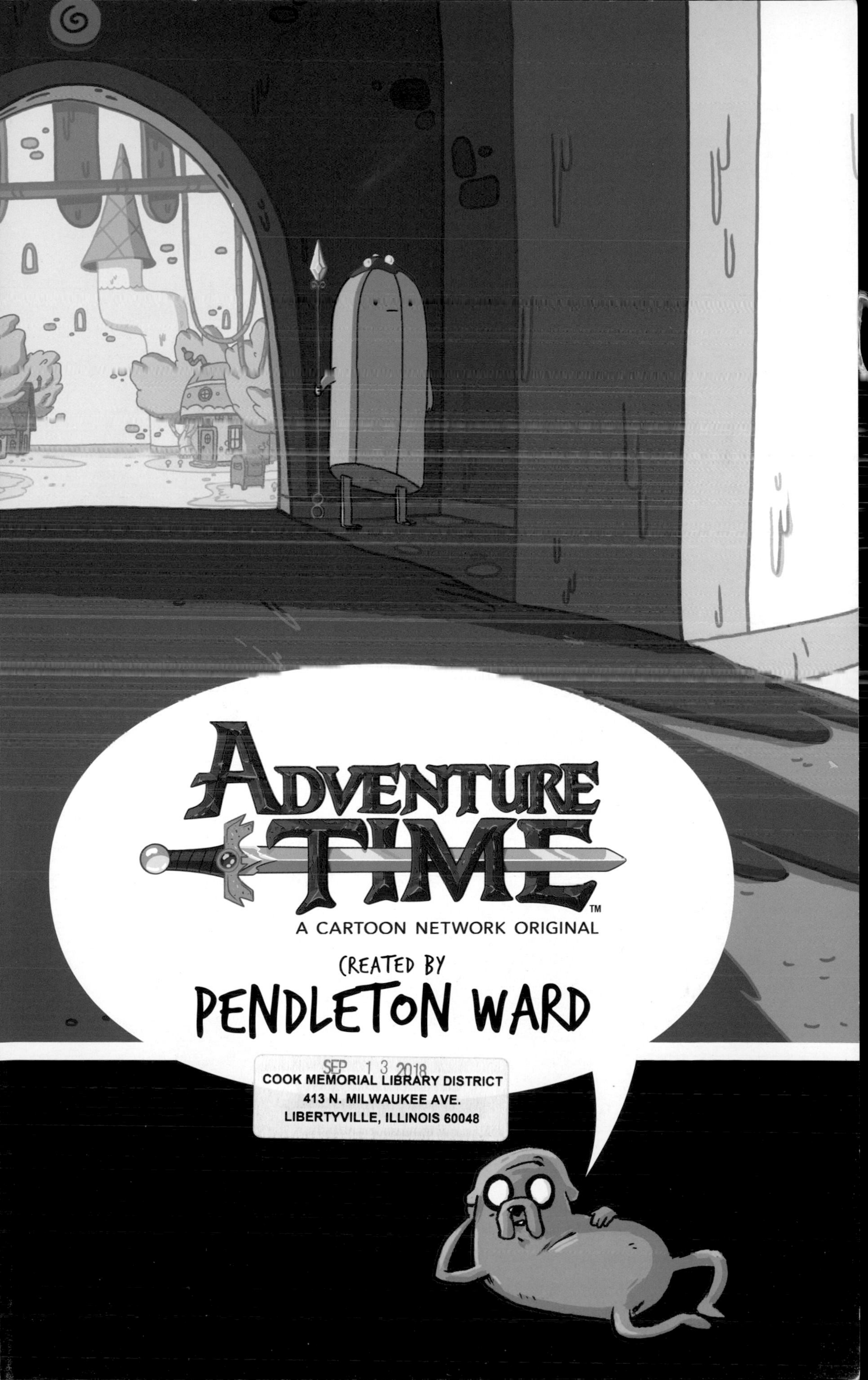
ADVENTURE TIME™
A CARTOON NETWORK ORIGINAL
CREATED BY
PENDLETON WARD

"DISH BEST SERVED GROSS"
Written by
JOSH TIERNEY
Illustrated by
MICHAEL DIALYNAS

"LEMONGRAB'S MAKEOVER"
Written by
SARA ELLIS & SAM ELLIS
Illustrated by
SAM ELLIS

"MYSTERY PLOP"
Written and Illustrated by
KAT LEYH

"GRAND PRIZE"
Written and Illustrated by
MICHELLE NUNNELLY
with Heather Nunnelly

"SAME MATH...DIFFERENT DAY"
Written and Illustrated by
TRAVIS J. HILL

"WORST DAY"
Written by
JAY EDIDIN
Illustrated by
KEL MCDONALD

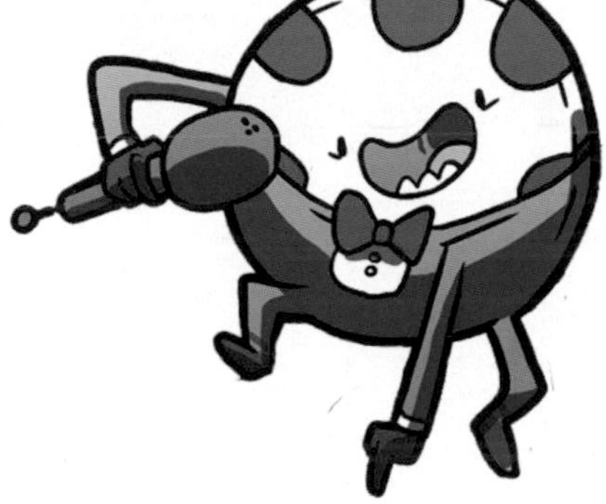

"GROCERY KINGDOM"
Written and Illustrated by
KAT LEYH

"AXE BEFORE TALKING"
Written and Illustrated by
JAKE WYATT

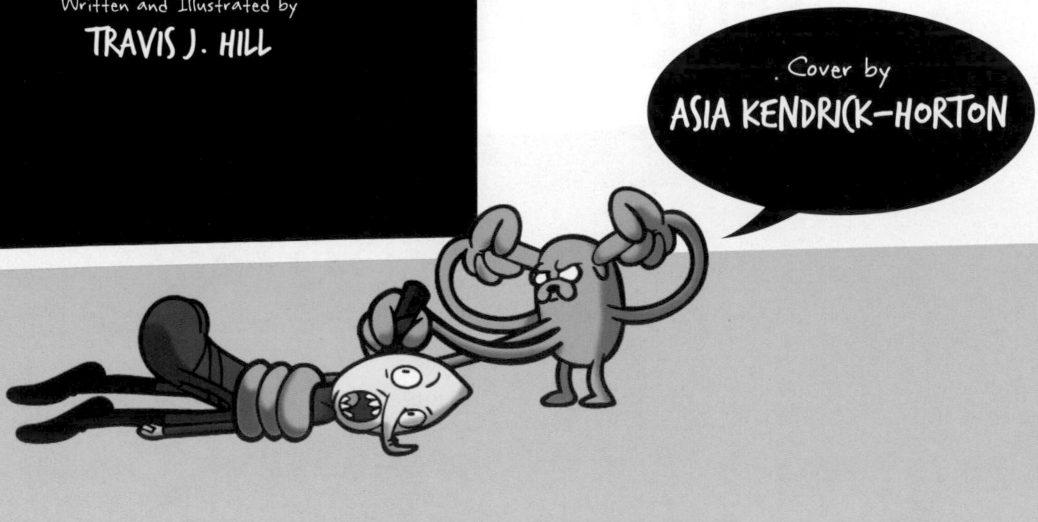
Cover by
ASIA KENDRICK-HORTON

"DAD OLYMPICS"
Written and Illustrated by
PHILLIP JACOBSON

"SIR BMO"
Written and Illustrated by
IAN MCGINTY
Colored by Fred C. Stresing

"OPEN MIC"
Written & Colored by
SHAWN STEVEN STRUBLE
Illustrated by
BEN SEARS

"TIGER AND THE MOON"
Written and Illustrated by
COLIN ANDERSEN

"FINDERS KEEPERS"
Written by
DAVID SCHEIDT
Illustrated by
JESS SMART SMILEY

"WATER STRIKE"
Written and Illustrated by
MADY MARTIN

"SICK DAY"
Written and Illustrated by
COLIN ANDERSEN

"FLOWERS FOR PAULTICORE"
Written by
DALE BERAN
Illustrated by
DAVID HELLMAN

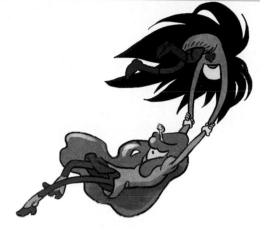

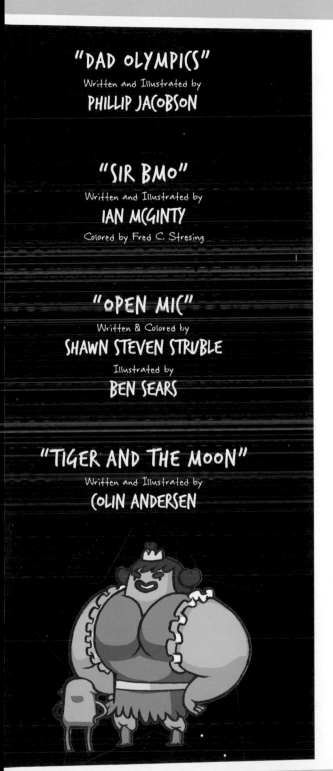

Designers
KARA LEOPARD
& GRACE PARK

Associate Editor
MATTHEW LEVINE

Editor
WHITNEY LEOPARD

With Special Thanks to Alex Galer, and A Very Special Thanks Marisa Marionakis, Janet No, Curtis Lelash, Conrad Montgomery, Meghan Bradley, Kelly Crews, Scott Malchus, Adam Muto and the wonderful folks at Cartoon Network.

DISH BEST SERVED GROSS

ISSUE TWENTY NINE, COVER D
CAREY PIETSCH

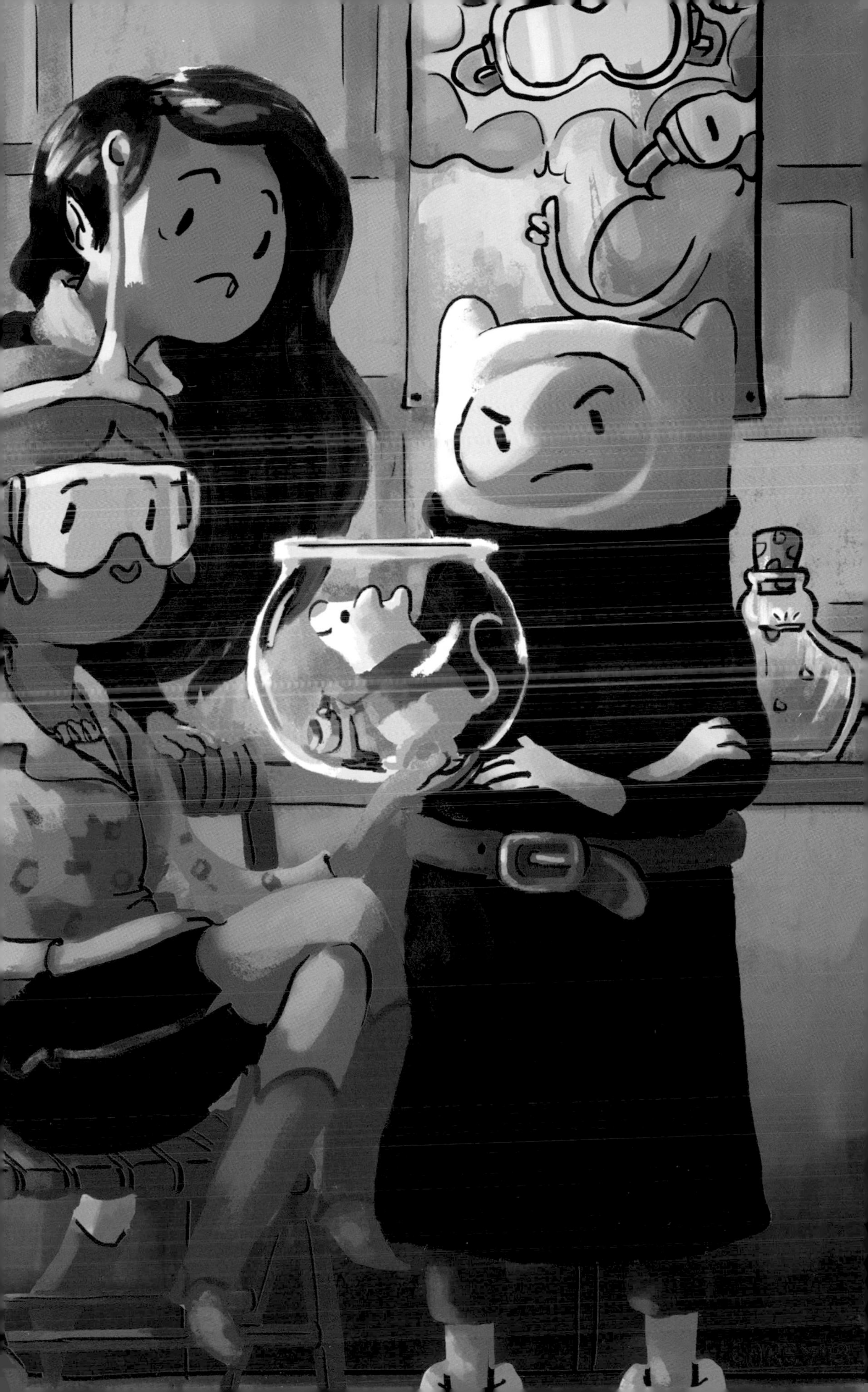

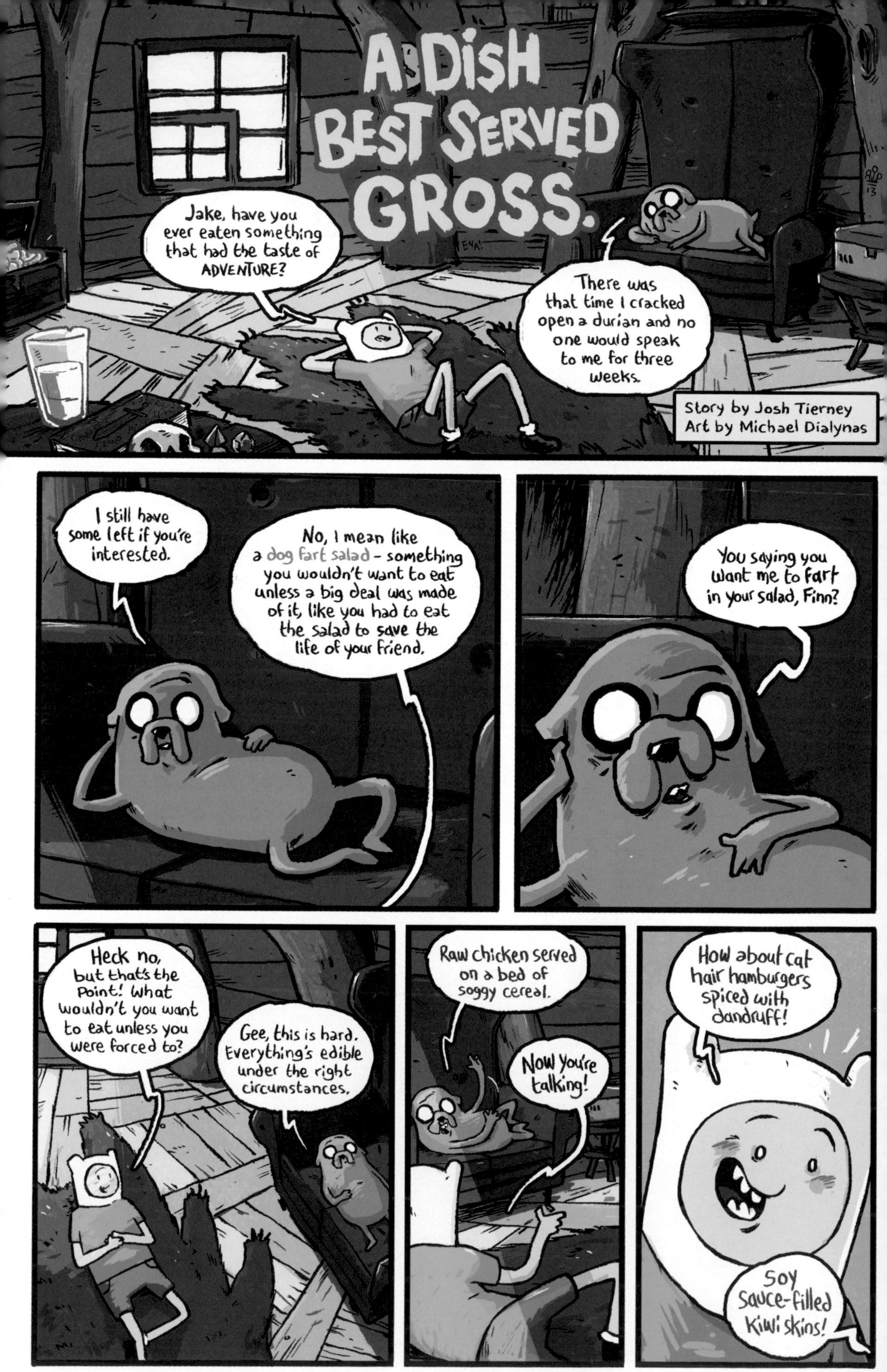

A DISH BEST SERVED GROSS.
Jake, have you ever eaten something that had the taste of ADVENTURE?
There was that time I cracked open a durian and no one would speak to me for three weeks.
Story by Josh Tierney
Art by Michael Dialynas
I still have some left if you're interested.
No, I mean like a dog fart salad - something you wouldn't want to eat unless a big deal was made of it, like you had to eat the salad to save the life of your friend.
You saying you want me to fart in your salad, Finn?
Heck no, but that's the point! What wouldn't you want to eat unless you were forced to?
Gee, this is hard. Everything's edible under the right circumstances.
Raw chicken served on a bed of soggy cereal.
Now you're talking!
How about cat hair hamburgers spiced with dandruff!
Soy sauce-filled kiwi skins!

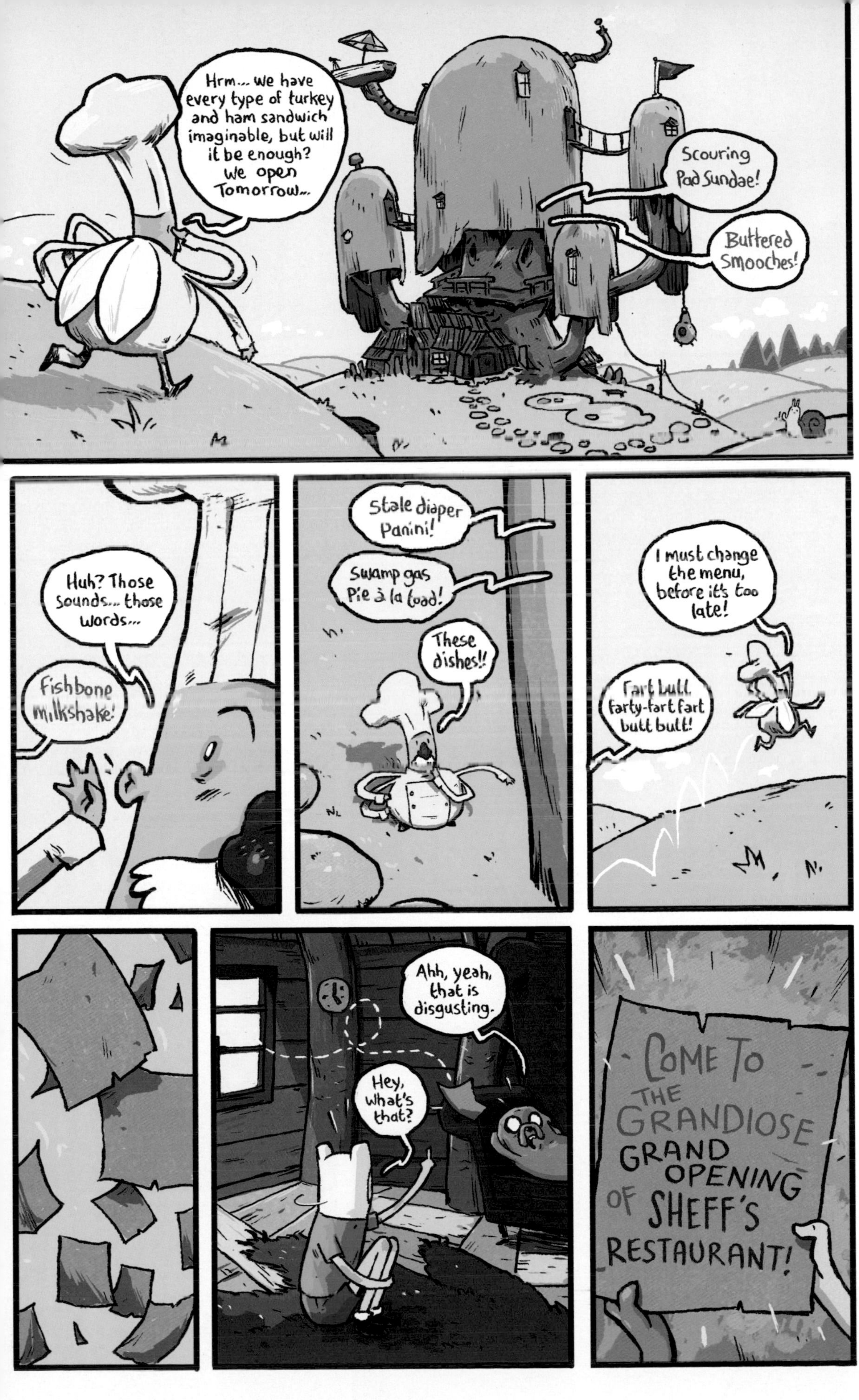
Hrm... we have every type of turkey and ham sandwich imaginable, but will it be enough? We open Tomorrow...
Scouring Pad Sundae!
Buttered Smooches!
Huh? Those sounds... those words...
Fishbone milkshake!
Stale diaper Panini!
Swamp gas Pie à la toad!
These dishes!!
I must change the menu, before it's too late!
Fart butt farty-fart fart butt butt!
Ahh, yeah, that is disgusting.
Hey, what's that?
COME TO THE GRANDIOSE GRAND OPENING OF SHEFF'S RESTAURANT!

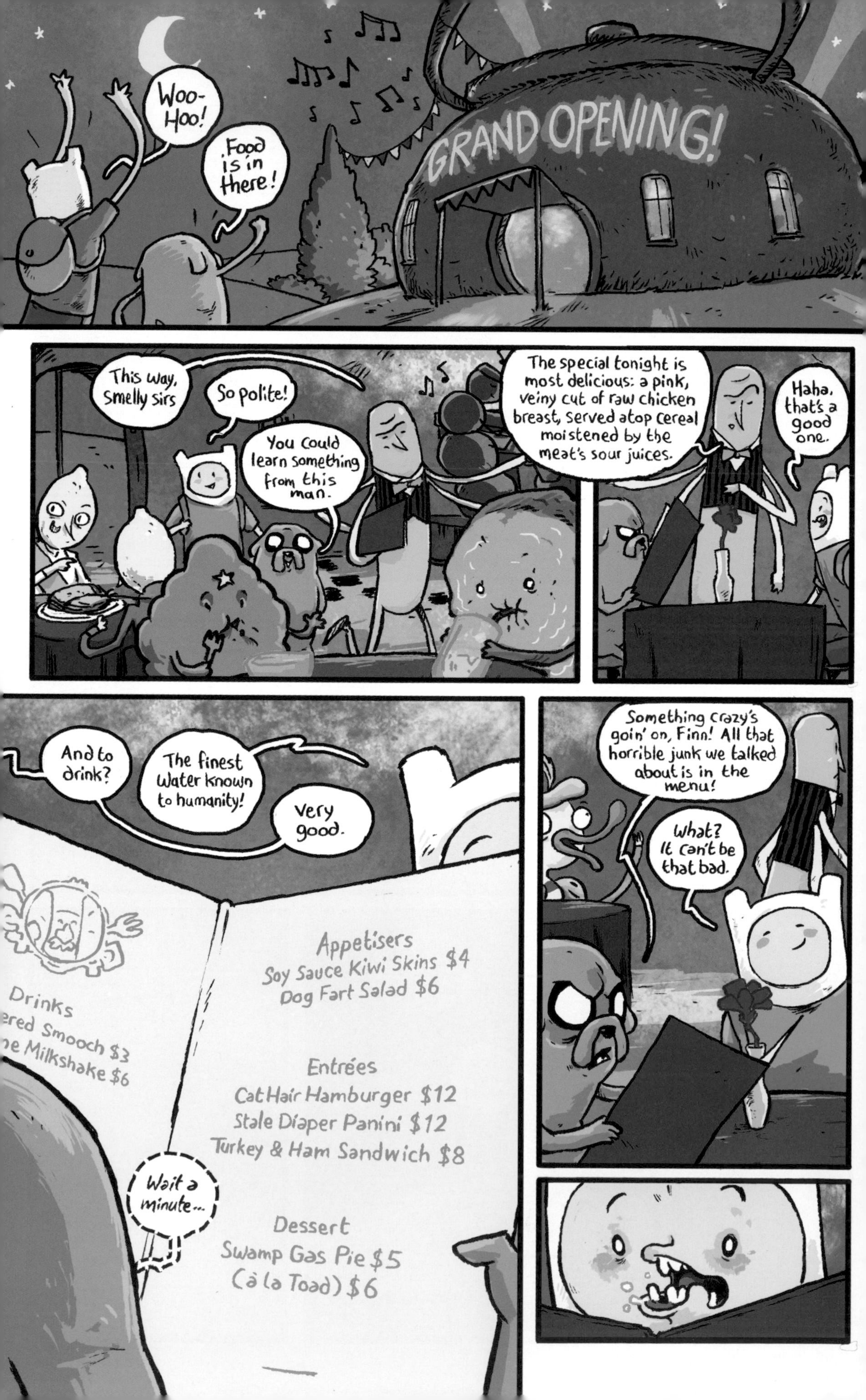

Woo-Hoo!
Food is in there!
GRAND OPENING!
This way, smelly sirs
So polite!
You could learn something from this man.
The special tonight is most delicious: a pink, veiny cut of raw chicken breast, served atop cereal moistened by the meat's sour juices.
Haha, that's a good one.
And to drink?
The finest water known to humanity!
Very good.
Drinks
ered Smooch $3
ne Milkshake $6
Appetisers
Soy Sauce Kiwi Skins $4
Dog Fart Salad $6
Entrées
Cat Hair Hamburger $12
Stale Diaper Panini $12
Turkey & Ham Sandwich $8
Dessert
Swamp Gas Pie $5
(à la Toad) $6
Wait a minute...
Something crazy's goin' on, Finn! All that horrible junk we talked about is in the menu!
What? It can't be that bad.

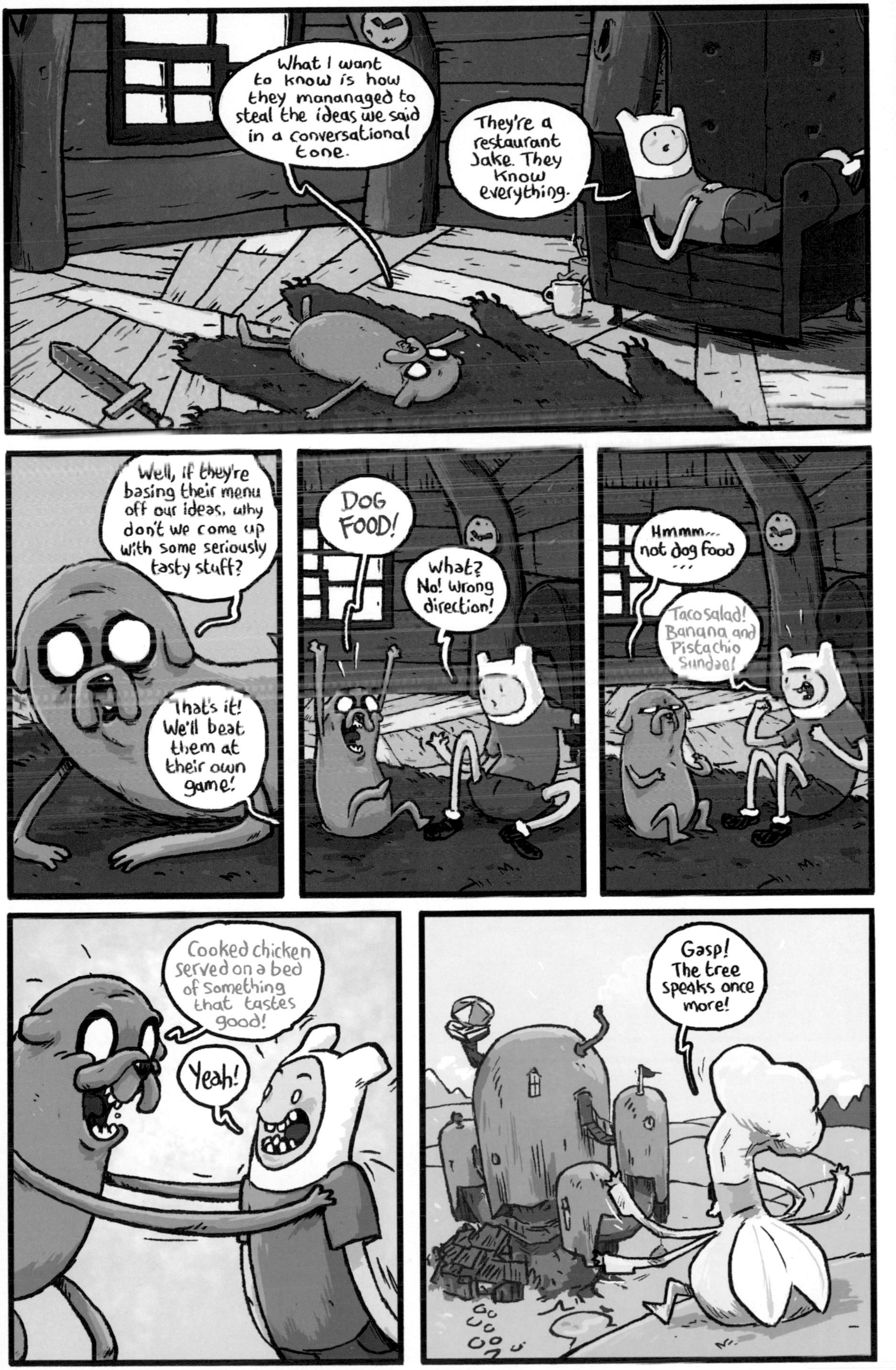

What I want to know is how they mananaged to steal the ideas we said in a conversational tone.
They're a restaurant Jake. They know everything.
Well, if they're basing their menu off our ideas, why don't we come up with some seriously tasty stuff?
That's it! We'll beat them at their own game!
DOG FOOD!
What? No! Wrong direction!
Hmmm... not dog food ...
Taco salad! Banana and Pistachio Sundae!
Cooked chicken served on a bed of something that tastes good!
Yeah!
Gasp! The tree speaks once more!

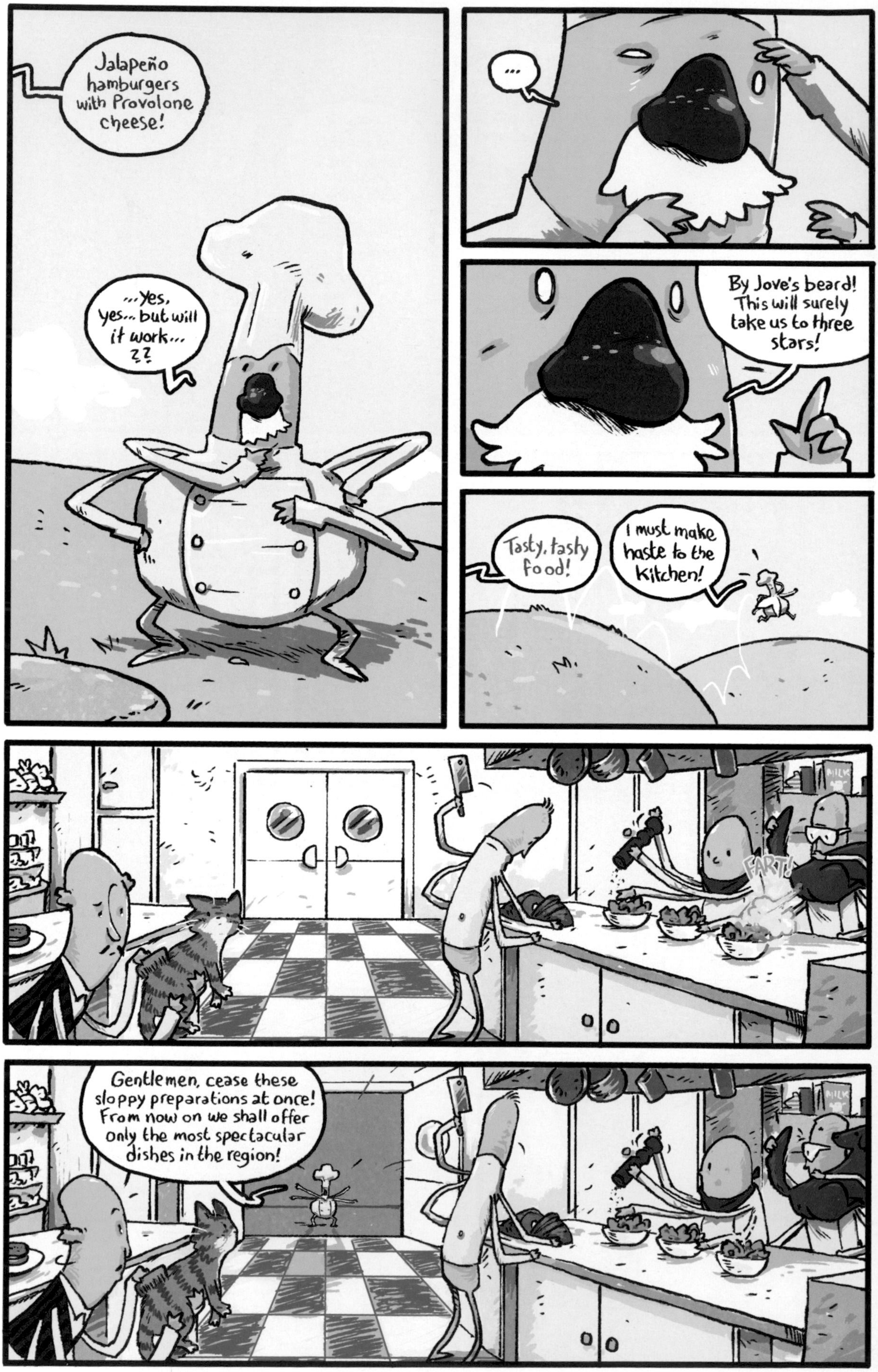
Jalapeño hamburgers with Provolone cheese!
...yes, yes... but will it work... ??
...
By Jove's beard! This will surely take us to three stars!
Tasty, tasty food!
I must make haste to the kitchen!
FART!
Gentlemen, cease these sloppy preparations at once! From now on we shall offer only the most spectacular dishes in the region!

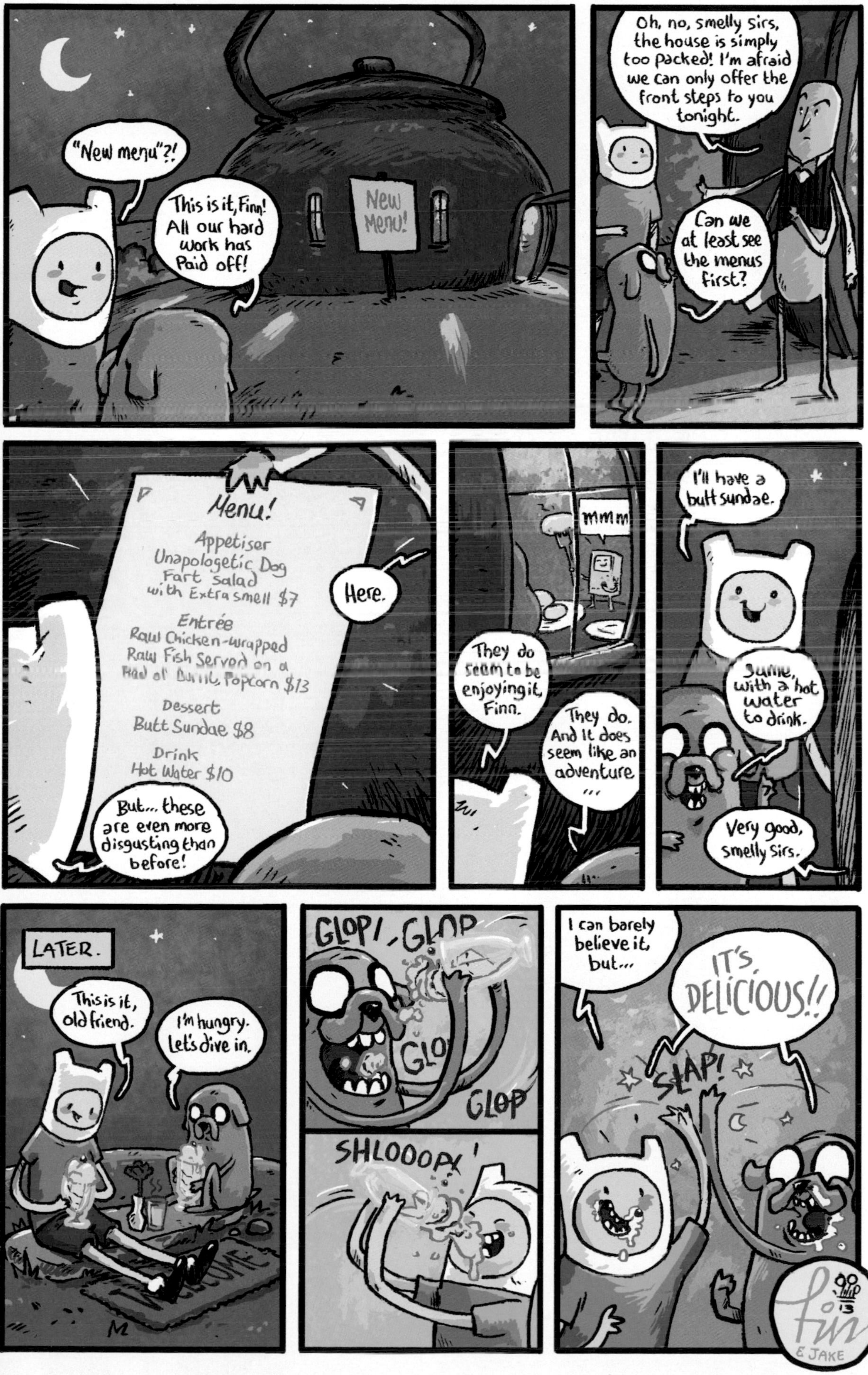
"New menu"?!
This is it, Finn! All our hard work has Paid off!
New Menu!
Oh, no, smelly sirs, the house is simply too packed! I'm afraid we can only offer the front steps to you tonight.
Can we at least see the menus first?
Here.
Menu!
Appetiser
Unapologetic Dog Fart salad with Extra smell $7
Entrée
Raw Chicken-wrapped Raw Fish Served on a
Popcorn $13
Dessert
Butt Sundae $8
Drink
Hot Water $10
But... these are even more disgusting than before!
mmm
They do seem to be enjoying it, Finn.
They do. And it does seem like an adventure ...
I'll have a butt sundae.
with a hot water to drink.
Very good, smelly Sirs.
LATER.
This is it, old friend.
I'm hungry. Let's dive in.
GLOP! GLOP
GLOP
GLOP
SHLOOOP!
I can barely believe it, but...
IT'S DELICIOUS!!
SLAP!
'13
FIN & JAKE

LEMONGRAB'S MAKEOVER

ISSUE THIRTY ONE, COVER B
SAM ELLIS

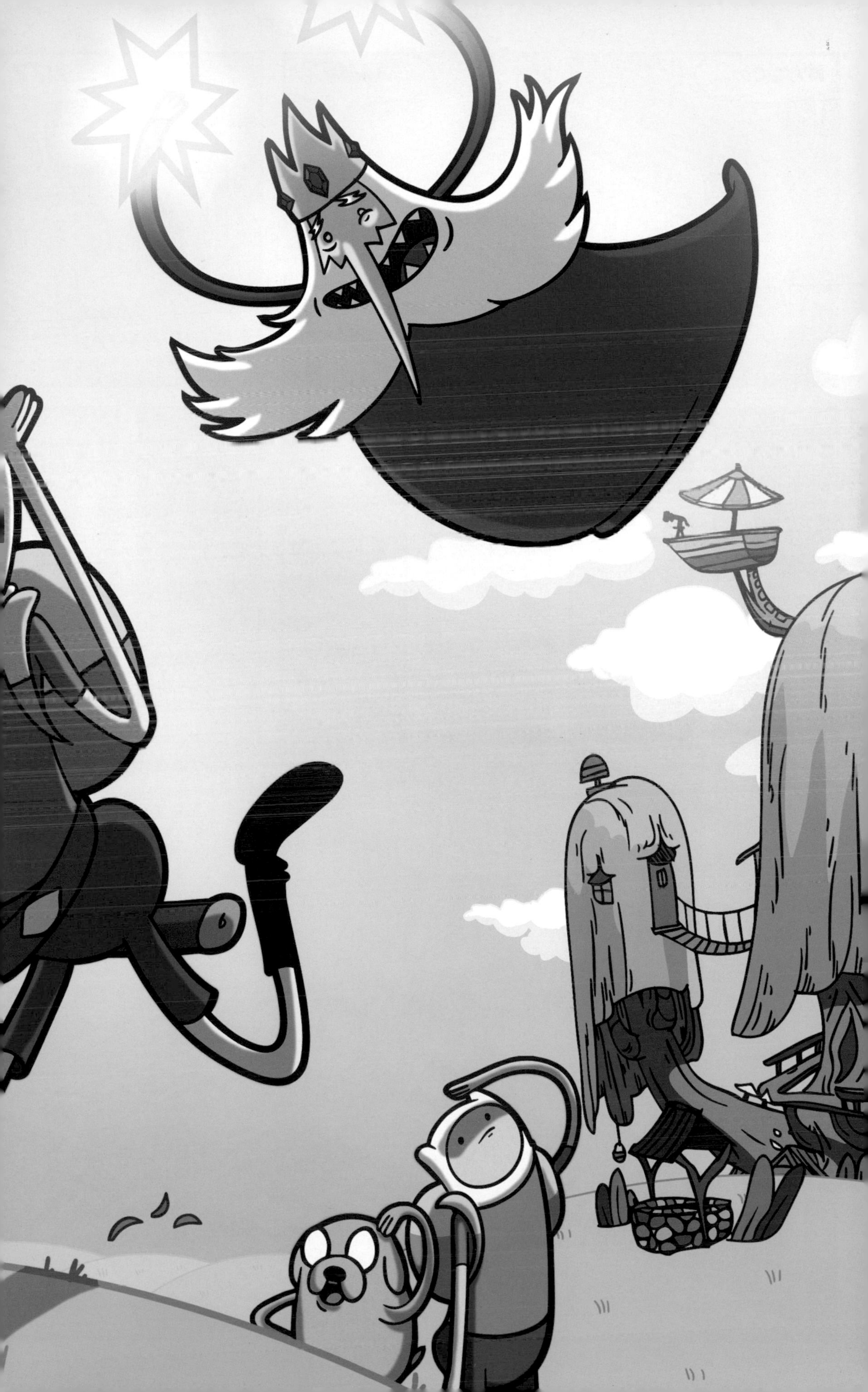

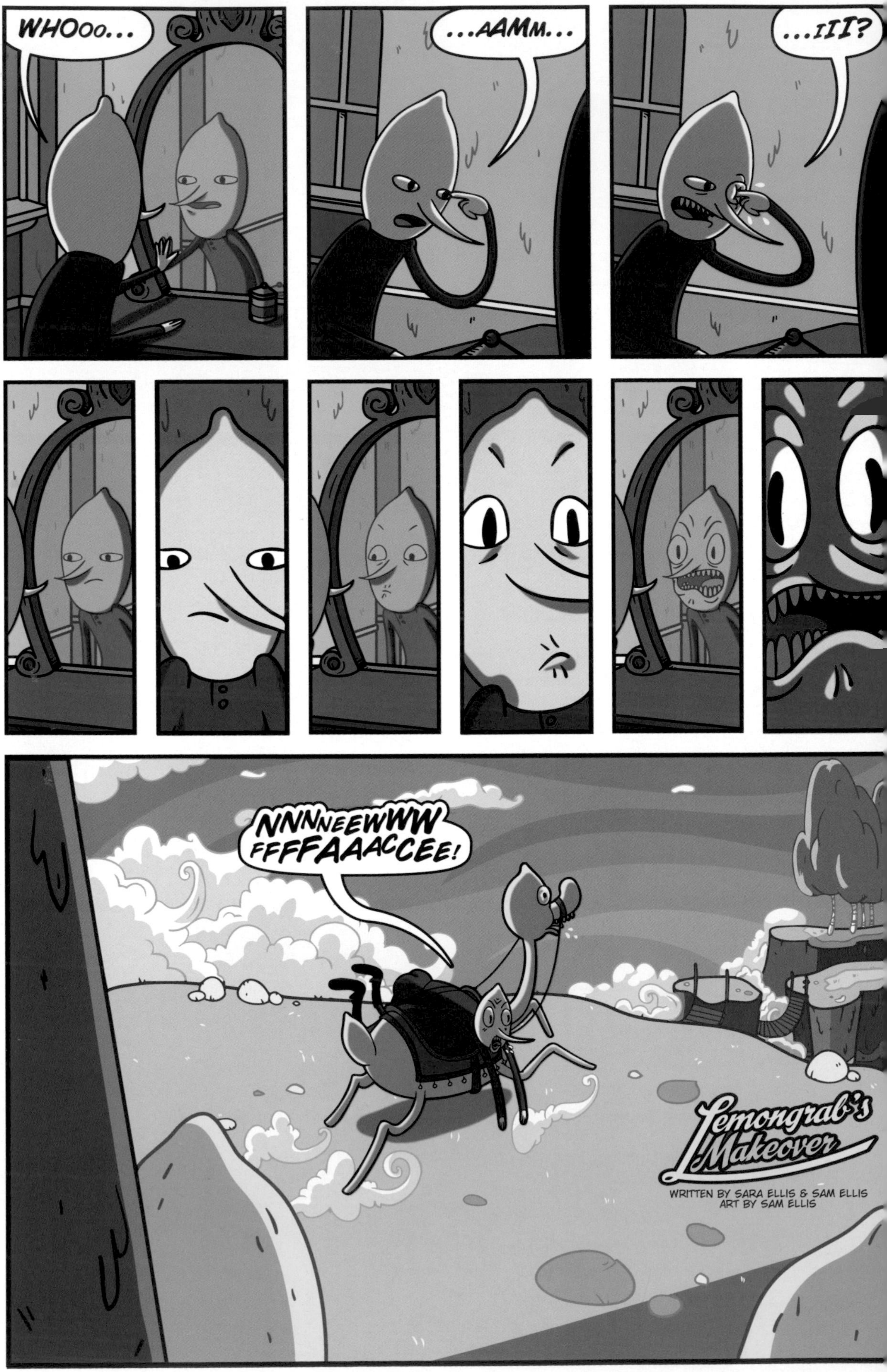
WHOoo...
...AAMM...
...III?
NNNNEEWWW FFFFAAACCEE!
Lemongrab's Makeover
WRITTEN BY SARA ELLIS & SAM ELLIS
ART BY SAM ELLIS

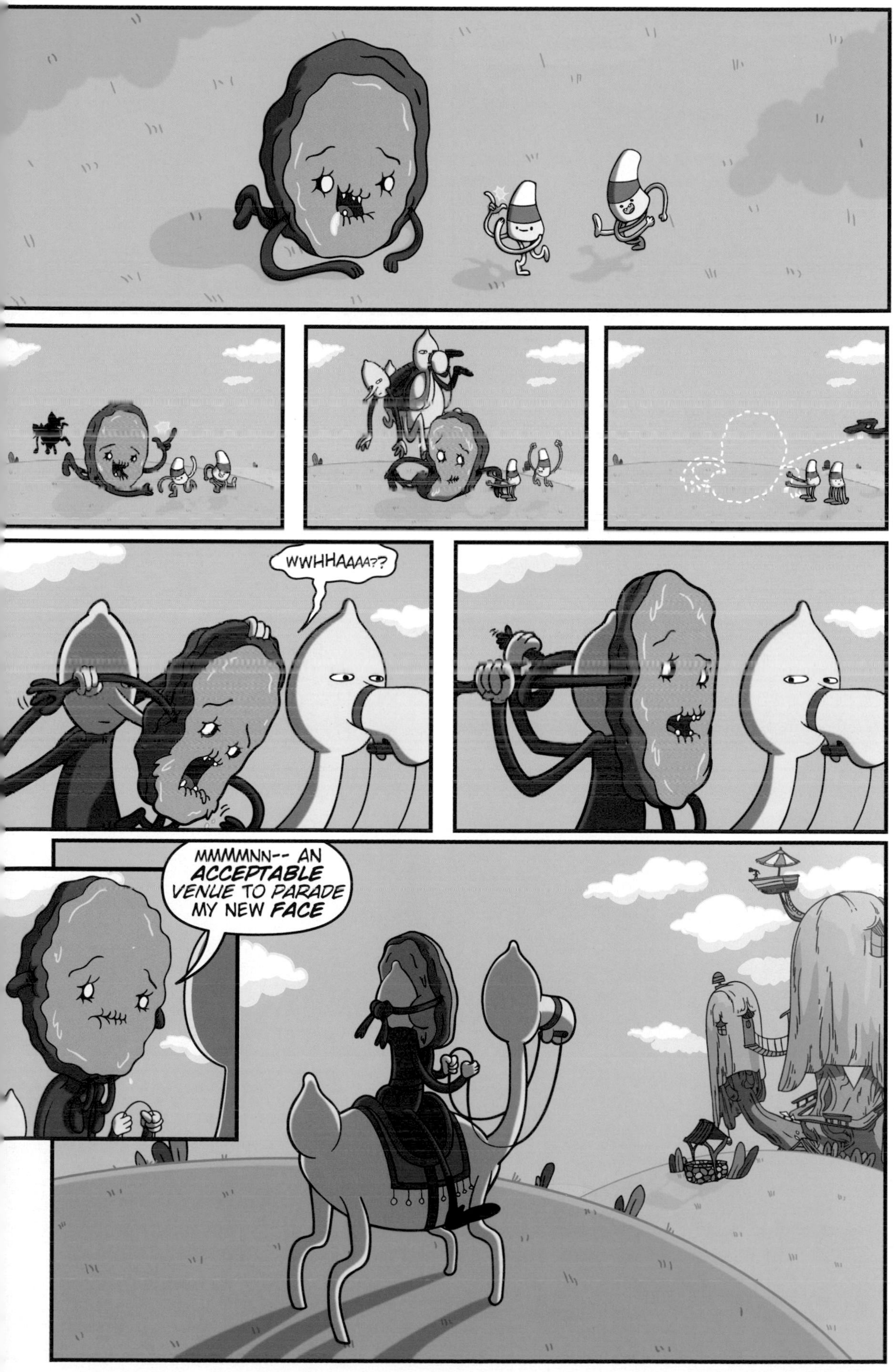
WWHHAAAA??
MMMMNN-- AN ACCEPTABLE VENUE TO PARADE MY NEW FACE

EVERYONE WINS AT *BURRITO* JENGA

KNOCK

KNOCK

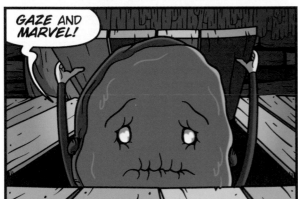

GAZE AND *MARVEL!*

CINNAMON BUN?

HHHEEELLLPPP MMEEEEE...

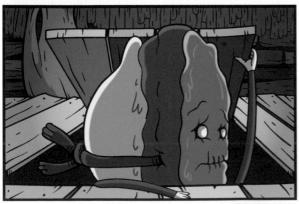

LEMONGRAB?

AAH, SICK *DUDE!*

LET HIM *GO!*

AAAAAAAAAAAAAAAAAAAAAAAAAAAA MY *FACE!* MY *FACE!* YOU MUST *REPLACE* WHAT HAS *BEEN* TAKEN!

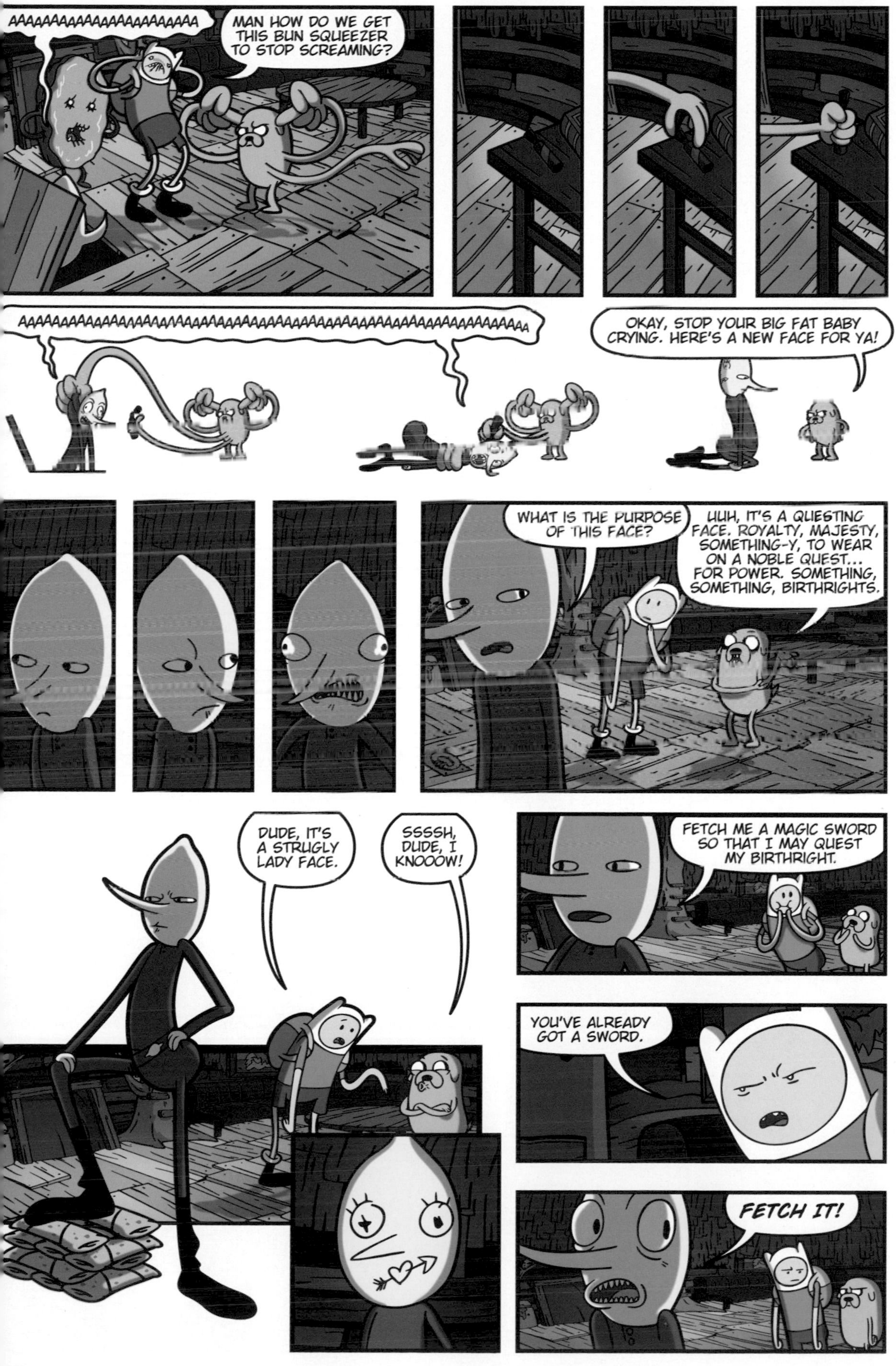
AAAAAAAAAAAAAAAAAAAAAAAA
MAN HOW DO WE GET THIS BUN SQUEEZER TO STOP SCREAMING?
AAAAAAAAAAAAAAAAAAAAAAAAAAAAAAAAAAAAAAAAAAAAAAAAAAAAAAAAAAAAAAAAAAAAAAAAA
OKAY, STOP YOUR BIG FAT BABY CRYING. HERE'S A NEW FACE FOR YA!
WHAT IS THE PURPOSE OF THIS FACE?
UUH, IT'S A QUESTING FACE. ROYALTY, MAJESTY, SOMETHING-Y, TO WEAR ON A NOBLE QUEST... FOR POWER. SOMETHING, SOMETHING, BIRTHRIGHTS.
DUDE, IT'S A STRUGLY LADY FACE.
SSSSH, DUDE, I KNOOOW!
FETCH ME A MAGIC SWORD SO THAT I MAY QUEST MY BIRTHRIGHT.
YOU'VE ALREADY GOT A SWORD.
FETCH IT!

SO ARE WE DITCHING HIM?

SURE THING, BUDDY.

I WANT A QUESTING FACE.

CHEESE AND BROS, CHEESE AND BROS, NOTHING *BETTER* THAN SOME FUN WITH YOUR *CHEESE AND BROS...*

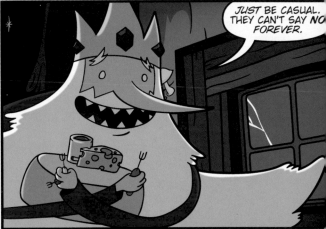

JUST BE CASUAL. THEY CAN'T SAY *NO* FOREVER.

HEY, FELLAS. WANNA DO SOME FONDUE UP IN THE BOAT? I BROUGHT THE CHEESE, WE JUST NEED A BAGUETTE AND--

...SAUSAGES.

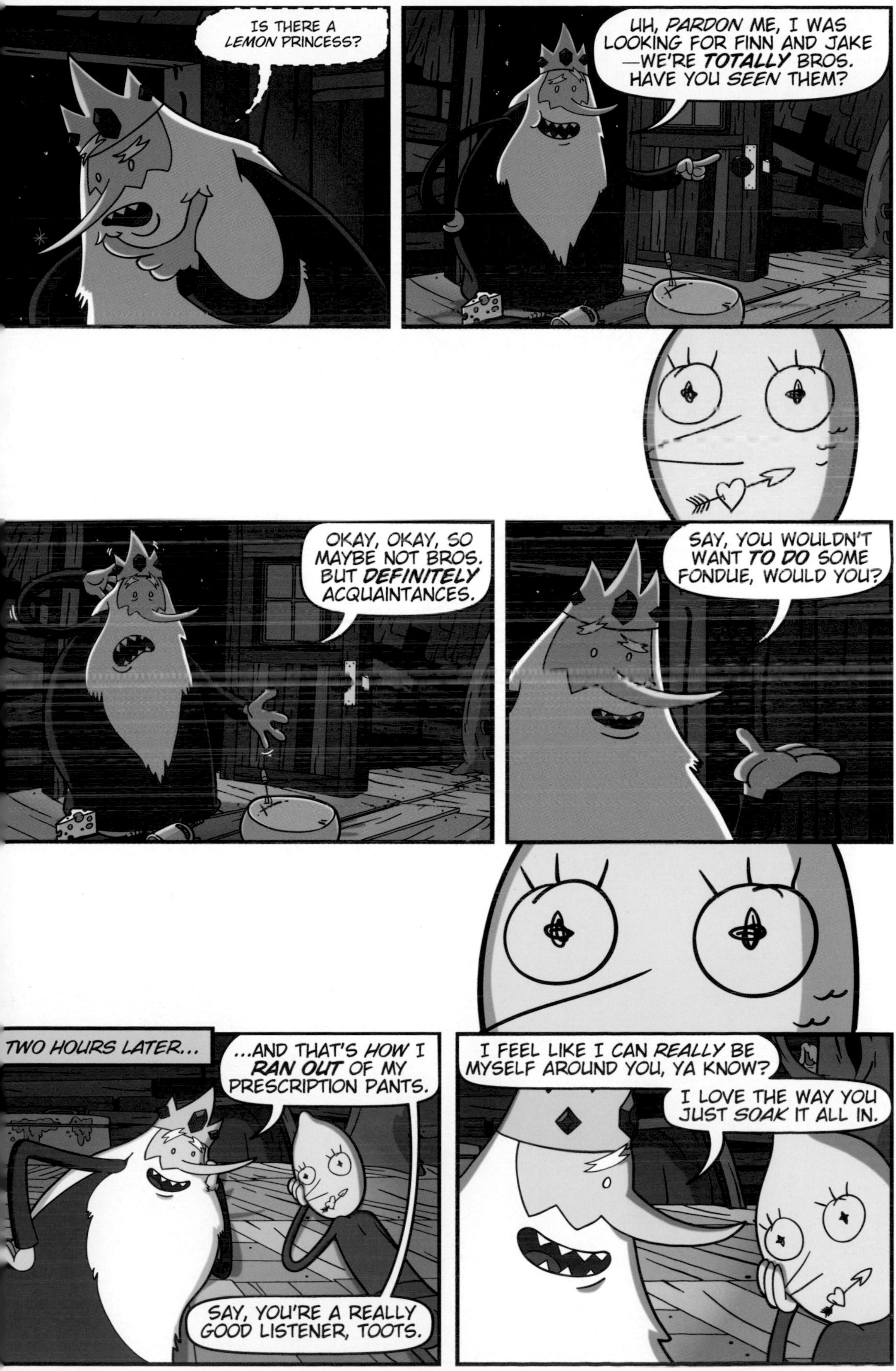
IS THERE A LEMON PRINCESS?
UH, PARDON ME, I WAS LOOKING FOR FINN AND JAKE —WE'RE TOTALLY BROS. HAVE YOU SEEN THEM?
OKAY, OKAY, SO MAYBE NOT BROS. BUT DEFINITELY ACQUAINTANCES.
SAY, YOU WOULDN'T WANT TO DO SOME FONDUE, WOULD YOU?
TWO HOURS LATER...
...AND THAT'S HOW I RAN OUT OF MY PRESCRIPTION PANTS.
SAY, YOU'RE A REALLY GOOD LISTENER, TOOTS.
I FEEL LIKE I CAN REALLY BE MYSELF AROUND YOU, YA KNOW?
I LOVE THE WAY YOU JUST SOAK IT ALL IN.

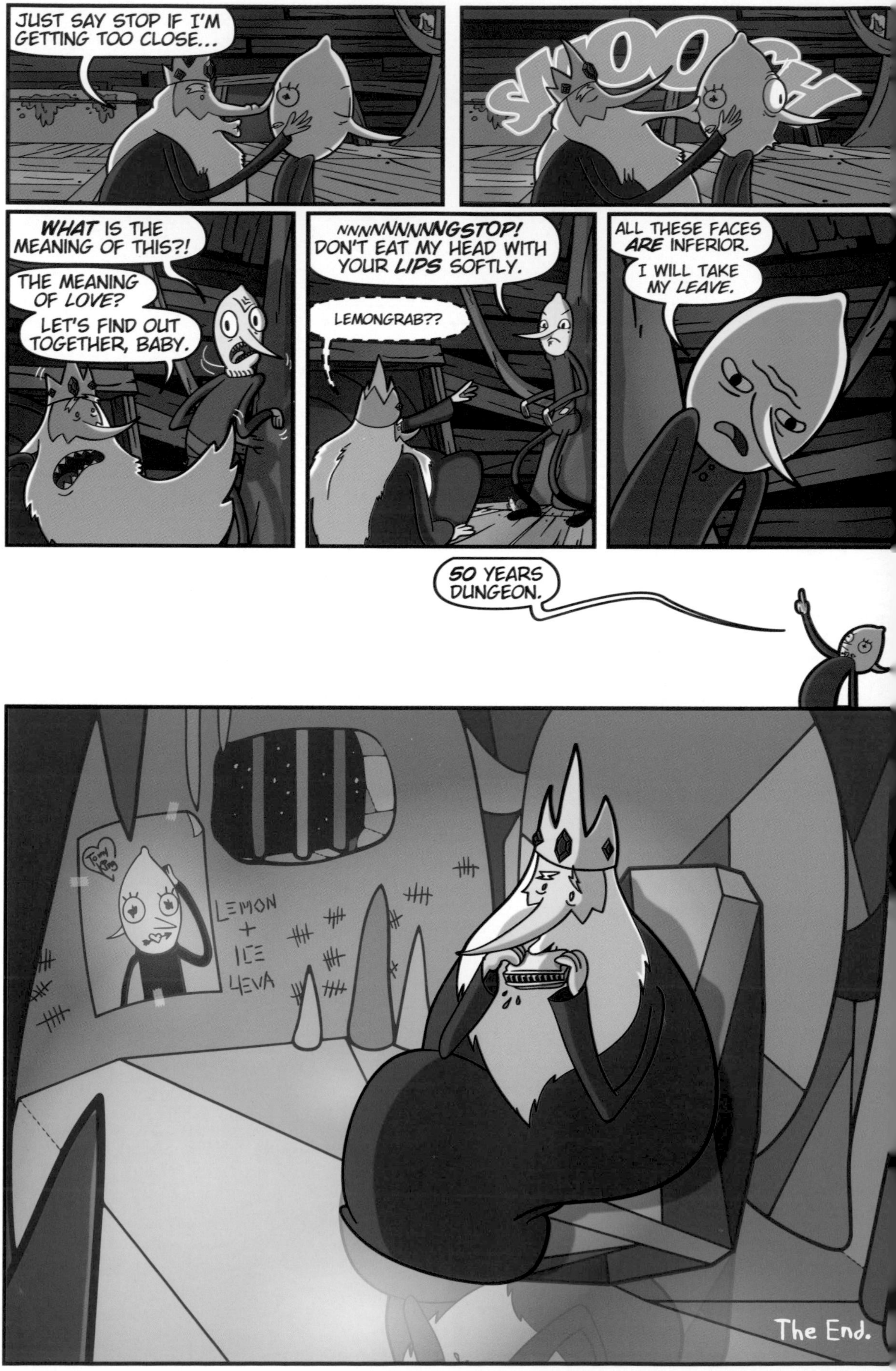
JUST SAY STOP IF I'M GETTING TOO CLOSE...
SMOOCH
WHAT IS THE MEANING OF THIS?!
THE MEANING OF LOVE?
LET'S FIND OUT TOGETHER, BABY.
NNNNNNNNNGSTOP! DON'T EAT MY HEAD WITH YOUR LIPS SOFTLY.
LEMONGRAB??
ALL THESE FACES ARE INFERIOR.
I WILL TAKE MY LEAVE.
50 YEARS DUNGEON.
LEMON + ICE 4EVA
The End.

MYSTERY PLOP

ISSUE THIRTY TWO COVER B
TAIT HOWARD

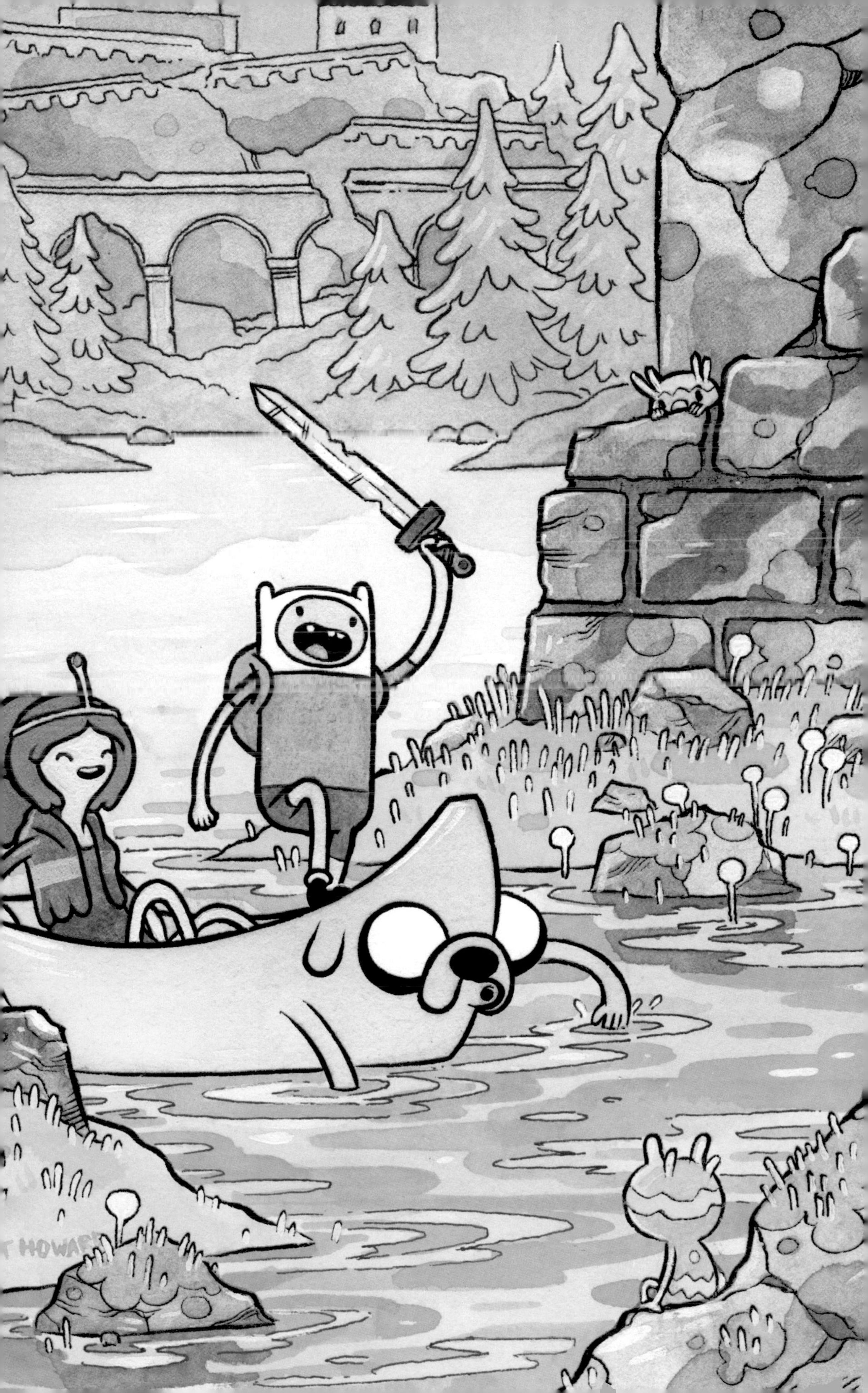

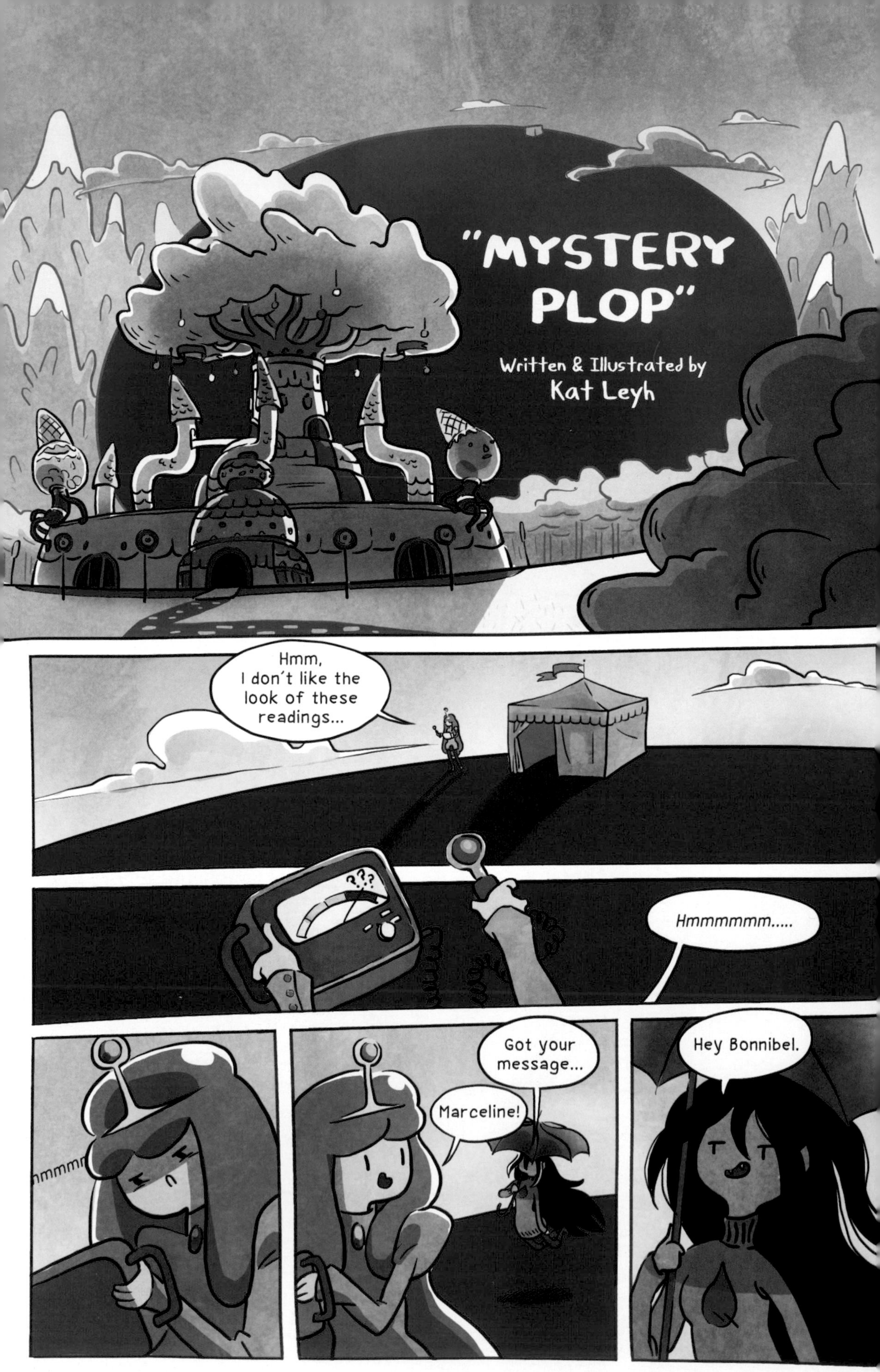
"MYSTERY PLOP"
Written & Illustrated by
Kat Leyh
Hmm, I don't like the look of these readings...
???
Hmmmmmm.....
hmmmm
Got your message...
Marceline!
Hey Bonnibel.

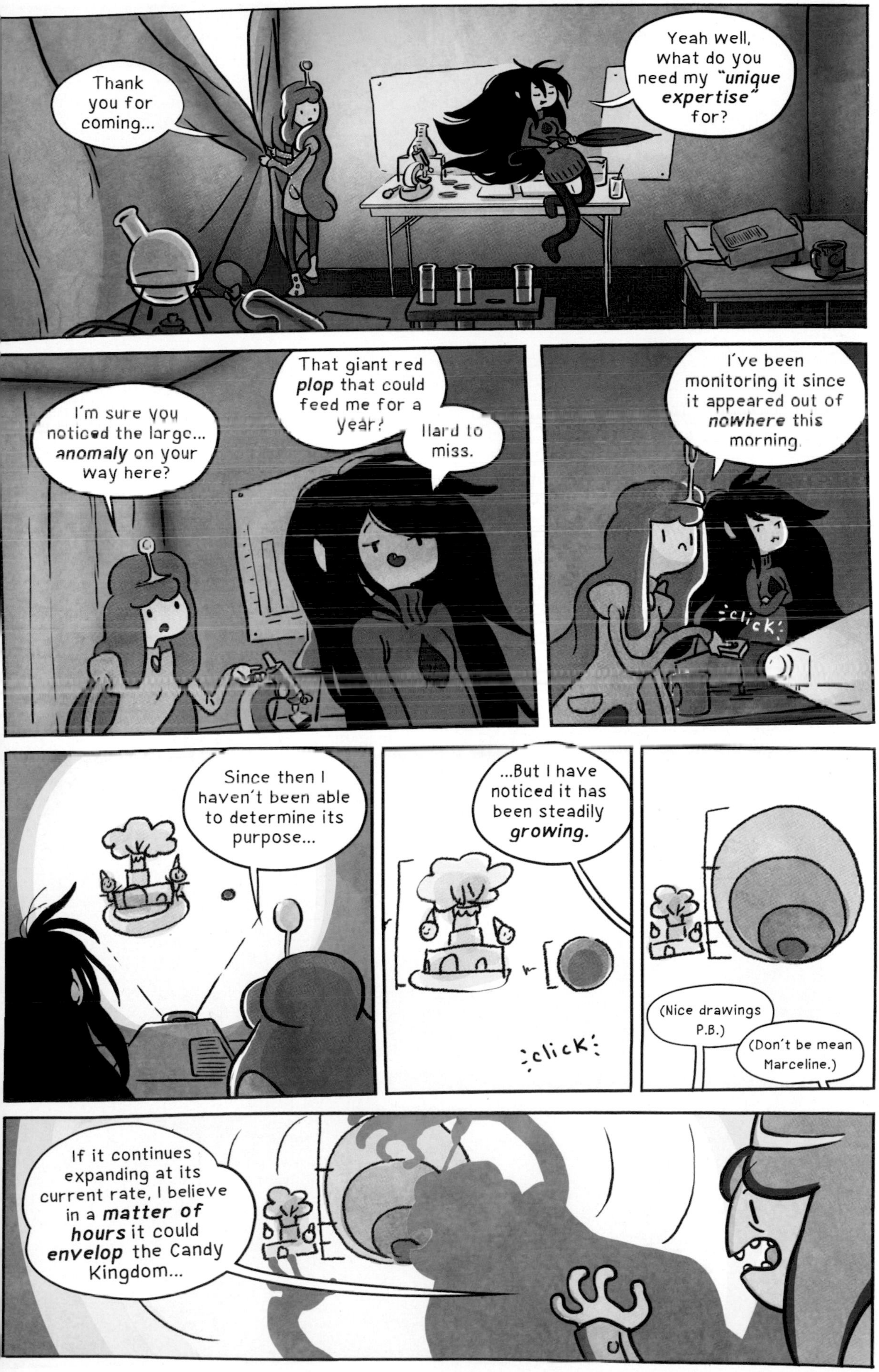
Thank you for coming...
Yeah well, what do you need my "unique expertise" for?
I'm sure you noticed the large... anomaly on your way here?
That giant red plop that could feed me for a year?
Hard to miss.
I've been monitoring it since it appeared out of nowhere this morning.
click
Since then I haven't been able to determine its purpose...
...But I have noticed it has been steadily growing.
click
(Nice drawings P.B.)
(Don't be mean Marceline.)
If it continues expanding at its current rate, I believe in a matter of hours it could envelop the Candy Kingdom...

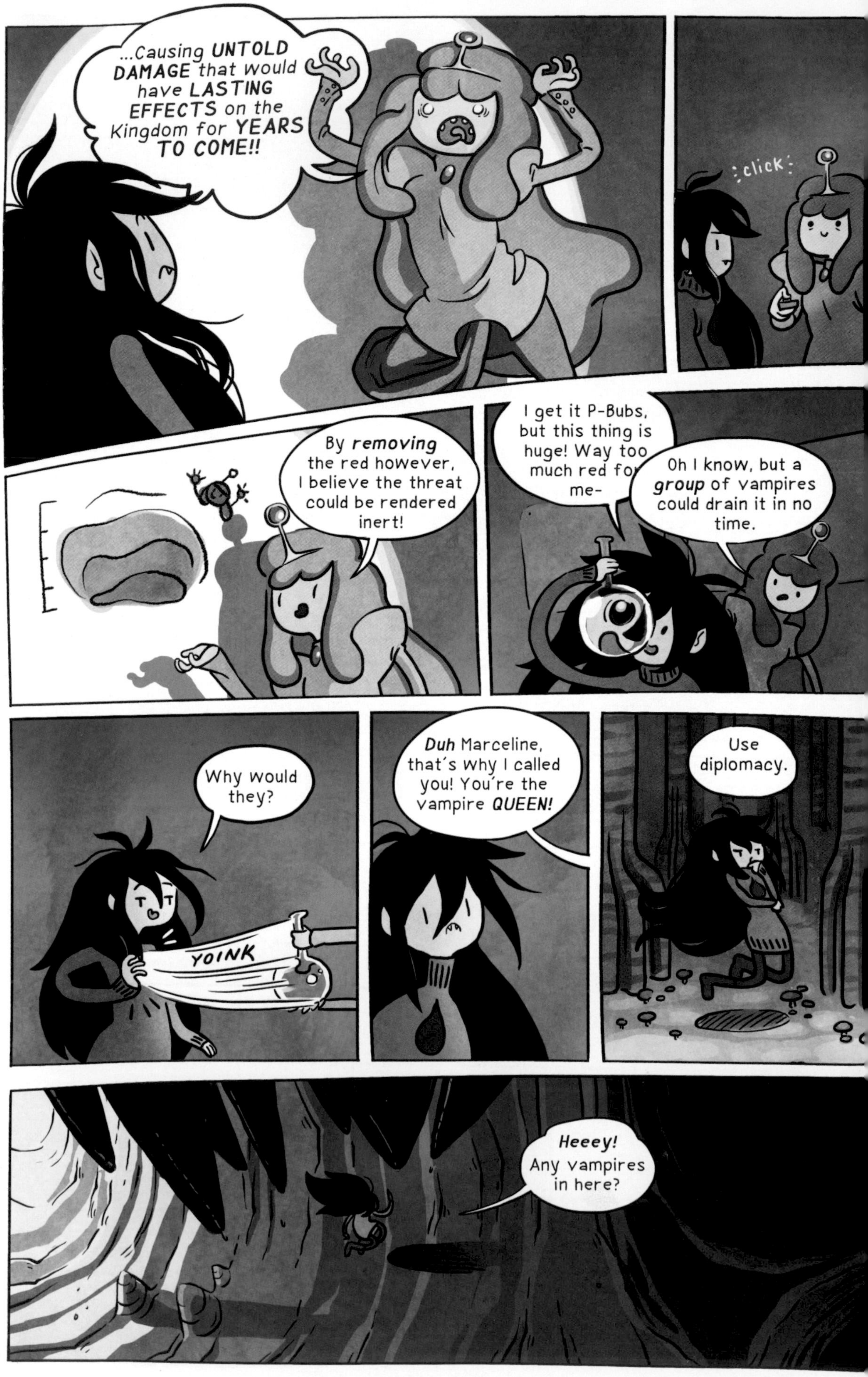
...Causing UNTOLD DAMAGE that would have LASTING EFFECTS on the Kingdom for YEARS TO COME!!
click
By removing the red however, I believe the threat could be rendered inert!
I get it P-Bubs, but this thing is huge! Way too much red for me-
Oh I know, but a group of vampires could drain it in no time.
Why would they?
YOINK
Duh Marceline, that's why I called you! You're the vampire QUEEN!
Use diplomacy.
Heeey! Any vampires in here?

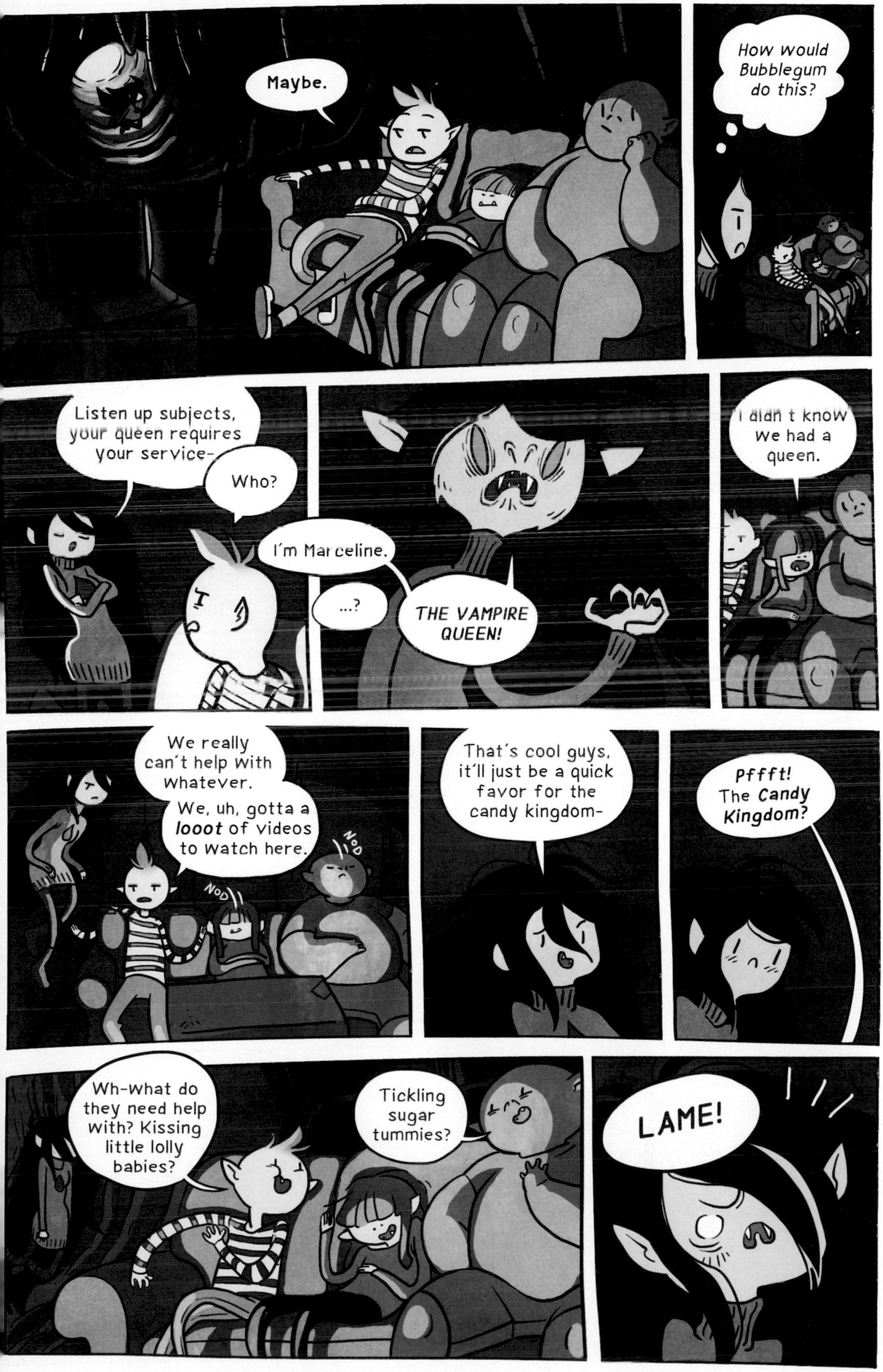
Maybe.
How would Bubblegum do this?
Listen up subjects, your queen requires your service-
Who?
I'm Marceline.
...?
THE VAMPIRE QUEEN!
I didn't know we had a queen.
We really can't help with whatever.
We, uh, gotta a looot of videos to watch here.
NOD
NOD
That's cool guys, it'll just be a quick favor for the candy kingdom-
Pffft! The Candy Kingdom?
Wh-what do they need help with? Kissing little lolly babies?
Tickling sugar tummies?
LAME!

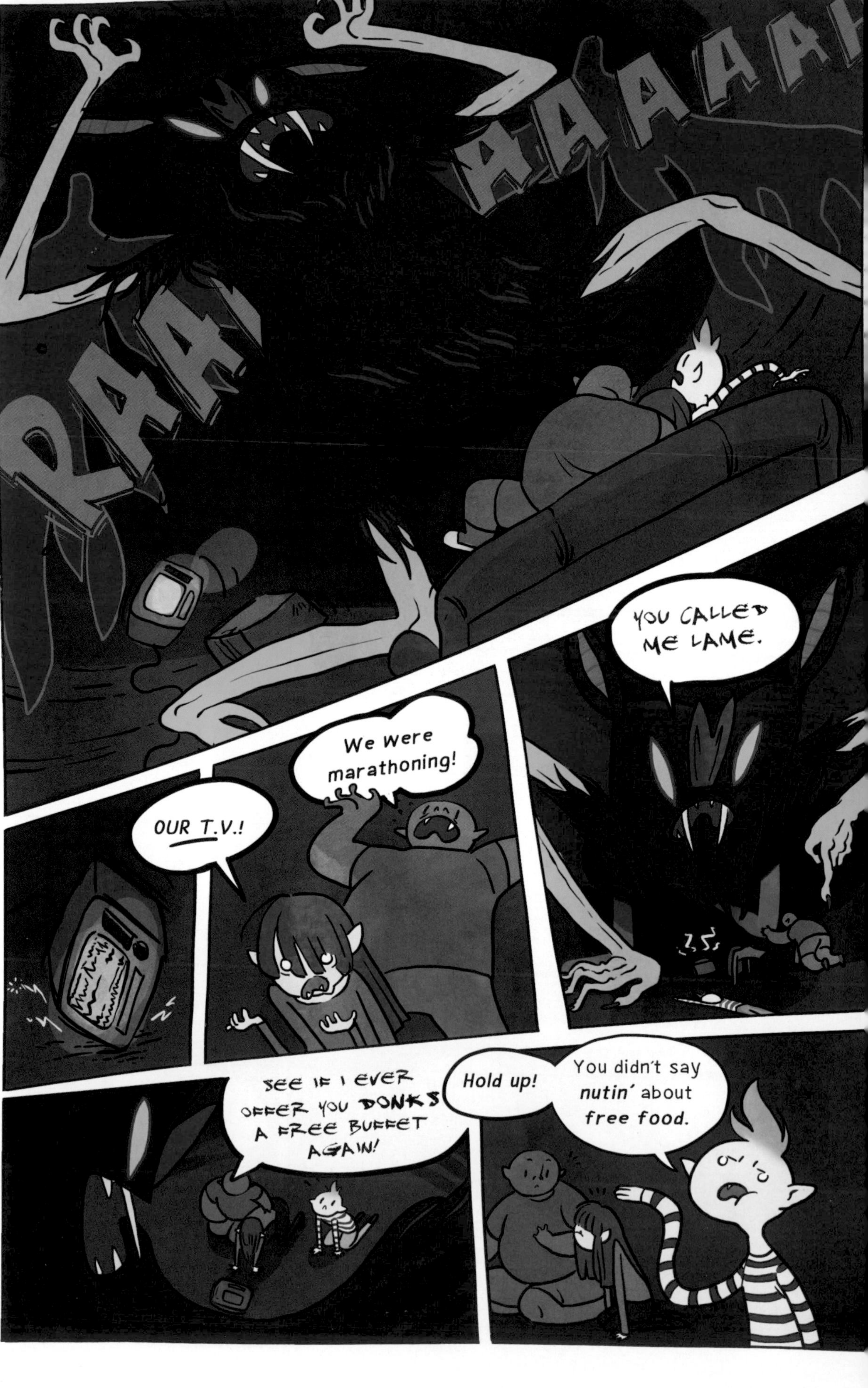
RAAAAAAAH
OUR T.V.!
We were marathoning!
YOU CALLED ME LAME.
SEE IF I EVER OFFER YOU DONKS A FREE BUFFET AGAIN!
Hold up!
You didn't say nutin' about free food.

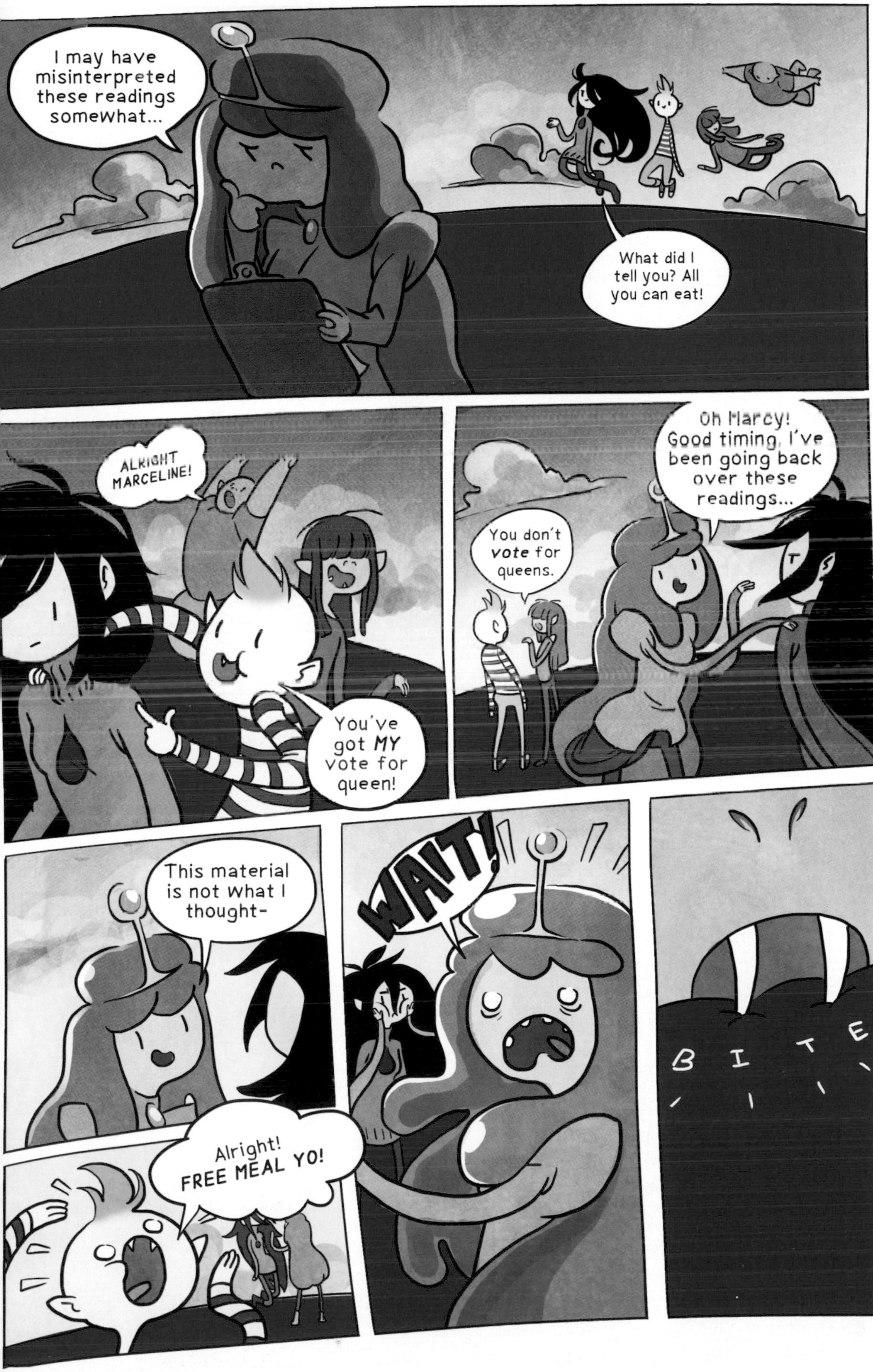
I may have misinterpreted these readings somewhat...
What did I tell you? All you can eat!
ALRIGHT MARCELINE!
You've got MY vote for queen!
You don't vote for queens.
Oh Marcy! Good timing, I've been going back over these readings...
This material is not what I thought-
Alright! FREE MEAL YO!
WAIT!
BITE

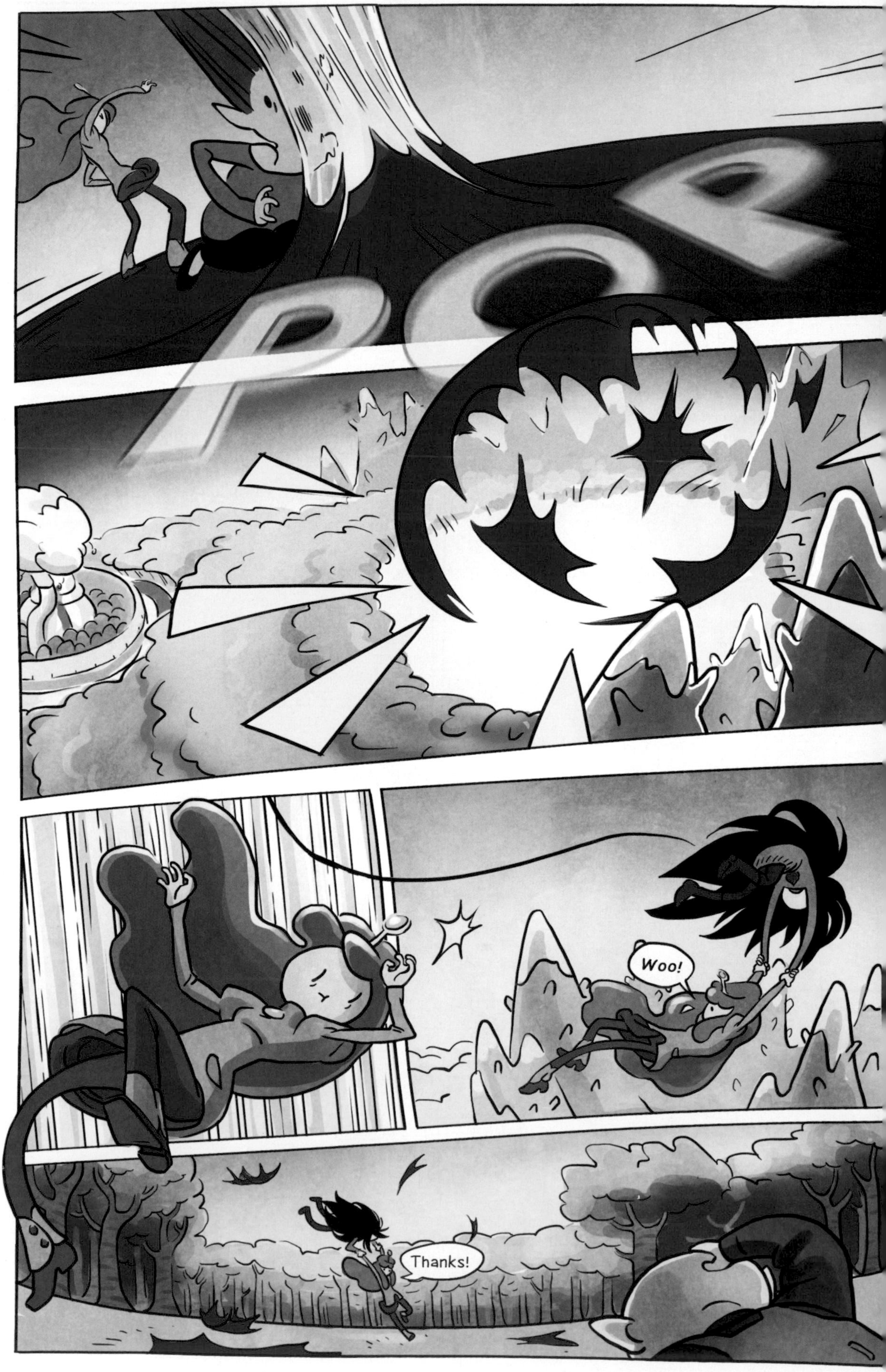
POP
Woo!
Thanks!

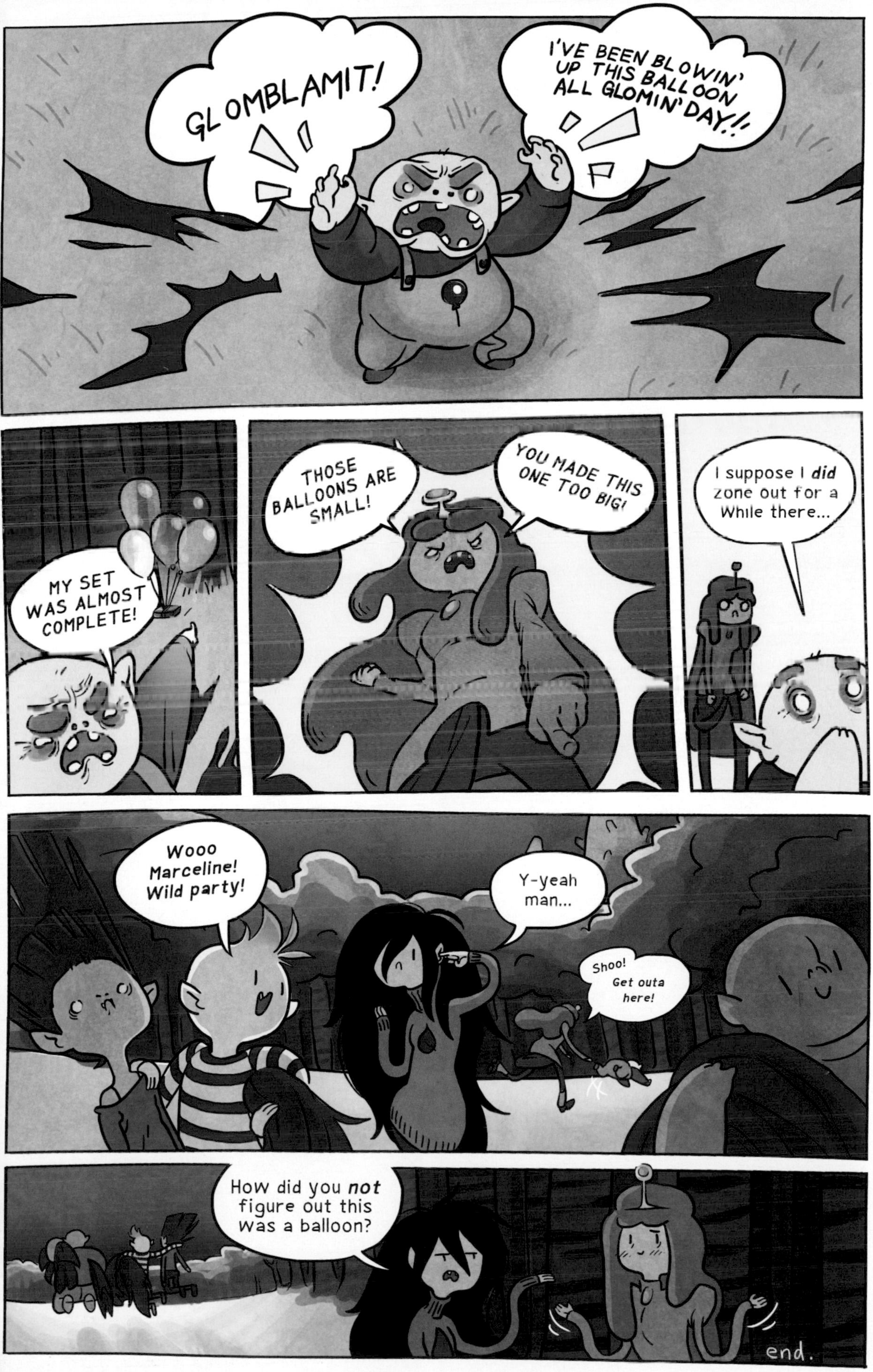
GLOMBLAMIT!
I'VE BEEN BLOWIN' UP THIS BALLOON ALL GLOMIN' DAY!!
MY SET WAS ALMOST COMPLETE!
THOSE BALLOONS ARE SMALL!
YOU MADE THIS ONE TOO BIG!
I suppose I *did* zone out for a While there...
Wooo Marceline! Wild party!
Y-yeah man...
Shoo! Get outa here!
How did you *not* figure out this was a balloon?
end.

GRAND PRIZE

ISSUE THIRTY SIX SUBSCRIPTION COVER
ALÉ GIORGINI

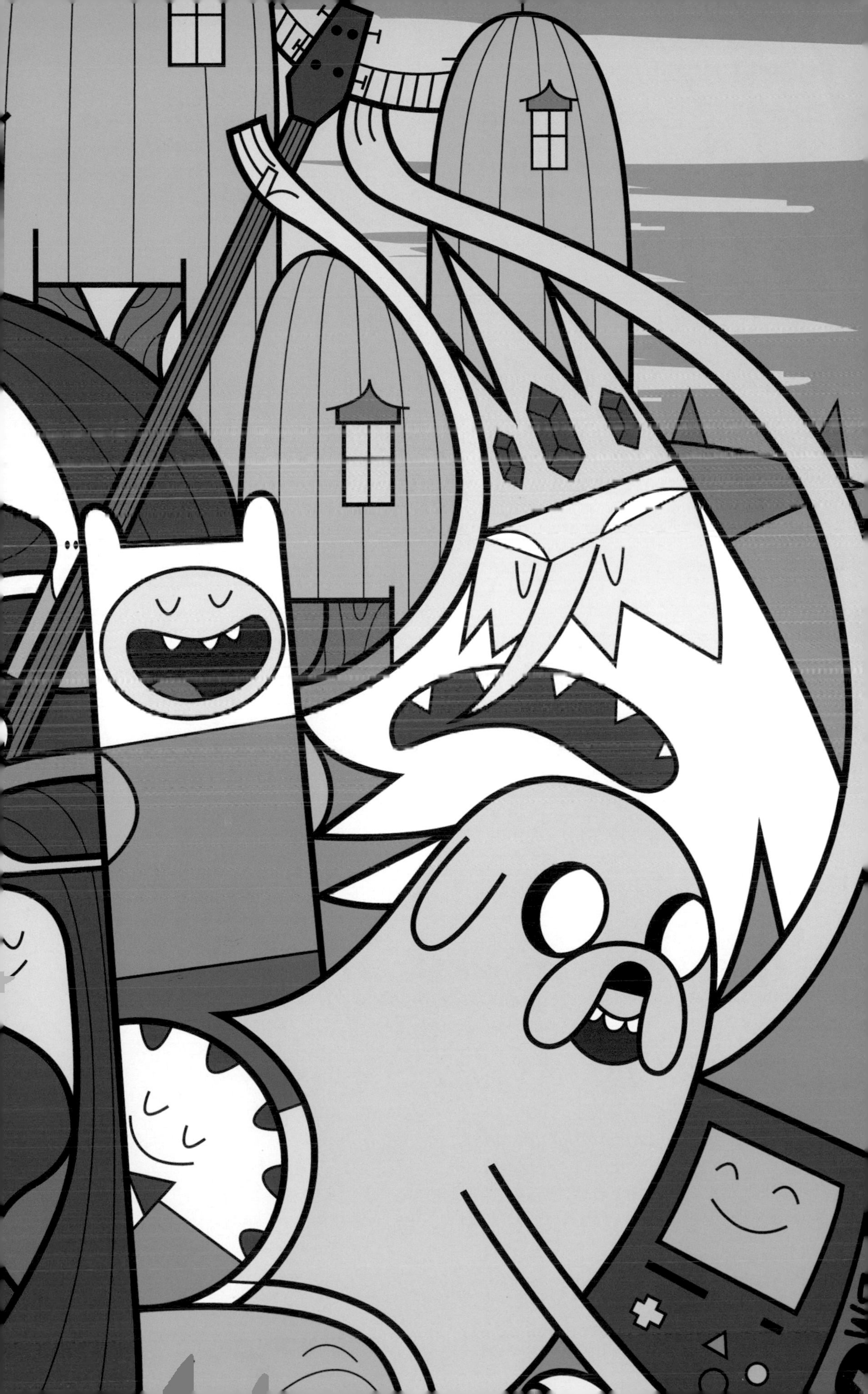

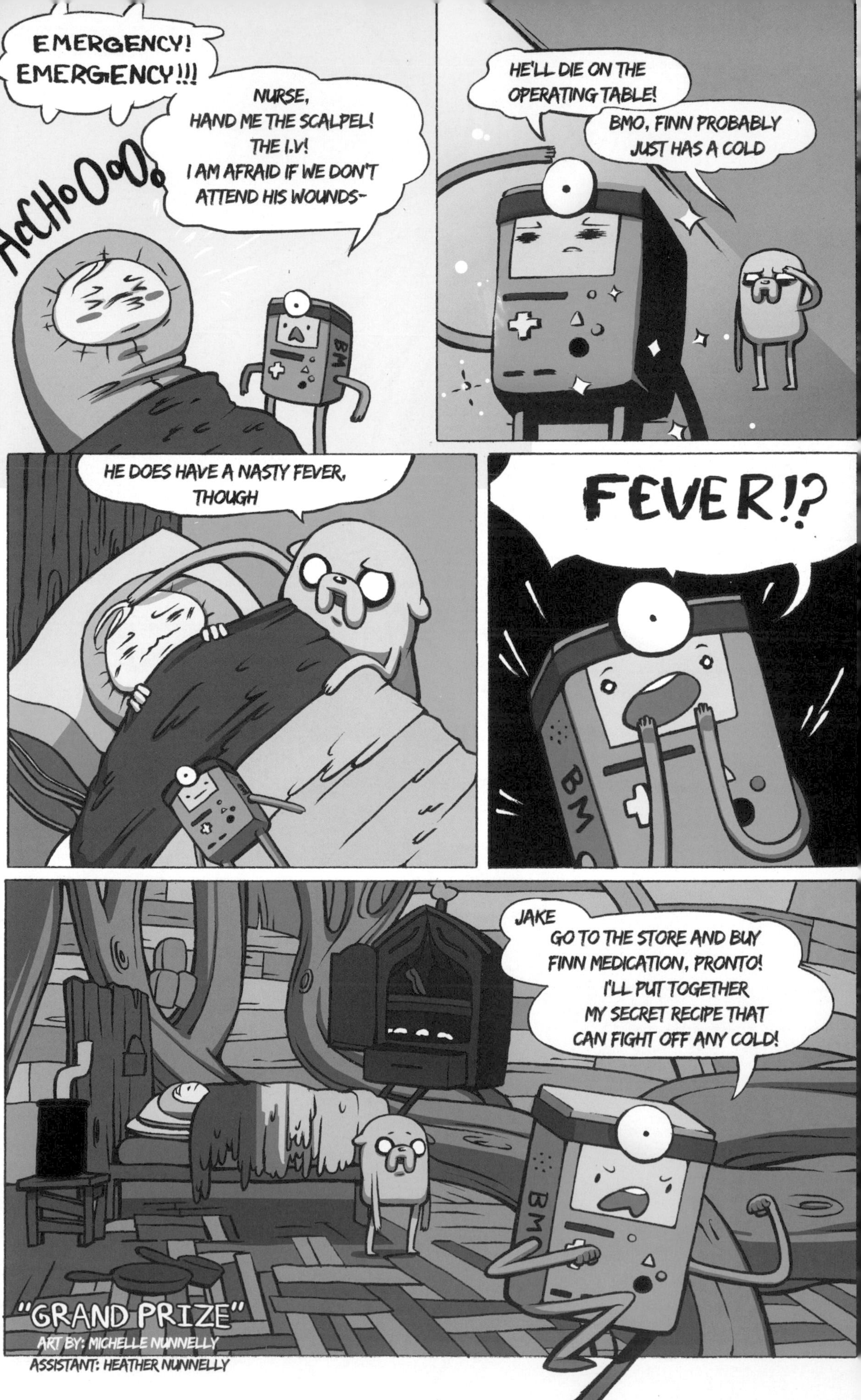
EMERGENCY!
EMERGENCY!!!
NURSE,
HAND ME THE SCALPEL!
THE I.V!
I AM AFRAID IF WE DON'T
ATTEND HIS WOUNDS-
ACCHOOOOO
HE'LL DIE ON THE
OPERATING TABLE!
BMO, FINN PROBABLY
JUST HAS A COLD
HE DOES HAVE A NASTY FEVER,
THOUGH
FEVER!?
JAKE
GO TO THE STORE AND BUY
FINN MEDICATION, PRONTO!
I'LL PUT TOGETHER
MY SECRET RECIPE THAT
CAN FIGHT OFF ANY COLD!
"GRAND PRIZE"
ART BY: MICHELLE NUNNELLY

ASSISTANT: HEATHER NUNNELLY

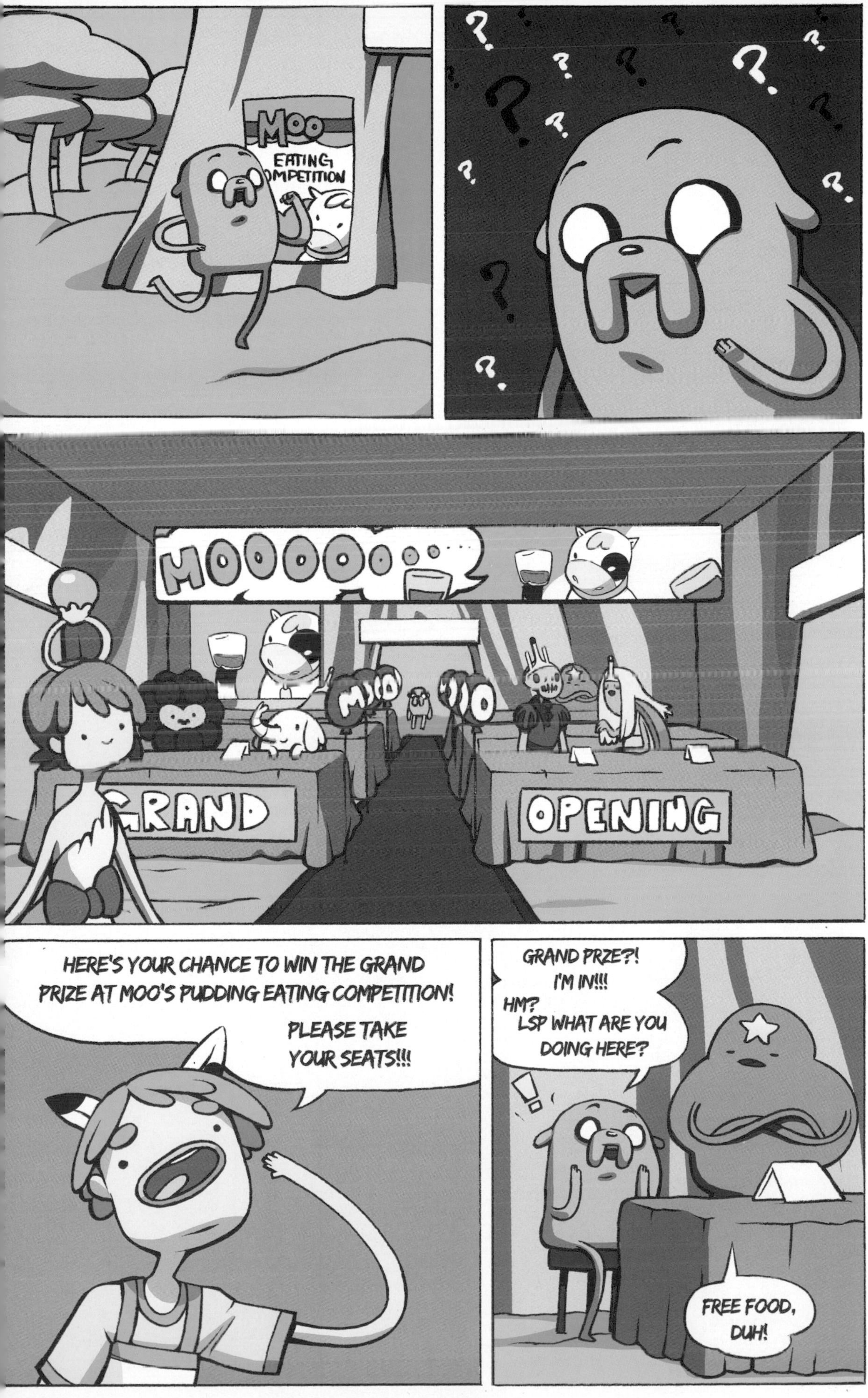
MOO
EATING
MOOOO...
GRAND
OPENING
HERE'S YOUR CHANCE TO WIN THE GRAND PRIZE AT MOO'S PUDDING EATING COMPETITION!
PLEASE TAKE YOUR SEATS!!!
GRAND PRZE?! I'M IN!!!
HM? LSP WHAT ARE YOU DOING HERE?
FREE FOOD, DUH!

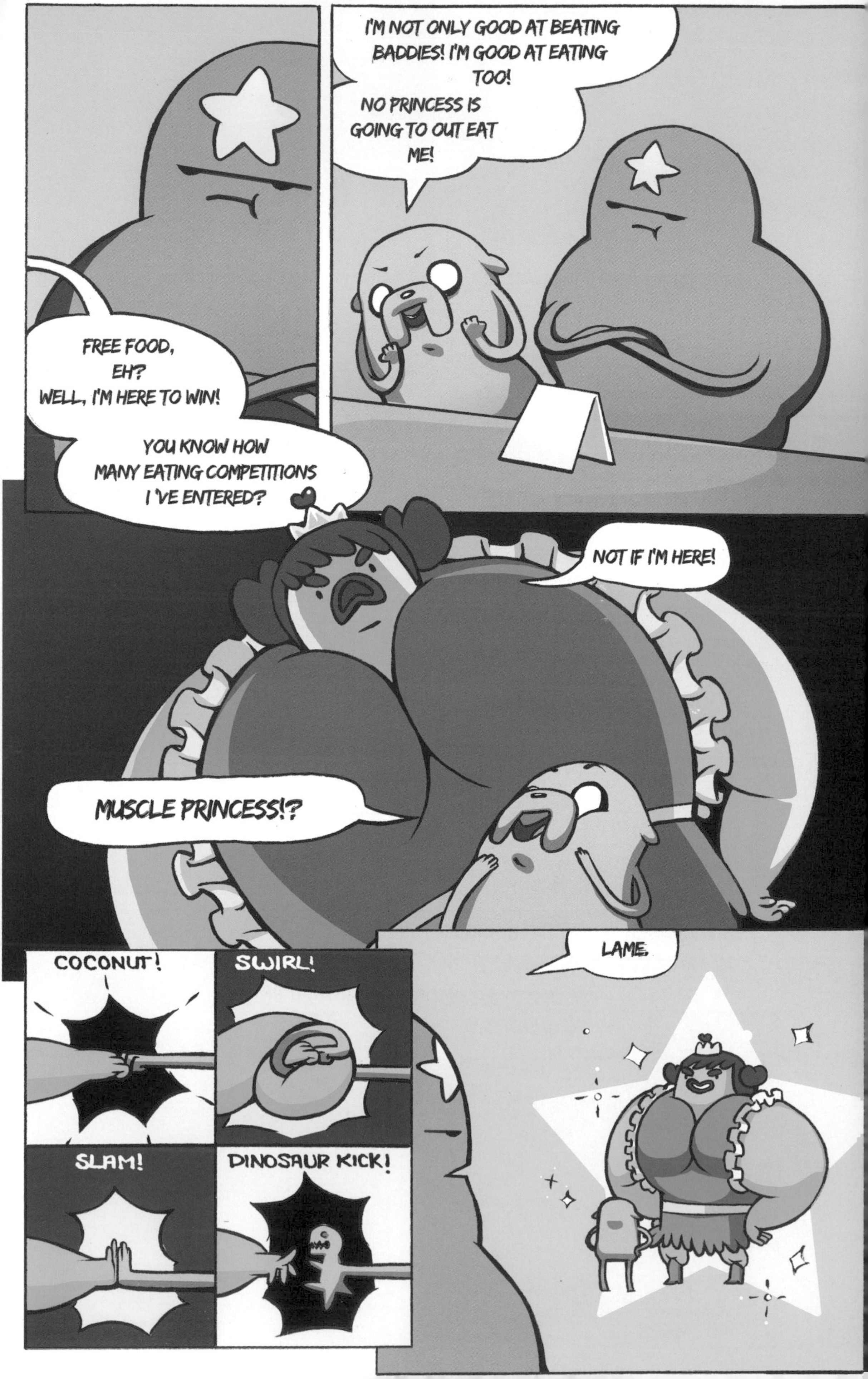

FREE FOOD,
EH?
WELL, I'M HERE TO WIN!
YOU KNOW HOW
MANY EATING COMPETITIONS
I'VE ENTERED?
I'M NOT ONLY GOOD AT BEATING BADDIES! I'M GOOD AT EATING TOO!
NO PRINCESS IS GOING TO OUT EAT ME!
NOT IF I'M HERE!
MUSCLE PRINCESS!?
COCONUT!
SWIRL!
SLAM!
DINOSAUR KICK!
LAME.

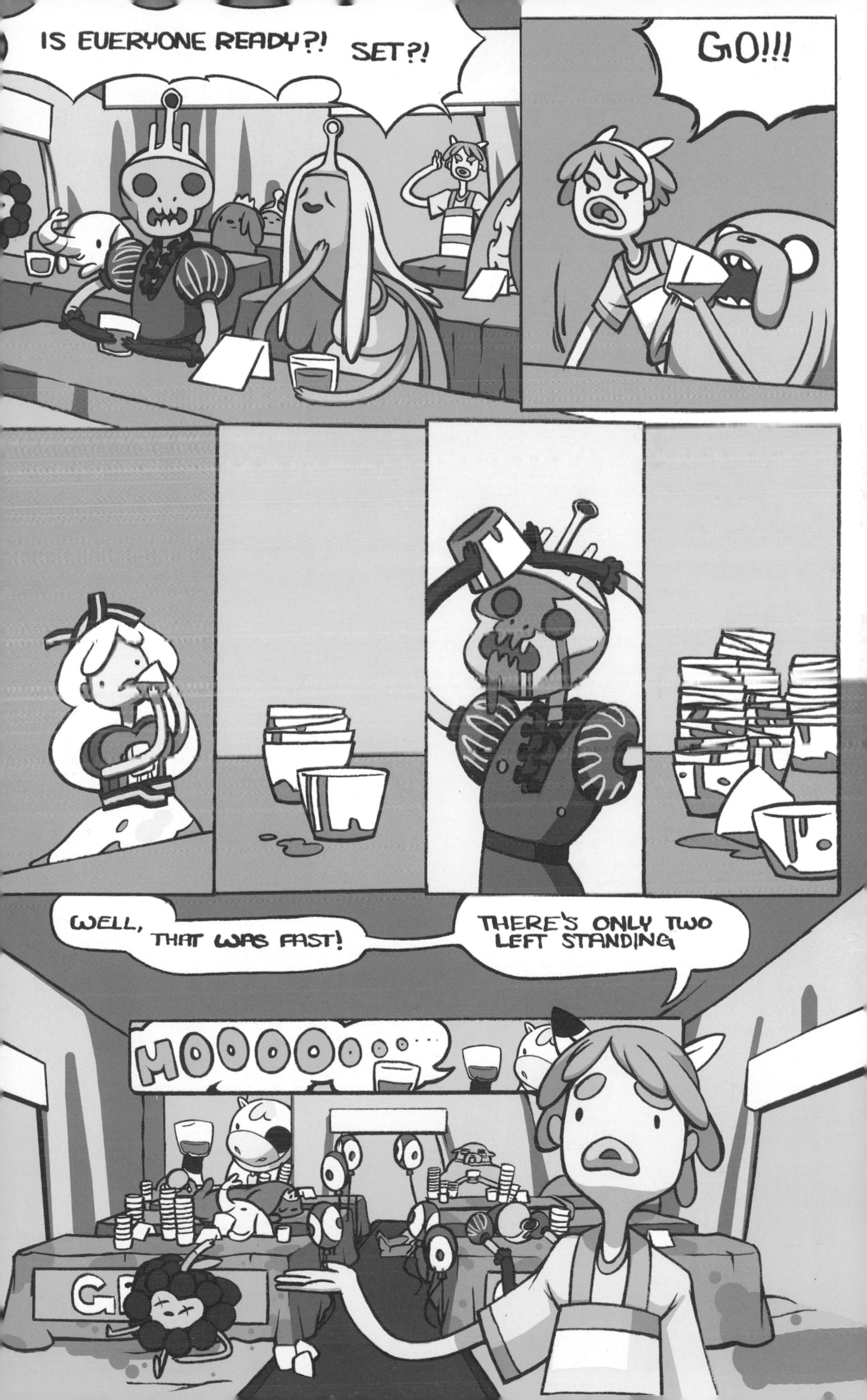
IS EVERYONE READY?!
SET?!
GO!!!
WELL, THAT WAS FAST!
THERE'S ONLY TWO LEFT STANDING
MOOOOo...

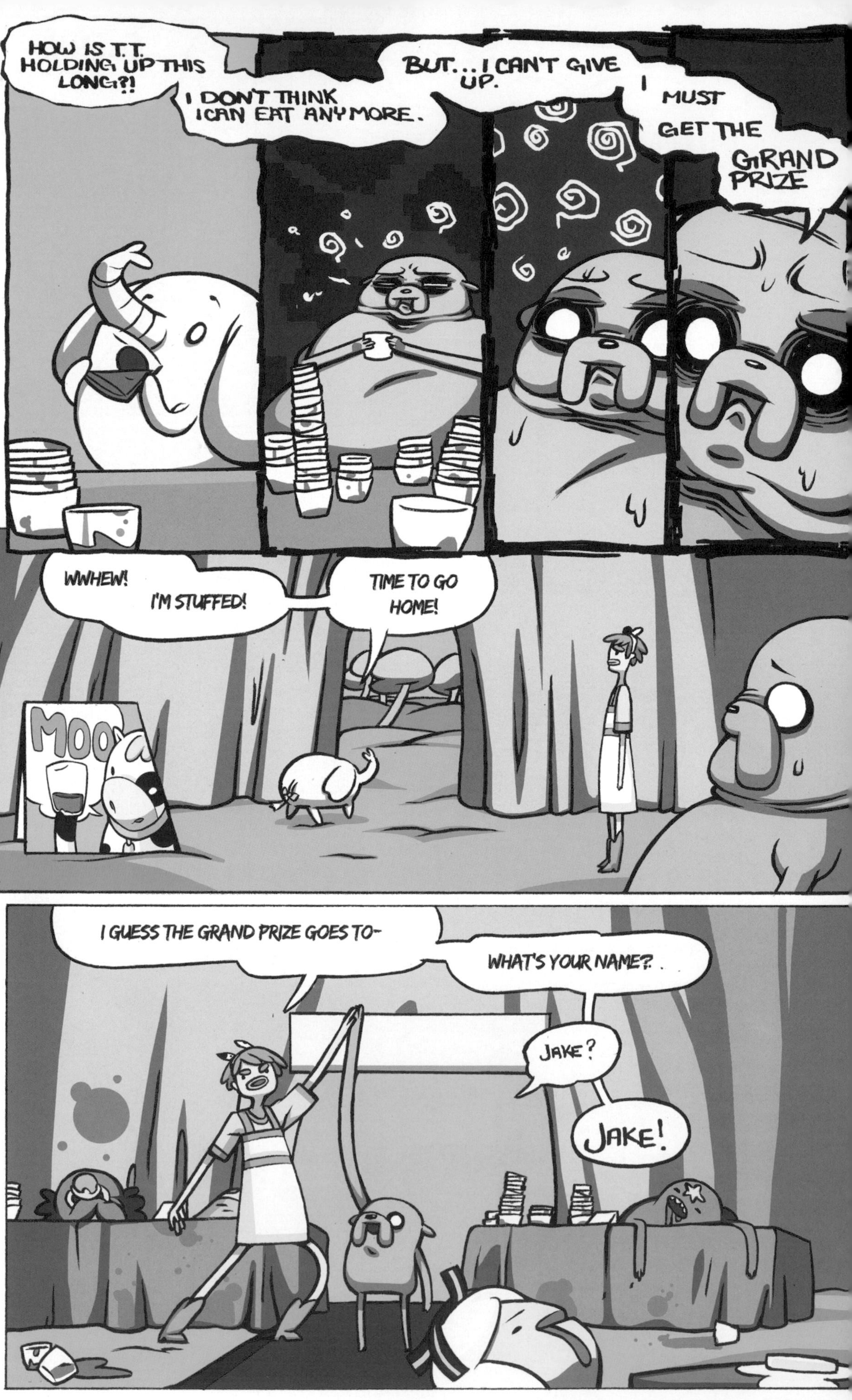
HOW IS T.T. HOLDING UP THIS LONG?!
I DON'T THINK I CAN EAT ANYMORE.
BUT... I CAN'T GIVE UP.
I
MUST
GET THE
GRAND PRIZE
WWHEW!
I'M STUFFED!
TIME TO GO HOME!
MOO
I GUESS THE GRAND PRIZE GOES TO-
WHAT'S YOUR NAME?
JAKE?
JAKE!

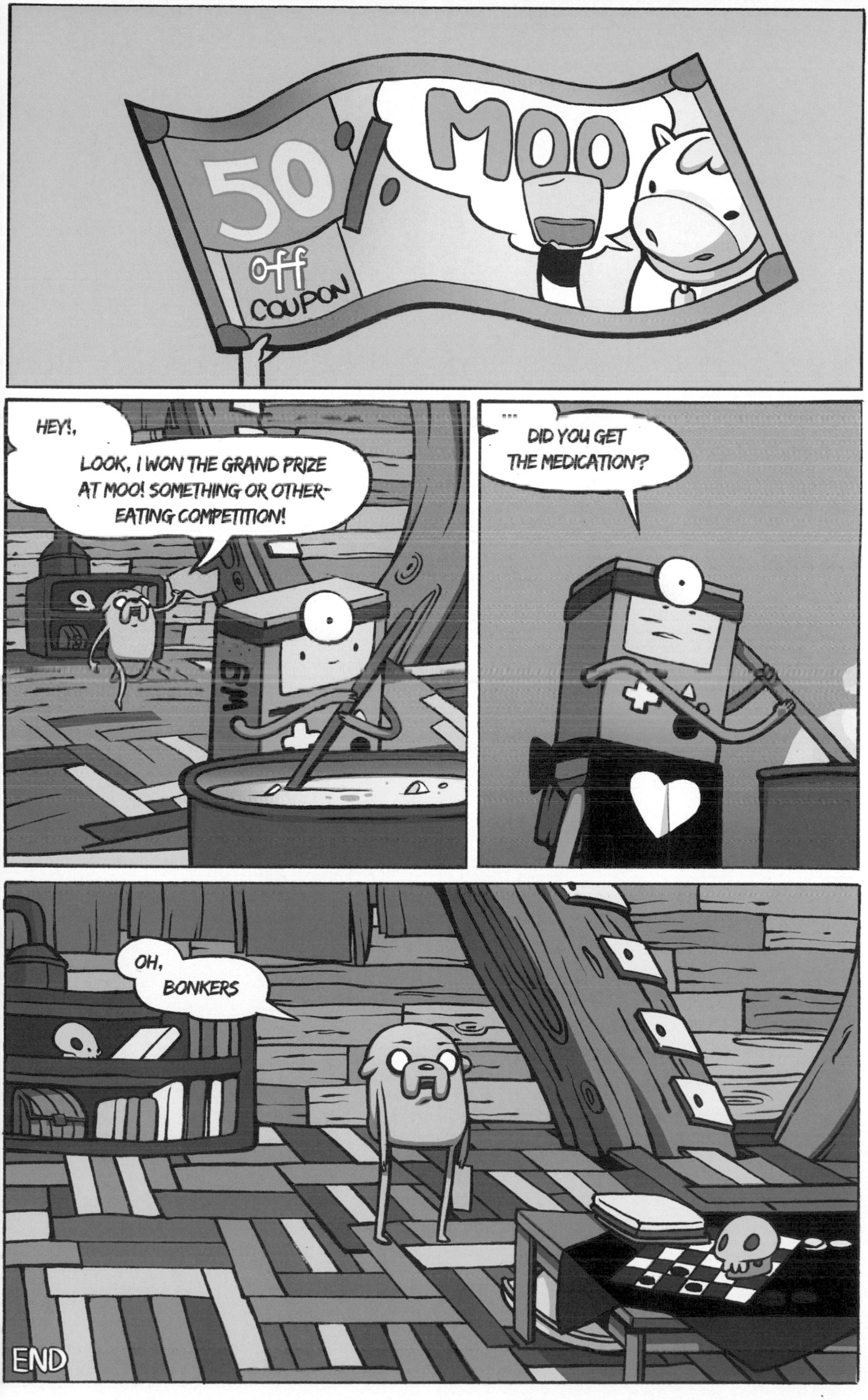
50% off COUPON
MOO
HEY!,
LOOK, I WON THE GRAND PRIZE AT MOO! SOMETHING OR OTHER-EATING COMPETITION!
...
DID YOU GET THE MEDICATION?
OH, BONKERS
END

SAME MATH...
DIFFERENT DAY

ISSUE THIRTY SEVEN VARIANT COVER
JUSTIN HILLGROVE

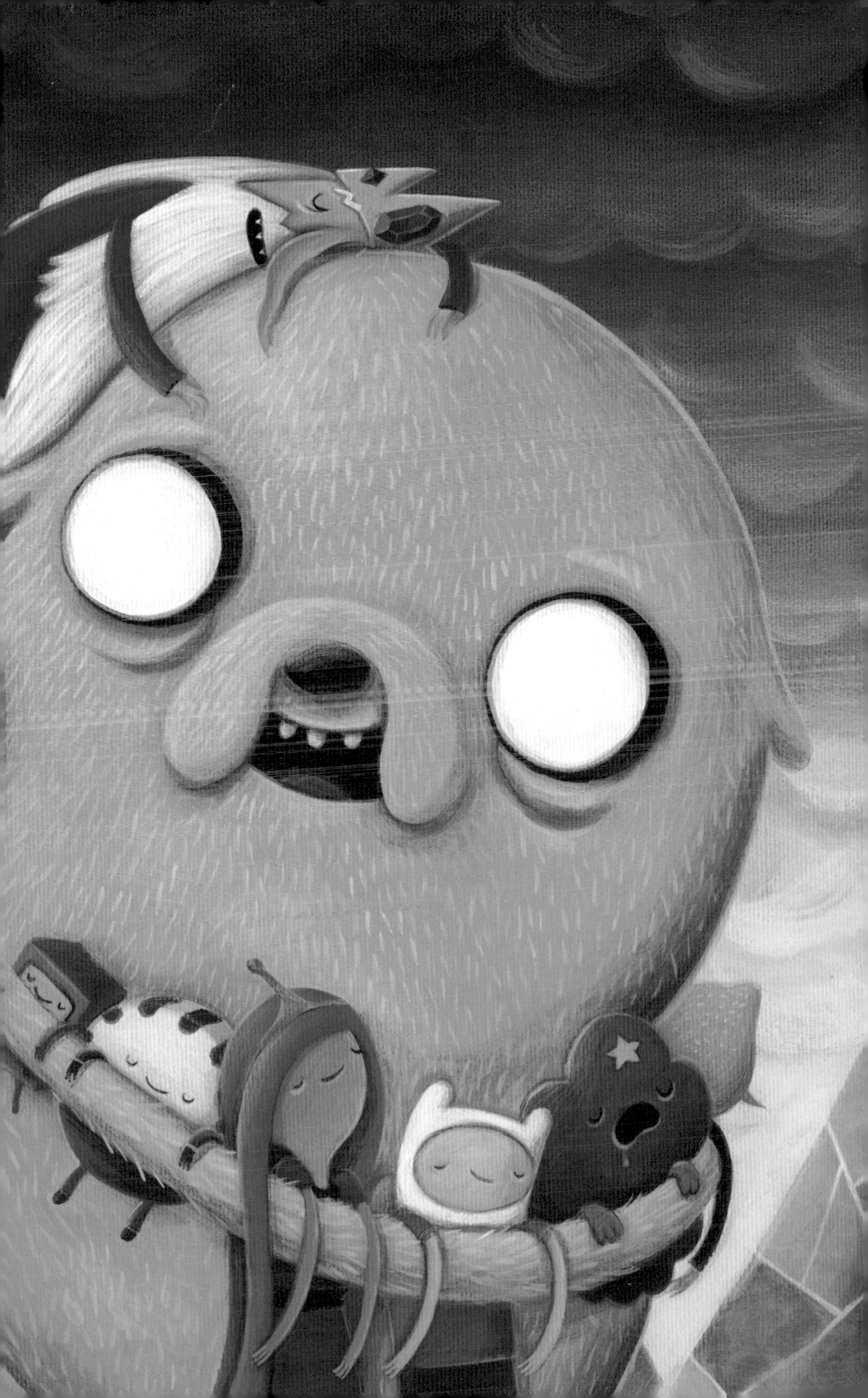

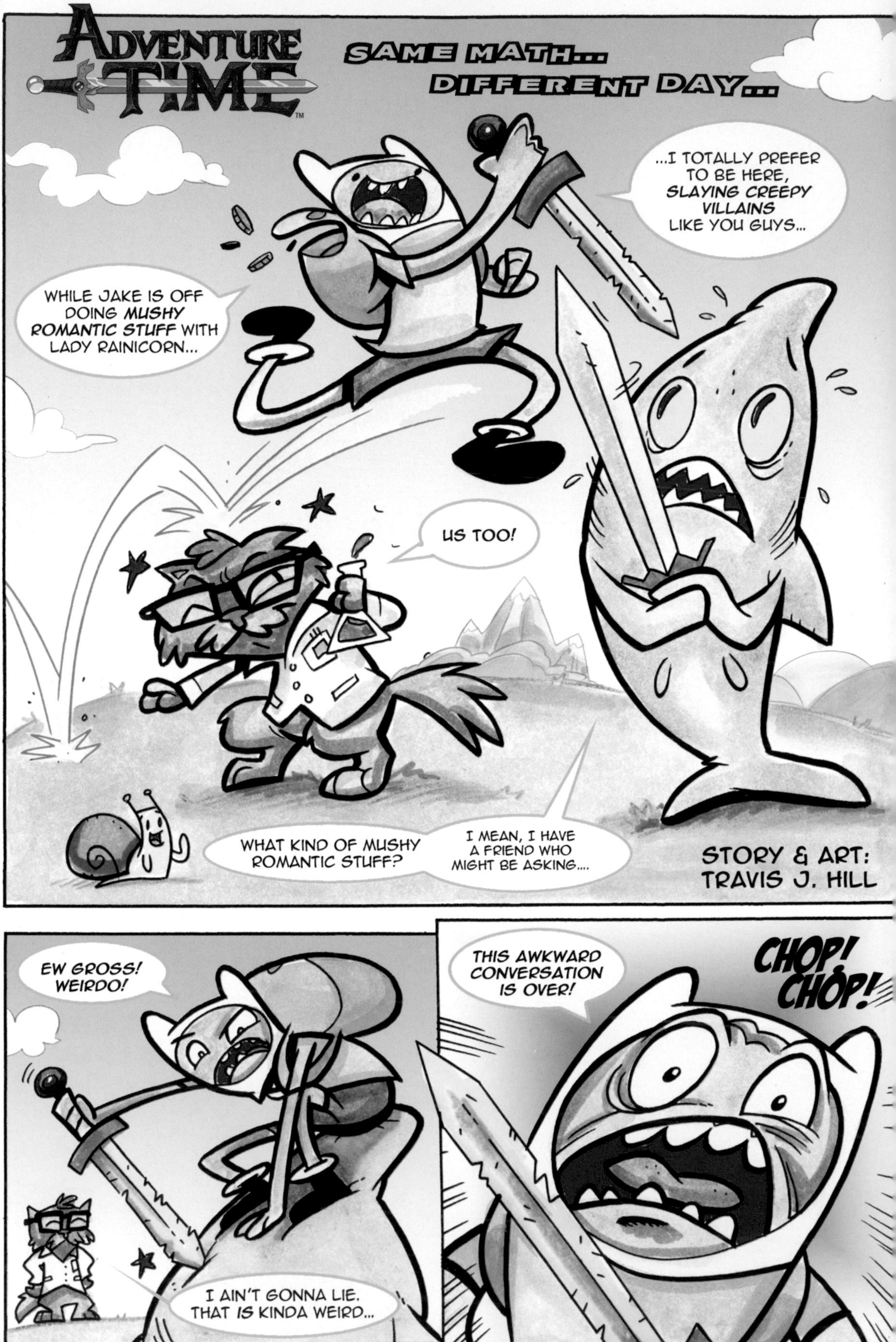
ADVENTURE TIME
SAME MATH... DIFFERENT DAY...
WHILE JAKE IS OFF DOING MUSHY ROMANTIC STUFF WITH LADY RAINICORN...
...I TOTALLY PREFER TO BE HERE, SLAYING CREEPY VILLAINS LIKE YOU GUYS...
US TOO!
WHAT KIND OF MUSHY ROMANTIC STUFF?
I MEAN, I HAVE A FRIEND WHO MIGHT BE ASKING....
STORY & ART: TRAVIS J. HILL
EW GROSS! WEIRDO!
I AIN'T GONNA LIE. THAT IS KINDA WEIRD...
THIS AWKWARD CONVERSATION IS OVER!
CHOP! CHOP!

SEE YOU TOMORROW AFTER YOU REGENERATE, YOU PATOOTS...

I'M DEFINITELY BLAMING TODAY'S LOSS ON *YOU*, SHARK. YOU SEEM DISTRACTED. WHAT GIVES?

POKE. POKE.

I DUNNO. I DON'T THINK MY HEART'S IN IT. DON'T *YOU* EVER GET TIRED OF THE SAME OLD SAME OLD?

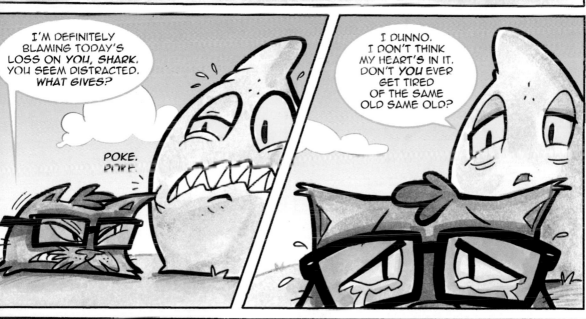

I DID MISS THE SCIENCE CONFERENCE IN VEGGIE VILLAGE LAST WEEK. SCIENCE *IS* KINDA MY THING....

...WHAT HAPPENED AFTER OUR HEADS WERE LOPPED OFF AND BEFORE THEY REGENERATED WAS AN INSULT TO INJURY. IT'S LIKE IT WAS YESTERDAY...

THIS DOES EVOKE A SATISFYING FEELING DEEP IN MY CANDY INSIDES... I HAD NO RIGHT TO JUDGE.

SMACK! SMACK!

YIPPEE!

SMACK! SMACK!

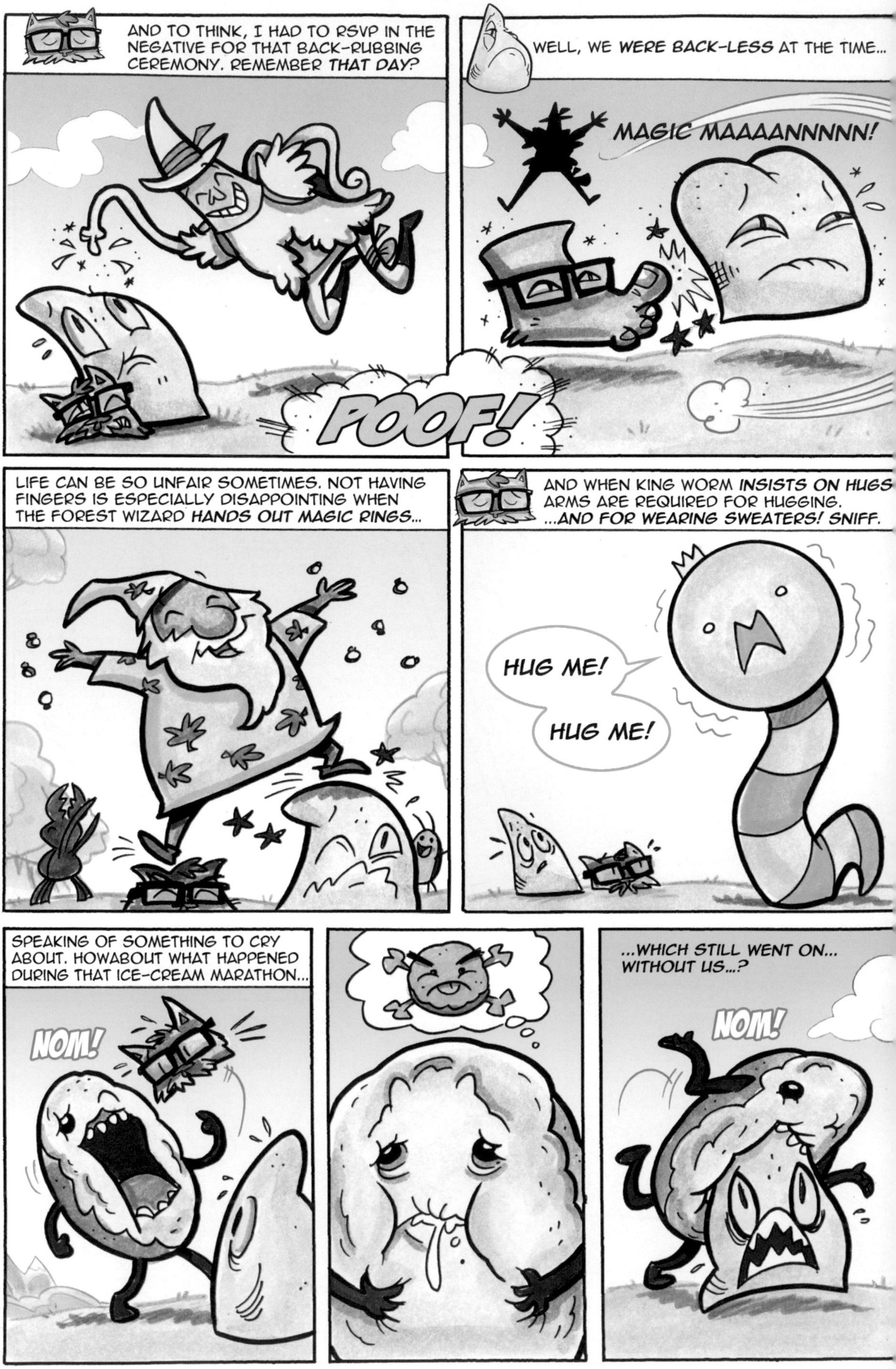
AND TO THINK, I HAD TO RSVP IN THE NEGATIVE FOR THAT BACK-RUBBING CEREMONY. REMEMBER THAT DAY?
WELL, WE WERE BACK-LESS AT THE TIME...
MAGIC MAAAANNNNN!
POOF!
LIFE CAN BE SO UNFAIR SOMETIMES. NOT HAVING FINGERS IS ESPECIALLY DISAPPOINTING WHEN THE FOREST WIZARD HANDS OUT MAGIC RINGS...
AND WHEN KING WORM INSISTS ON HUGS ARMS ARE REQUIRED FOR HUGGING. ...AND FOR WEARING SWEATERS! SNIFF.
HUG ME!
HUG ME!
SPEAKING OF SOMETHING TO CRY ABOUT. HOWABOUT WHAT HAPPENED DURING THAT ICE-CREAM MARATHON...
NOM!
...WHICH STILL WENT ON... WITHOUT US...?
NOM!

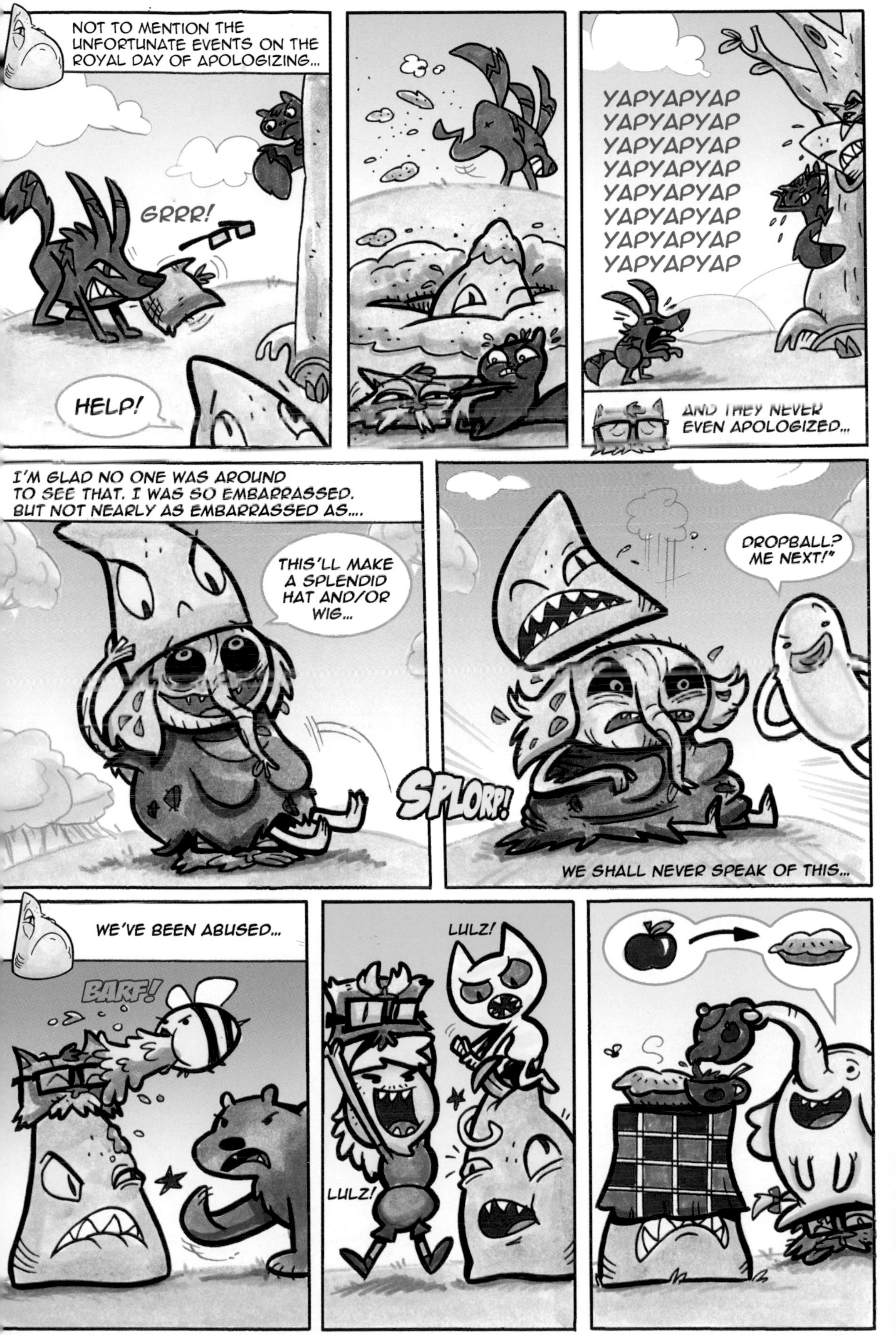
NOT TO MENTION THE UNFORTUNATE EVENTS ON THE ROYAL DAY OF APOLOGIZING...
GRRR!
HELP!
YAPYAPYAP YAPYAPYAP YAPYAPYAP YAPYAPYAP YAPYAPYAP YAPYAPYAP YAPYAPYAP YAPYAPYAP
AND THEY NEVER EVEN APOLOGIZED...
I'M GLAD NO ONE WAS AROUND TO SEE THAT. I WAS SO EMBARRASSED. BUT NOT NEARLY AS EMBARRASSED AS....
THIS'LL MAKE A SPLENDID HAT AND/OR WIG...
SPLORP!
DROPBALL? ME NEXT!"
WE SHALL NEVER SPEAK OF THIS...
WE'VE BEEN ABUSED...
BARF!
LULZ!
LULZ!

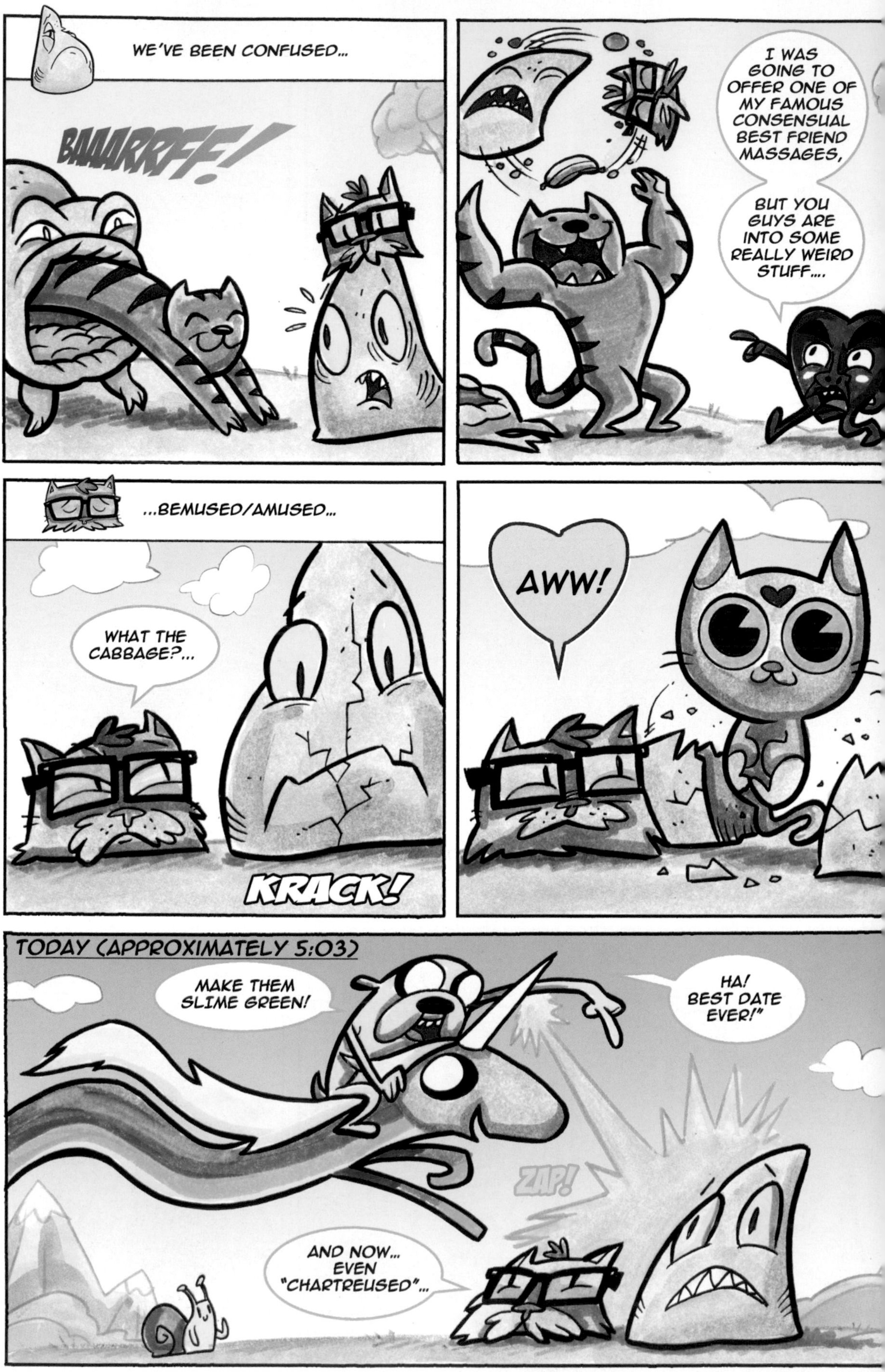

WE'VE BEEN CONFUSED...
BAAARRRFF!
I WAS GOING TO OFFER ONE OF MY FAMOUS CONSENSUAL BEST FRIEND MASSAGES,
BUT YOU GUYS ARE INTO SOME REALLY WEIRD STUFF....
...BEMUSED/AMUSED...
WHAT THE CABBAGE?...
KRACK!
AWW!
TODAY (APPROXIMATELY 5:03)
MAKE THEM SLIME GREEN!
HA! BEST DATE EVER!"
ZAP!
AND NOW... EVEN "CHARTREUSED"...

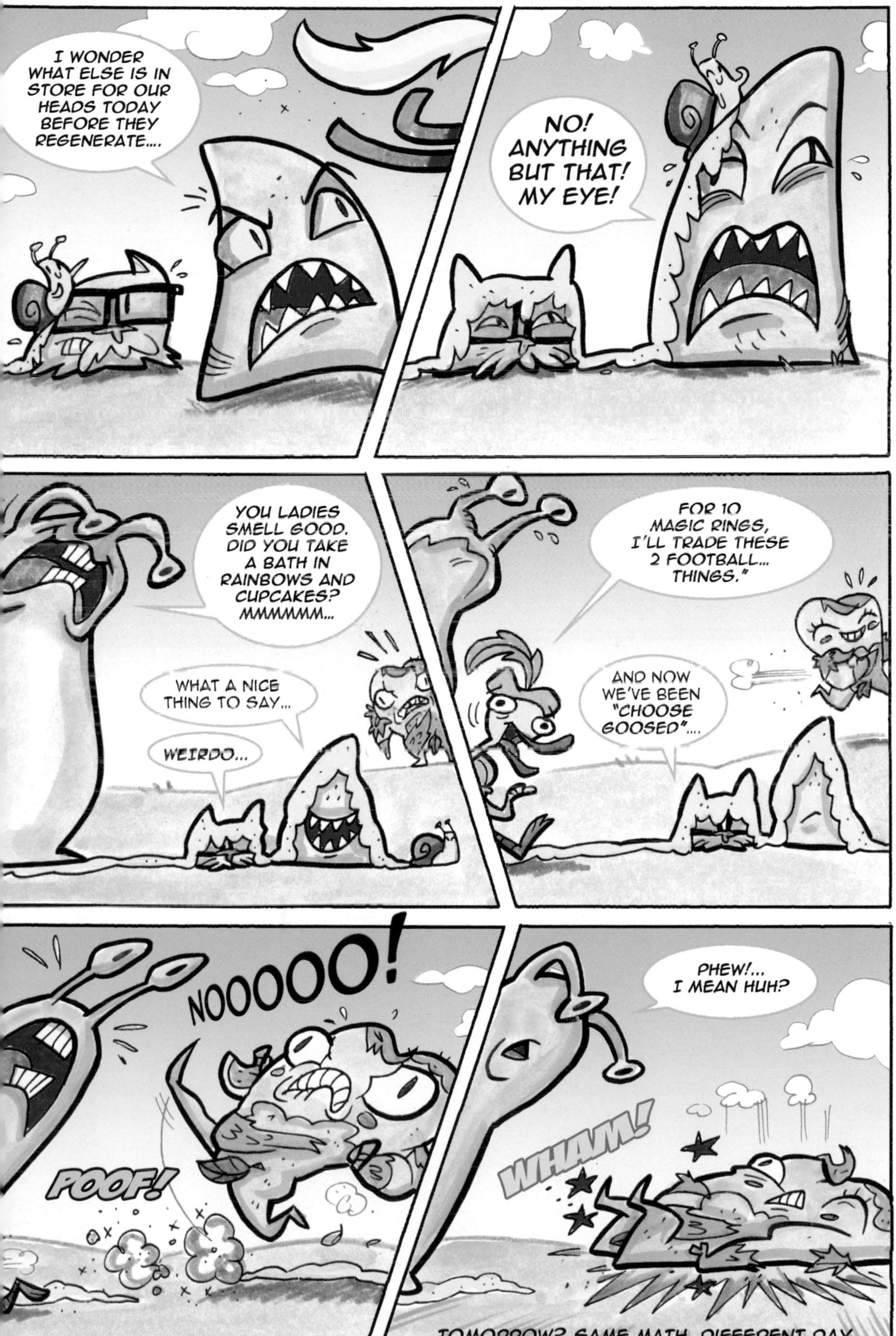
I WONDER WHAT ELSE IS IN STORE FOR OUR HEADS TODAY BEFORE THEY REGENERATE....
NO! ANYTHING BUT THAT! MY EYE!
YOU LADIES SMELL GOOD. DID YOU TAKE A BATH IN RAINBOWS AND CUPCAKES? MMMMMM...
WHAT A NICE THING TO SAY...
WEIRDO...
FOR 10 MAGIC RINGS, I'LL TRADE THESE 2 FOOTBALL... THINGS."
AND NOW WE'VE BEEN "CHOOSE GOOSED"....
NOOOOO!
POOF!
PHEW!... I MEAN HUH?
WHAM!
TOMORROW? SAME MATH. DIFFERENT DAY...

WORST DAY

ISSUE THIRTY EIGHT VARIANT COVER
ZÉ BURNAY

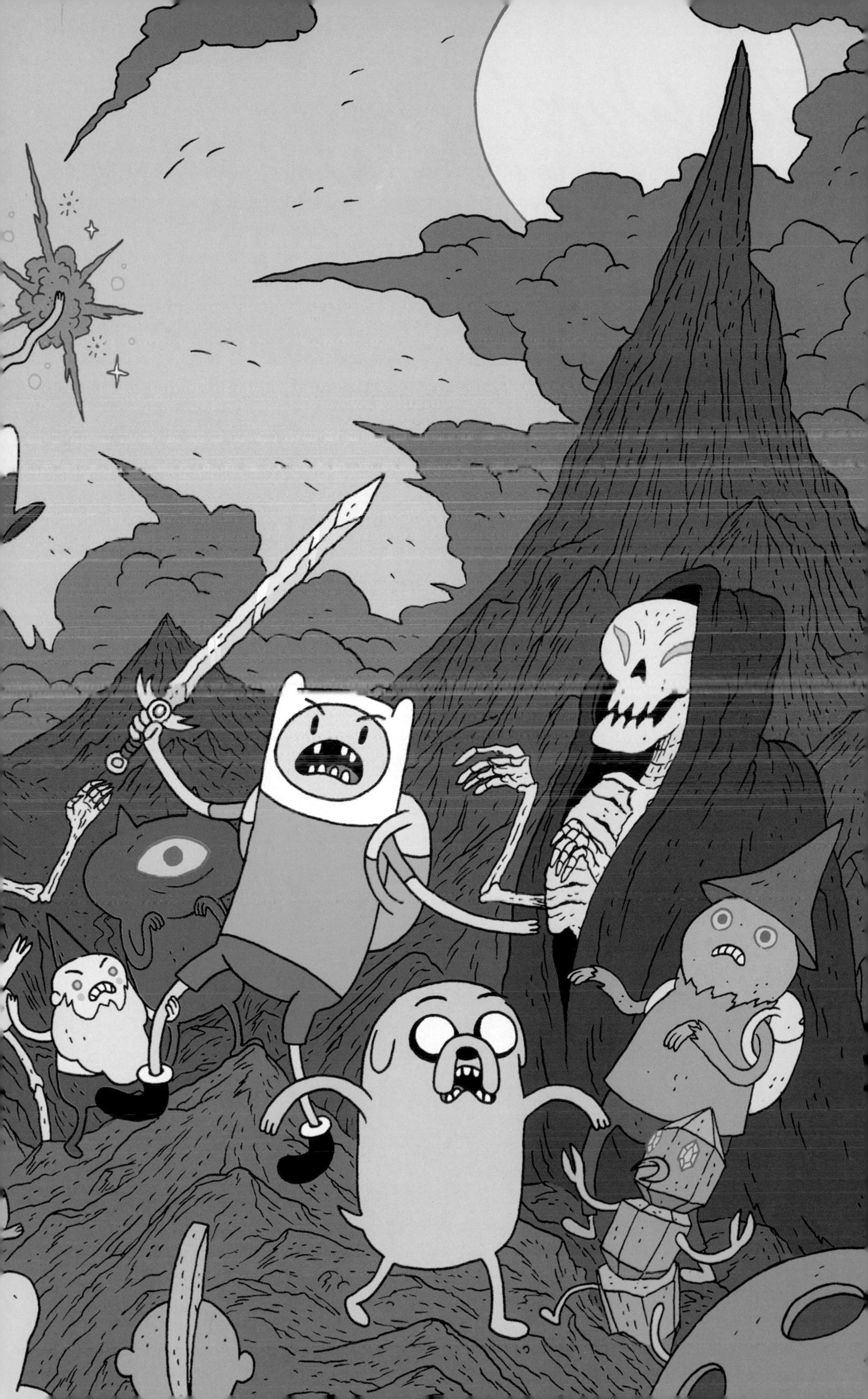

The Worst Day

Starring Marceline the Vampire Queen.

Written by Jay Edidin

Drawn by Kel McDonald

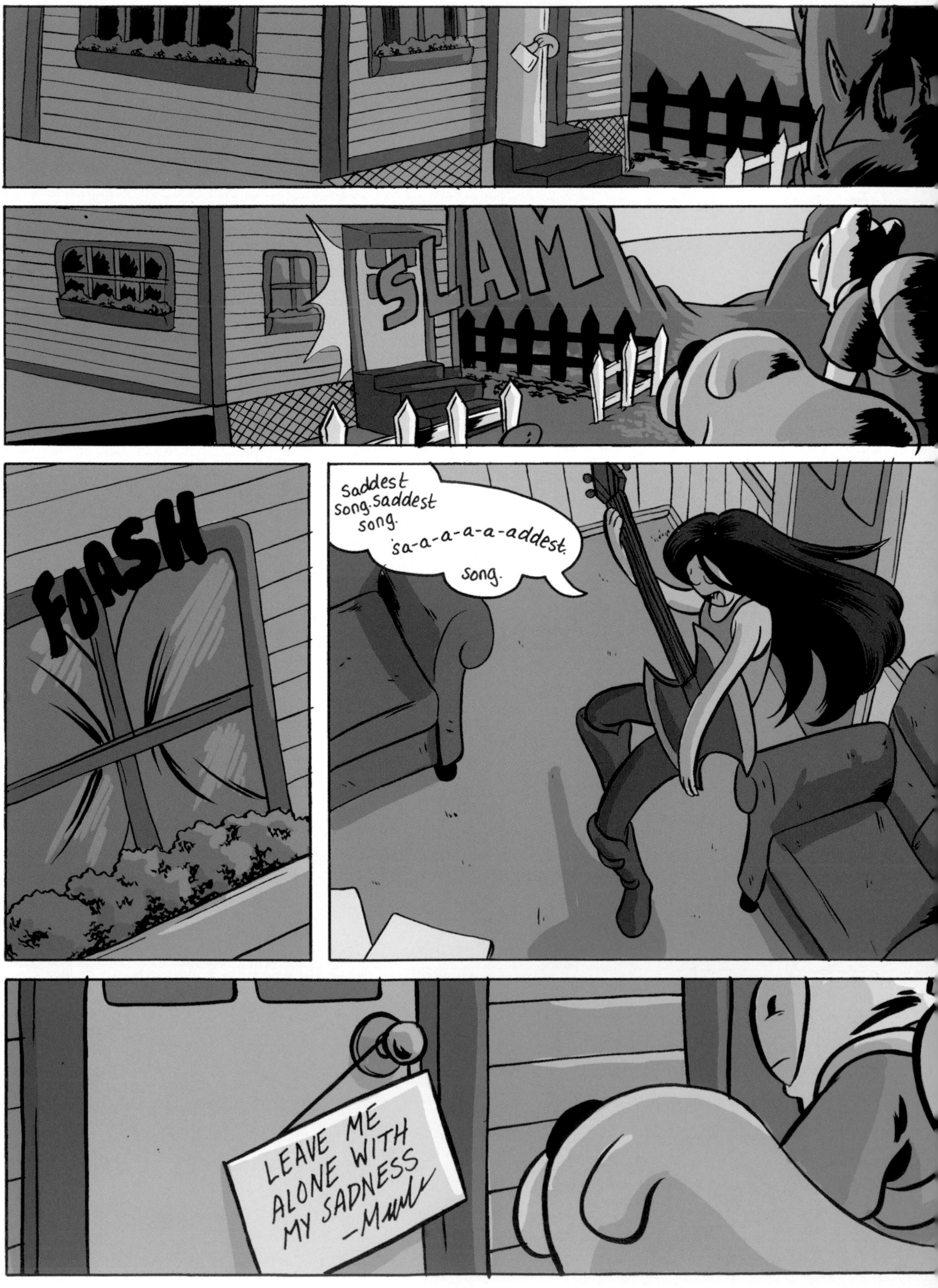

SLAM
FOASH
saddest song. saddest song. sa-a-a-a-a-addest. song.
LEAVE ME ALONE WITH MY SADNESS

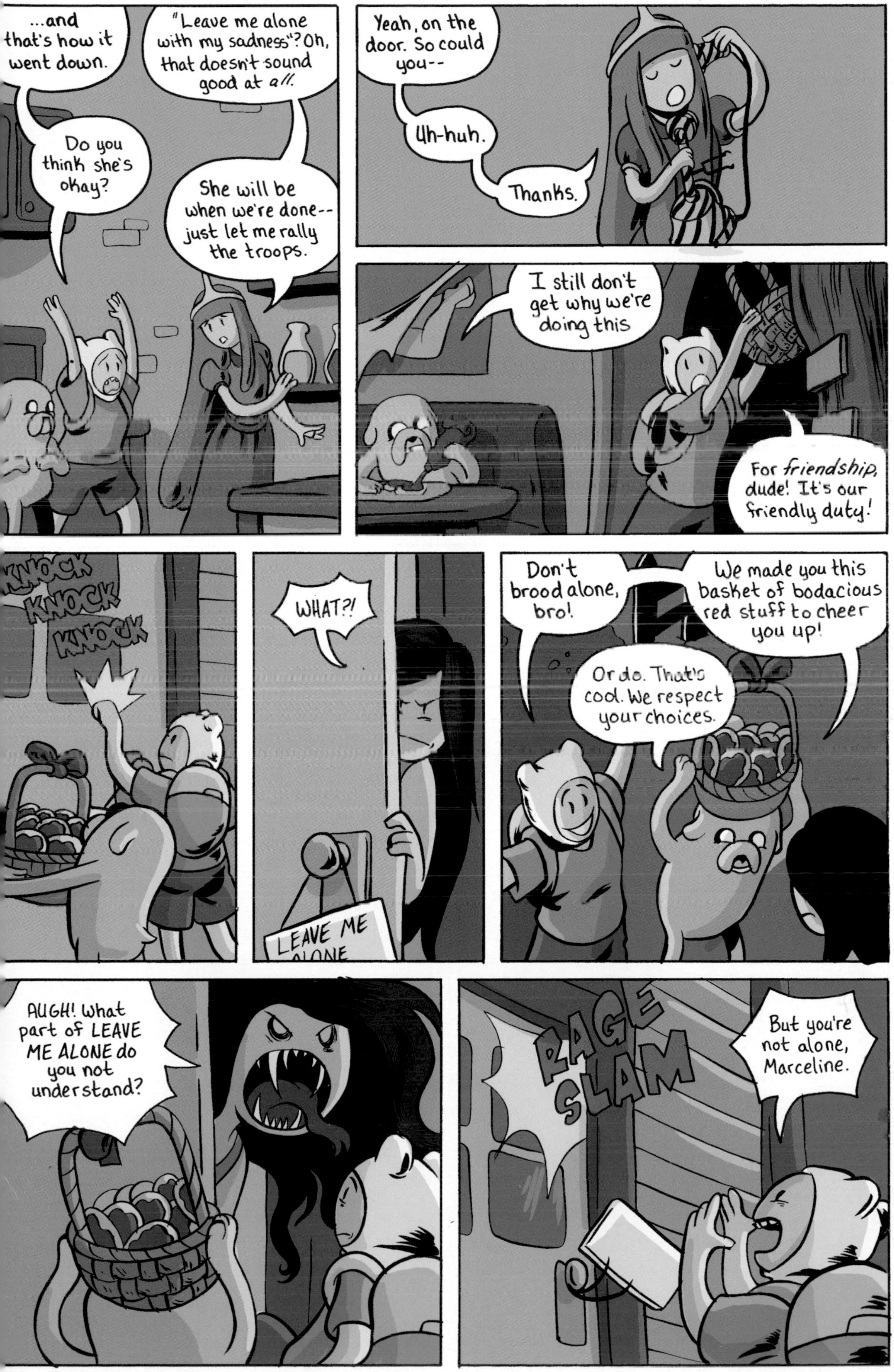
...and that's how it went down.
"Leave me alone with my sadness"? Oh, that doesn't sound good at *all*.
Do you think she's okay?
She will be when we're done-- just let me rally the troops.
Yeah, on the door. So could you--
Uh-huh.
Thanks.
I still don't get why we're doing this
For *friendship*, dude! It's our friendly duty!
KNOCK KNOCK KNOCK
WHAT?!
LEAVE ME ALONE
Don't brood alone, bro!
We made you this basket of bodacious red stuff to cheer you up!
Or do. That's cool. We respect your choices.
AUGH! What part of LEAVE ME ALONE do you not understand?
RAGE SLAM
But you're not alone, Marceline.

Ugh. Of all the stupid inconsiderate...

Now I have to start *all* over again.

SO MANY ORPHANS

ENCYCLOPEDIA OF MISERY

LIQUID TEARS

That's not even *sad* so much as *stupid*.

Maybe it's time to pull out the big guns.

Okay, orphans. It's up to you, now.

Yessss, ophrans. Your sad little parentless eyes and artfully smudge faces will fuel the bonfire of my sorrow.

SKRITCH SKRITCH

Ugh, what *now?*

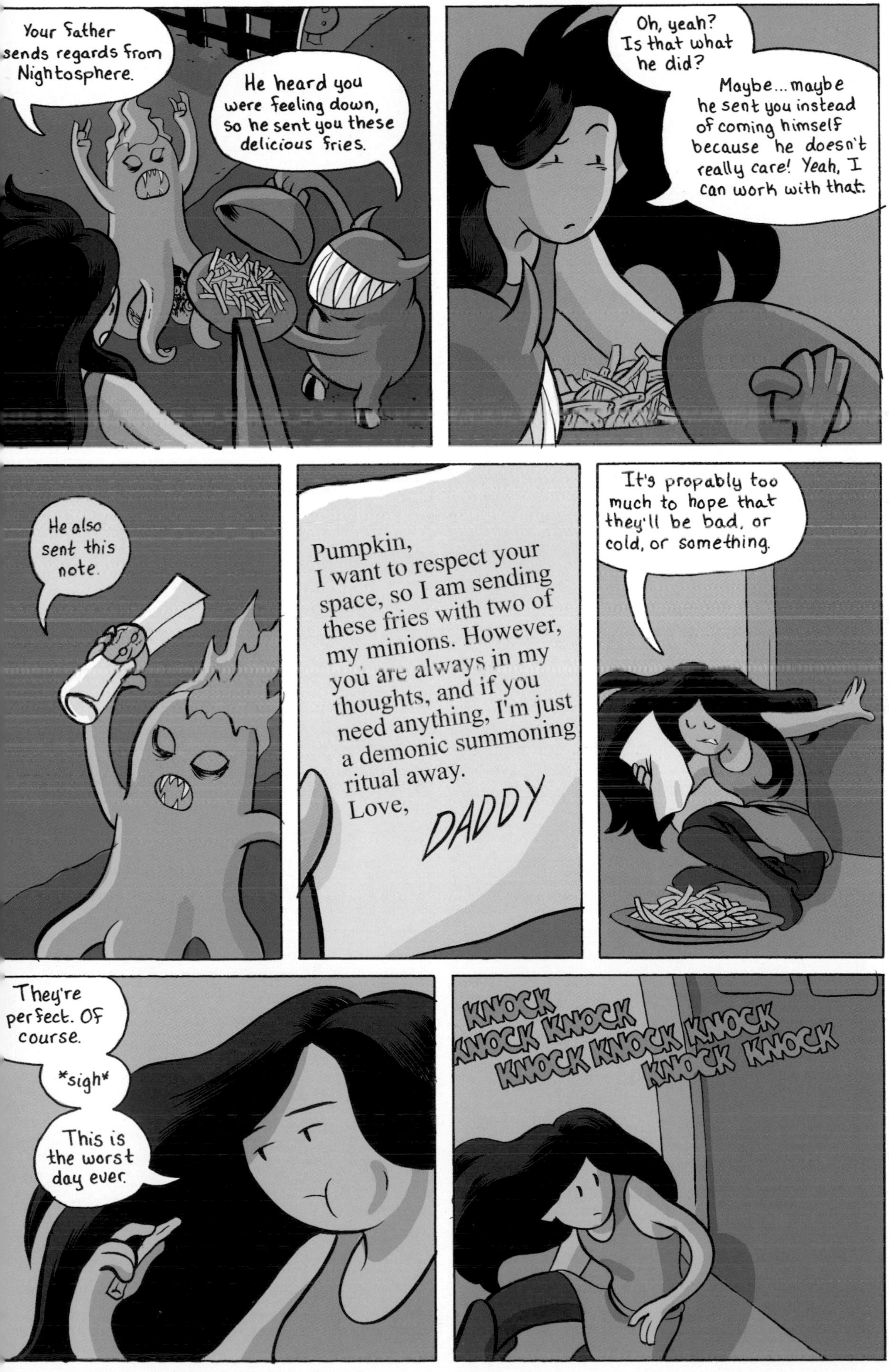

Your father sends regards from Nightosphere.
He heard you were feeling down, so he sent you these delicious fries.
Oh, yeah? Is that what he did?
Maybe... maybe he sent you instead of coming himself because he doesn't really care! Yeah, I can work with that.
He also sent this note.
Pumpkin,
I want to respect your space, so I am sending these fries with two of my minions. However, you are always in my thoughts, and if you need anything, I'm just a demonic summoning ritual away.
Love,
DADDY
It's propably too much to hope that they'll be bad, or cold, or something.
They're perfect. Of course.
sigh
This is the worst day ever.
KNOCK KNOCK KNOCK KNOCK KNOCK KNOCK KNOCK KNOCK

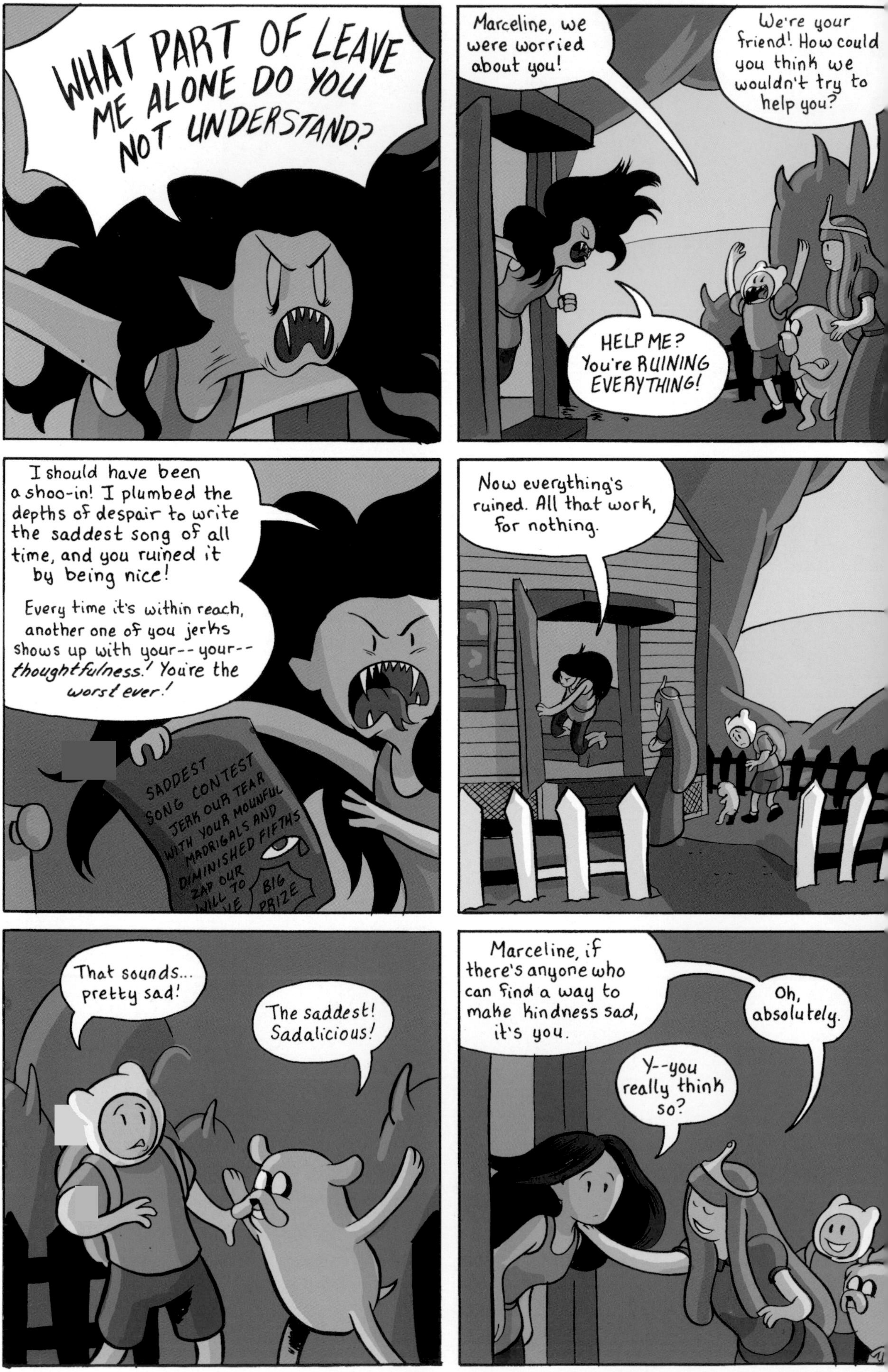

WHAT PART OF LEAVE ME ALONE DO YOU NOT UNDERSTAND?
Marceline, we were worried about you!
We're your friend! How could you think we wouldn't try to help you?
HELP ME? You're RUINING EVERYTHING!
I should have been a shoo-in! I plumbed the depths of despair to write the saddest song of all time, and you ruined it by being nice!
Every time it's within reach, another one of you jerks shows up with your-- your-- *thoughtfulness!* You're the *worst ever!*
SADDEST SONG CONTEST
JERK OUR TEAR WITH YOUR MOUNFUL MADRIGALS AND DIMINISHED FIFTHS
ZAP OUR WILL TO
BIG PRIZE
Now everything's ruined. All that work, for nothing.
That sounds... pretty sad!
The saddest! Sadalicious!
Marceline, if there's anyone who can find a way to make kindness sad, it's you.
Oh, absolutely.
Y--you really think so?

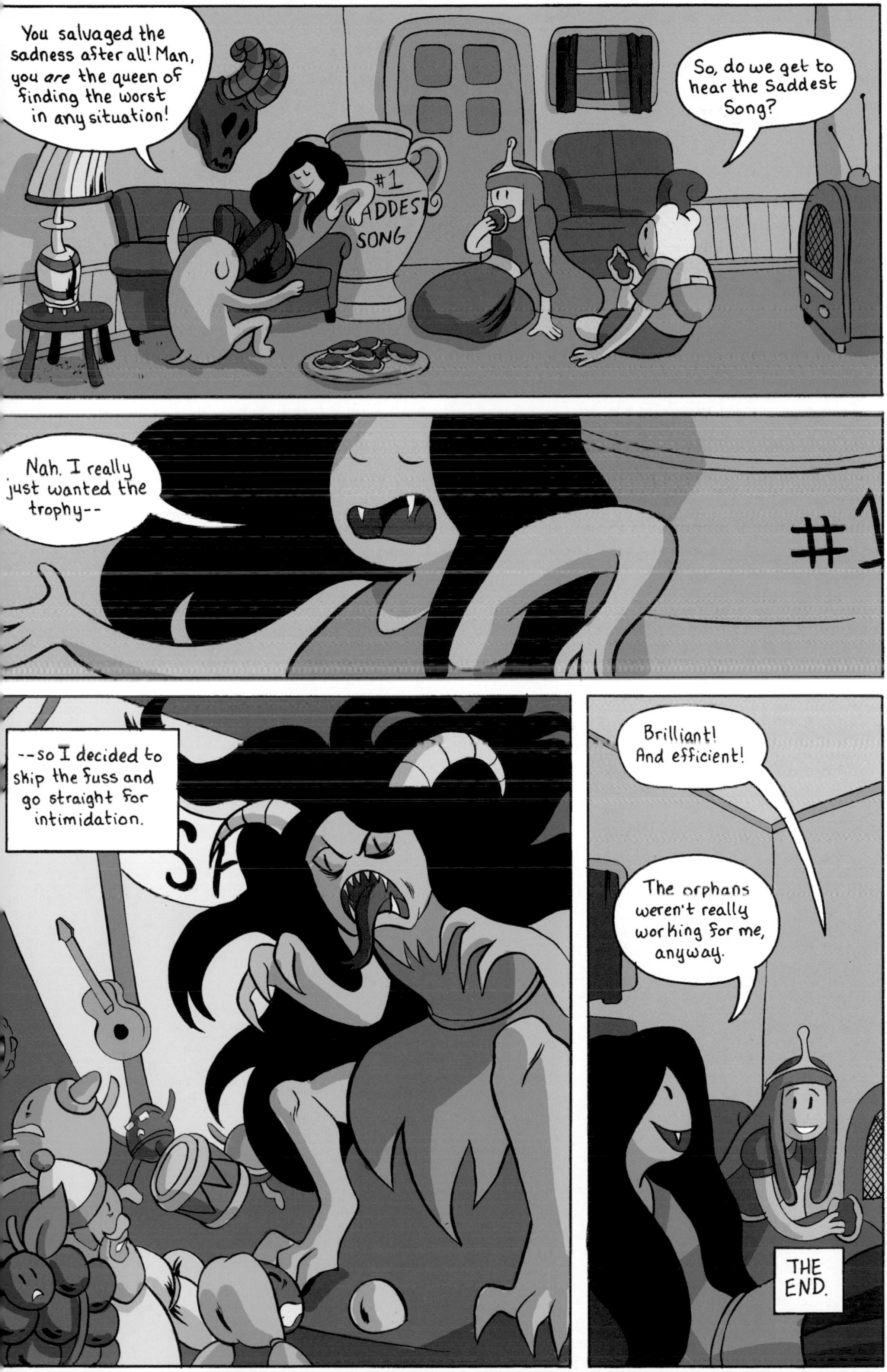
You salvaged the sadness after all! Man, you *are* the queen of finding the worst in any situation!
#1 SADDEST SONG
So, do we get to hear the Saddest Song?
Nah. I really just wanted the trophy--
--so I decided to skip the fuss and go straight for intimidation.
Brilliant! And efficient!
The orphans weren't really working for me, anyway.
THE END.

GROCERY KINGDOM

ISSUE THIRTY NINE SUBSCRIPTION COVER
ANNA STRAIN

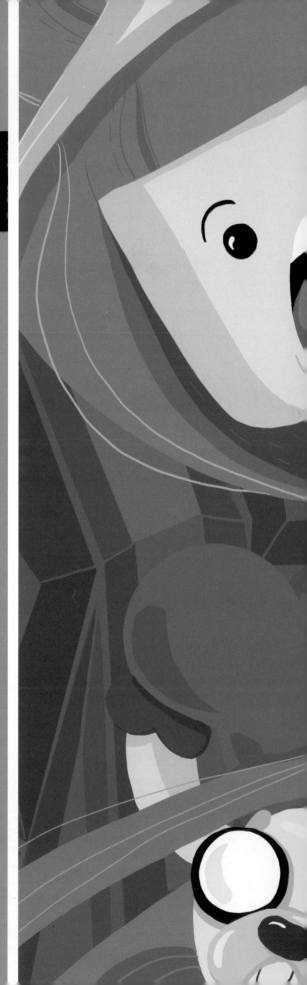

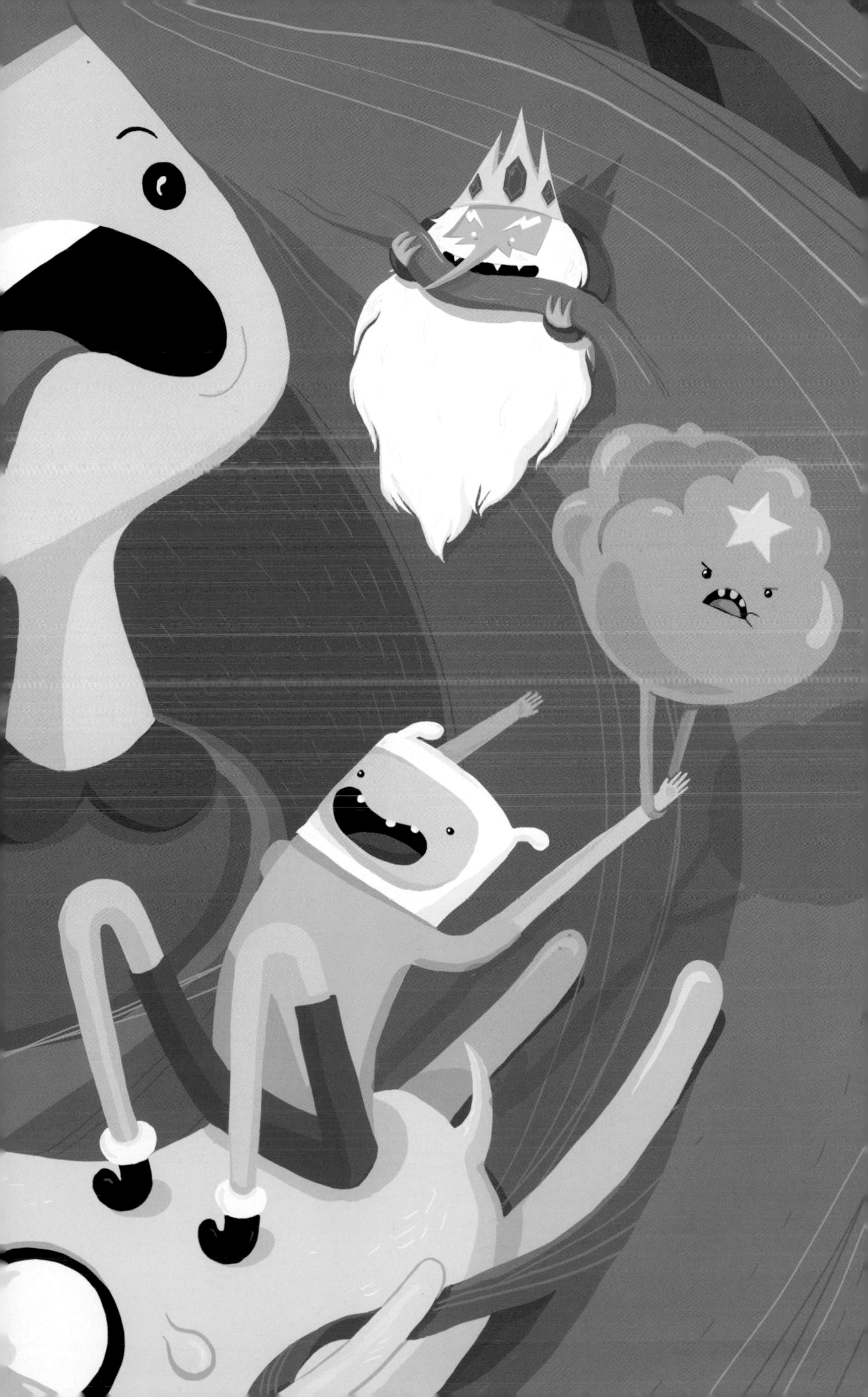

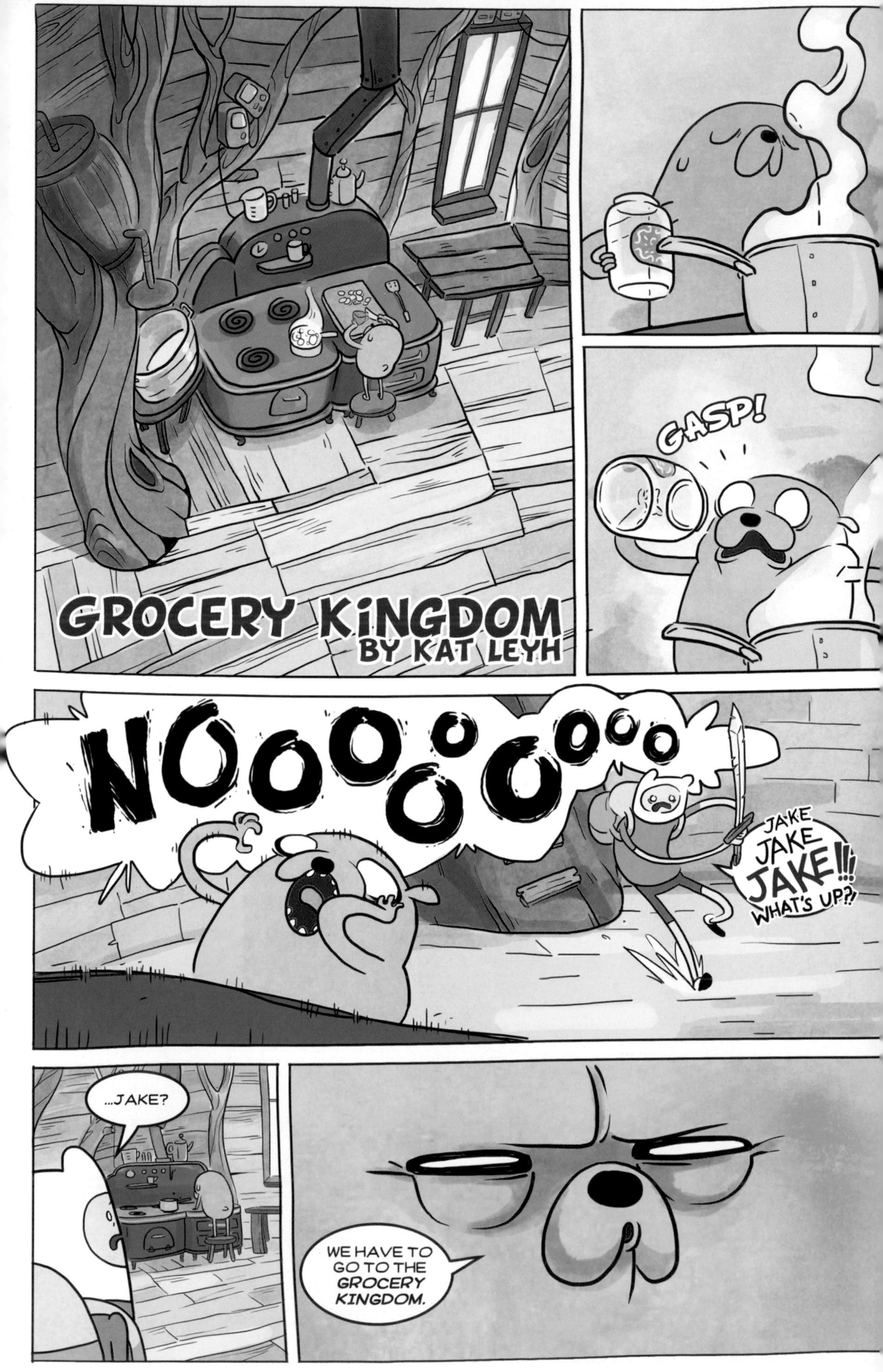
GROCERY KINGDOM
BY KAT LEYH
GASP!
NOOOOOOOooo
JAKE
JAKE
JAKE!!!
WHAT'S UP?!
...JAKE?
WE HAVE TO GO TO THE GROCERY KINGDOM.

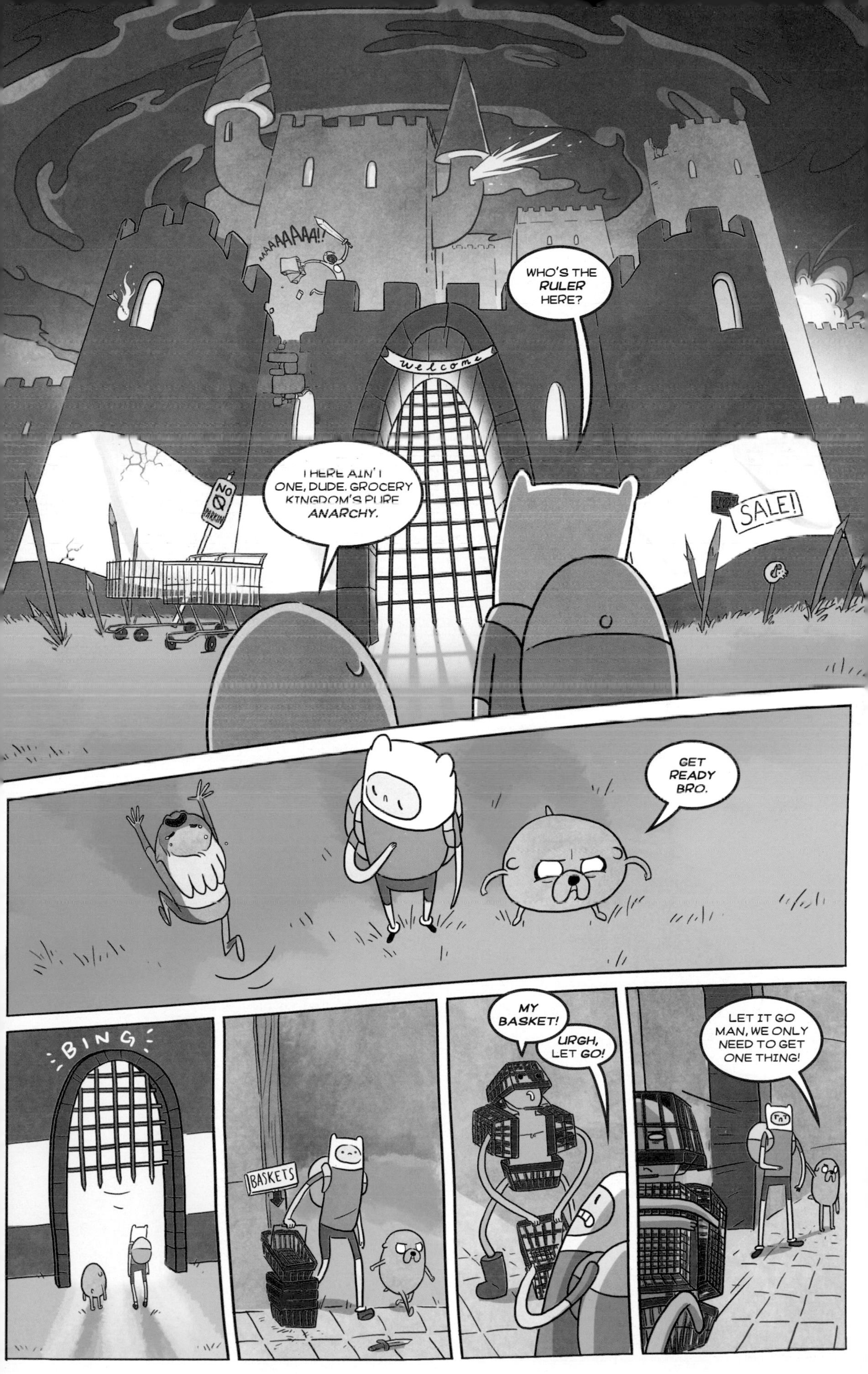
AAAAAAAAAA!!
WELCOME
NO PARKING
SALE!
WHO'S THE RULER HERE?
THERE AIN'T ONE, DUDE. GROCERY KINGDOM'S PURE ANARCHY.
GET READY BRO.
BING
BASKETS
MY BASKET!
URGH, LET GO!
LET IT GO MAN, WE ONLY NEED TO GET ONE THING!

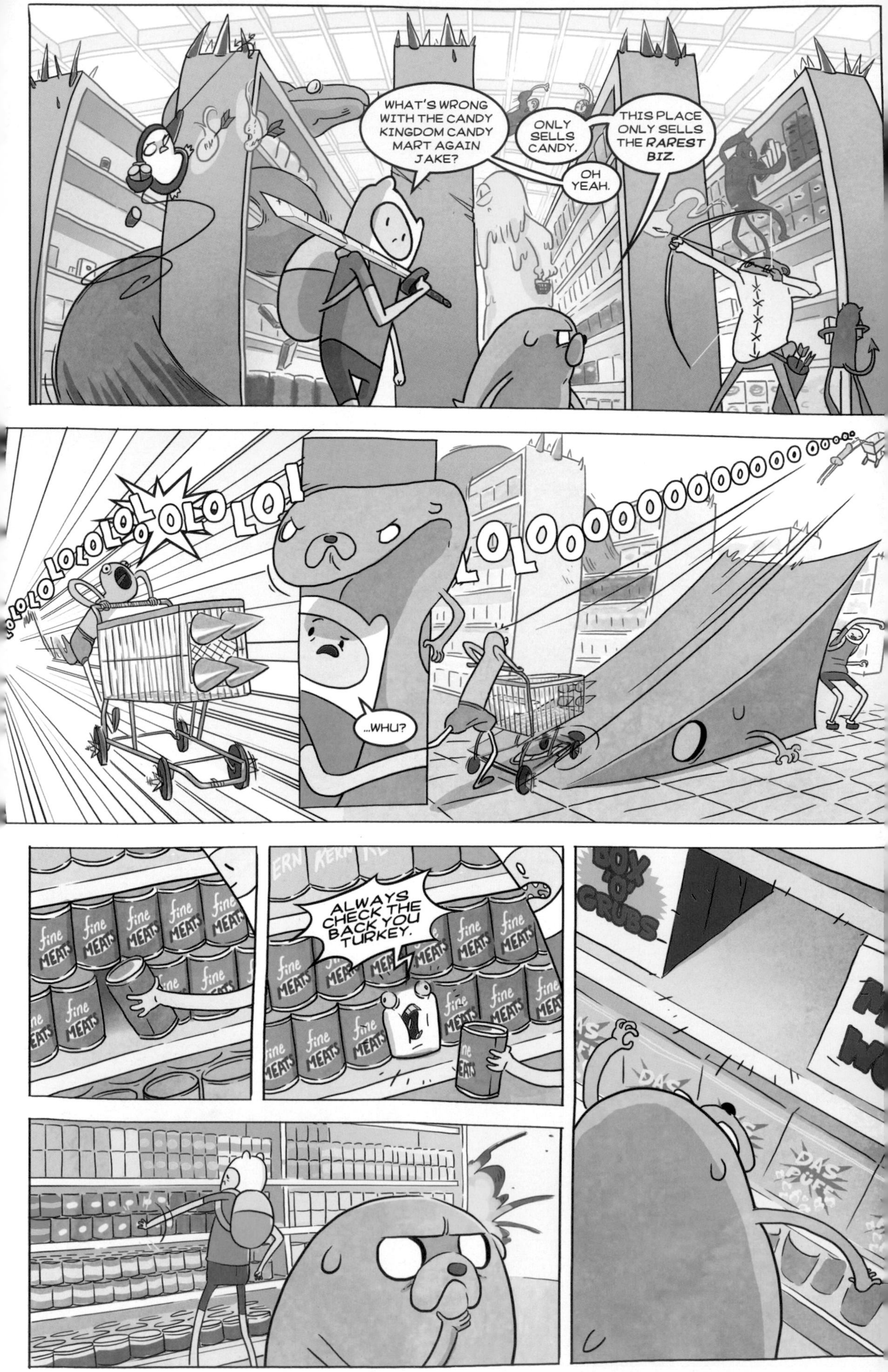
WHAT'S WRONG WITH THE CANDY KINGDOM CANDY MART AGAIN JAKE?
ONLY SELLS CANDY.
OH YEAH.
THIS PLACE ONLY SELLS THE RAREST BIZ.
LOLOLOLOLOLOLOLOLO!
LOLOOOOOOOOOOOOOOOOOOOO
...WHU?
ALWAYS CHECK THE BACK YOU TURKEY.
fine MEATS
BOX 'O' GRUBS

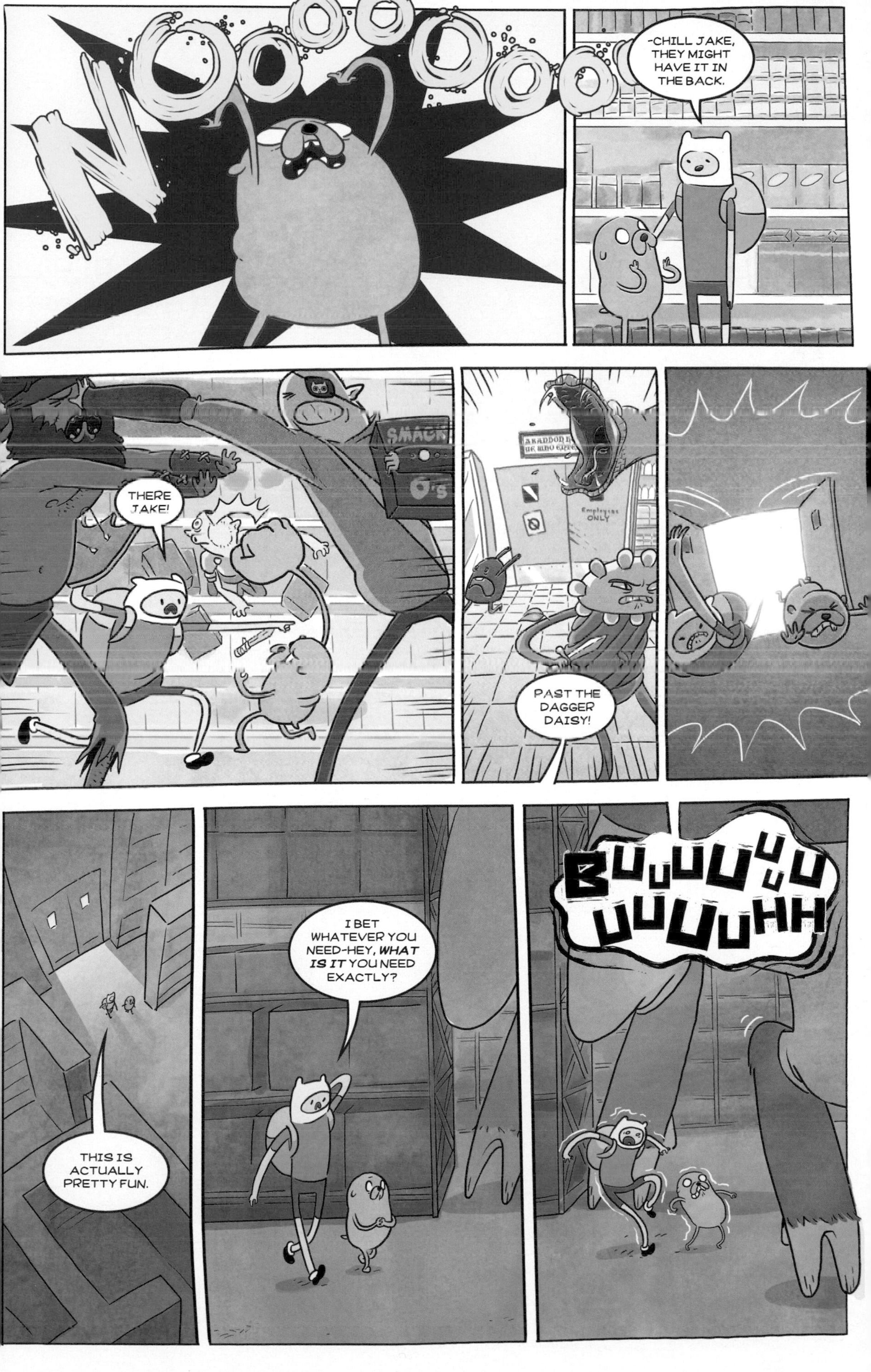
NOOOOOOOO
-CHILL JAKE, THEY MIGHT HAVE IT IN THE BACK.
SMACK
THERE JAKE!
Employees ONLY
PAST THE DAGGER DAISY!
THIS IS ACTUALLY PRETTY FUN.
I BET WHATEVER YOU NEED-HEY, ***WHAT IS IT*** YOU NEED EXACTLY?
BUUUUUUU
UUUUUHH

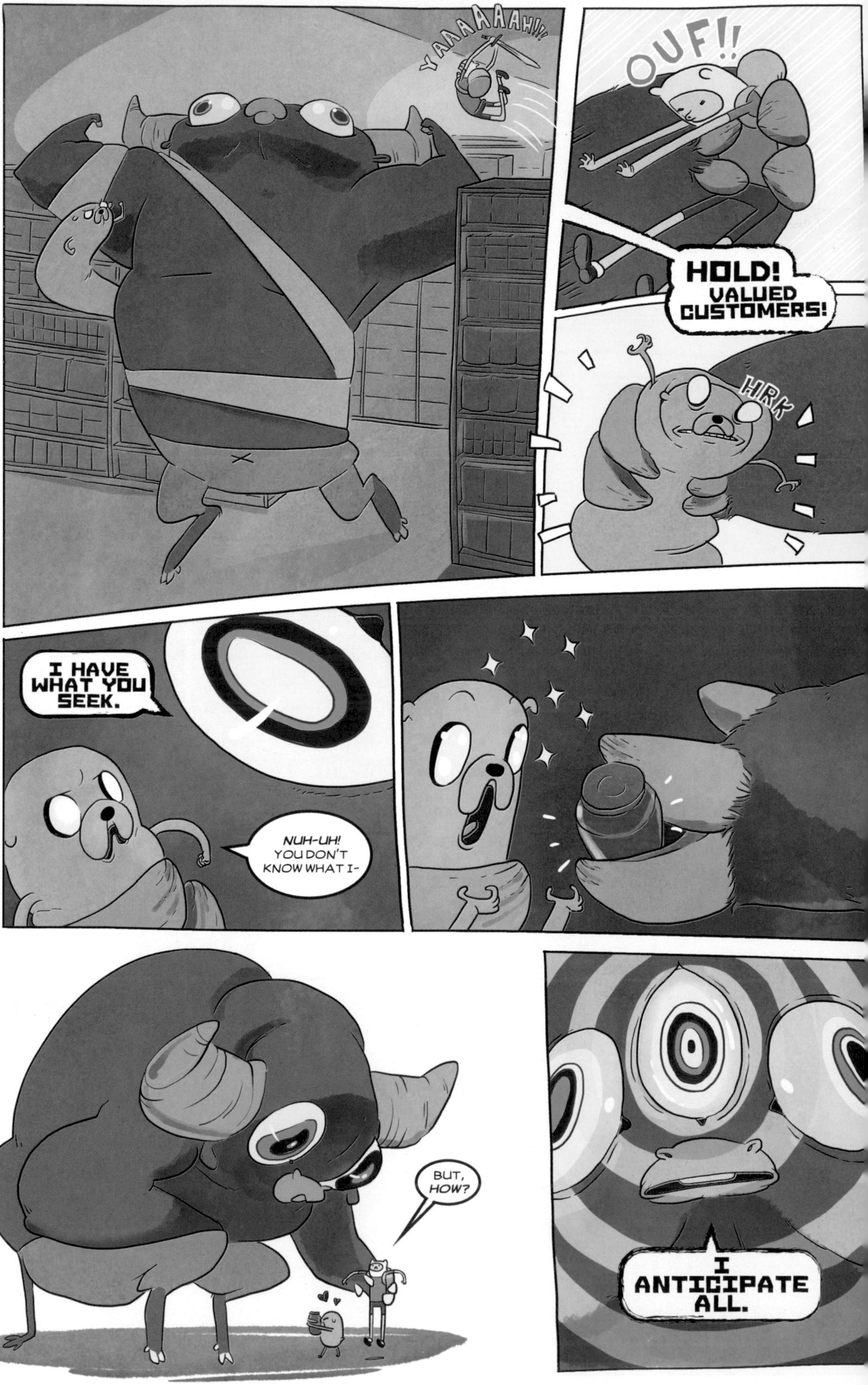
YAAAAAAAH!!!
OUF!!
HOLD! VALUED CUSTOMERS!
HRK
I HAVE WHAT YOU SEEK.
NUH-UH! YOU DON'T KNOW WHAT I-
BUT, HOW?
I ANTICIPATE ALL.

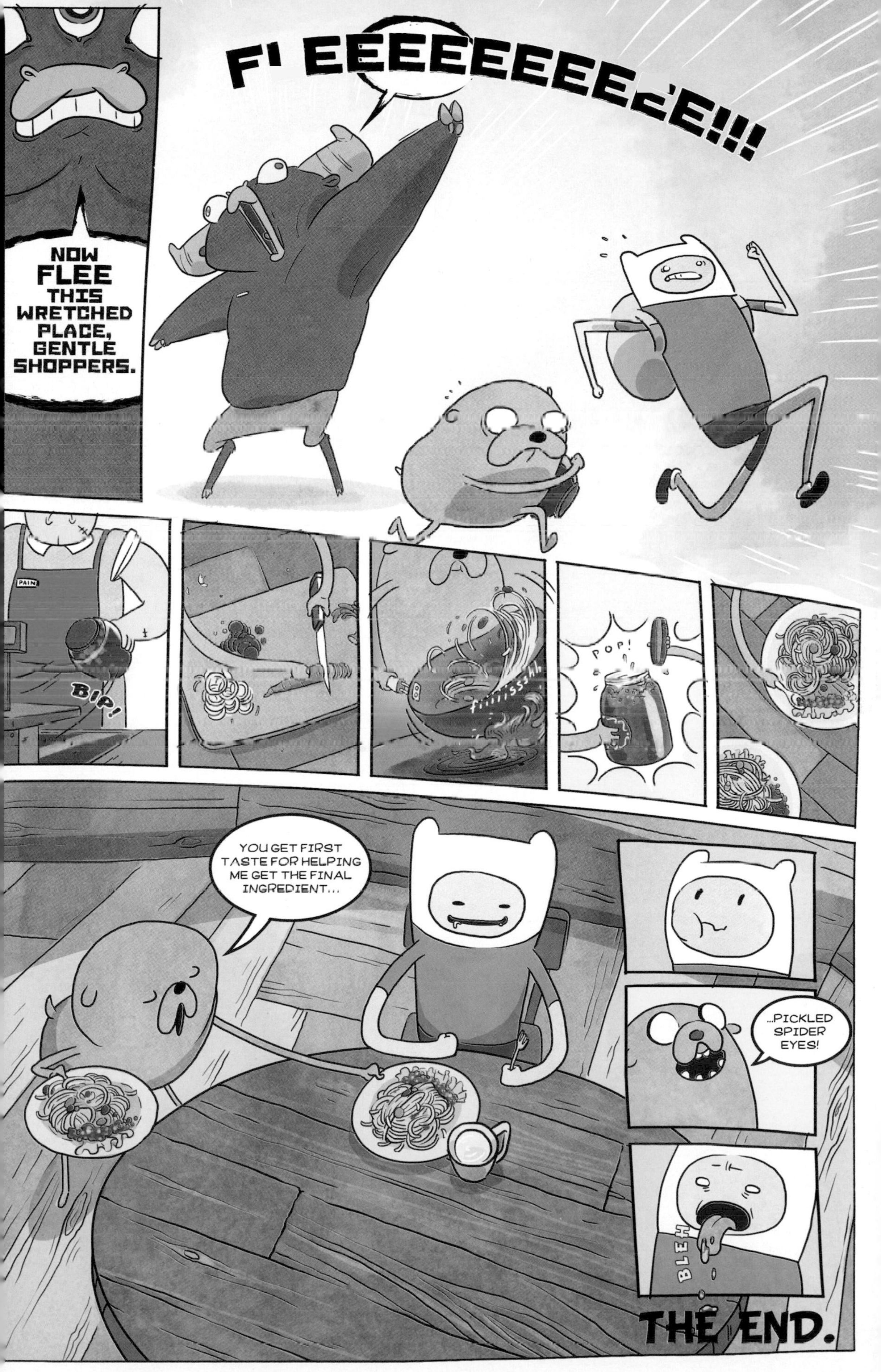
NOW FLEE THIS WRETCHED PLACE, GENTLE SHOPPERS.
FEEEEEEEEEEEE!!!
PAIN
BIP!
POP!
YOU GET FIRST TASTE FOR HELPING ME GET THE FINAL INGREDIENT...
...PICKLED SPIDER EYES!
BLEH
THE END.

AXE BEFORE TALKING

ISSUE FORTY HASTINGS EXCLUSIVE COVER
VIVIAN NG

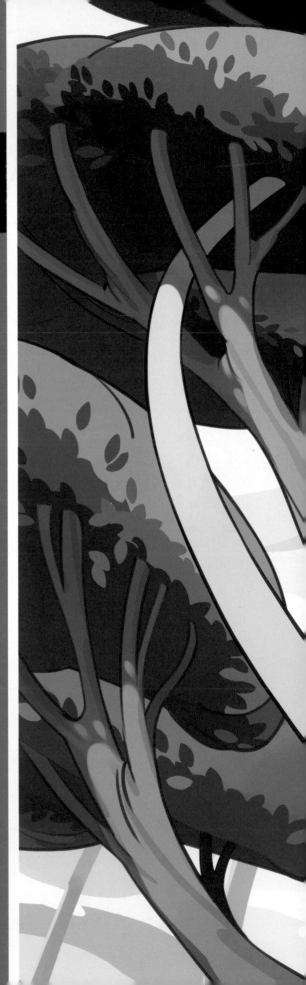

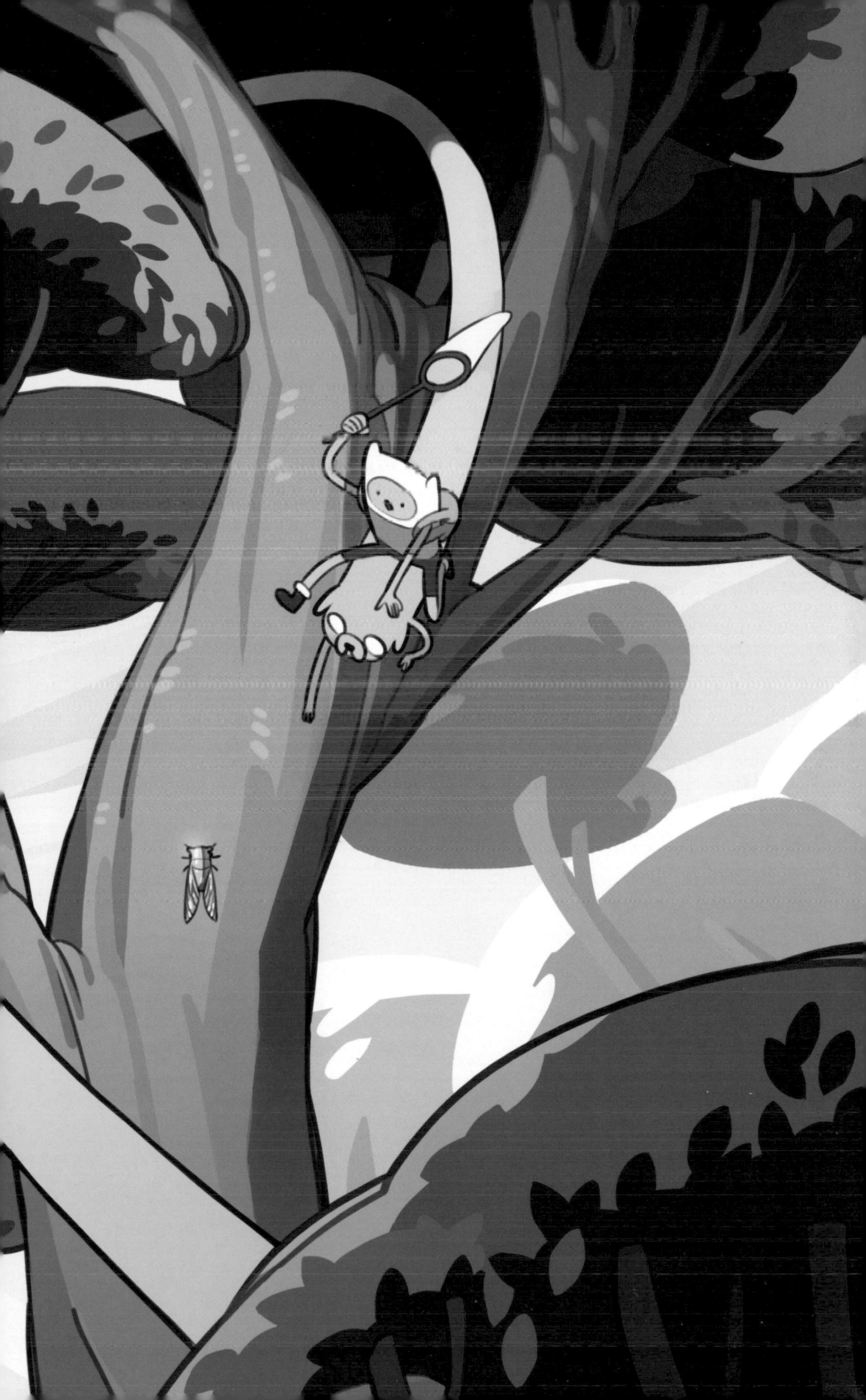

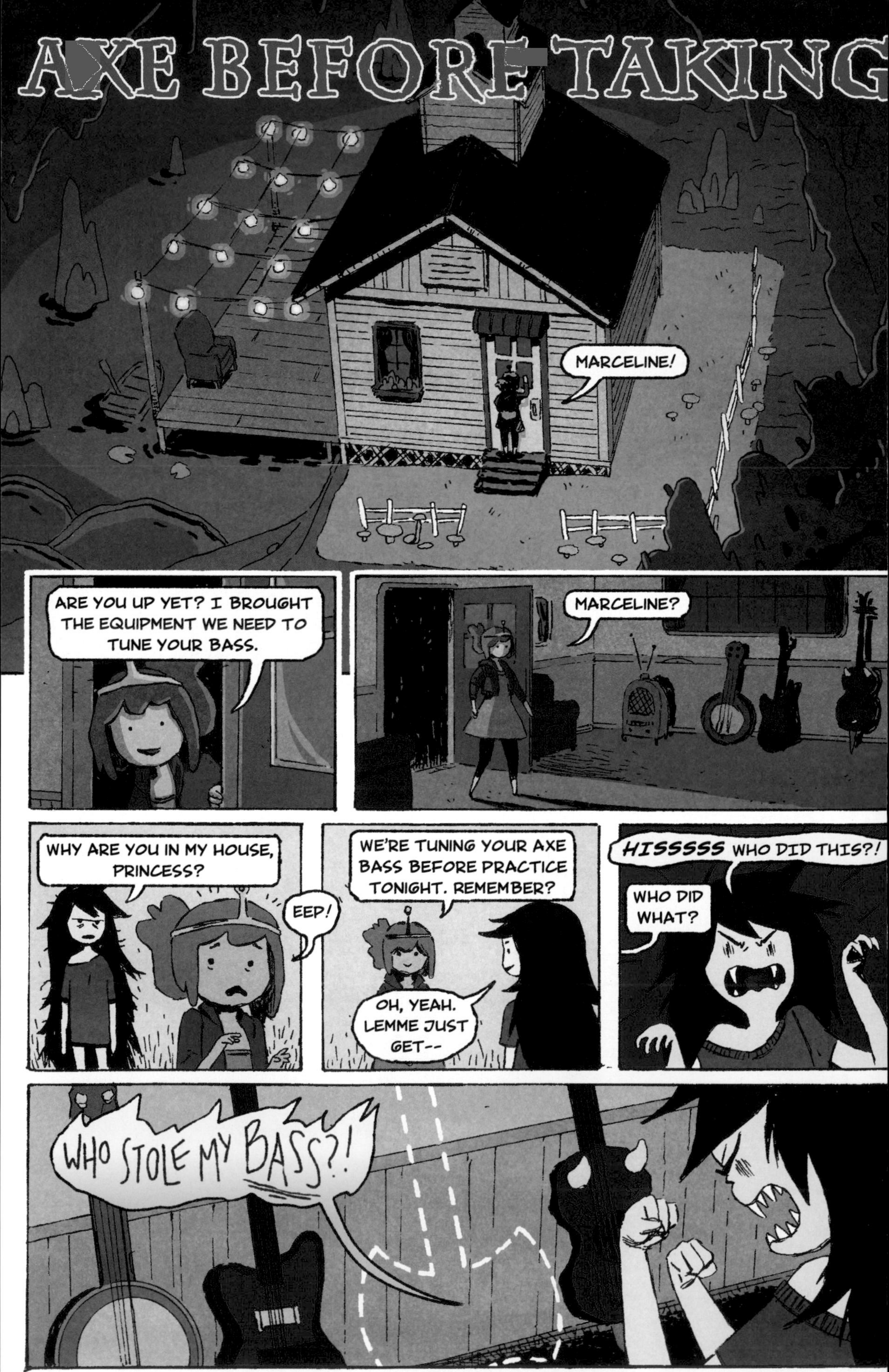
AXE BEFORE TAKING
MARCELINE!
ARE YOU UP YET? I BROUGHT THE EQUIPMENT WE NEED TO TUNE YOUR BASS.
MARCELINE?
WHY ARE YOU IN MY HOUSE, PRINCESS?
EEP!
WE'RE TUNING YOUR AXE BASS BEFORE PRACTICE TONIGHT. REMEMBER?
OH, YEAH. LEMME JUST GET--
HISSSSS WHO DID THIS?!
WHO DID WHAT?
WHO STOLE MY BASS?!

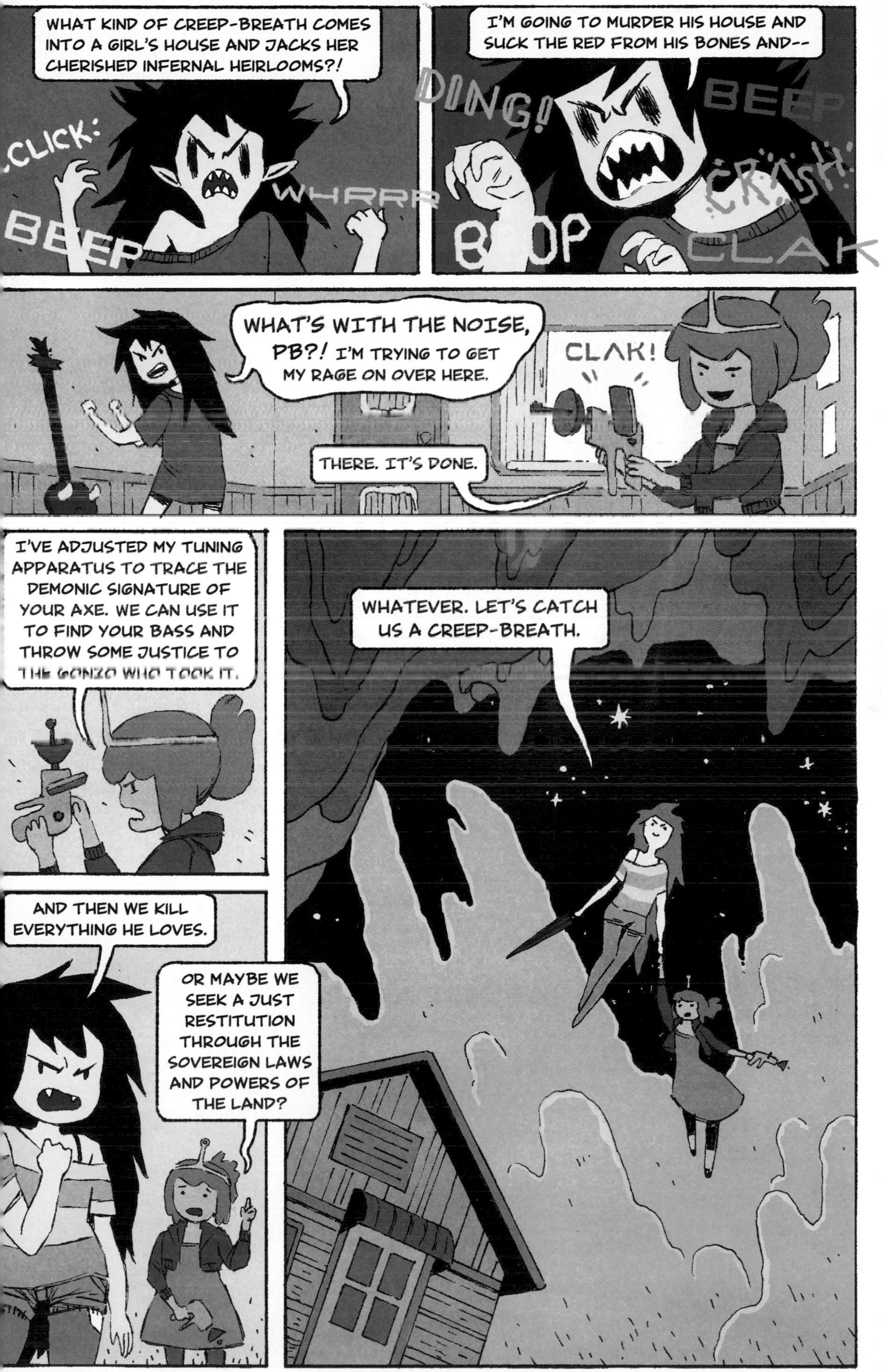
WHAT KIND OF CREEP-BREATH COMES INTO A GIRL'S HOUSE AND JACKS HER CHERISHED INFERNAL HEIRLOOMS?!
CLICK:
WHRRR
BEEP
I'M GOING TO MURDER HIS HOUSE AND SUCK THE RED FROM HIS BONES AND--
DING!
BEEP
CRASH!
CLAK
WHAT'S WITH THE NOISE, PB?! I'M TRYING TO GET MY RAGE ON OVER HERE.
CLAK!
THERE. IT'S DONE.
I'VE ADJUSTED MY TUNING APPARATUS TO TRACE THE DEMONIC SIGNATURE OF YOUR AXE. WE CAN USE IT TO FIND YOUR BASS AND THROW SOME JUSTICE TO THE GONZO WHO TOOK IT.
AND THEN WE KILL EVERYTHING HE LOVES.
OR MAYBE WE SEEK A JUST RESTITUTION THROUGH THE SOVEREIGN LAWS AND POWERS OF THE LAND?
WHATEVER. LET'S CATCH US A CREEP-BREATH.

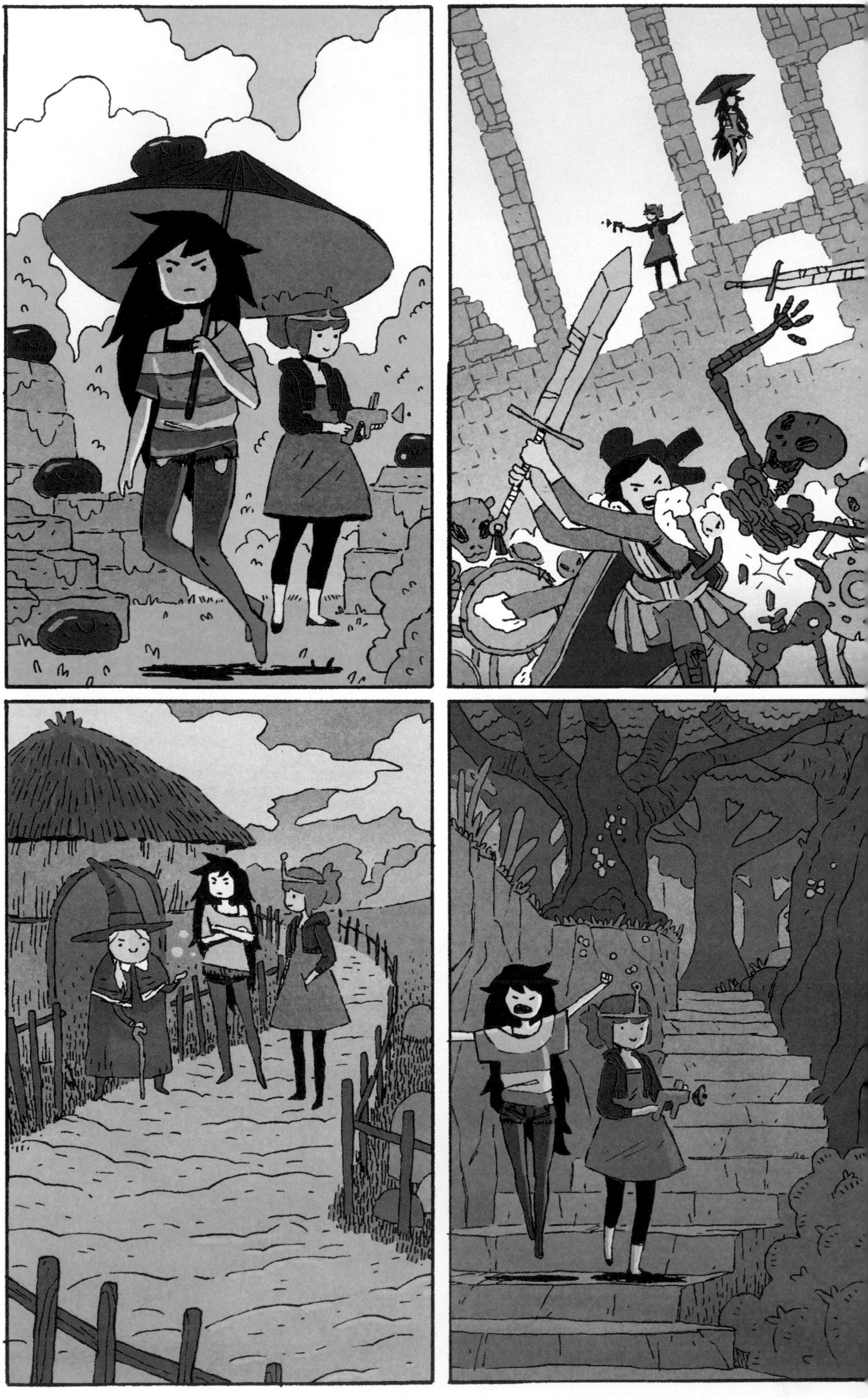

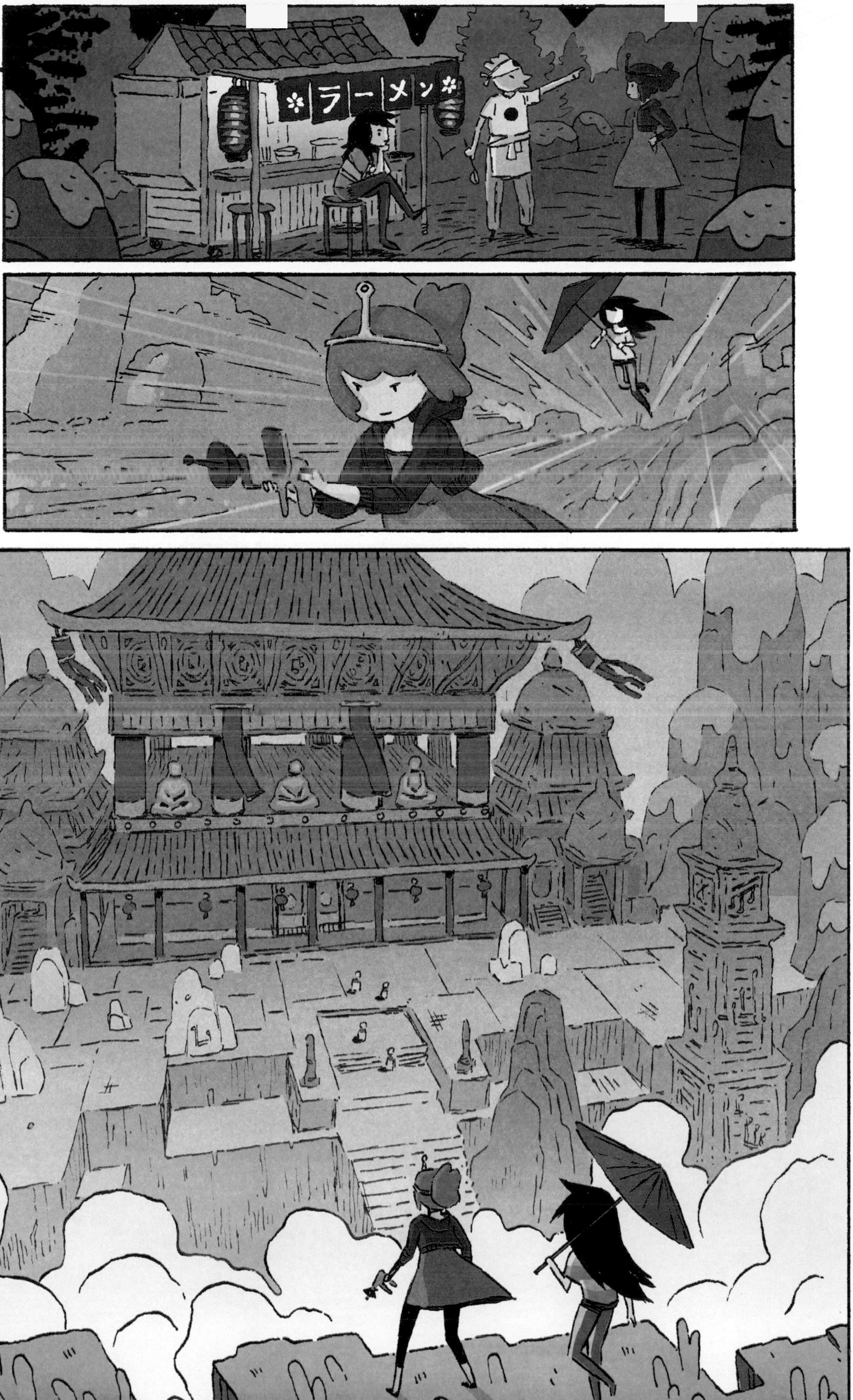
ラーメン

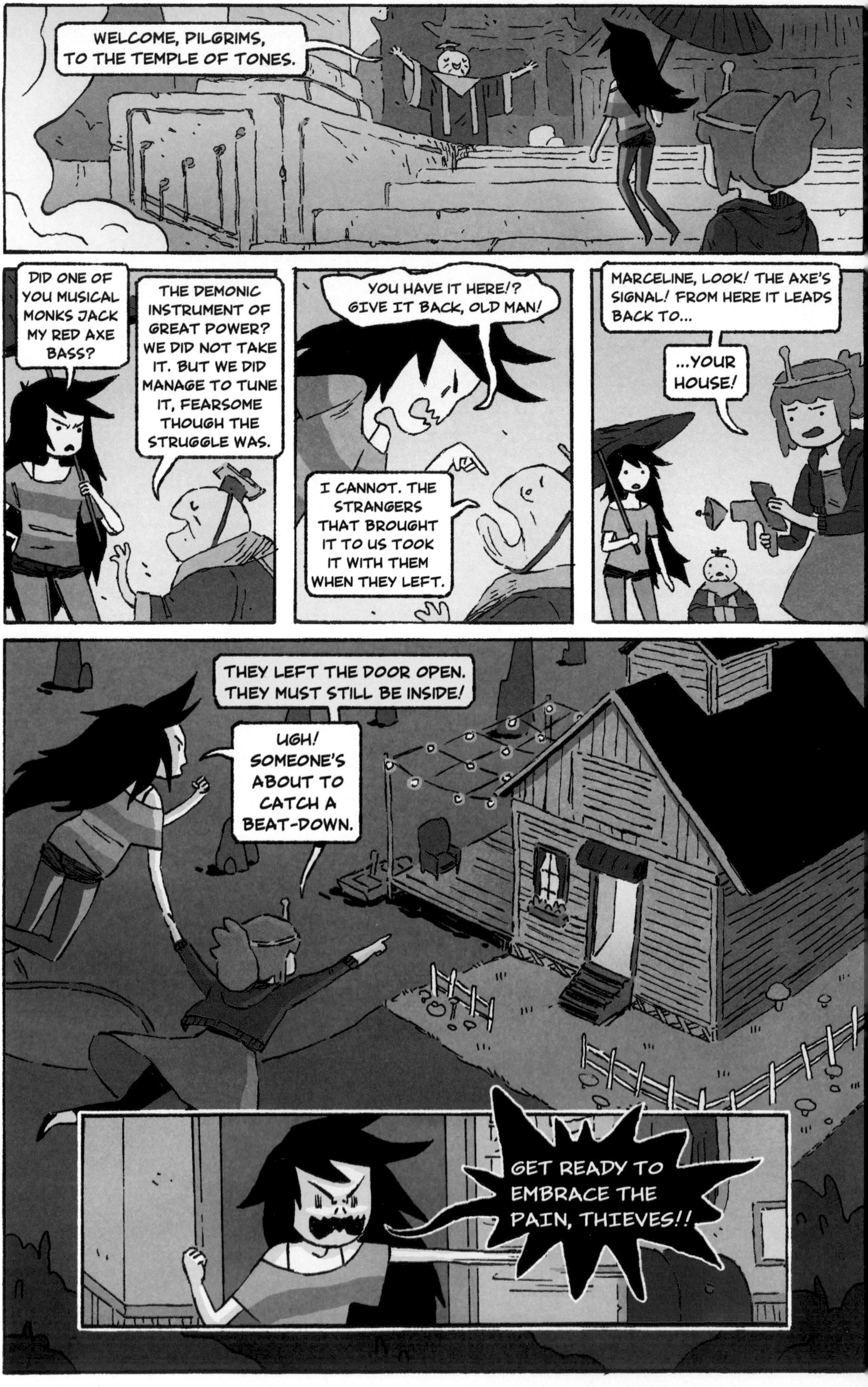
WELCOME, PILGRIMS, TO THE TEMPLE OF TONES.
DID ONE OF YOU MUSICAL MONKS JACK MY RED AXE BASS?
THE DEMONIC INSTRUMENT OF GREAT POWER? WE DID NOT TAKE IT. BUT WE DID MANAGE TO TUNE IT, FEARSOME THOUGH THE STRUGGLE WAS.
YOU HAVE IT HERE!? GIVE IT BACK, OLD MAN!
I CANNOT. THE STRANGERS THAT BROUGHT IT TO US TOOK IT WITH THEM WHEN THEY LEFT.
MARCELINE, LOOK! THE AXE'S SIGNAL! FROM HERE IT LEADS BACK TO...
...YOUR HOUSE!
THEY LEFT THE DOOR OPEN. THEY MUST STILL BE INSIDE!
UGH! SOMEONE'S ABOUT TO CATCH A BEAT-DOWN.
GET READY TO EMBRACE THE PAIN, THIEVES!!

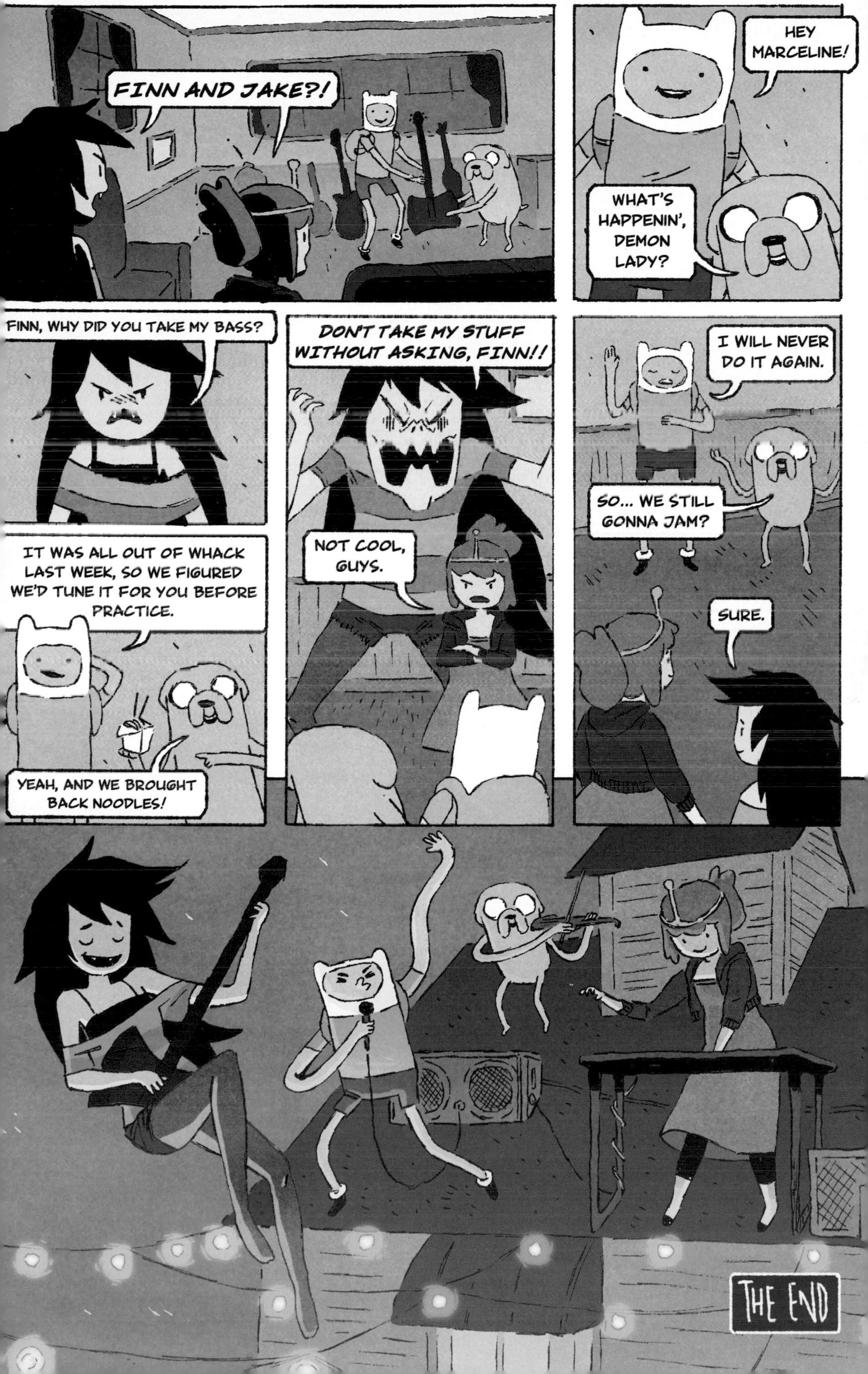
FINN AND JAKE?!
HEY MARCELINE!
WHAT'S HAPPENIN', DEMON LADY?
FINN, WHY DID YOU TAKE MY BASS?
IT WAS ALL OUT OF WHACK LAST WEEK, SO WE FIGURED WE'D TUNE IT FOR YOU BEFORE PRACTICE.
YEAH, AND WE BROUGHT BACK NOODLES!
DON'T TAKE MY STUFF WITHOUT ASKING, FINN!!
NOT COOL, GUYS.
I WILL NEVER DO IT AGAIN.
SO... WE STILL GONNA JAM?
SURE.
THE END

DAD OLYMPICS

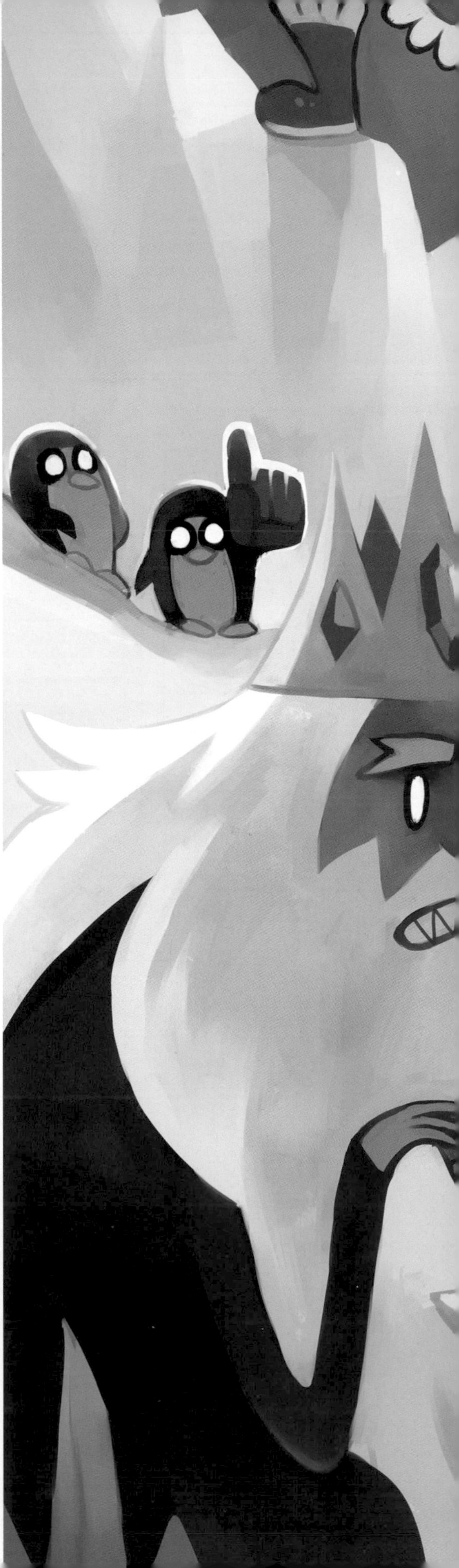

ISSUE FORTY ONE SUBSCRIPTION COVER
MELANIE HERRING

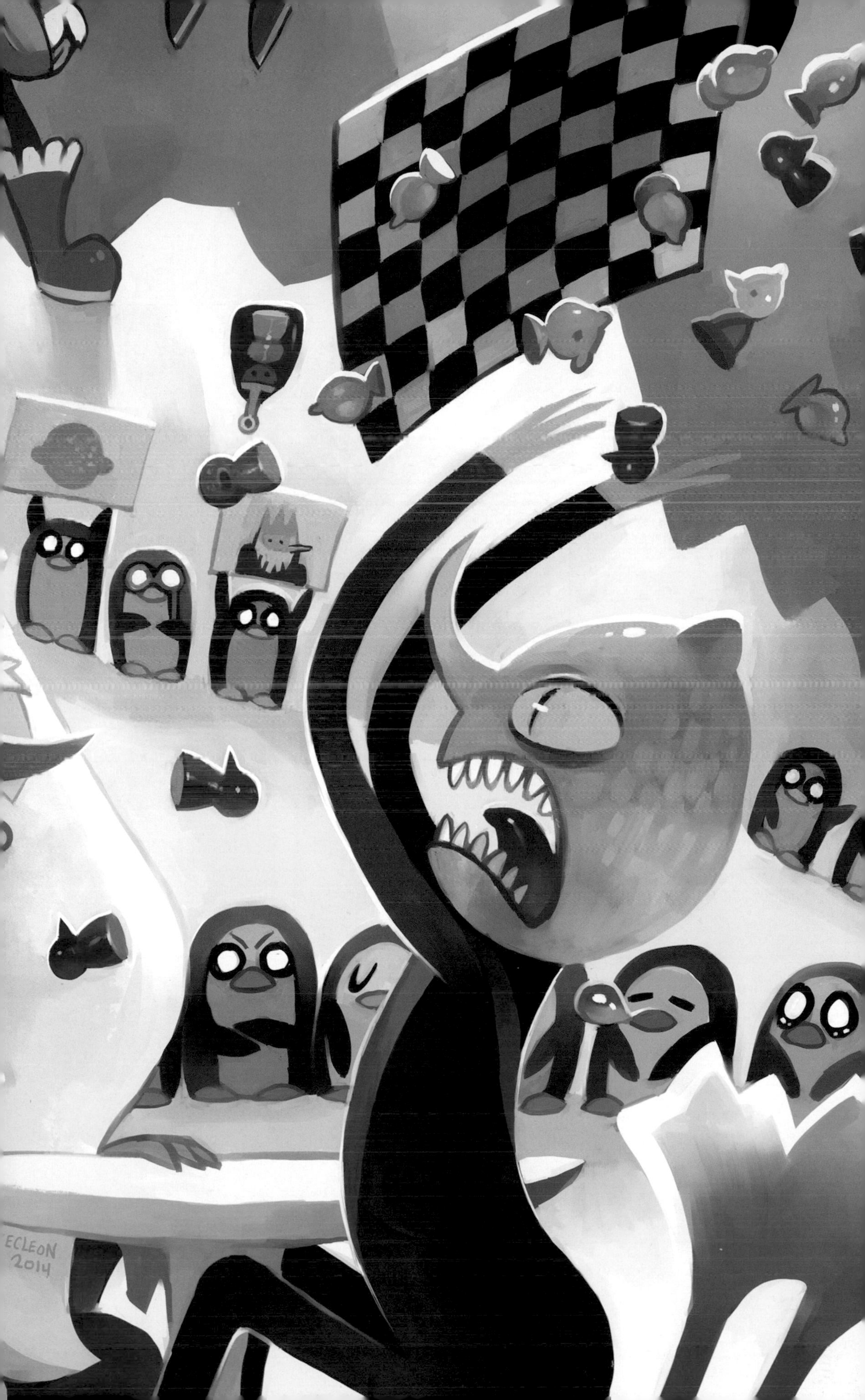
ECLEON
2014

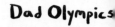

WELCOME, CITIZENS OF OOO! TODAY MARKS THE OPENING OF THE FIRST EVER DAD OLYMPICS!

IT'S TIME TO WELCOME YOUR CHAMPIONS! AND THE LIKE.. FOUR PEOPLE WHO ACTUALLY HAVE DADS.

FIRST UP, PRINCESS BUBBLEGUM AND HER CANDY GOLEM FATHER!

TOTALLY COUNTS, GUYS!

NEXT WE HAVE MARCELINE AND HER FATHER, THE DARK LORD OF THE NIGHTOSPHERE!

AND LAST BUT NOT LEAST, JAKE THE DOG AND HIS HOLOGRAM DAD!

WHAT ABOUT FLAME PRINCESS AND HER DAD?

SHE DOESN'T COUNT!!!

OOP! CAN'T FORGET ABOUT THE SPIRIT SQUAD! GO TEAM!

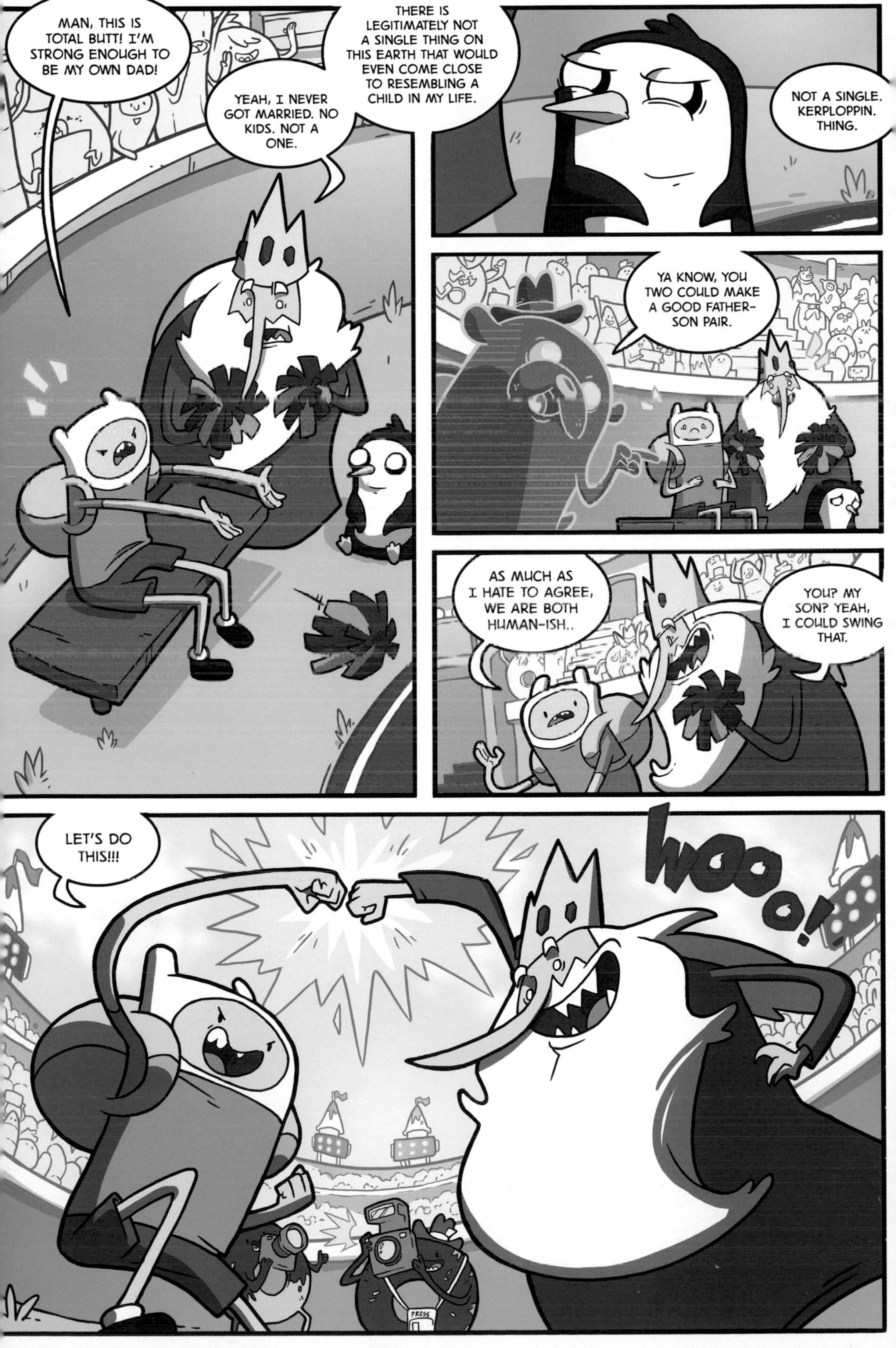
MAN, THIS IS TOTAL BUTT! I'M STRONG ENOUGH TO BE MY OWN DAD!
YEAH, I NEVER GOT MARRIED. NO KIDS. NOT A ONE.
THERE IS LEGITIMATELY NOT A SINGLE THING ON THIS EARTH THAT WOULD EVEN COME CLOSE TO RESEMBLING A CHILD IN MY LIFE.
NOT A SINGLE. KERPLOPPIN. THING.
YA KNOW, YOU TWO COULD MAKE A GOOD FATHER-SON PAIR.
AS MUCH AS I HATE TO AGREE, WE ARE BOTH HUMAN-ISH..
YOU? MY SON? YEAH, I COULD SWING THAT.
LET'S DO THIS!!!
WOOO!
PRESS

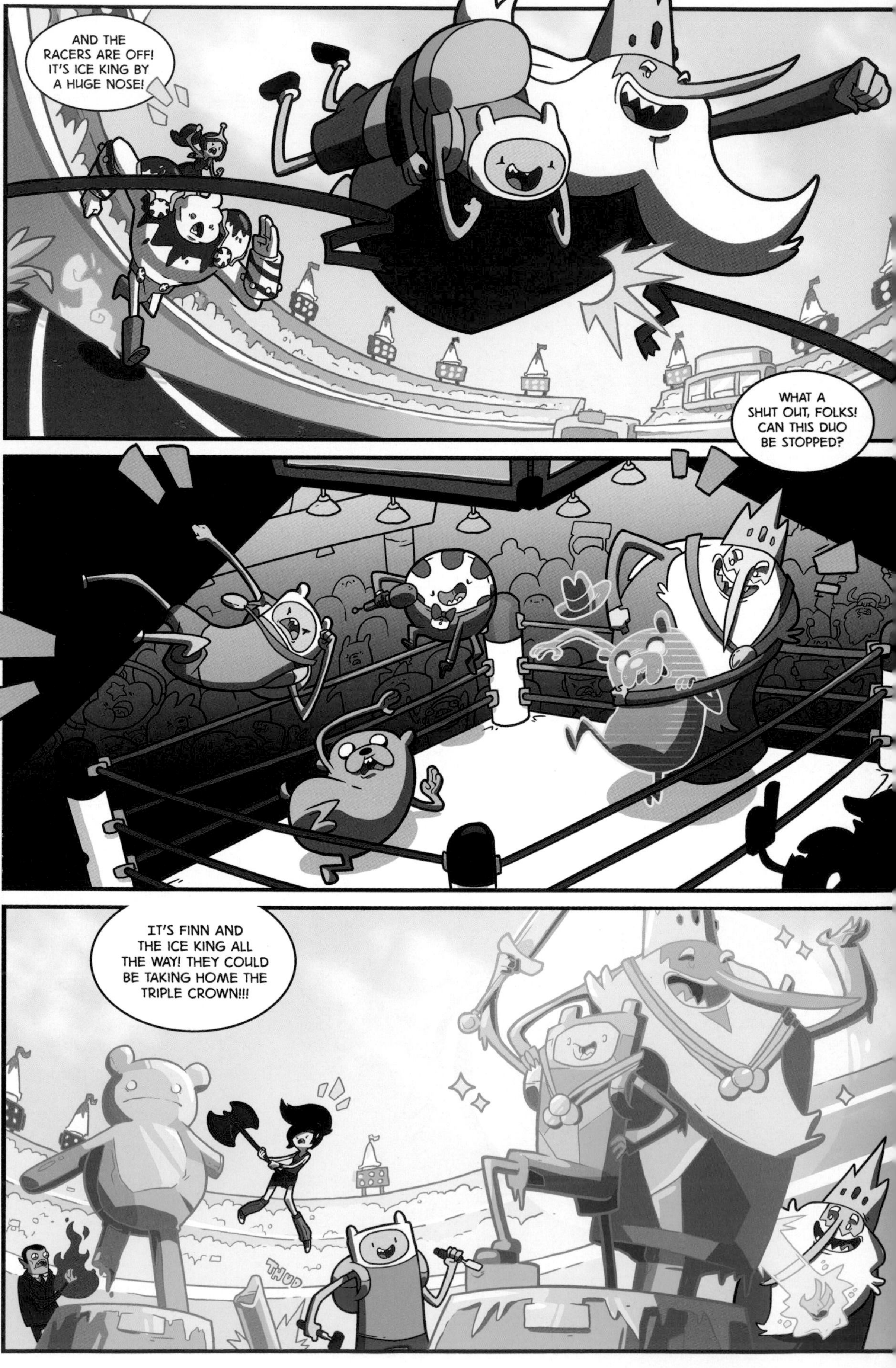
AND THE RACERS ARE OFF! IT'S ICE KING BY A HUGE NOSE!
WHAT A SHUT OUT, FOLKS! CAN THIS DUO BE STOPPED?
IT'S FINN AND THE ICE KING ALL THE WAY! THEY COULD BE TAKING HOME THE TRIPLE CROWN!!!
THUD

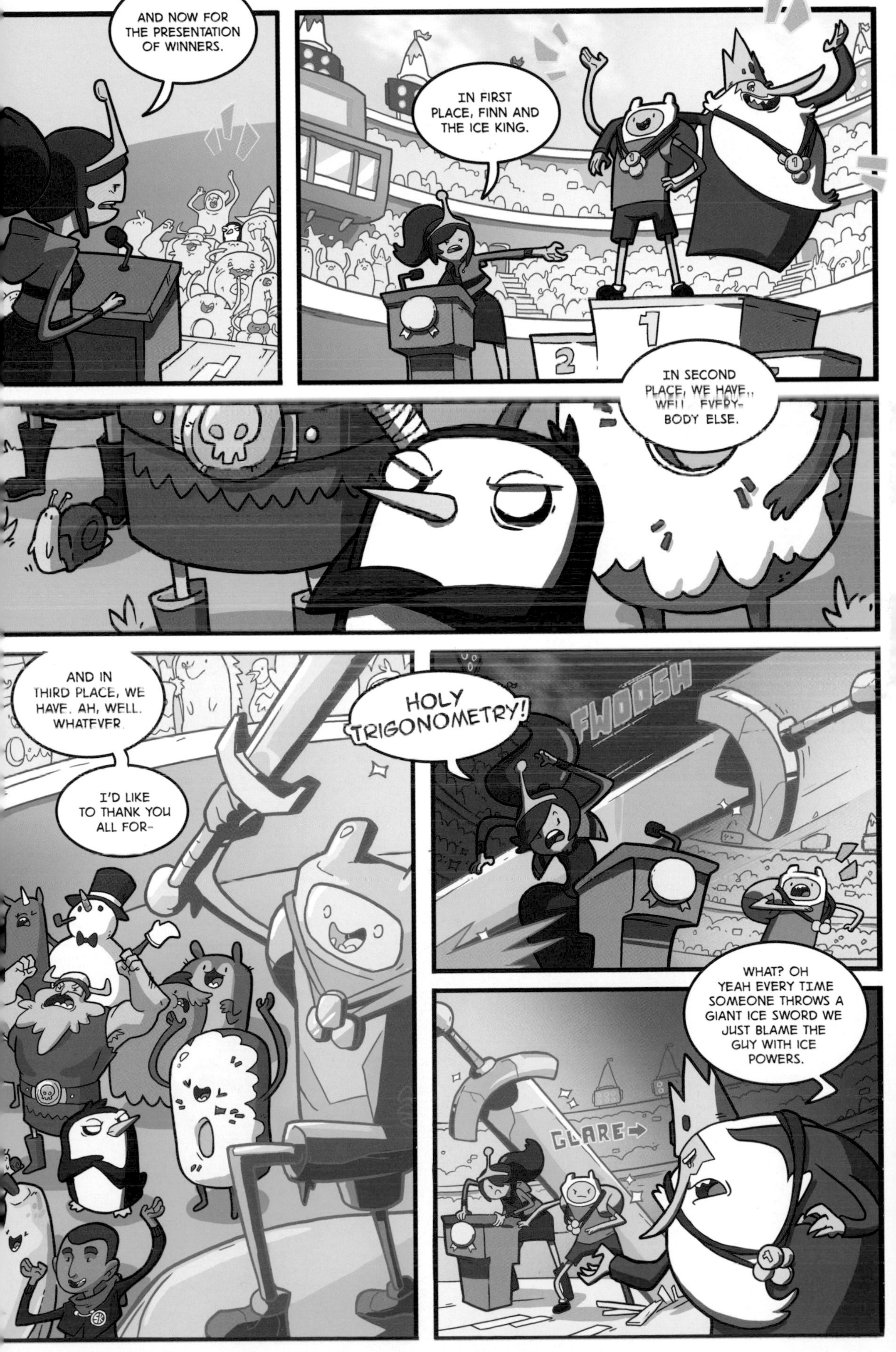
AND NOW FOR THE PRESENTATION OF WINNERS.
IN FIRST PLACE, FINN AND THE ICE KING.
IN SECOND PLACE, WE HAVE.. WELL, EVERY-BODY ELSE.
AND IN THIRD PLACE, WE HAVE. AH, WELL. WHATEVER.
I'D LIKE TO THANK YOU ALL FOR-
HOLY TRIGONOMETRY!
FWOOSH
WHAT? OH YEAH EVERY TIME SOMEONE THROWS A GIANT ICE SWORD WE JUST BLAME THE GUY WITH ICE POWERS.
GLARE

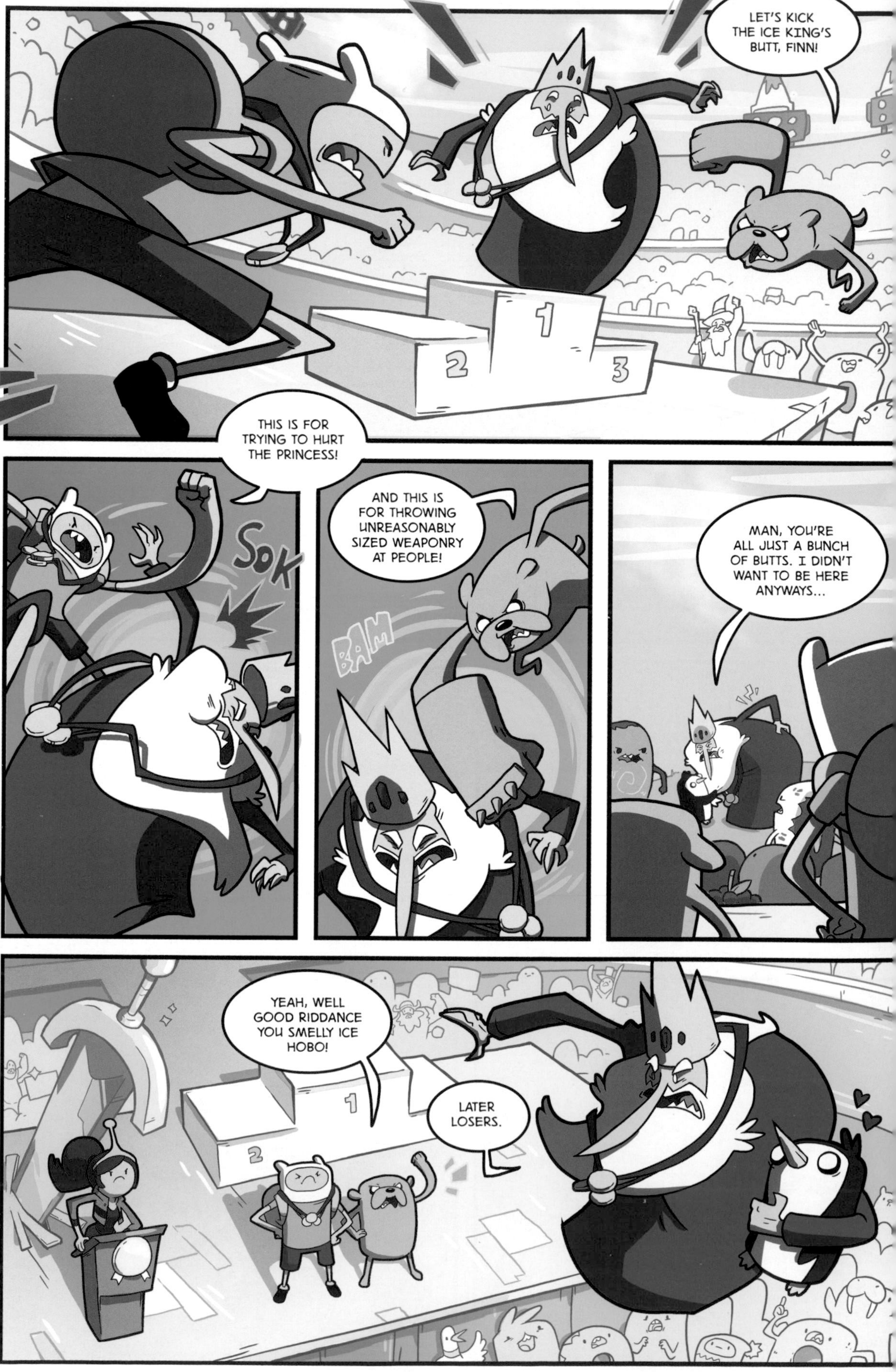
LET'S KICK THE ICE KING'S BUTT, FINN!
THIS IS FOR TRYING TO HURT THE PRINCESS!
SOK
AND THIS IS FOR THROWING UNREASONABLY SIZED WEAPONRY AT PEOPLE!
BAM
MAN, YOU'RE ALL JUST A BUNCH OF BUTTS. I DIDN'T WANT TO BE HERE ANYWAYS...
YEAH, WELL GOOD RIDDANCE YOU SMELLY ICE HOBO!
LATER LOSERS.

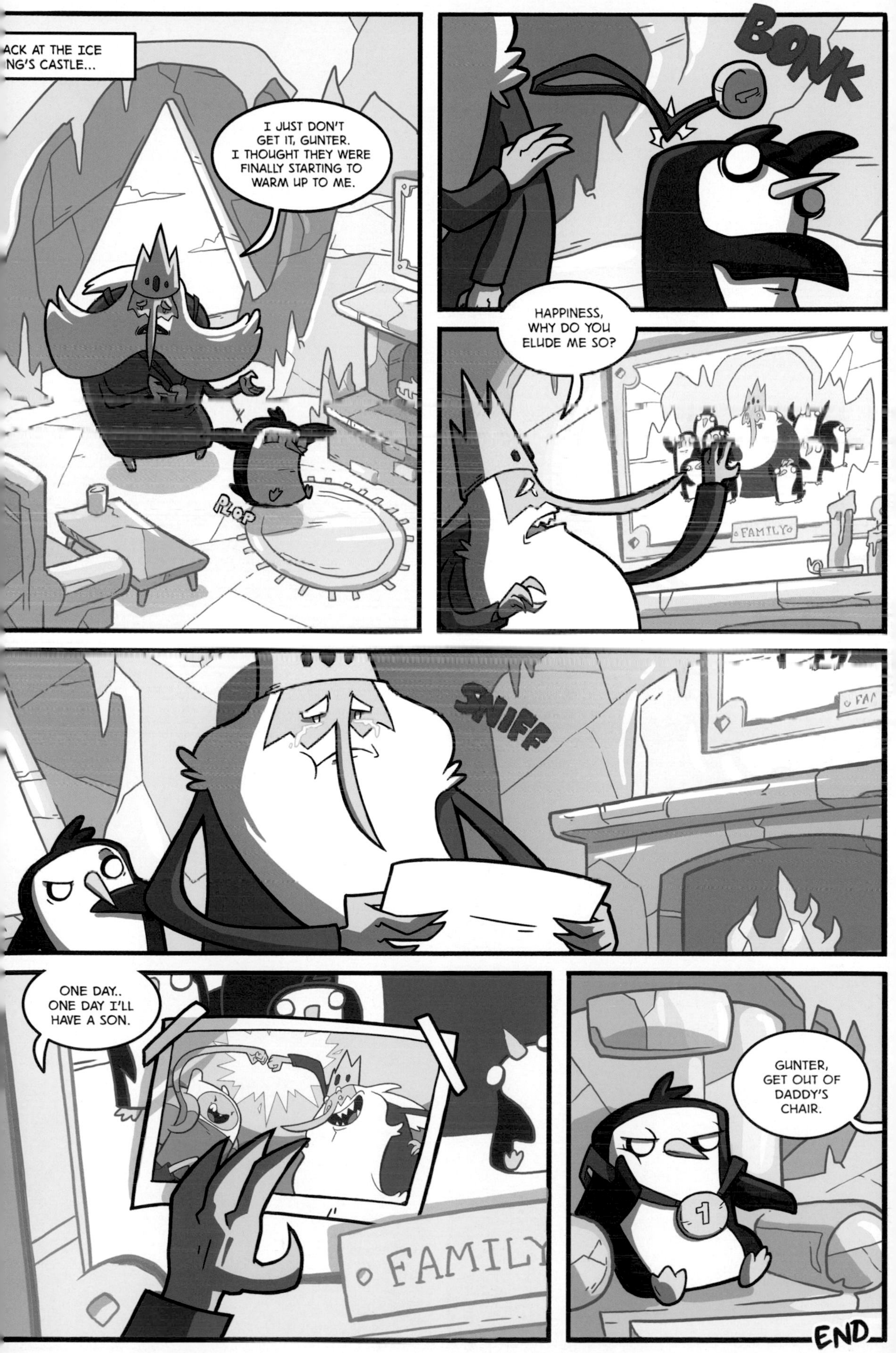
ACK AT THE ICE
NG'S CASTLE...
I JUST DON'T GET IT, GUNTER. I THOUGHT THEY WERE FINALLY STARTING TO WARM UP TO ME.
PLOP
BONK
HAPPINESS, WHY DO YOU ELUDE ME SO?
FAMILY
SNIFF
ONE DAY.. ONE DAY I'LL HAVE A SON.
FAMILY
GUNTER, GET OUT OF DADDY'S CHAIR.
1
END

SIR BMO

ISSUE FORTY TWO SUBSCRIPTION COVER
MYCHAL AMANN

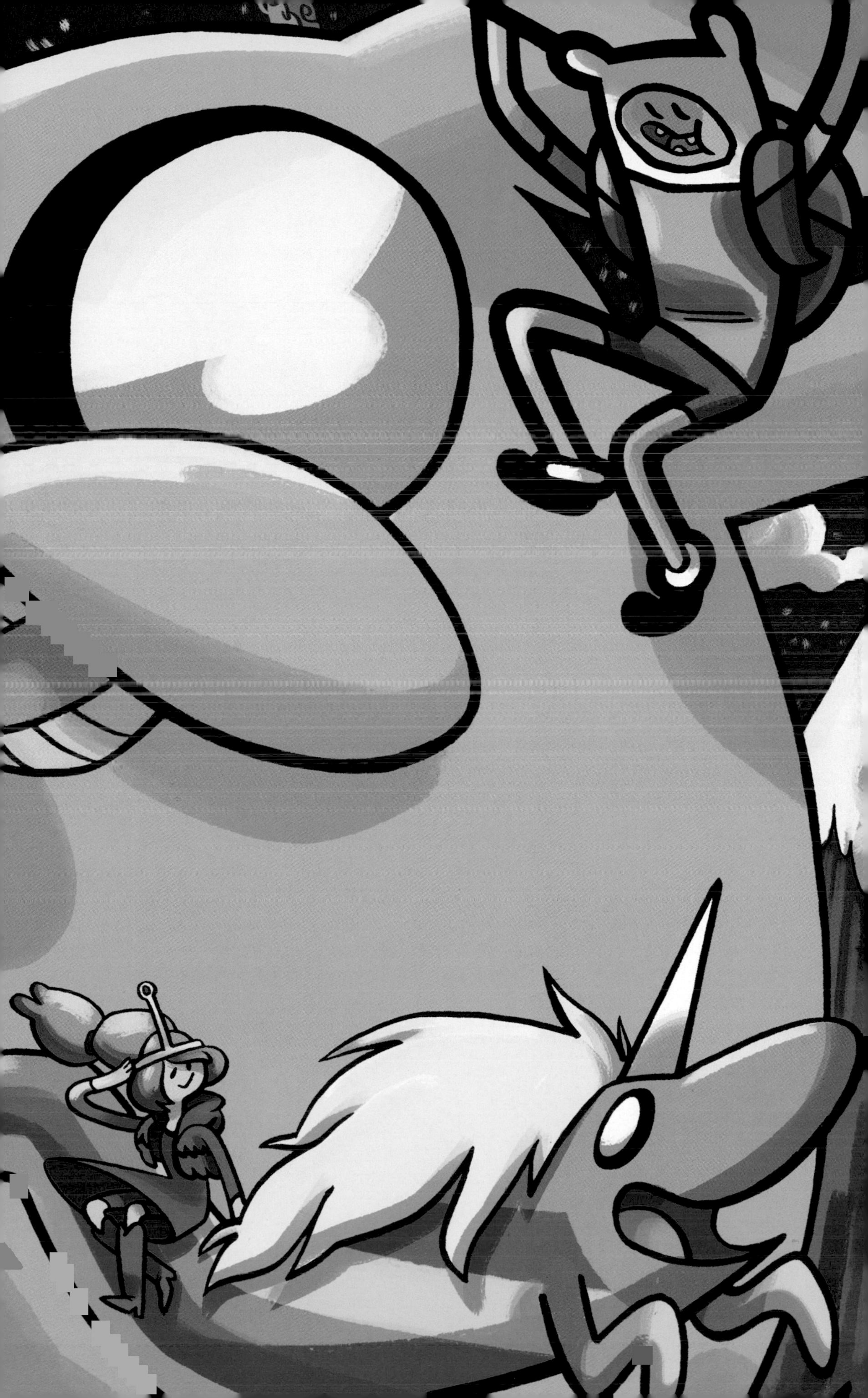

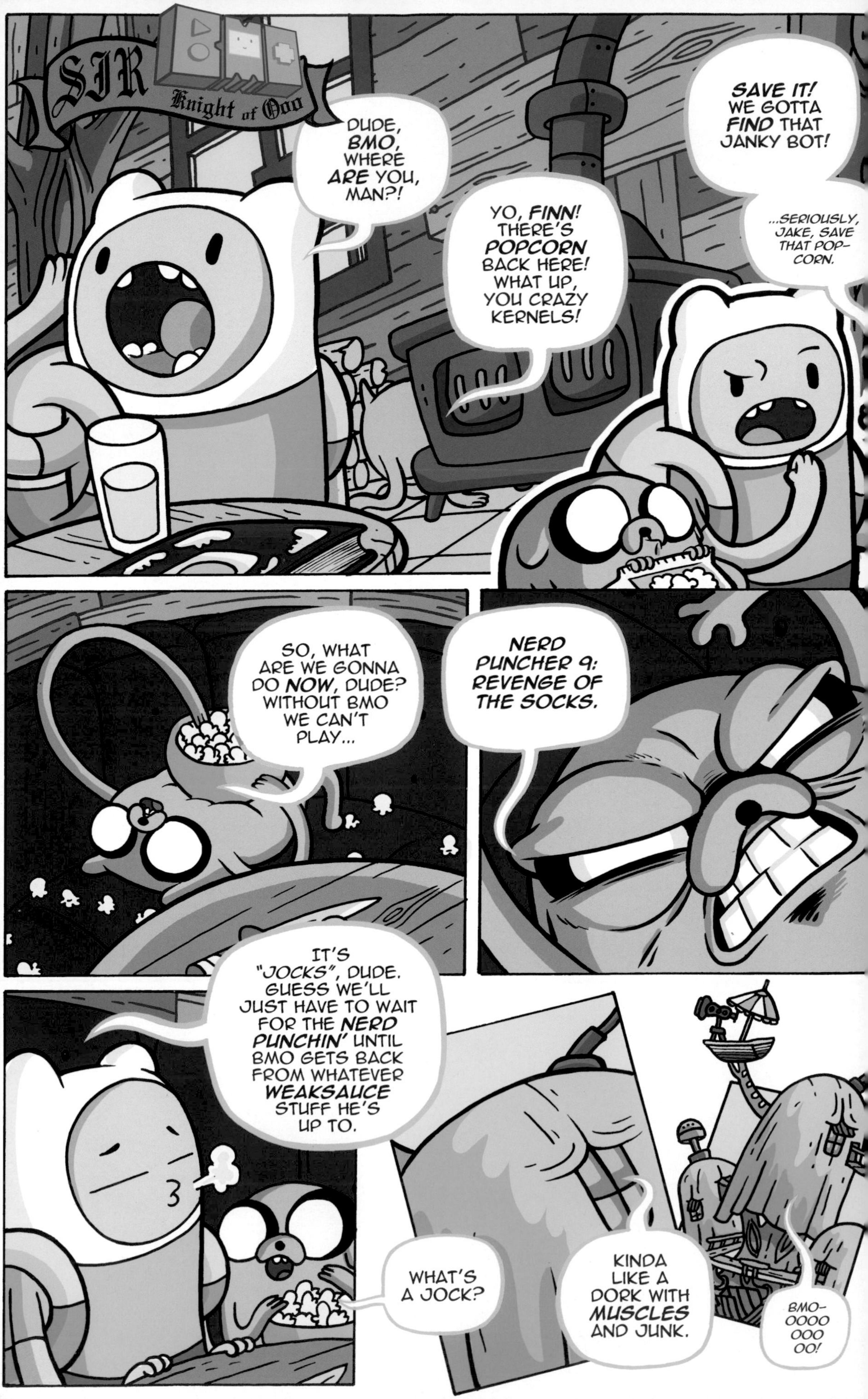
SIR
Knight of Ooo
DUDE, BMO, WHERE ARE YOU, MAN?!
YO, FINN! THERE'S POPCORN BACK HERE! WHAT UP, YOU CRAZY KERNELS!
SAVE IT! WE GOTTA FIND THAT JANKY BOT!
...SERIOUSLY, JAKE, SAVE THAT POP-CORN.
SO, WHAT ARE WE GONNA DO NOW, DUDE? WITHOUT BMO WE CAN'T PLAY...
NERD PUNCHER 9: REVENGE OF THE SOCKS.
IT'S "JOCKS", DUDE. GUESS WE'LL JUST HAVE TO WAIT FOR THE NERD PUNCHIN' UNTIL BMO GETS BACK FROM WHATEVER WEAKSAUCE STUFF HE'S UP TO.
WHAT'S A JOCK?
KINDA LIKE A DORK WITH MUSCLES AND JUNK.
BMO-OOOOOOOOO!

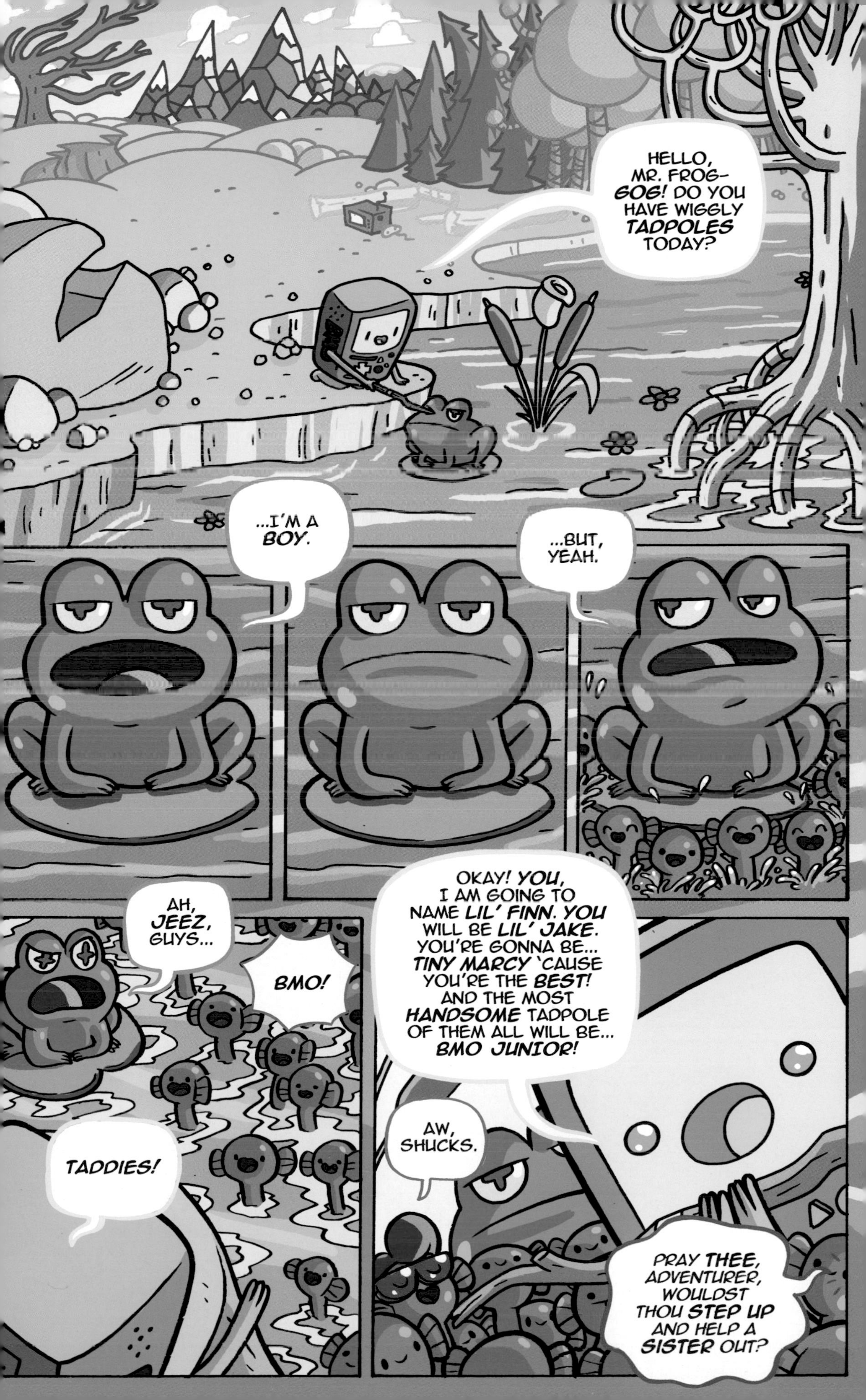
HELLO, MR. FROG-GOG! DO YOU HAVE WIGGLY TADPOLES TODAY?
...I'M A BOY.
...BUT, YEAH.
AH, JEEZ, GUYS...
BMO!
TADDIES!
OKAY! YOU, I AM GOING TO NAME LIL' FINN. YOU WILL BE LIL' JAKE. YOU'RE GONNA BE... TINY MARCY 'CAUSE YOU'RE THE BEST! AND THE MOST HANDSOME TADPOLE OF THEM ALL WILL BE... BMO JUNIOR!
AW, SHUCKS.
PRAY THEE, ADVENTURER, WOULDST THOU STEP UP AND HELP A SISTER OUT?

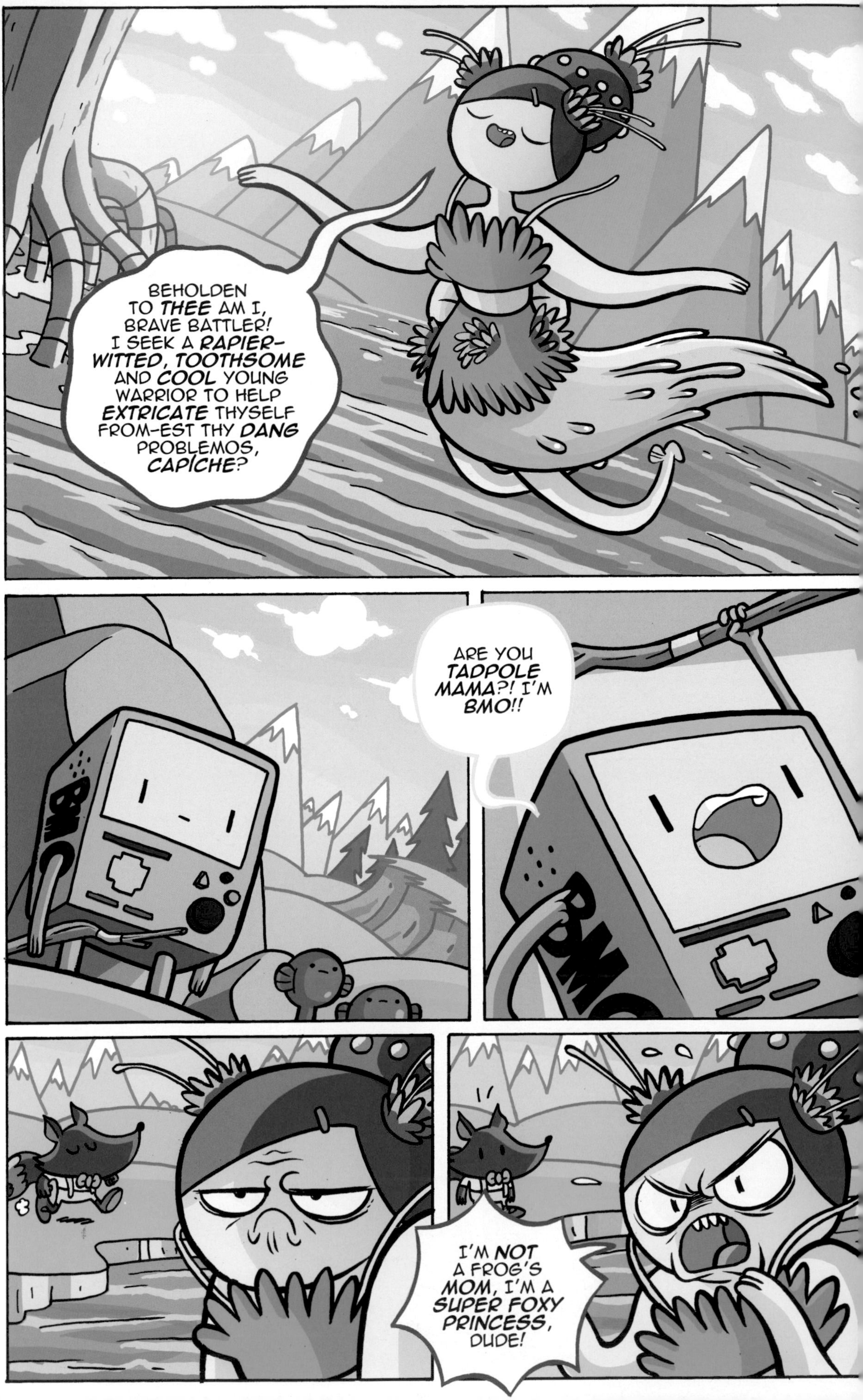
BEHOLDEN TO THEE AM I, BRAVE BATTLER! I SEEK A RAPIER-WITTED, TOOTHSOME AND COOL YOUNG WARRIOR TO HELP EXTRICATE THYSELF FROM-EST THY DANG PROBLEMOS, CAPICHE?
ARE YOU TADPOLE MAMA?! I'M BMO!!
BMO
BMO
I'M NOT A FROG'S MOM, I'M A SUPER FOXY PRINCESS, DUDE!

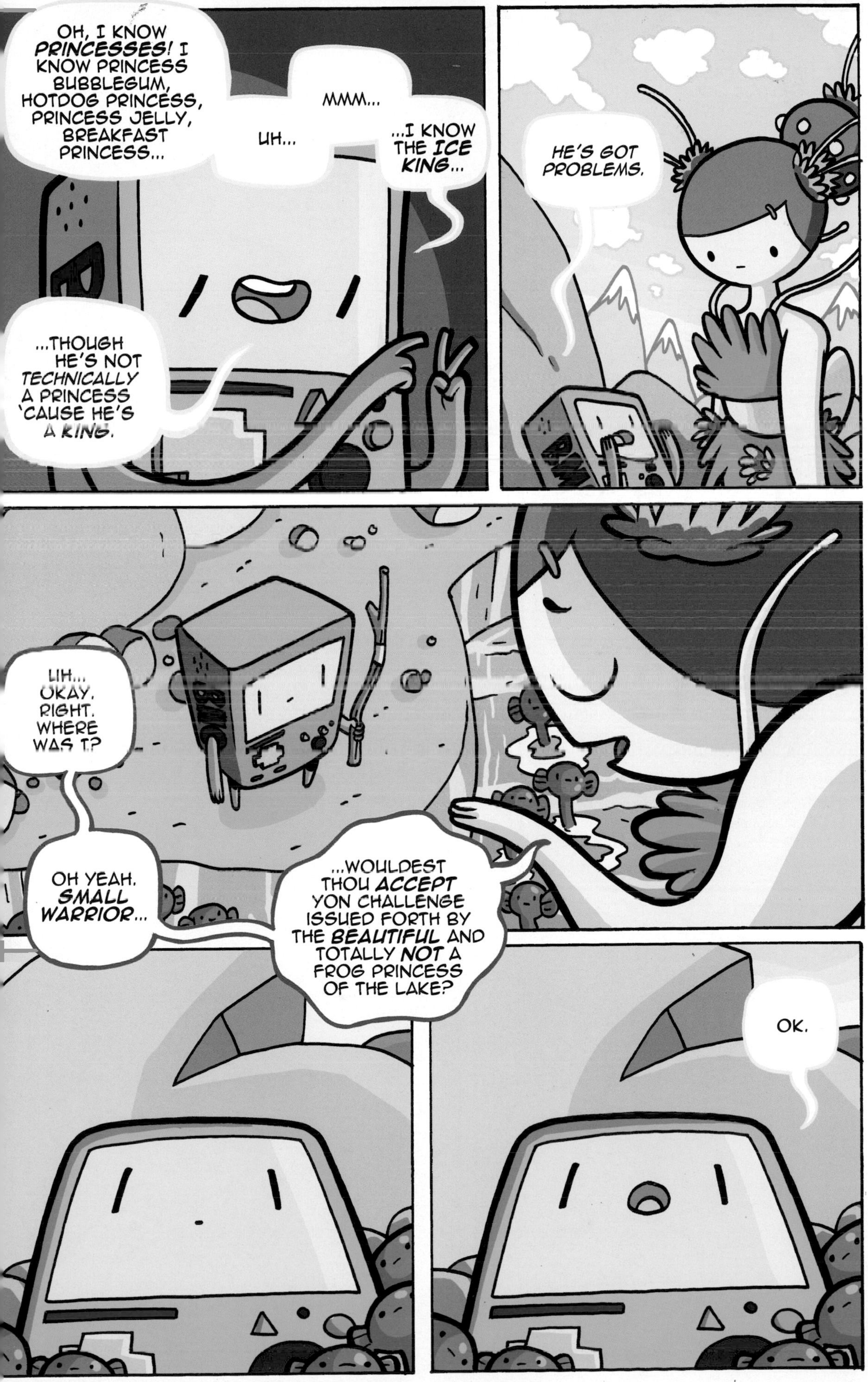
OH, I KNOW PRINCESSES! I KNOW PRINCESS BUBBLEGUM, HOTDOG PRINCESS, PRINCESS JELLY, BREAKFAST PRINCESS...
UH...
MMM...
...I KNOW THE ICE KING...
...THOUGH HE'S NOT TECHNICALLY A PRINCESS 'CAUSE HE'S A KING.
HE'S GOT PROBLEMS.
UH... OKAY. RIGHT. WHERE WAS I?
OH YEAH. SMALL WARRIOR...
...WOULDEST THOU ACCEPT YON CHALLENGE ISSUED FORTH BY THE BEAUTIFUL AND TOTALLY NOT A FROG PRINCESS OF THE LAKE?
OK.

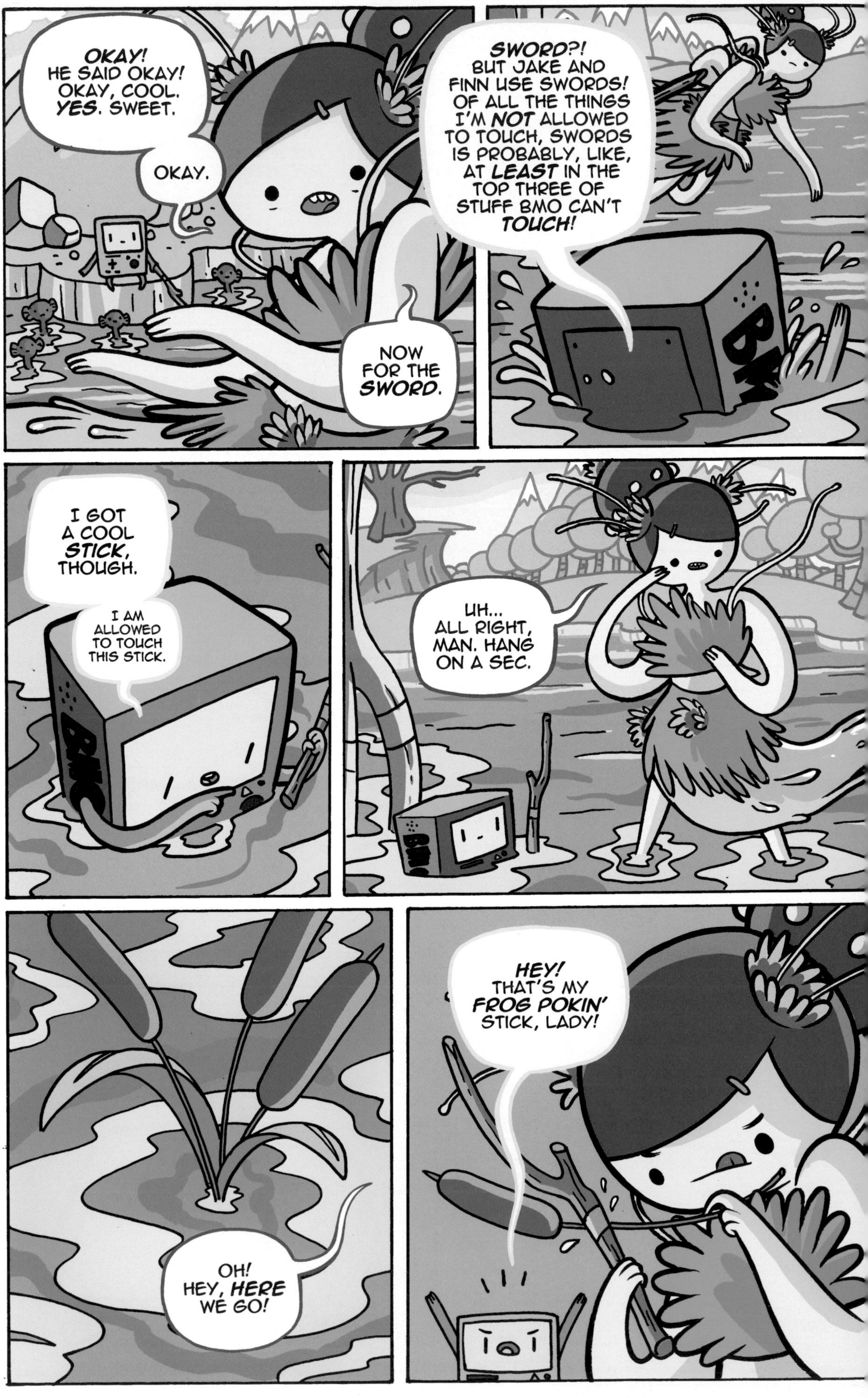
OKAY! HE SAID OKAY! OKAY, COOL. YES. SWEET.
OKAY.
NOW FOR THE SWORD.
SWORD?! BUT JAKE AND FINN USE SWORDS! OF ALL THE THINGS I'M NOT ALLOWED TO TOUCH, SWORDS IS PROBABLY, LIKE, AT LEAST IN THE TOP THREE OF STUFF BMO CAN'T TOUCH!
I GOT A COOL STICK, THOUGH.
I AM ALLOWED TO TOUCH THIS STICK.
UH... ALL RIGHT, MAN. HANG ON A SEC.
OH! HEY, HERE WE GO!
HEY! THAT'S MY FROG POKIN' STICK, LADY!

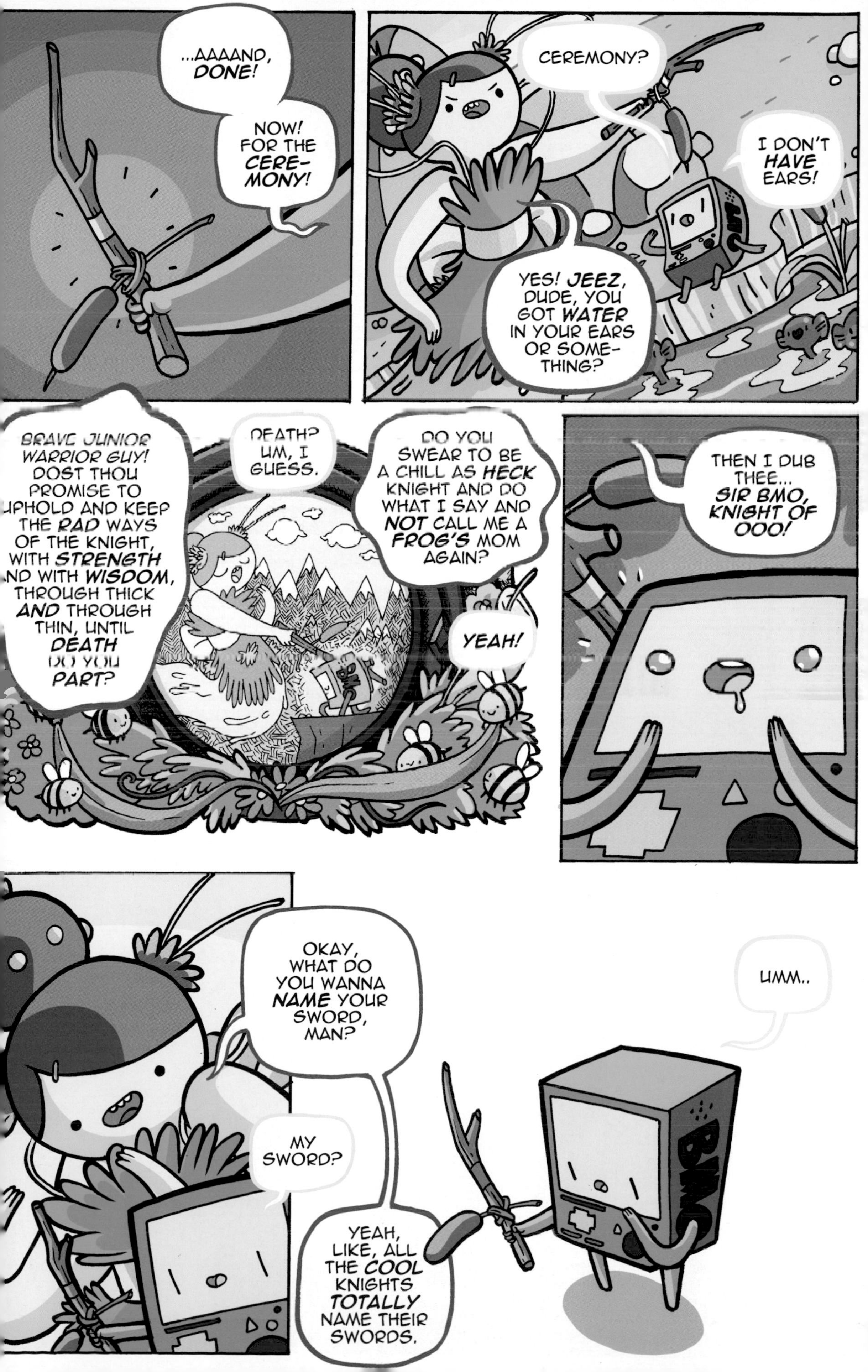
...AAAAND, DONE!
NOW! FOR THE CERE-MONY!
CEREMONY?
I DON'T HAVE EARS!
YES! JEEZ, DUDE, YOU GOT WATER IN YOUR EARS OR SOME-THING?
BRAVE JUNIOR WARRIOR GUY! DOST THOU PROMISE TO UPHOLD AND KEEP THE RAD WAYS OF THE KNIGHT, WITH STRENGTH AND WITH WISDOM, THROUGH THICK AND THROUGH THIN, UNTIL DEATH DO YOU PART?
DEATH? UM, I GUESS.
DO YOU SWEAR TO BE A CHILL AS HECK KNIGHT AND DO WHAT I SAY AND NOT CALL ME A FROG'S MOM AGAIN?
YEAH!
THEN I DUB THEE... SIR BMO, KNIGHT OF OOO!
OKAY, WHAT DO YOU WANNA NAME YOUR SWORD, MAN?
MY SWORD?
YEAH, LIKE, ALL THE COOL KNIGHTS TOTALLY NAME THEIR SWORDS.
UMM..

FROG POKER!

OKAY, KNIGHT! YOUR VERY **FIRST** TASK IS A **DOOZY**, BUT I **KNOW** YOU CAN DO IT! ARE YOU READY FOR **ADVENTURE**, SIR BMO??

JUST **ONE** QUESTION, M'LADY.

...DO I GET A **SASH**?

FINE, HERE.

THY **FIRST** TASK, IS TO ASSEMBLE A BRAVE BAND OF **WARRIORS**, **THIEVES**, AND **RUFFIANS**!

THEN! SIR BMO MUST DEFEAT THE **SCOURGE** OF THE LAKE KINGDOM...

...THE **NOT RAD** AND BAD **DUMB** FIRE DRAGON, MEAN-MUG SKULL-BITER!

SO **AWA** WITH THE **AWAY** T FIGHT—

...SIR BMO?

BMO! WHERE'VE YOU **BEEN** ALL DAY, MAN? ME AND JAKE WANTED TO PLAY **NERD PUNCHER 9**!

HEY, HOW COME YOU GOT THAT COOL **SASH**?

I GOT IT...

FOR BRAVERY!

OPEN MIC

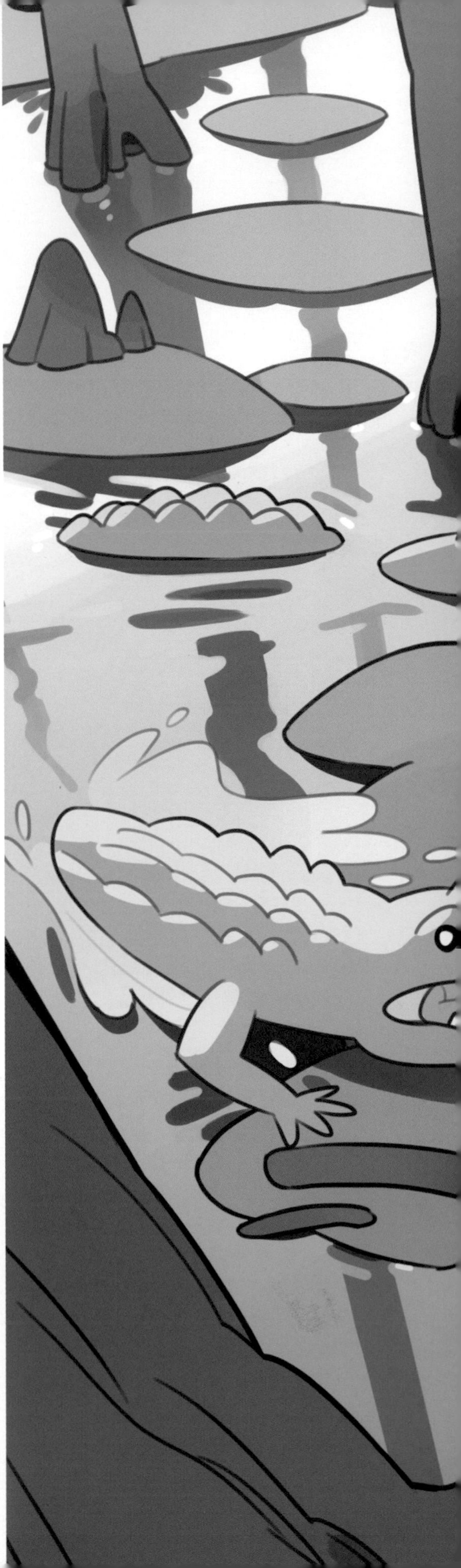

ISSUE FORTY THREE SUBSCRIPTION COVER
VIVIAN NG

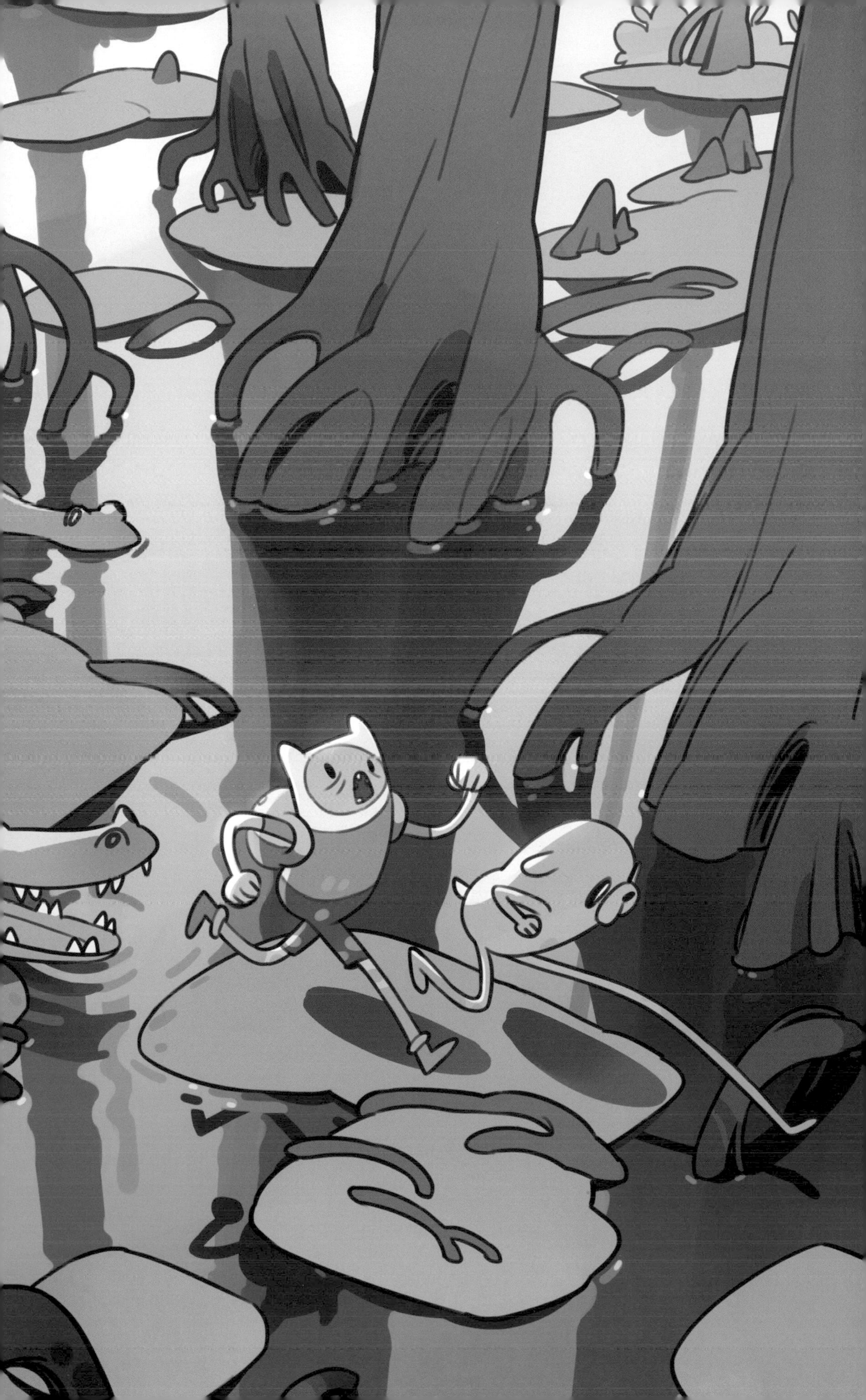

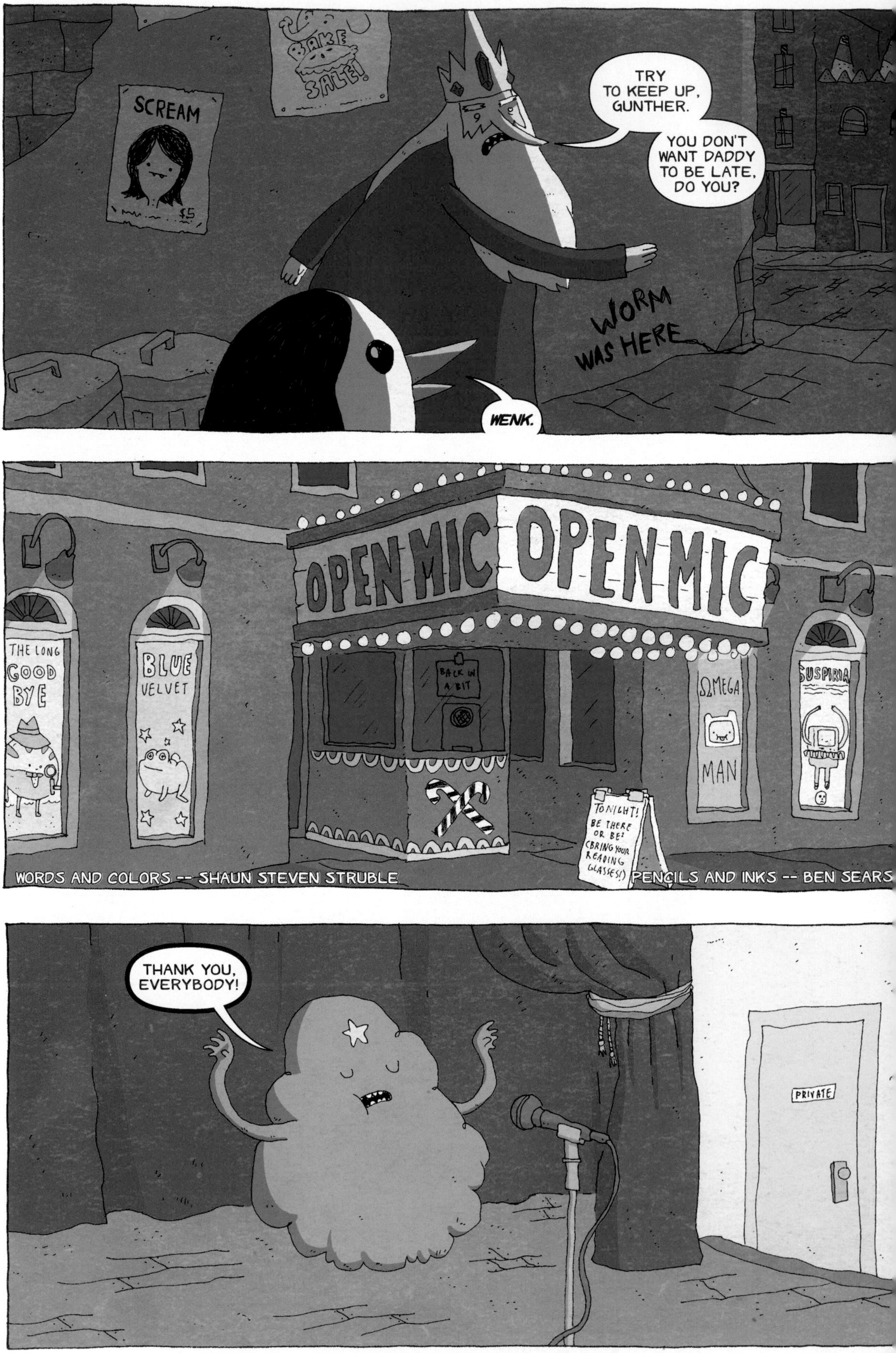

SCREAM
$5
BAKE SALE!
TRY TO KEEP UP, GUNTHER.
YOU DON'T WANT DADDY TO BE LATE, DO YOU?
WORM WAS HERE
WENK.
OPEN MIC
OPEN MIC
THE LONG GOOD BYE
BLUE VELVET
BACK IN A BIT
ΩMEGA MAN
SUSPIRIA
TONIGHT! BE THERE OR BE² (BRING YOUR READING GLASSES!)
WORDS AND COLORS -- SHAUN STEVEN STRUBLE
PENCILS AND INKS -- BEN SEARS
THANK YOU, EVERYBODY!
PRIVATE

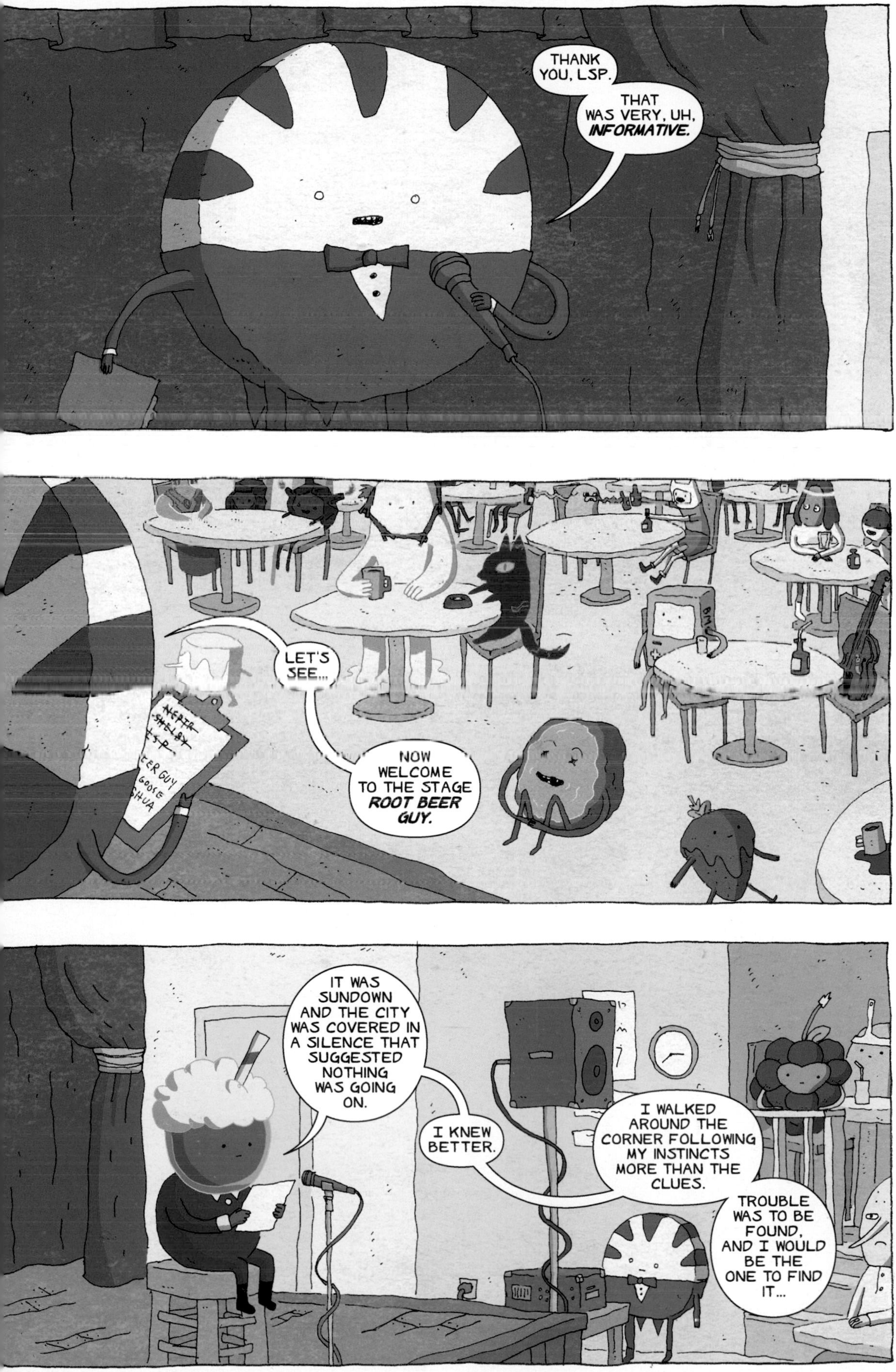
THANK YOU, LSP.
THAT WAS VERY, UH, ***INFORMATIVE.***
LET'S SEE...
NOW WELCOME TO THE STAGE ***ROOT BEER GUY.***
IT WAS SUNDOWN AND THE CITY WAS COVERED IN A SILENCE THAT SUGGESTED NOTHING WAS GOING ON.
I KNEW BETTER.
I WALKED AROUND THE CORNER FOLLOWING MY INSTINCTS MORE THAN THE CLUES.
TROUBLE WAS TO BE FOUND, AND I WOULD BE THE ONE TO FIND IT...

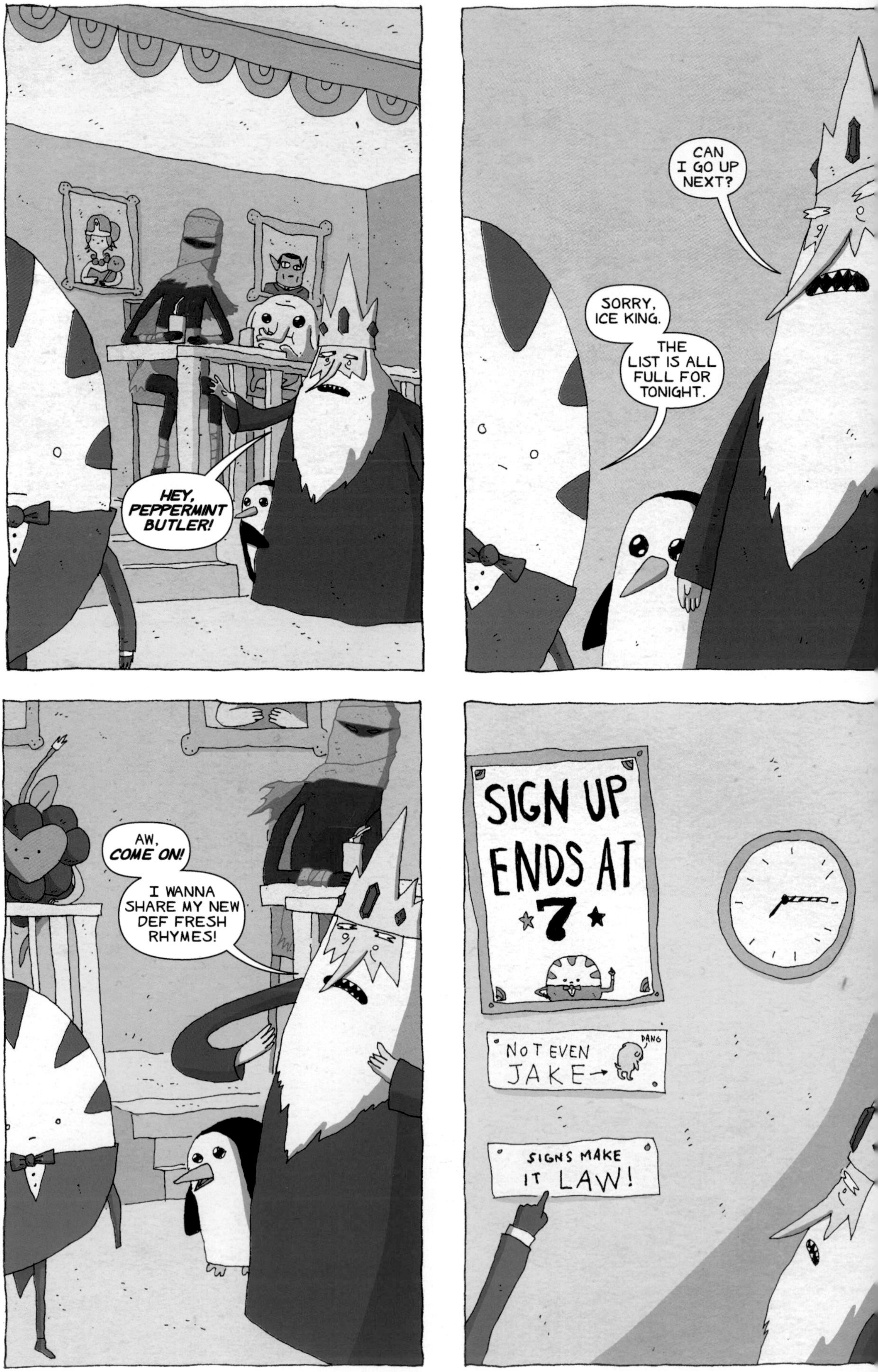

HEY, PEPPERMINT BUTLER!
CAN I GO UP NEXT?
SORRY, ICE KING.
THE LIST IS ALL FULL FOR TONIGHT.
AW, COME ON!
I WANNA SHARE MY NEW DEF FRESH RHYMES!
SIGN UP ENDS AT 7
NOT EVEN JAKE →
DANO
SIGNS MAKE IT LAW!

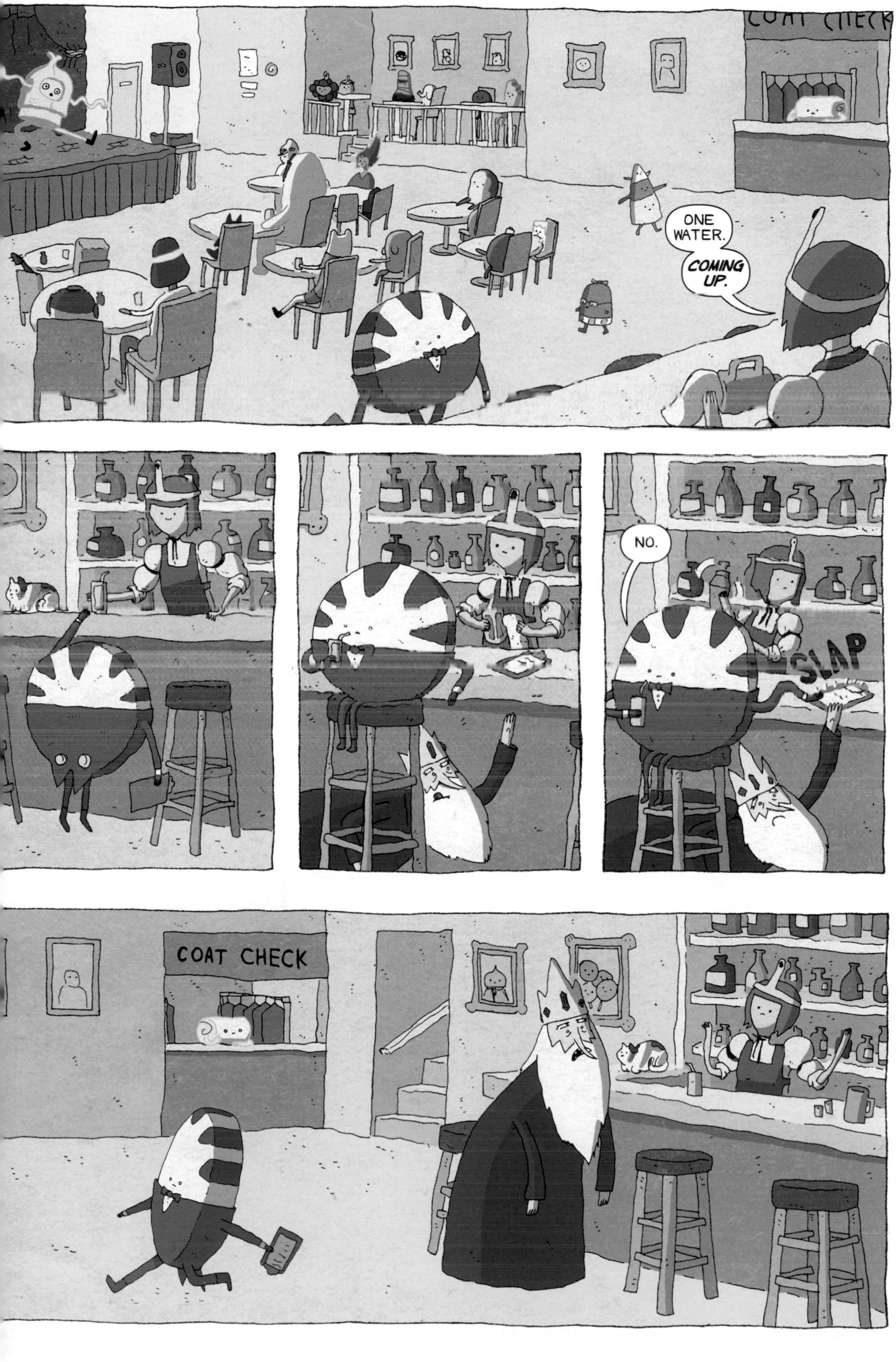
COAT CHECK
ONE WATER.
COMING UP.
NO.
SLAP
COAT CHECK

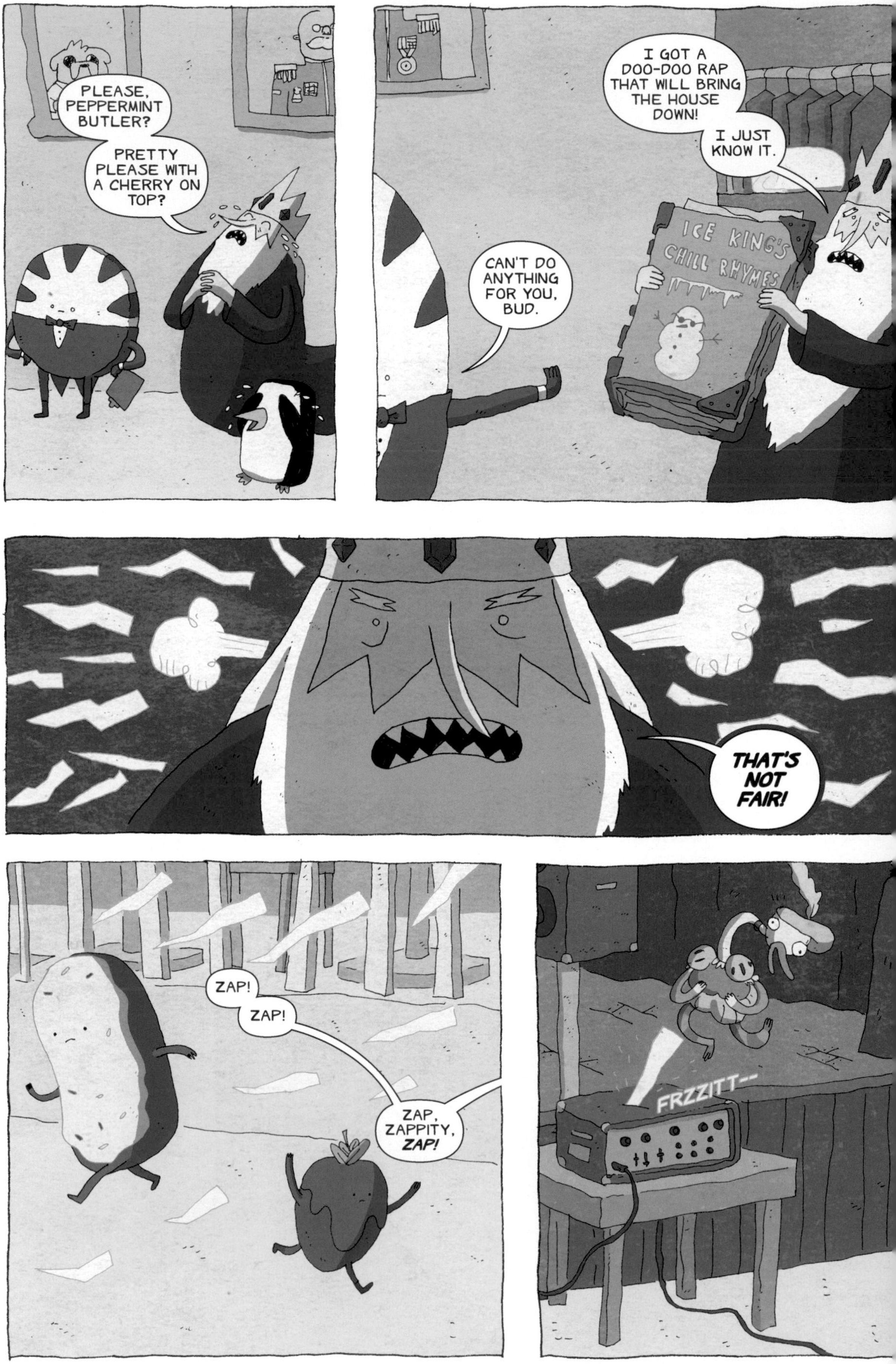

PLEASE, PEPPERMINT BUTLER?
PRETTY PLEASE WITH A CHERRY ON TOP?
CAN'T DO ANYTHING FOR YOU, BUD.
I GOT A DOO-DOO RAP THAT WILL BRING THE HOUSE DOWN!
I JUST KNOW IT.
ICE KING'S CHILL RHYMES
THAT'S NOT FAIR!
ZAP!
ZAP!
ZAP, ZAPPITY, ZAP!
FRZZITT--

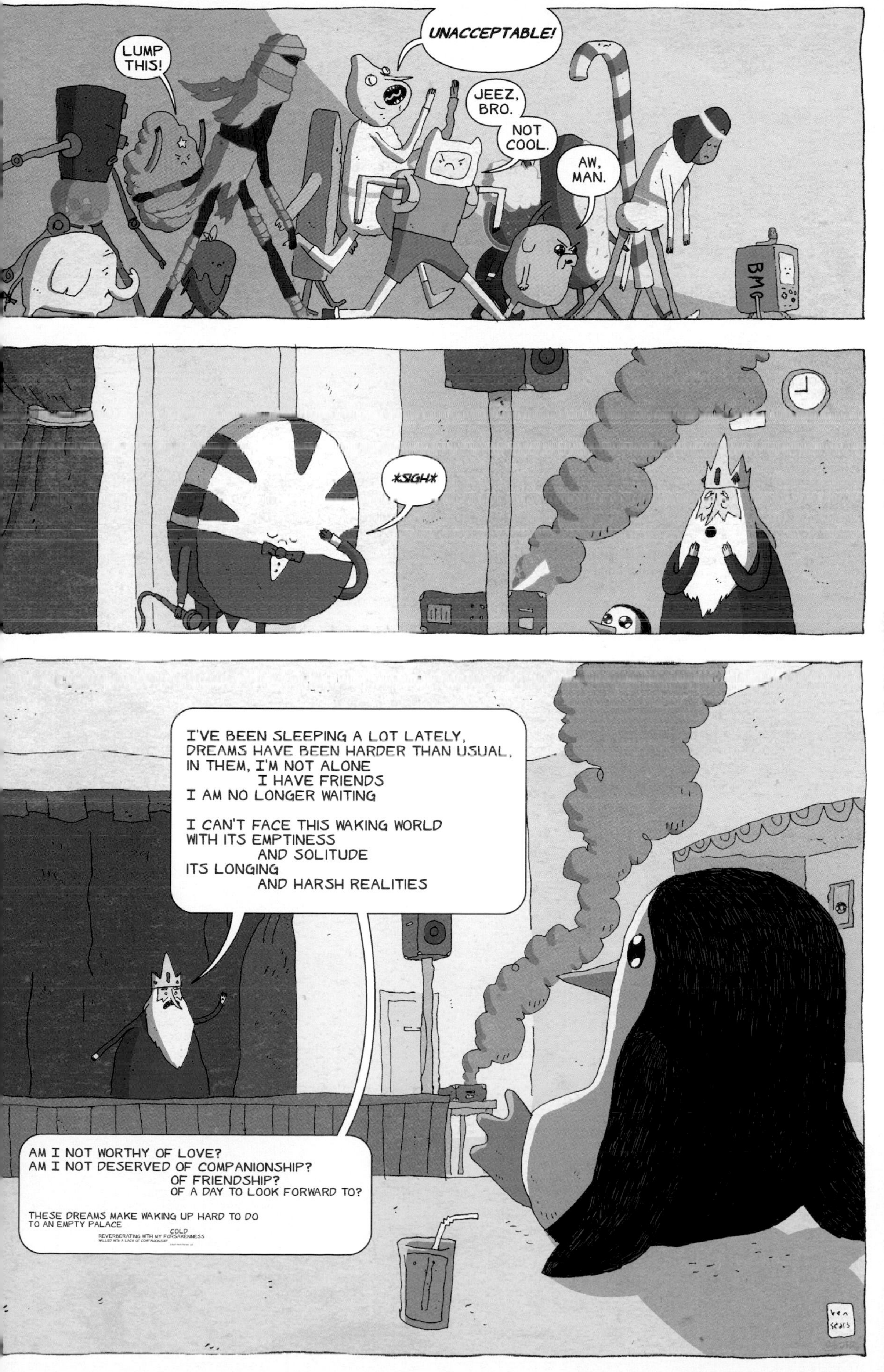
LUMP THIS!
UNACCEPTABLE!
JEEZ, BRO.
NOT COOL.
AW, MAN.
BMO
SIGH
I'VE BEEN SLEEPING A LOT LATELY,
DREAMS HAVE BEEN HARDER THAN USUAL,
IN THEM, I'M NOT ALONE
I HAVE FRIENDS
I AM NO LONGER WAITING
I CAN'T FACE THIS WAKING WORLD
WITH ITS EMPTINESS
AND SOLITUDE
ITS LONGING
AND HARSH REALITIES
AM I NOT WORTHY OF LOVE?
AM I NOT DESERVED OF COMPANIONSHIP?
OF FRIENDSHIP?
OF A DAY TO LOOK FORWARD TO?
THESE DREAMS MAKE WAKING UP HARD TO DO
TO AN EMPTY PALACE
COLD
REVERBERATING WITH MY FORSAKENNESS
WALLED WITH A LACK OF COMPANIONSHIP
ben sears

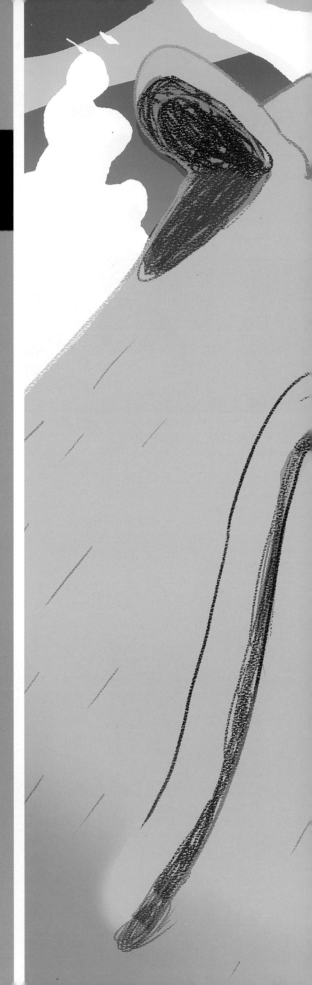

TIGER AND THE MOON

ISSUE FORTY FOUR SUBSCRIPTION COVER
CHRIS KINDRED

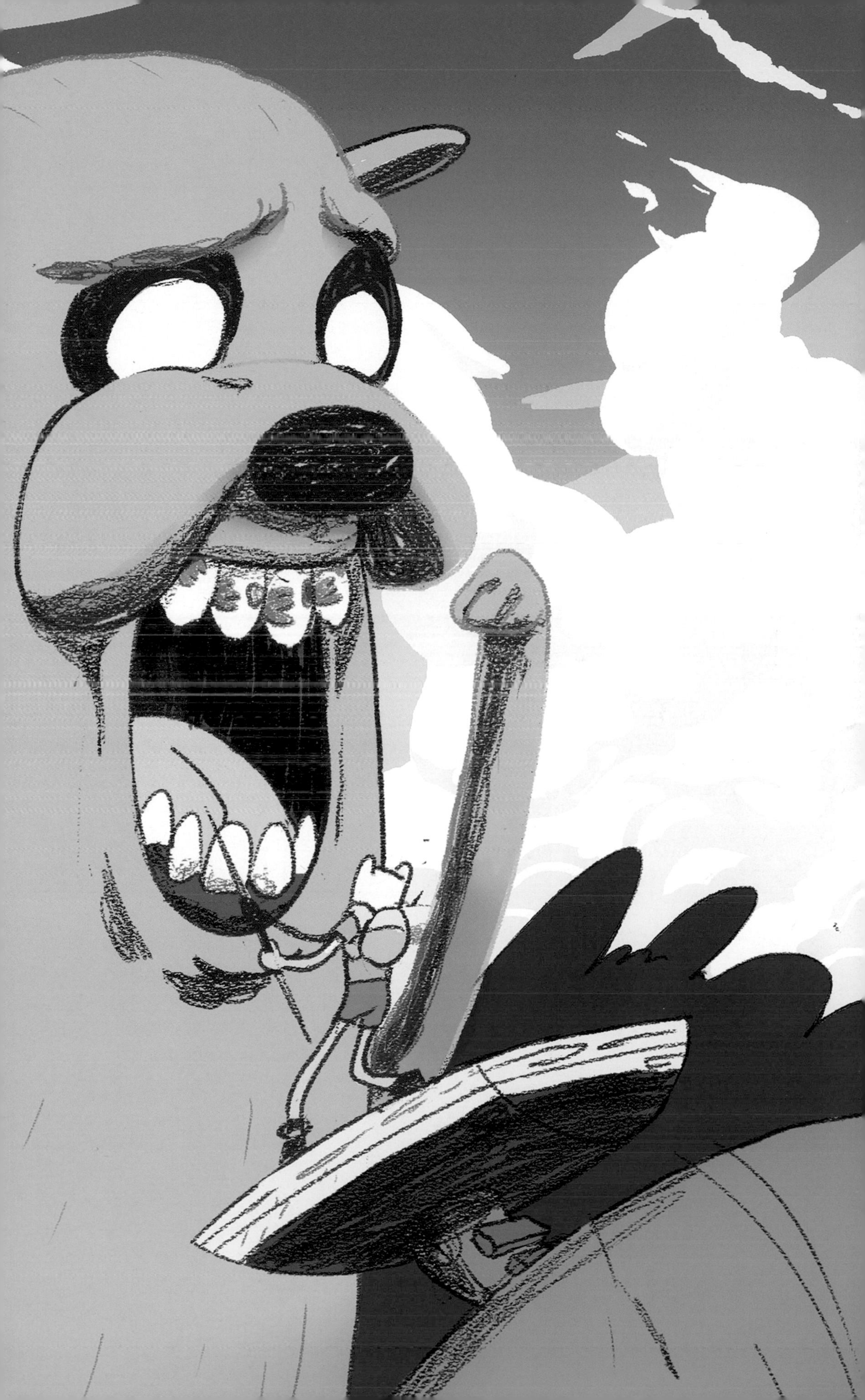

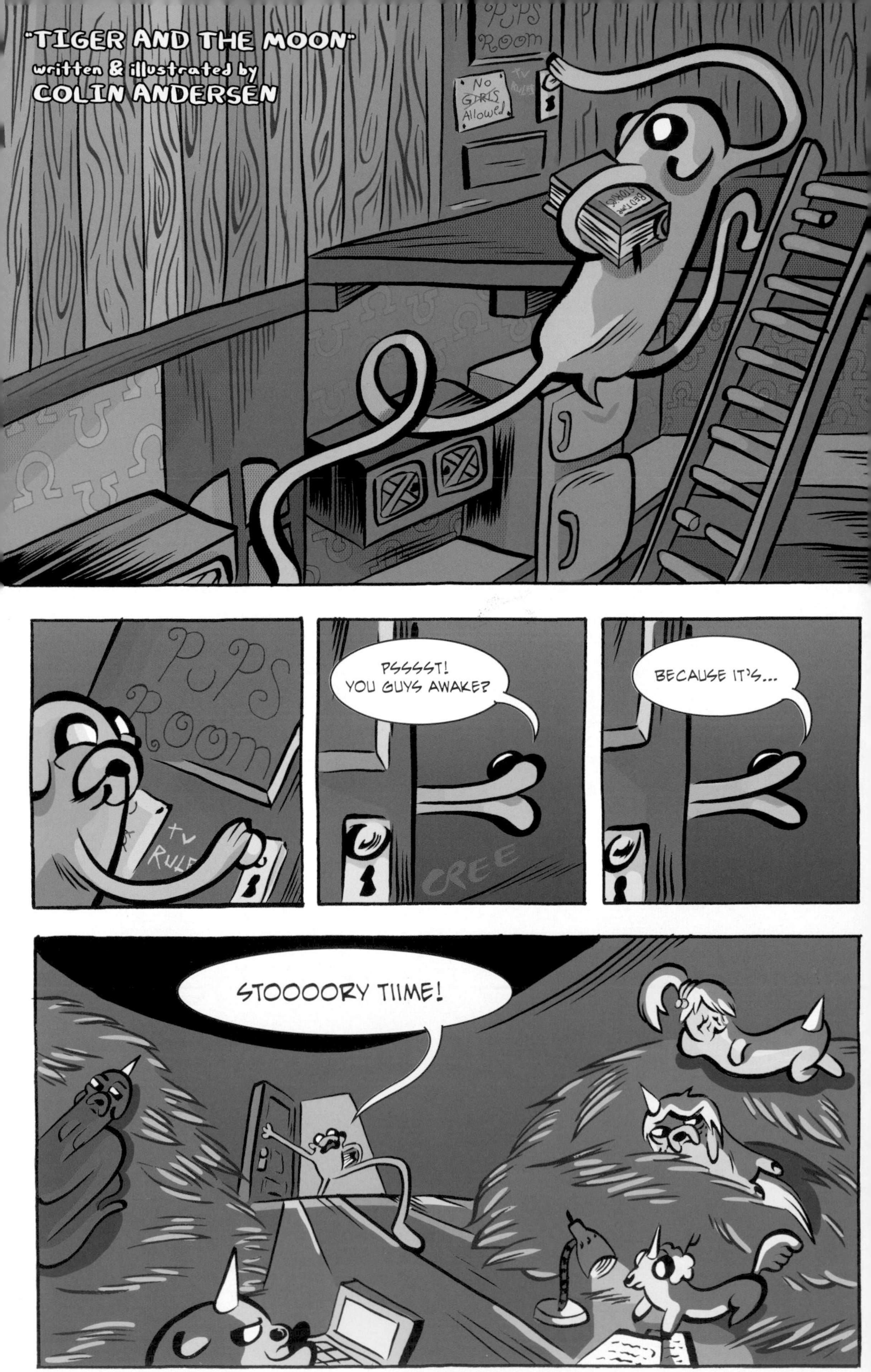
"TIGER AND THE MOON"
written & illustrated by
COLIN ANDERSEN
PSSSST! YOU GUYS AWAKE?
CREE
BECAUSE IT'S...
STOOOORY TIIME!

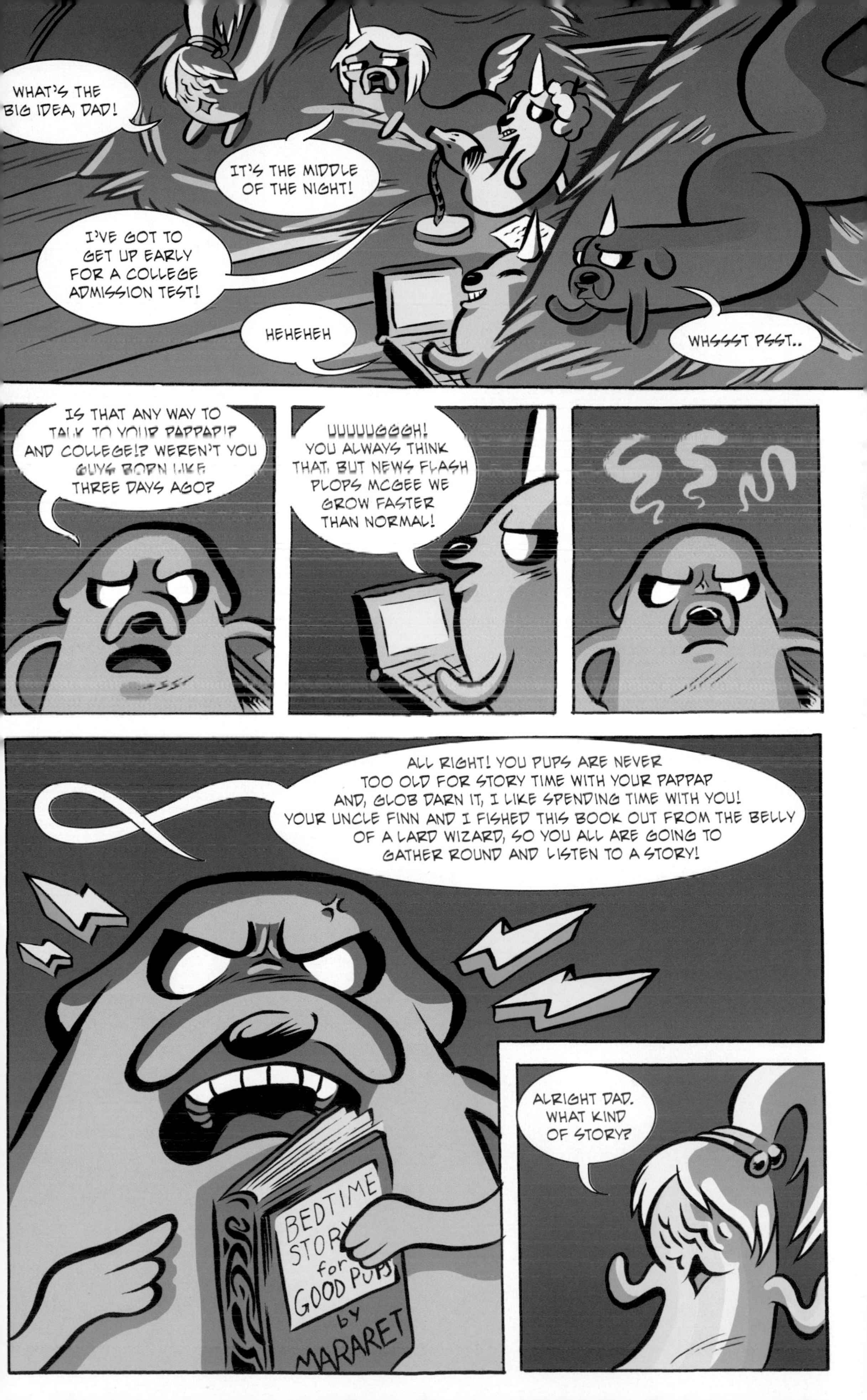
WHAT'S THE BIG IDEA, DAD!
IT'S THE MIDDLE OF THE NIGHT!
I'VE GOT TO GET UP EARLY FOR A COLLEGE ADMISSION TEST!
HEHEHEH
WHSSST PSST..
IS THAT ANY WAY TO TALK TO YOUR PAPPAP!? AND COLLEGE!? WEREN'T YOU GUYS BORN LIKE THREE DAYS AGO?
UUUUUGGGH! YOU ALWAYS THINK THAT, BUT NEWS FLASH PLOPS MCGEE WE GROW FASTER THAN NORMAL!
ALL RIGHT! YOU PUPS ARE NEVER TOO OLD FOR STORY TIME WITH YOUR PAPPAP AND, GLOB DARN IT, I LIKE SPENDING TIME WITH YOU! YOUR UNCLE FINN AND I FISHED THIS BOOK OUT FROM THE BELLY OF A LARD WIZARD, SO YOU ALL ARE GOING TO GATHER ROUND AND LISTEN TO A STORY!
BEDTIME STORY for GOOD PUPS by MARARET
ALRIGHT DAD. WHAT KIND OF STORY?

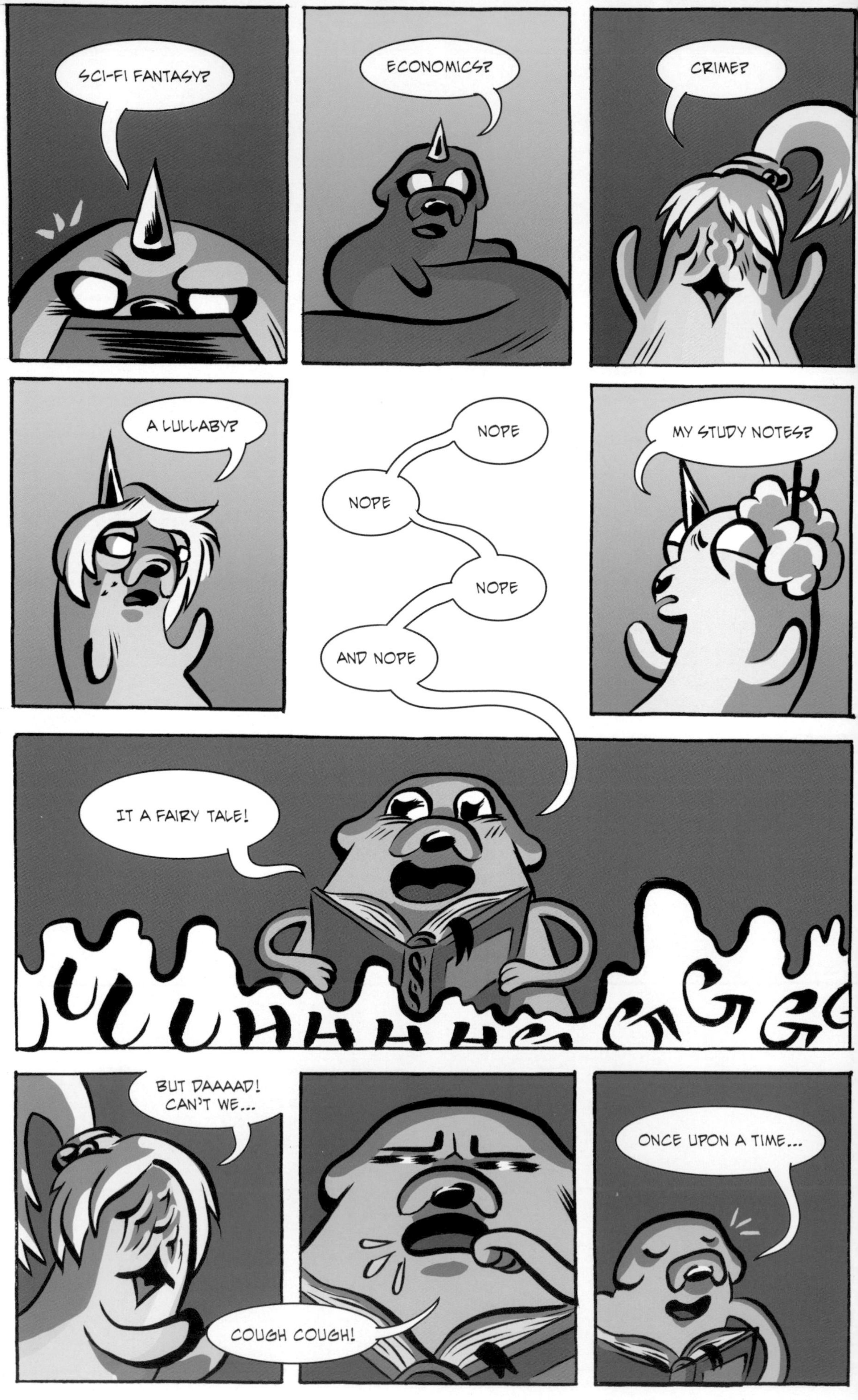

SCI-FI FANTASY?
ECONOMICS?
CRIME?
A LULLABY?
NOPE
NOPE
NOPE
AND NOPE
MY STUDY NOTES?
IT A FAIRY TALE!
UUHHHHGGGGG
BUT DAAAAD! CAN'T WE...
COUGH COUGH!
ONCE UPON A TIME...

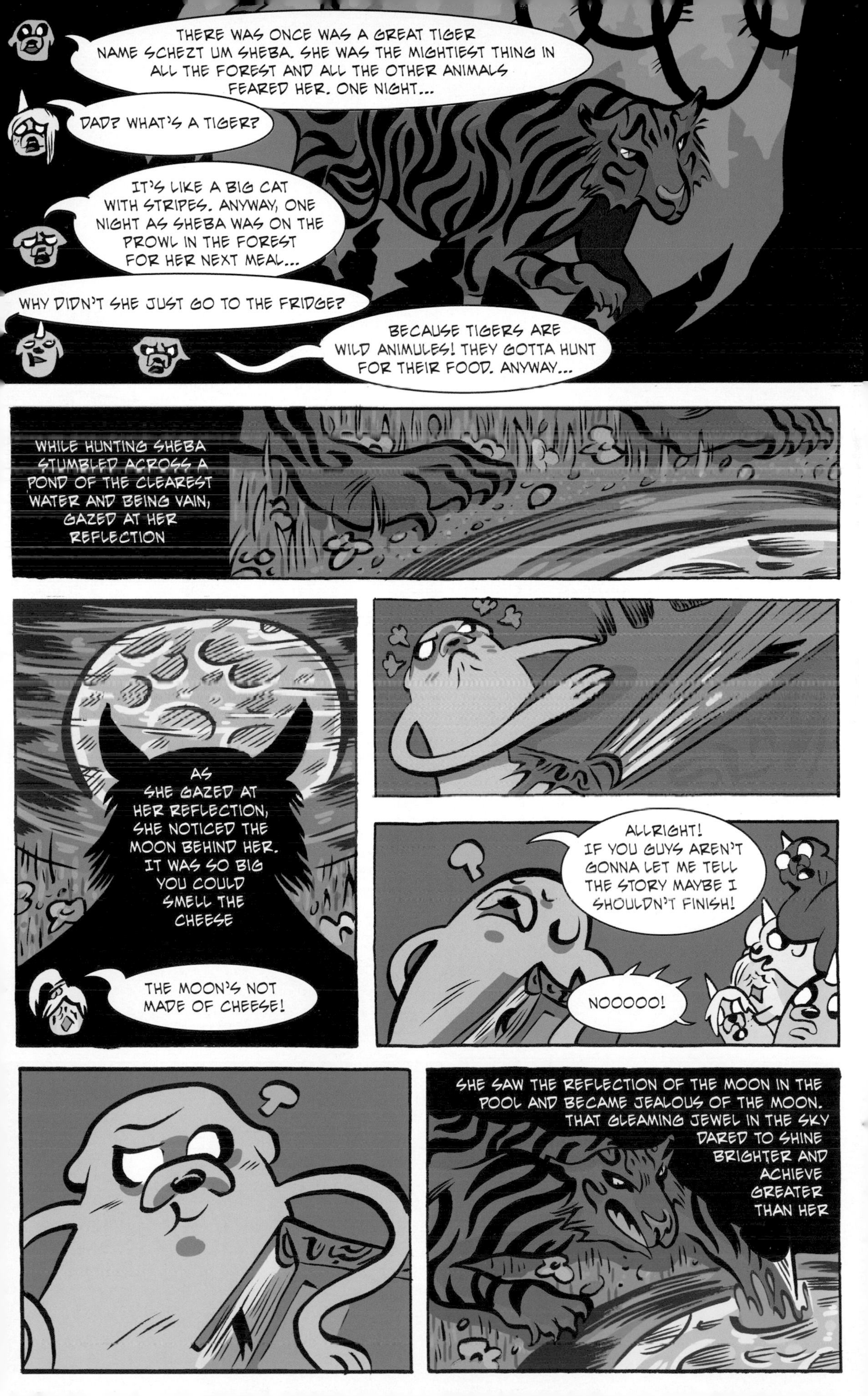

THERE WAS ONCE WAS A GREAT TIGER NAME SCHEZT UM SHEBA. SHE WAS THE MIGHTIEST THING IN ALL THE FOREST AND ALL THE OTHER ANIMALS FEARED HER. ONE NIGHT...
DAD? WHAT'S A TIGER?
IT'S LIKE A BIG CAT WITH STRIPES. ANYWAY, ONE NIGHT AS SHEBA WAS ON THE PROWL IN THE FOREST FOR HER NEXT MEAL...
WHY DIDN'T SHE JUST GO TO THE FRIDGE?
BECAUSE TIGERS ARE WILD ANIMULES! THEY GOTTA HUNT FOR THEIR FOOD. ANYWAY...
WHILE HUNTING SHEBA STUMBLED ACROSS A POND OF THE CLEAREST WATER AND BEING VAIN, GAZED AT HER REFLECTION
AS SHE GAZED AT HER REFLECTION, SHE NOTICED THE MOON BEHIND HER. IT WAS SO BIG YOU COULD SMELL THE CHEESE
THE MOON'S NOT MADE OF CHEESE!
ALLRIGHT! IF YOU GUYS AREN'T GONNA LET ME TELL THE STORY MAYBE I SHOULDN'T FINISH!
NOOOOO!
SHE SAW THE REFLECTION OF THE MOON IN THE POOL AND BECAME JEALOUS OF THE MOON. THAT GLEAMING JEWEL IN THE SKY DARED TO SHINE BRIGHTER AND ACHIEVE GREATER THAN HER

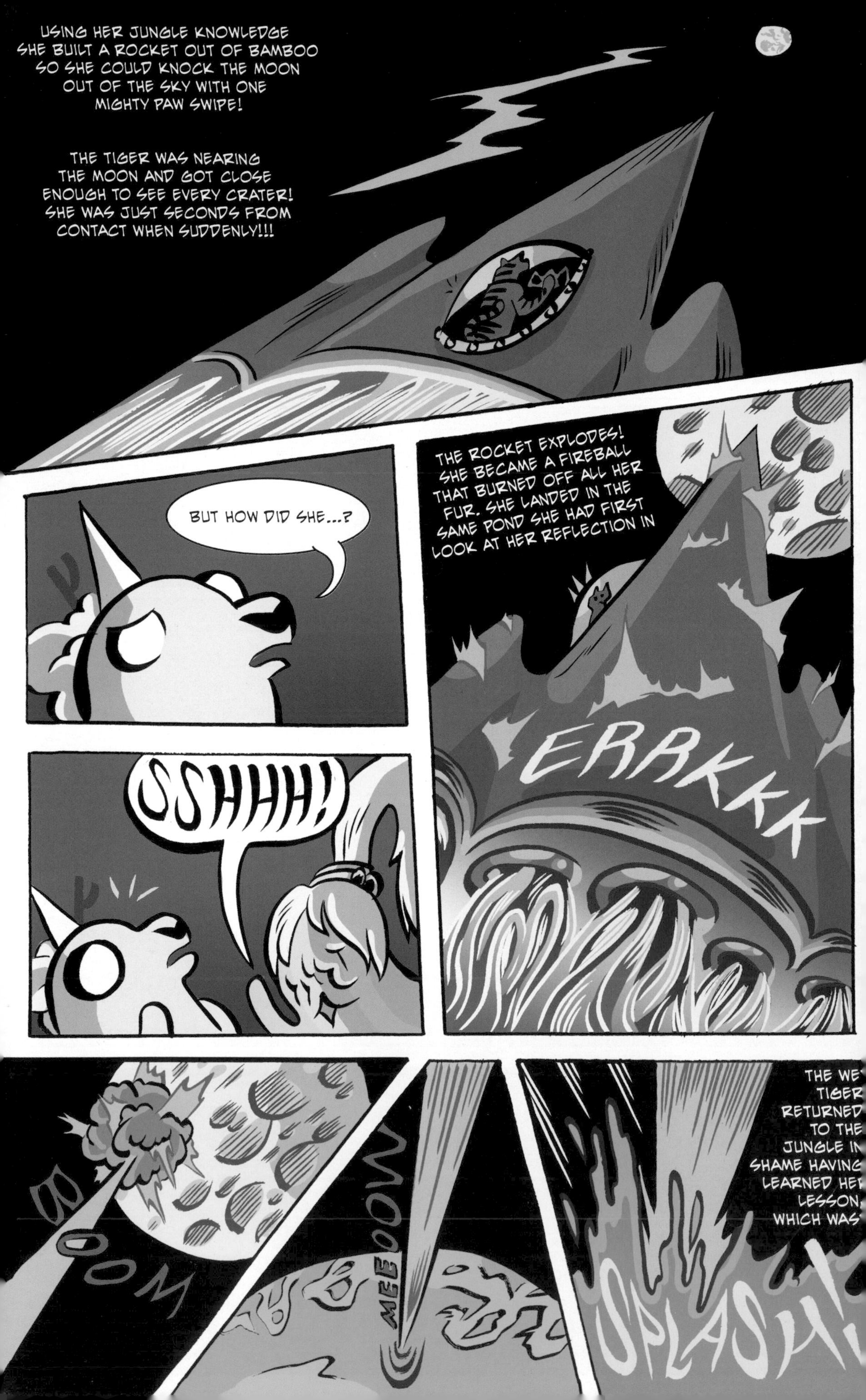
USING HER JUNGLE KNOWLEDGE SHE BUILT A ROCKET OUT OF BAMBOO SO SHE COULD KNOCK THE MOON OUT OF THE SKY WITH ONE MIGHTY PAW SWIPE!
THE TIGER WAS NEARING THE MOON AND GOT CLOSE ENOUGH TO SEE EVERY CRATER! SHE WAS JUST SECONDS FROM CONTACT WHEN SUDDENLY!!!
BUT HOW DID SHE...?
SSHHH!
THE ROCKET EXPLODES! SHE BECAME A FIREBALL THAT BURNED OFF ALL HER FUR. SHE LANDED IN THE SAME POND SHE HAD FIRST LOOK AT HER REFLECTION IN
ERRKKK
BOOOM
MEEOOOOW
THE WE TIGER RETURNED TO THE JUNGLE IN SHAME HAVING LEARNED HE LESSON, WHICH WAS
SPLASH!

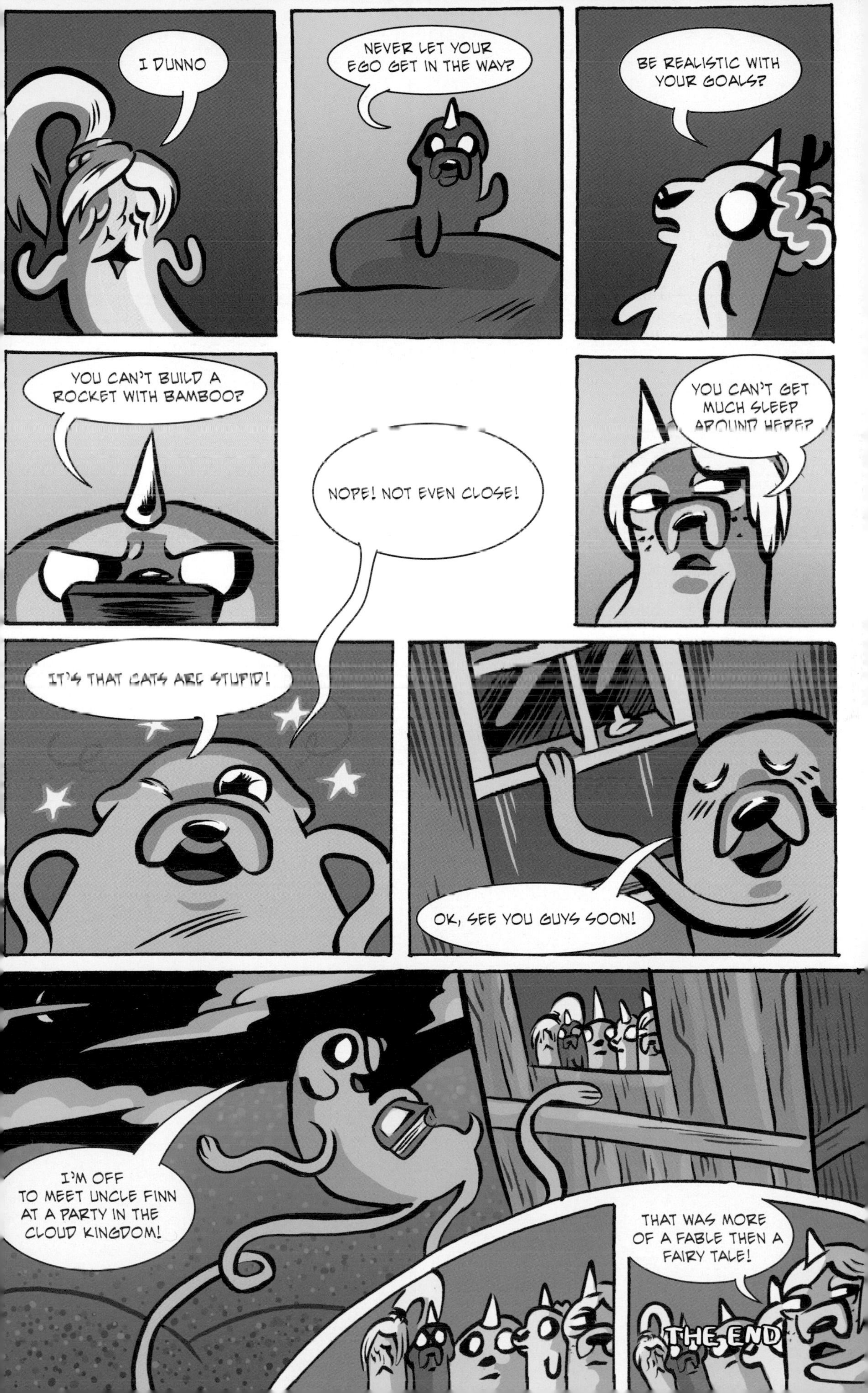
I DUNNO
NEVER LET YOUR EGO GET IN THE WAY?
BE REALISTIC WITH YOUR GOALS?
YOU CAN'T BUILD A ROCKET WITH BAMBOO?
YOU CAN'T GET MUCH SLEEP AROUND HERE?
NOPE! NOT EVEN CLOSE!
IT'S THAT CATS ARE STUPID!
OK, SEE YOU GUYS SOON!
I'M OFF TO MEET UNCLE FINN AT A PARTY IN THE CLOUD KINGDOM!
THAT WAS MORE OF A FABLE THEN A FAIRY TALE!
THE END

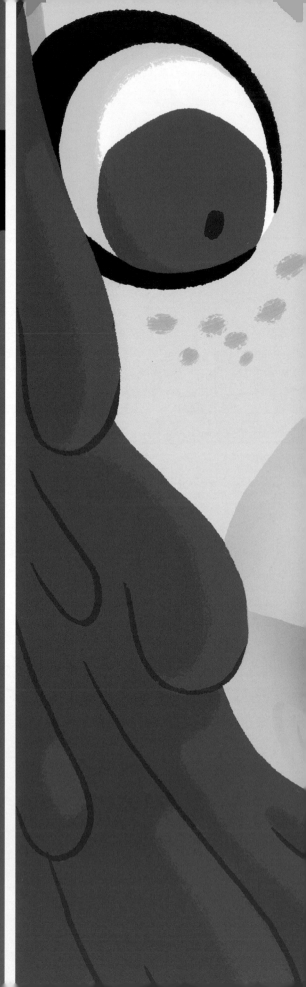

FINDERS KEEPERS

ISSUE FORTY FIVE SUBSCRIPTION COVER
ANDRE

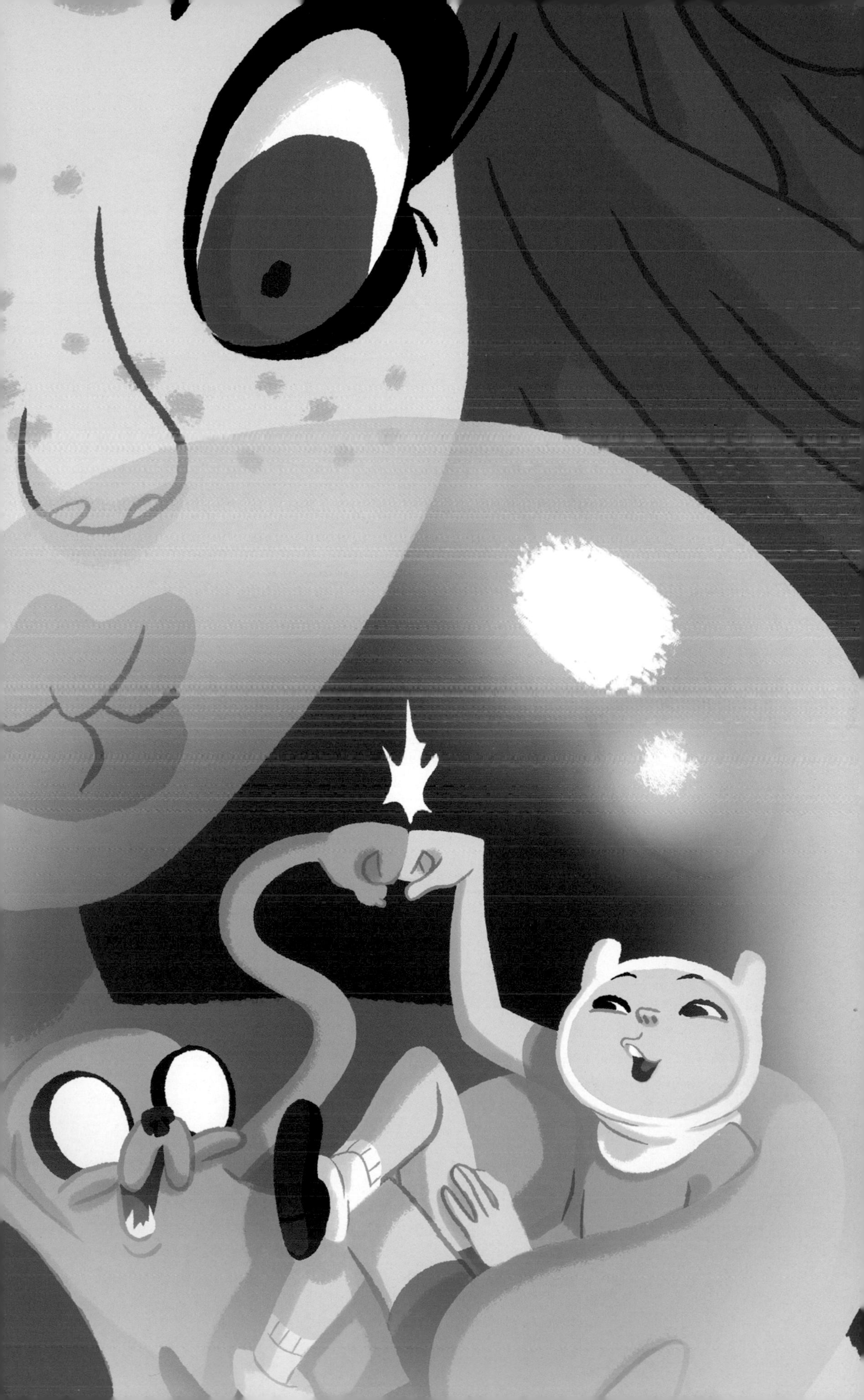

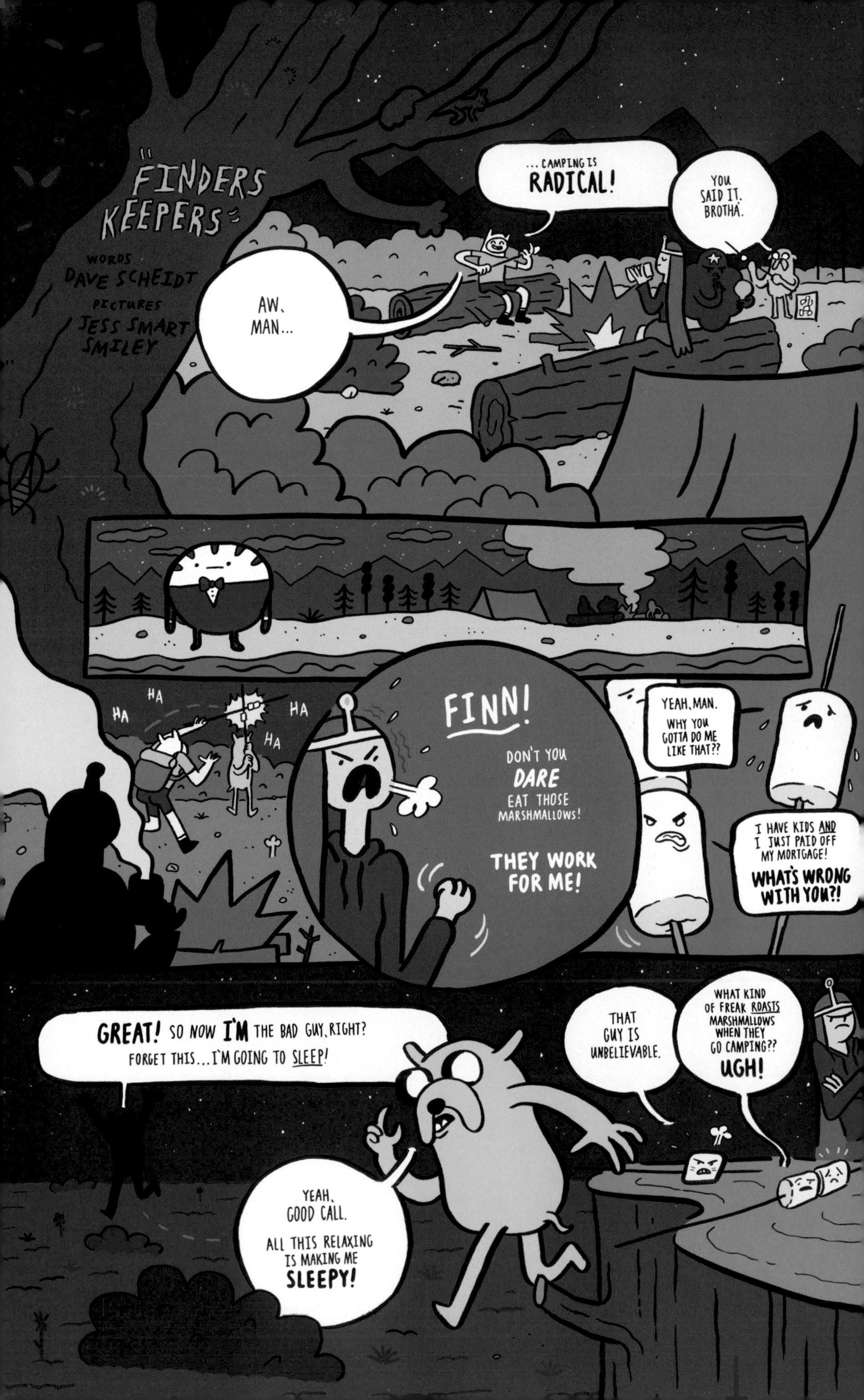
"FINDERS KEEPERS"
WORDS DAVE SCHEIDT
PICTURES JESS SMART SMILEY
... CAMPING IS RADICAL!
YOU SAID IT, BROTHA.
AW, MAN...
HA HA HA HA
FINN! DON'T YOU DARE EAT THOSE MARSHMALLOWS! THEY WORK FOR ME!
YEAH, MAN. WHY YOU GOTTA DO ME LIKE THAT??
I HAVE KIDS AND I JUST PAID OFF MY MORTGAGE! WHAT'S WRONG WITH YOU?!
GREAT! SO NOW I'M THE BAD GUY, RIGHT? FORGET THIS... I'M GOING TO SLEEP!
THAT GUY IS UNBELIEVABLE.
WHAT KIND OF FREAK ROASTS MARSHMALLOWS WHEN THEY GO CAMPING?? UGH!
YEAH, GOOD CALL. ALL THIS RELAXING IS MAKING ME SLEEPY!

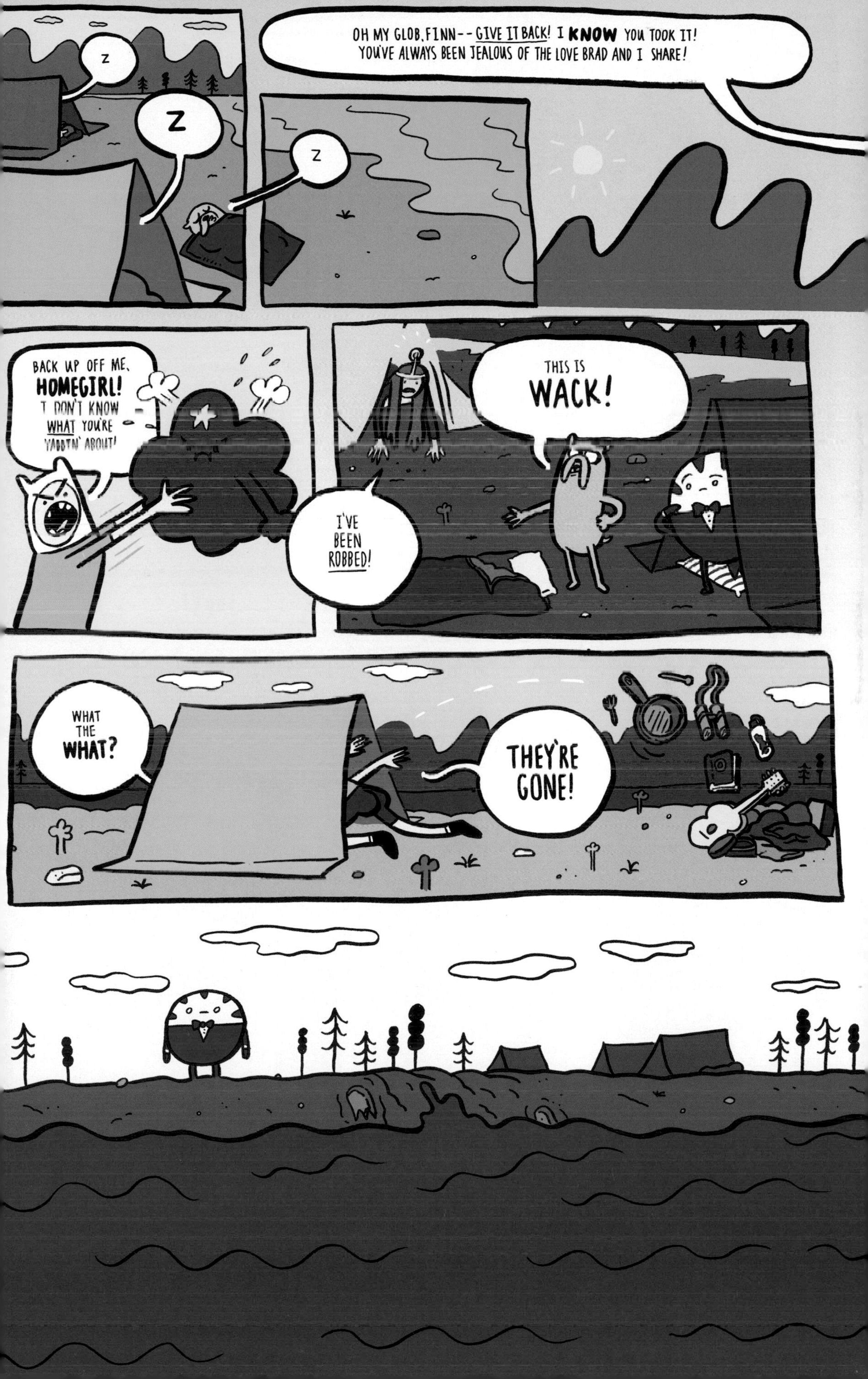
Z
Z
Z
OH MY GLOB, FINN-- GIVE IT BACK! I KNOW YOU TOOK IT! YOU'VE ALWAYS BEEN JEALOUS OF THE LOVE BRAD AND I SHARE!
BACK UP OFF ME, HOMEGIRL! I DON'T KNOW WHAT YOU'RE YABBIN' ABOUT!
I'VE BEEN ROBBED!
THIS IS WACK!
WHAT THE WHAT?
THEY'RE GONE!

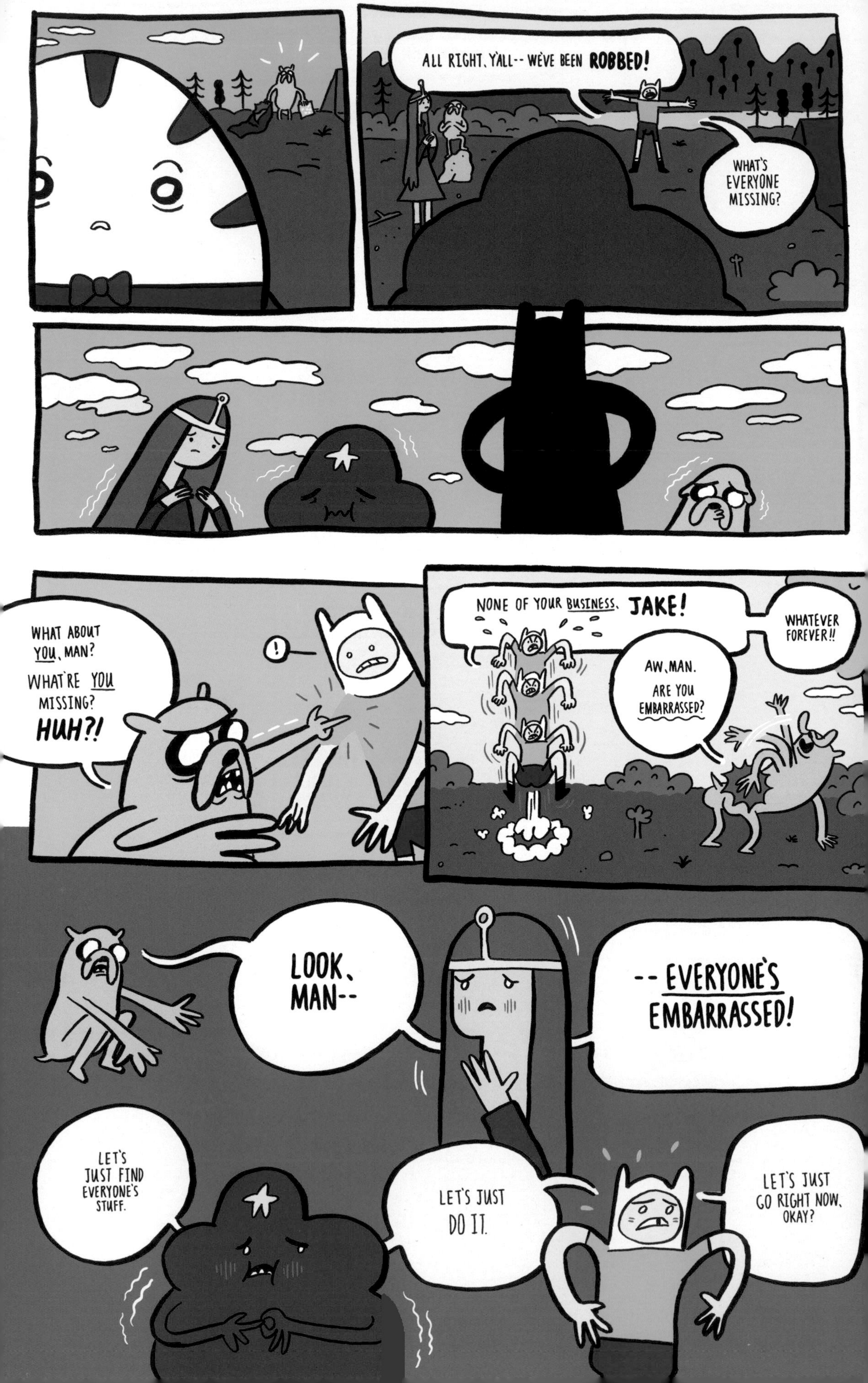

ALL RIGHT, Y'ALL-- WE'VE BEEN ROBBED!
WHAT'S EVERYONE MISSING?
WHAT ABOUT YOU, MAN? WHAT'RE YOU MISSING? HUH?!
!
NONE OF YOUR BUSINESS, JAKE!
WHATEVER FOREVER!!
AW, MAN. ARE YOU EMBARRASSED?
LOOK, MAN--
-- EVERYONE'S EMBARRASSED!
LET'S JUST FIND EVERYONE'S STUFF.
LET'S JUST DO IT.
LET'S JUST GO RIGHT NOW, OKAY?

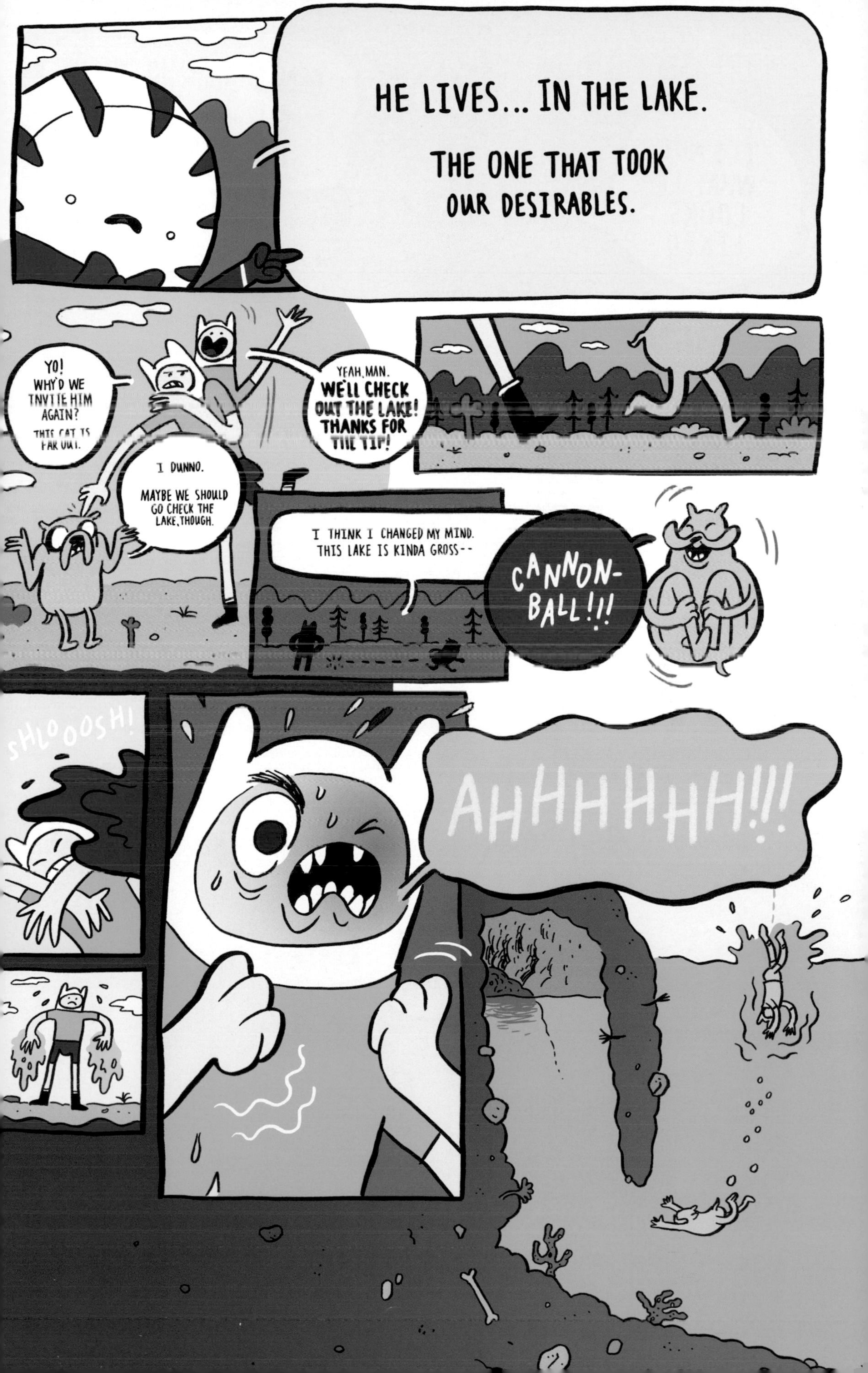
HE LIVES... IN THE LAKE.
THE ONE THAT TOOK OUR DESIRABLES.
YO! WHY'D WE INVITE HIM AGAIN? THIS CAT IS FAR OUT.
YEAH, MAN. WE'LL CHECK OUT THE LAKE! THANKS FOR THE TIP!
I DUNNO. MAYBE WE SHOULD GO CHECK THE LAKE, THOUGH.
I THINK I CHANGED MY MIND. THIS LAKE IS KINDA GROSS--
CANNON-BALL!!!
SHLOOOSH!
AHHHHHHH!!!

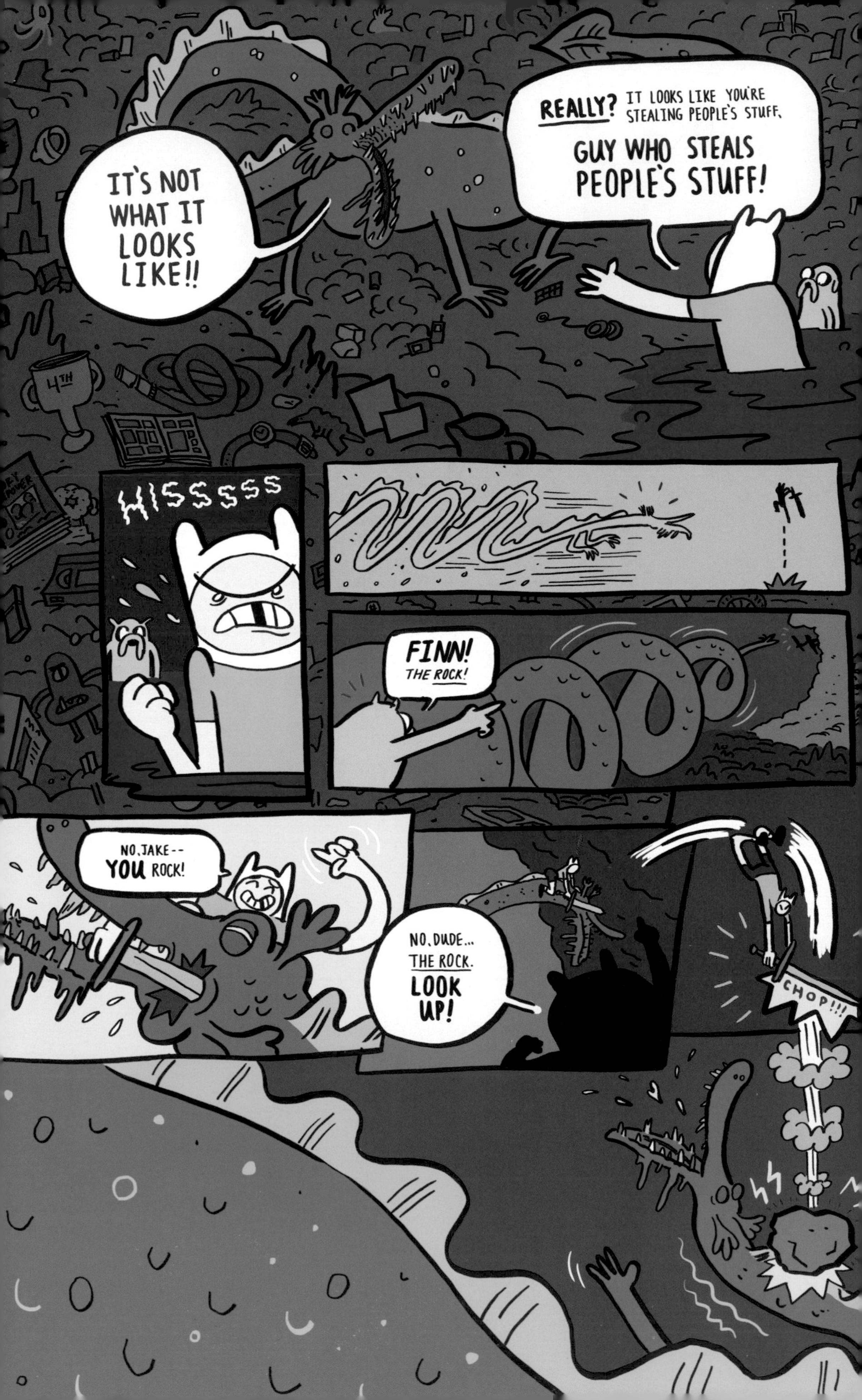
IT'S NOT WHAT IT LOOKS LIKE!!
REALLY? IT LOOKS LIKE YOU'RE STEALING PEOPLE'S STUFF, GUY WHO STEALS PEOPLE'S STUFF!
4TH
HISSSSSS
FINN! THE ROCK!
NO, JAKE-- YOU ROCK!
NO, DUDE... THE ROCK. LOOK UP!
CHOP!!!

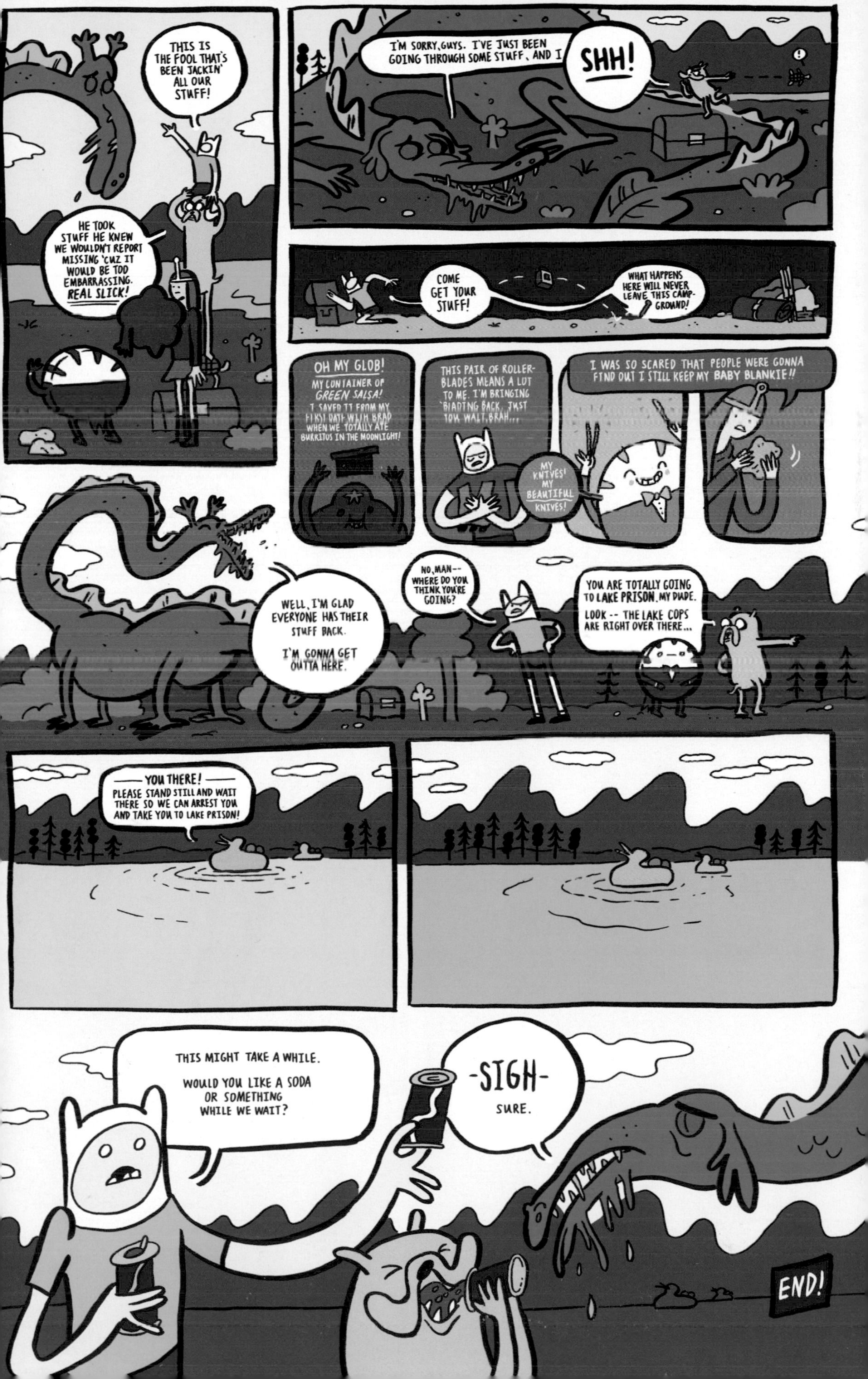
THIS IS THE FOOL THAT'S BEEN JACKIN' ALL OUR STUFF!
HE TOOK STUFF HE KNEW WE WOULDN'T REPORT MISSING 'CUZ IT WOULD BE TOO EMBARRASSING. REAL SLICK!
I'M SORRY, GUYS. I'VE JUST BEEN GOING THROUGH SOME STUFF, AND I
SHH!
COME GET YOUR STUFF!
WHAT HAPPENS HERE WILL NEVER LEAVE THIS CAMP-GROUND!
OH MY GLOB! MY CONTAINER OF GREEN SALSA! I SAVED IT FROM MY FIRST DATE WITH BRAD WHEN WE TOTALLY ATE BURRITOS IN THE MOONLIGHT!
THIS PAIR OF ROLLER-BLADES MEANS A LOT TO ME. I'M BRINGING 'BLADING BACK, JUST YOU WAIT, BRAH...
MY KNIVES! MY BEAUTIFUL KNIVES!
I WAS SO SCARED THAT PEOPLE WERE GONNA FIND OUT I STILL KEEP MY BABY BLANKIE!!
WELL, I'M GLAD EVERYONE HAS THEIR STUFF BACK.
I'M GONNA GET OUTTA HERE.
NO, MAN-- WHERE DO YOU THINK YOU'RE GOING?
YOU ARE TOTALLY GOING TO LAKE PRISON, MY DUDE.
LOOK -- THE LAKE COPS ARE RIGHT OVER THERE...
YOU THERE!
PLEASE STAND STILL AND WAIT THERE SO WE CAN ARREST YOU AND TAKE YOU TO LAKE PRISON!
THIS MIGHT TAKE A WHILE.
WOULD YOU LIKE A SODA OR SOMETHING WHILE WE WAIT?
-SIGH-
SURE.
END!

WATER STRIKE

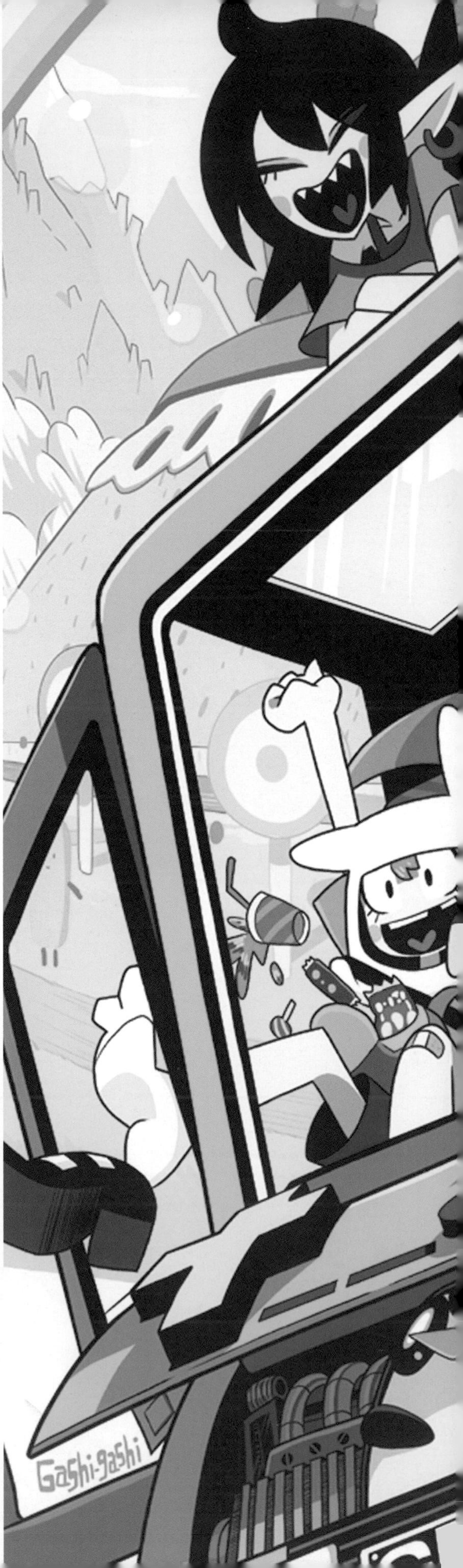
Gashi-gashi

ISSUE FORTY SIX EUGENE COMIC CON 2015 EXCLUSIVE COVER
GASHI GASHI

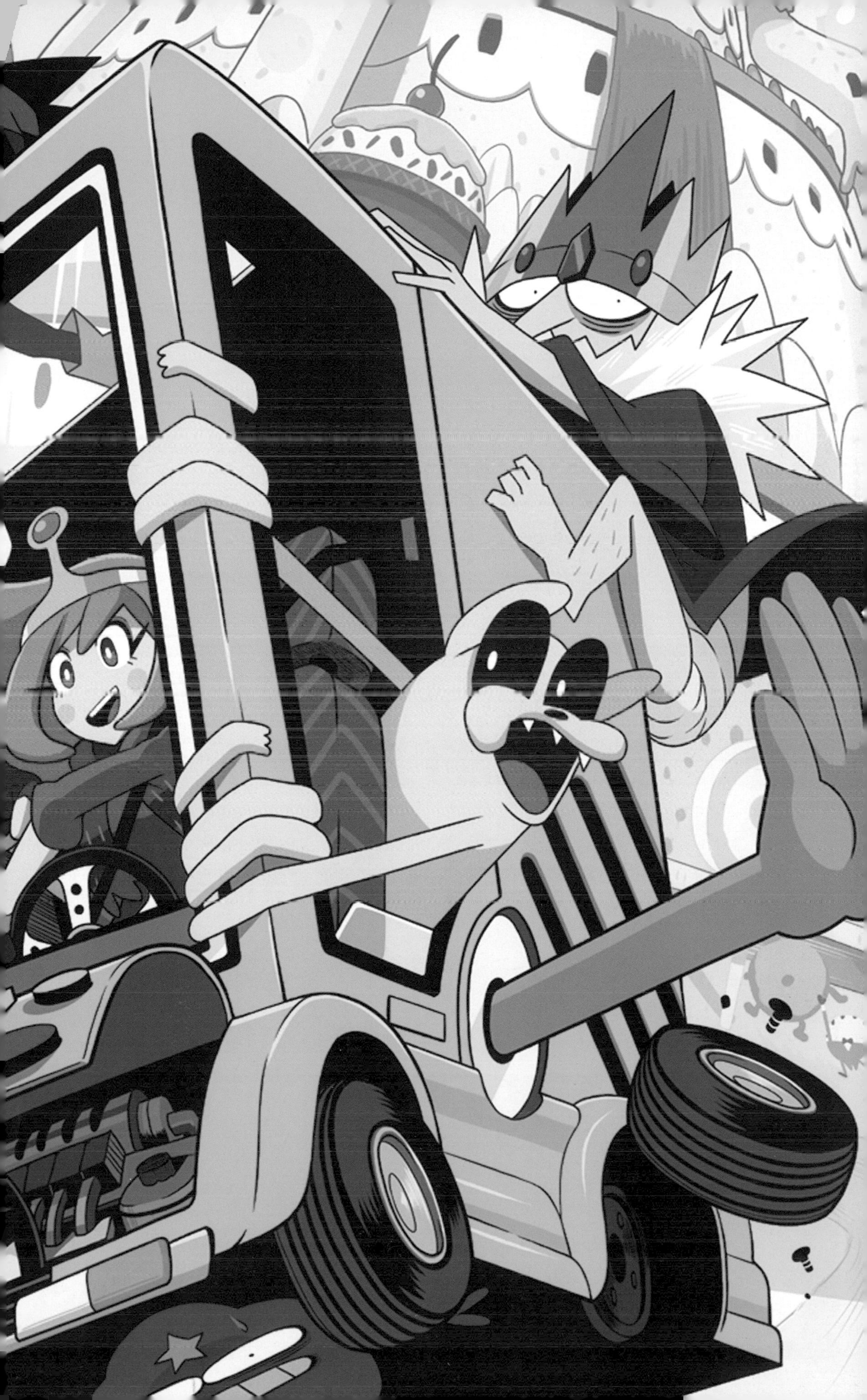

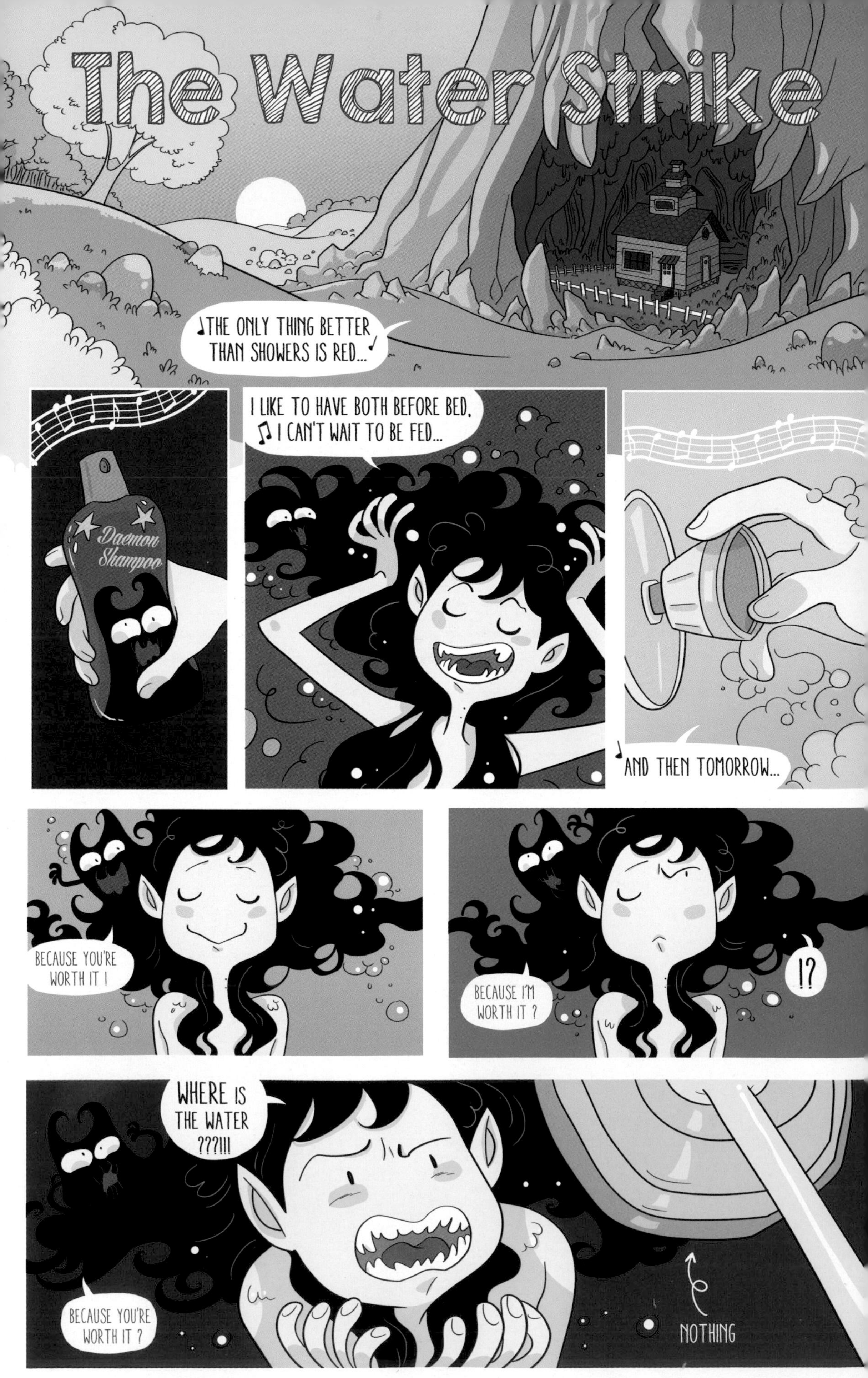
The Water Strike
THE ONLY THING BETTER THAN SHOWERS IS RED...
Daemon Shampoo
I LIKE TO HAVE BOTH BEFORE BED, I CAN'T WAIT TO BE FED...
AND THEN TOMORROW...
BECAUSE YOU'RE WORTH IT !
BECAUSE I'M WORTH IT ?
!?
WHERE IS THE WATER ???!!!
BECAUSE YOU'RE WORTH IT ?
NOTHING

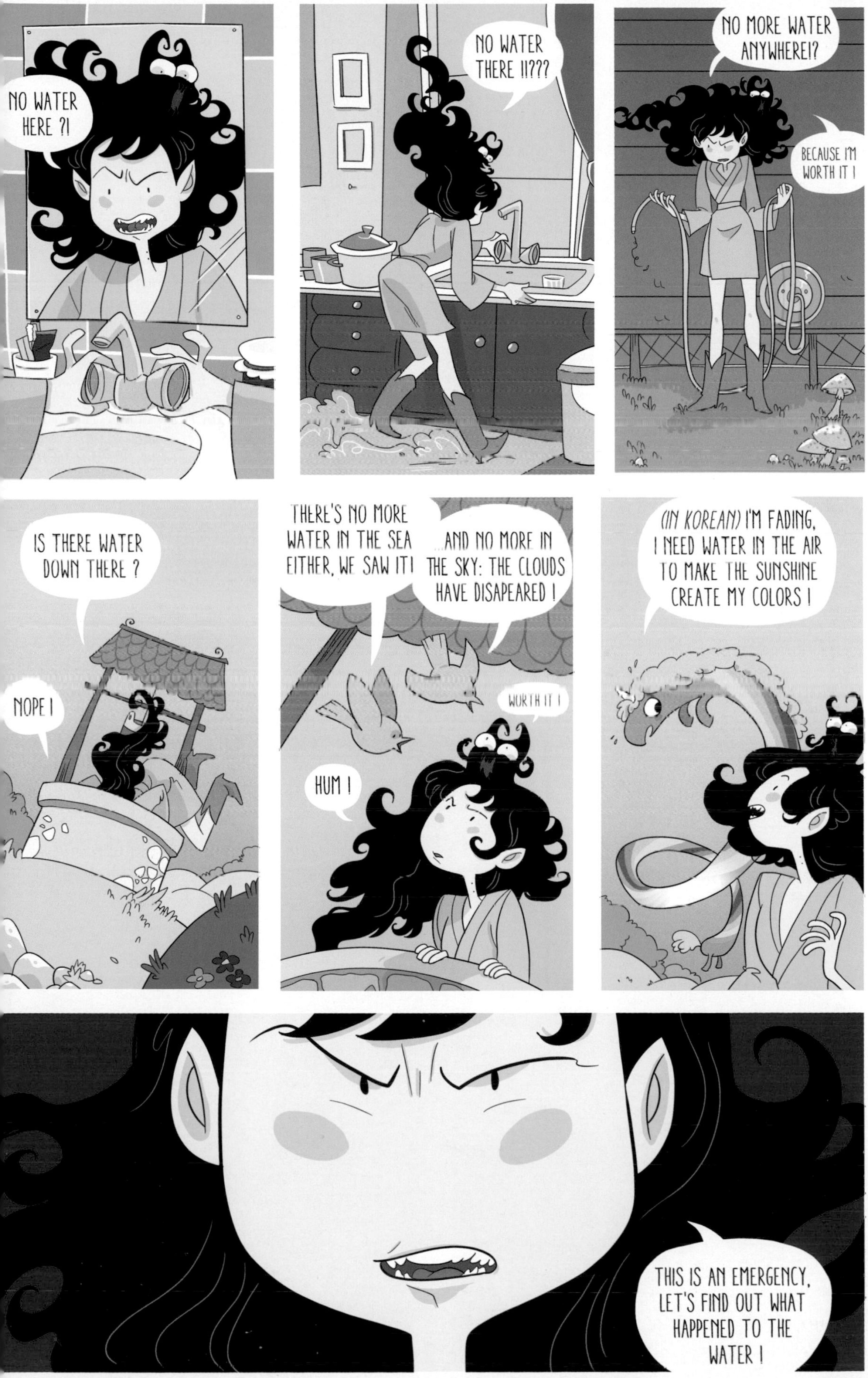
NO WATER
HERE ?!
NO WATER
THERE !!???
NO MORE WATER
ANYWHERE!?
BECAUSE I'M
WORTH IT !
IS THERE WATER
DOWN THERE ?
NOPE !
THERE'S NO MORE
WATER IN THE SEA
EITHER, WE SAW IT!
...AND NO MORE IN
THE SKY: THE CLOUDS
HAVE DISAPEARED !
WORTH IT !
HUM !
(IN KOREAN) I'M FADING,
I NEED WATER IN THE AIR
TO MAKE THE SUNSHINE
CREATE MY COLORS !
THIS IS AN EMERGENCY,
LET'S FIND OUT WHAT
HAPPENED TO THE
WATER !

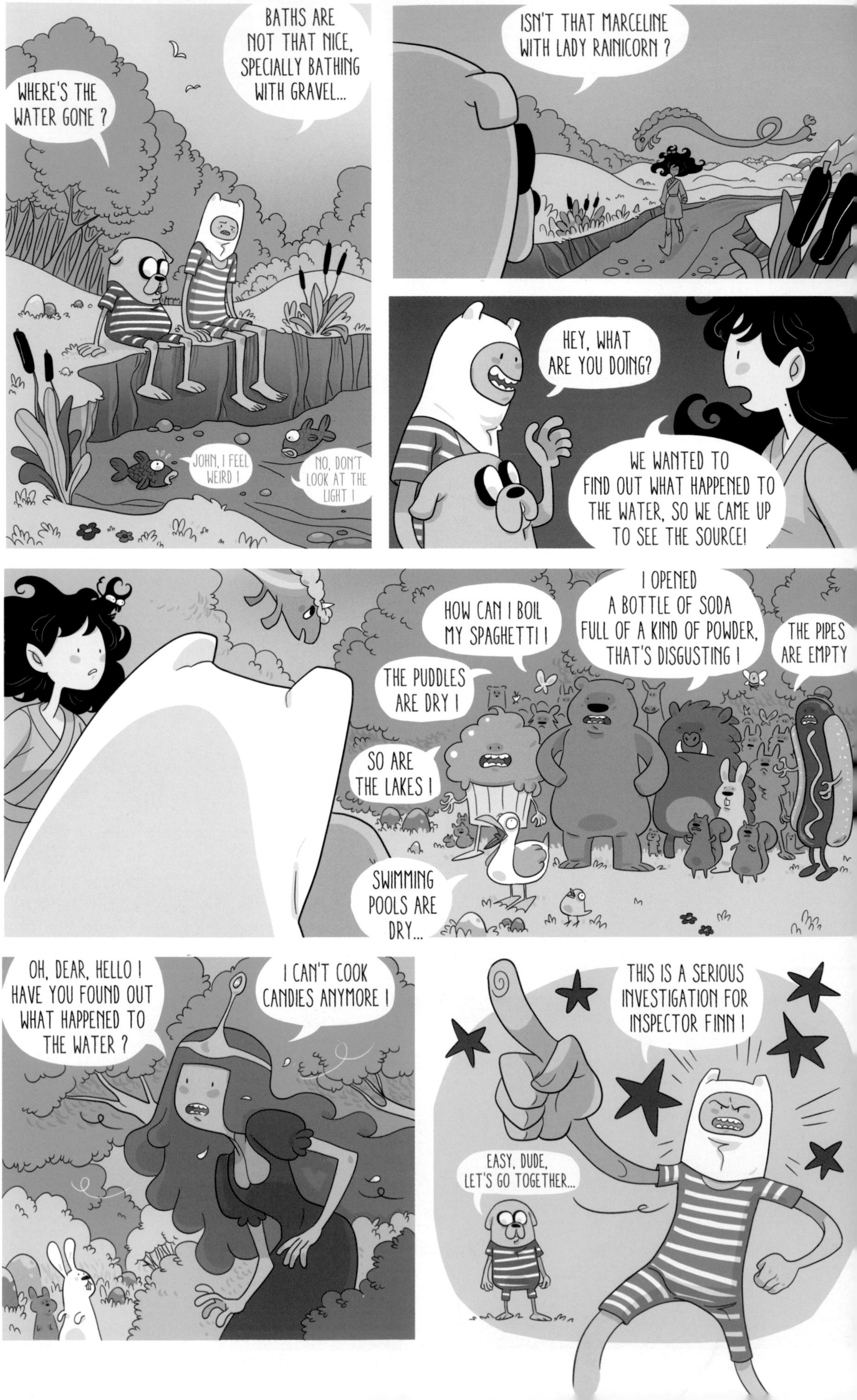
WHERE'S THE WATER GONE ?
BATHS ARE NOT THAT NICE, SPECIALLY BATHING WITH GRAVEL...
JOHN, I FEEL WEIRD !
NO, DON'T LOOK AT THE LIGHT !
ISN'T THAT MARCELINE WITH LADY RAINICORN ?
HEY, WHAT ARE YOU DOING?
WE WANTED TO FIND OUT WHAT HAPPENED TO THE WATER, SO WE CAME UP TO SEE THE SOURCE!
HOW CAN I BOIL MY SPAGHETTI !
I OPENED A BOTTLE OF SODA FULL OF A KIND OF POWDER, THAT'S DISGUSTING !
THE PIPES ARE EMPTY
THE PUDDLES ARE DRY !
SO ARE THE LAKES !
SWIMMING POOLS ARE DRY...
OH, DEAR, HELLO ! HAVE YOU FOUND OUT WHAT HAPPENED TO THE WATER ?
I CAN'T COOK CANDIES ANYMORE !
THIS IS A SERIOUS INVESTIGATION FOR INSPECTOR FINN !
EASY, DUDE, LET'S GO TOGETHER...

FEW HOURS LATER...

SLURP, SLURP...

JAKE, WHAT ARE YOU DOING ?!!

I'M SO THIRSTY, SO I FIND WATER WHERE THERE'S STILL SOME: MY SWEAT !

YERK ! THAT'S GROSS !

...AND PRETTY CLEVER !

BETTER WITH NO SHIRT, YOU KNOW...

WORTH IT!

SHHH, I HEAR SOMETHING !

BOUHOUHOUHOU... SOB, SOB.....SNRFL

II??

SOUNDS LIKE SOMEONE IS CRYING OVER THERE !

MHH ??

WATER !!

BOUHOU SOB...

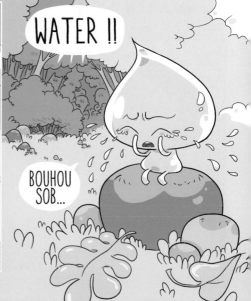

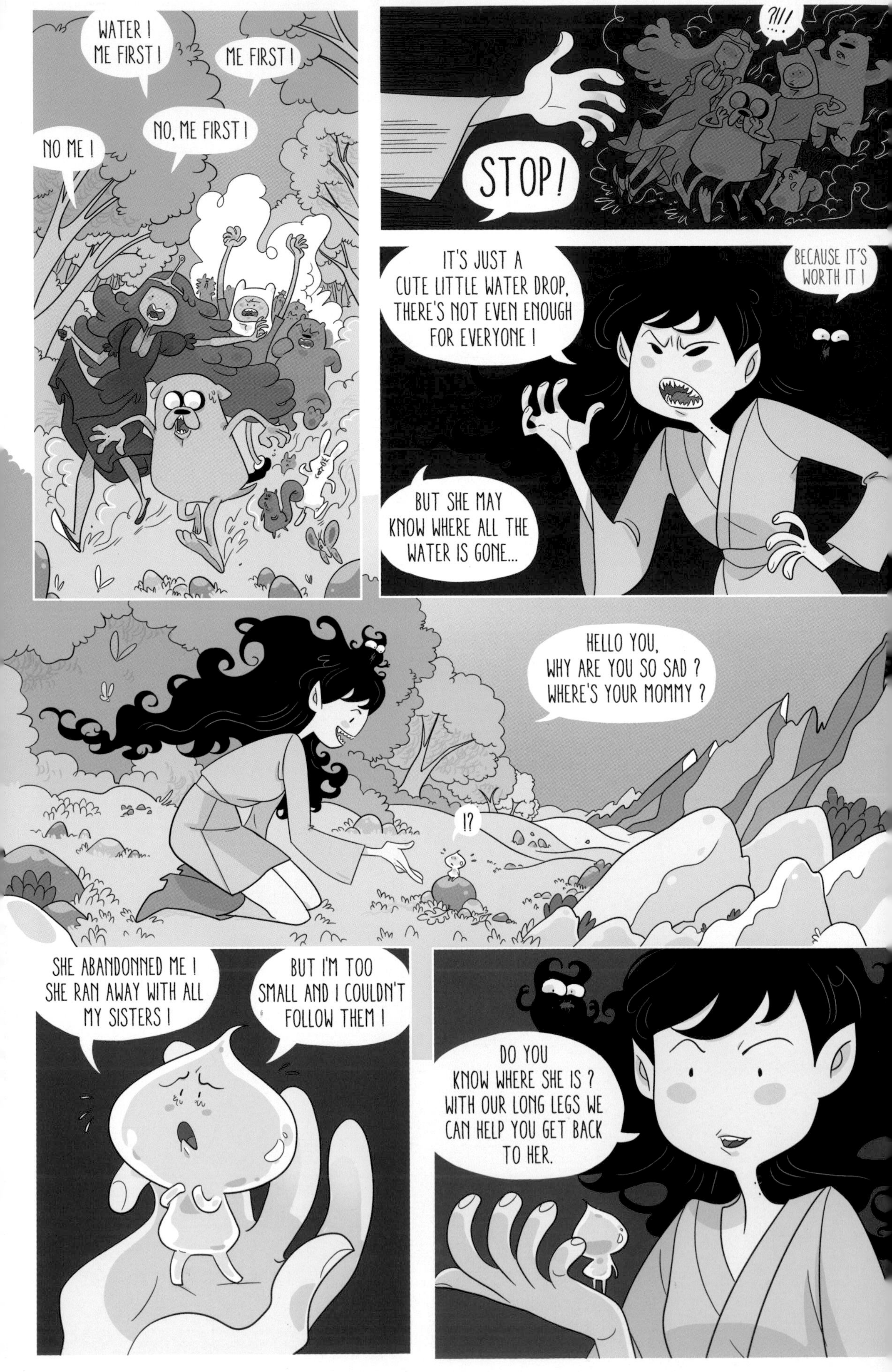
WATER ! ME FIRST !
ME FIRST !
NO, ME FIRST !
NO ME !
?!! !
STOP !
IT'S JUST A CUTE LITTLE WATER DROP, THERE'S NOT EVEN ENOUGH FOR EVERYONE !
BECAUSE IT'S WORTH IT !
BUT SHE MAY KNOW WHERE ALL THE WATER IS GONE...
HELLO YOU, WHY ARE YOU SO SAD ? WHERE'S YOUR MOMMY ?
!?
SHE ABANDONNED ME ! SHE RAN AWAY WITH ALL MY SISTERS !
BUT I'M TOO SMALL AND I COULDN'T FOLLOW THEM !
DO YOU KNOW WHERE SHE IS ? WITH OUR LONG LEGS WE CAN HELP YOU GET BACK TO HER.

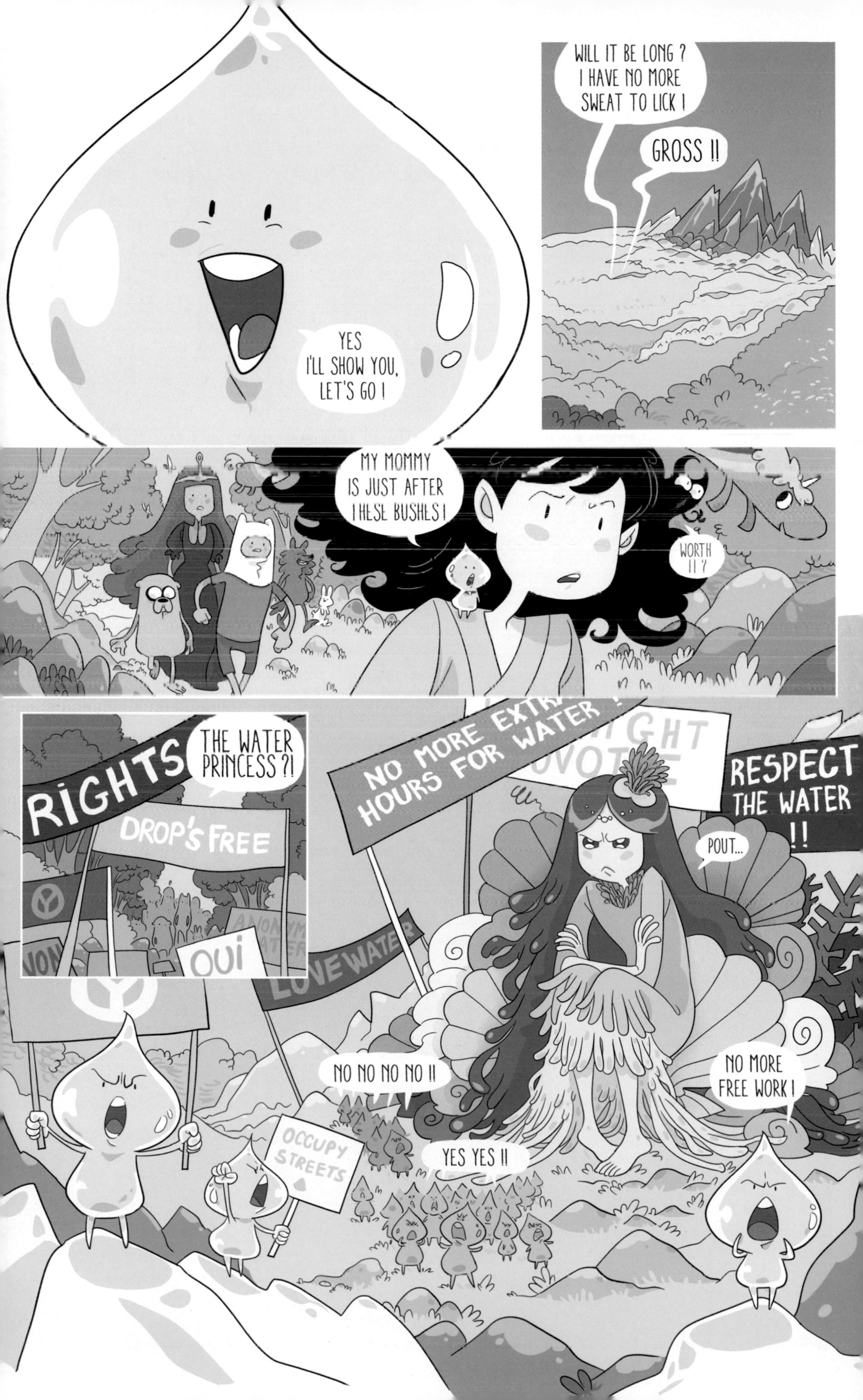
YES I'LL SHOW YOU, LET'S GO !
WILL IT BE LONG ? I HAVE NO MORE SWEAT TO LICK !
GROSS !!
MY MOMMY IS JUST AFTER THESE BUSHES !
WORTH IT ?
THE WATER PRINCESS ?!
RIGHTS
DROP'S FREE
OUI
NO MORE EXTRA HOURS FOR WATER !
RESPECT THE WATER !!
POUT...
LOVE WATER
NO NO NO NO !!
OCCUPY STREETS
YES YES !!
NO MORE FREE WORK !

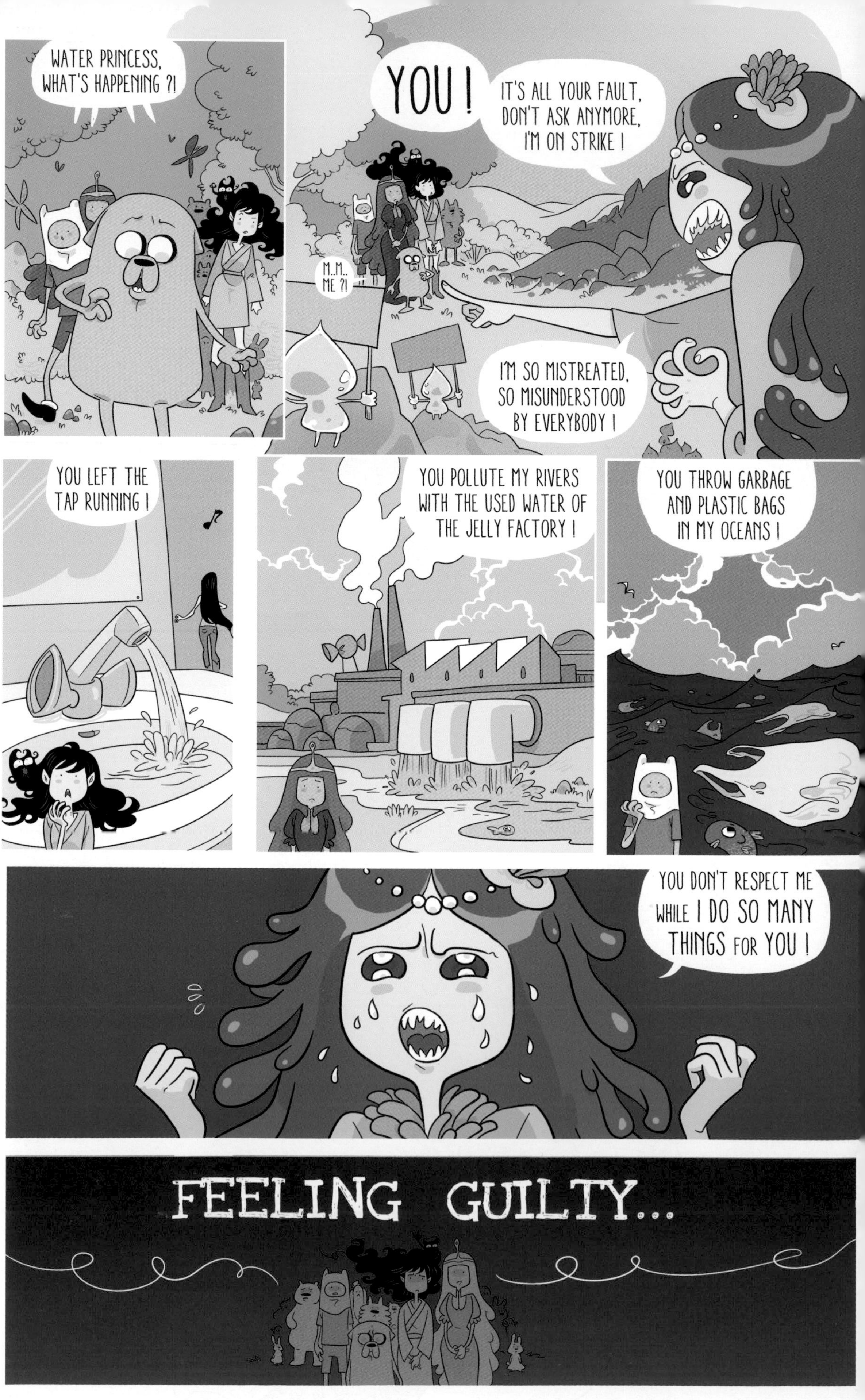
WATER PRINCESS, WHAT'S HAPPENING ?!
YOU !
IT'S ALL YOUR FAULT, DON'T ASK ANYMORE, I'M ON STRIKE !
M..M.. ME ?!
I'M SO MISTREATED, SO MISUNDERSTOOD BY EVERYBODY !
YOU LEFT THE TAP RUNNING !
YOU POLLUTE MY RIVERS WITH THE USED WATER OF THE JELLY FACTORY !
YOU THROW GARBAGE AND PLASTIC BAGS IN MY OCEANS !
YOU DON'T RESPECT ME WHILE I DO SO MANY THINGS FOR YOU !
FEELING GUILTY...

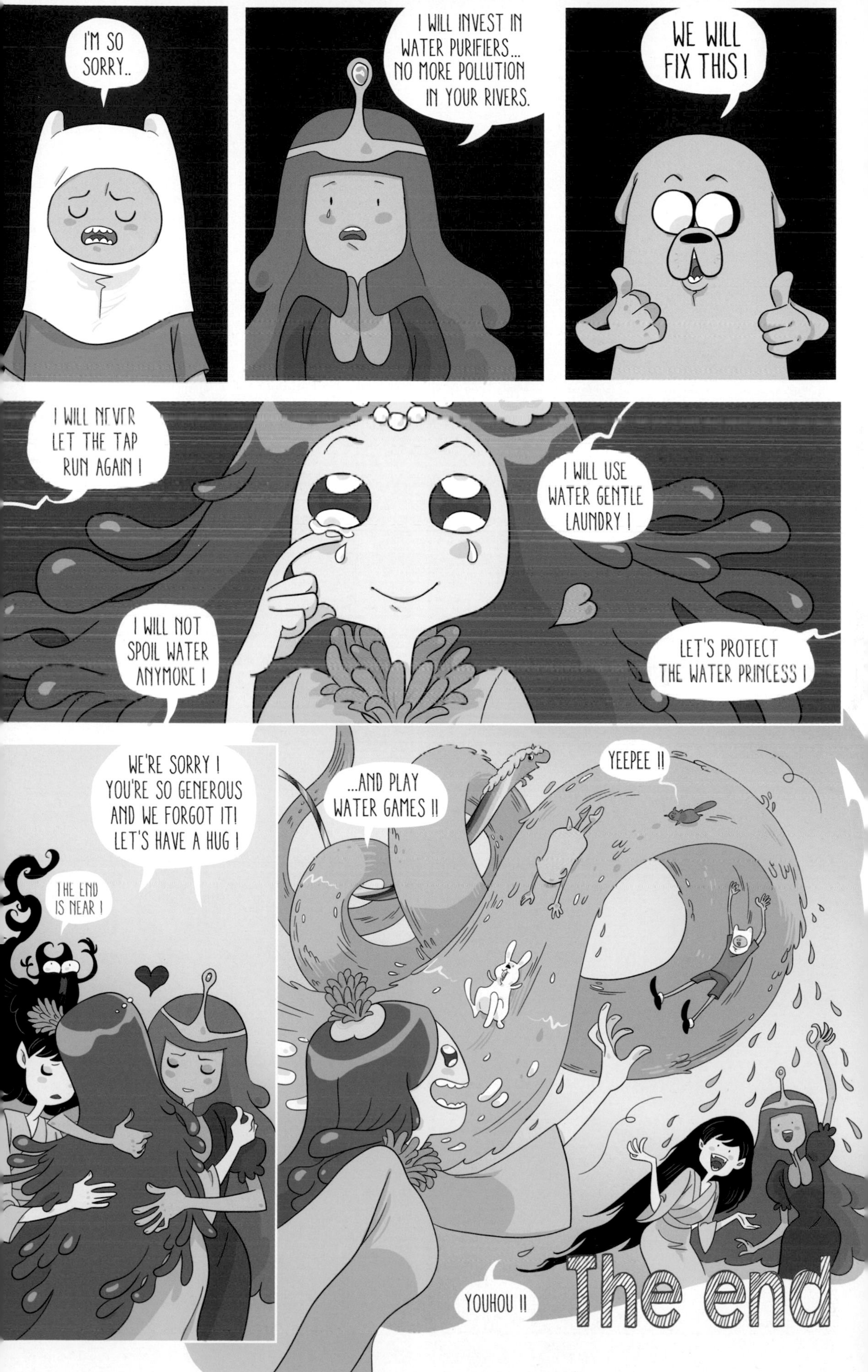
I'M SO SORRY..
I WILL INVEST IN WATER PURIFIERS... NO MORE POLLUTION IN YOUR RIVERS.
WE WILL FIX THIS!
I WILL NEVER LET THE TAP RUN AGAIN!
I WILL USE WATER GENTLE LAUNDRY!
I WILL NOT SPOIL WATER ANYMORE!
LET'S PROTECT THE WATER PRINCESS!
WE'RE SORRY! YOU'RE SO GENEROUS AND WE FORGOT IT! LET'S HAVE A HUG!
THE END IS NEAR!
...AND PLAY WATER GAMES!!
YEEPEE!!
YOUHOU!!
The end

SICK DAY

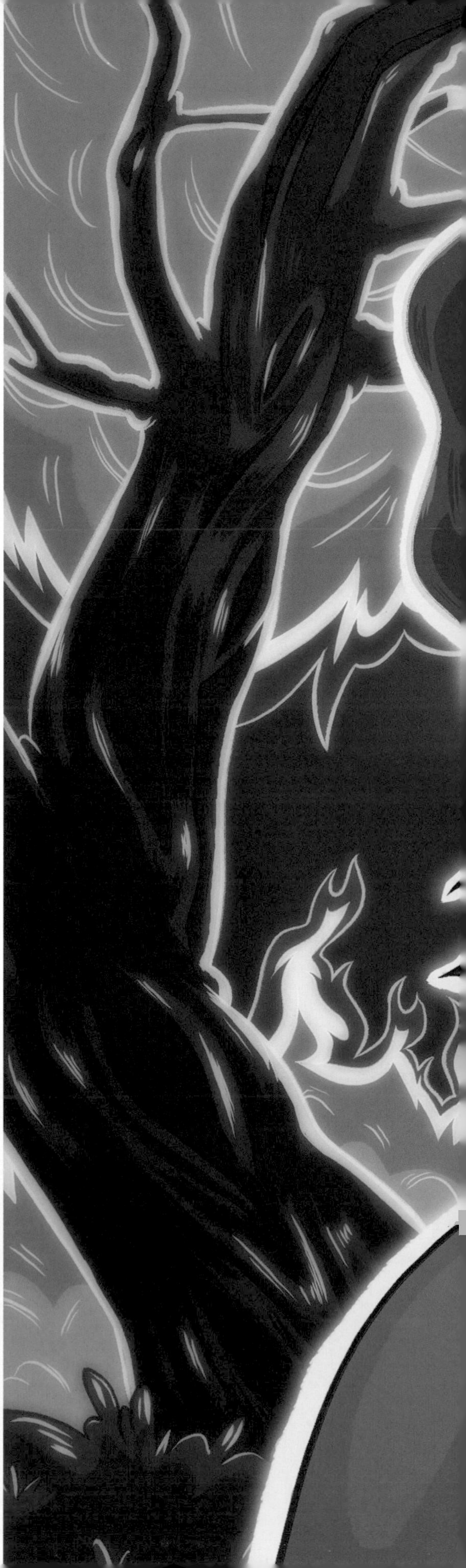

ISSUE FORTY SEVEN SUBSCRIPTION COVER

LISA DUBOIS

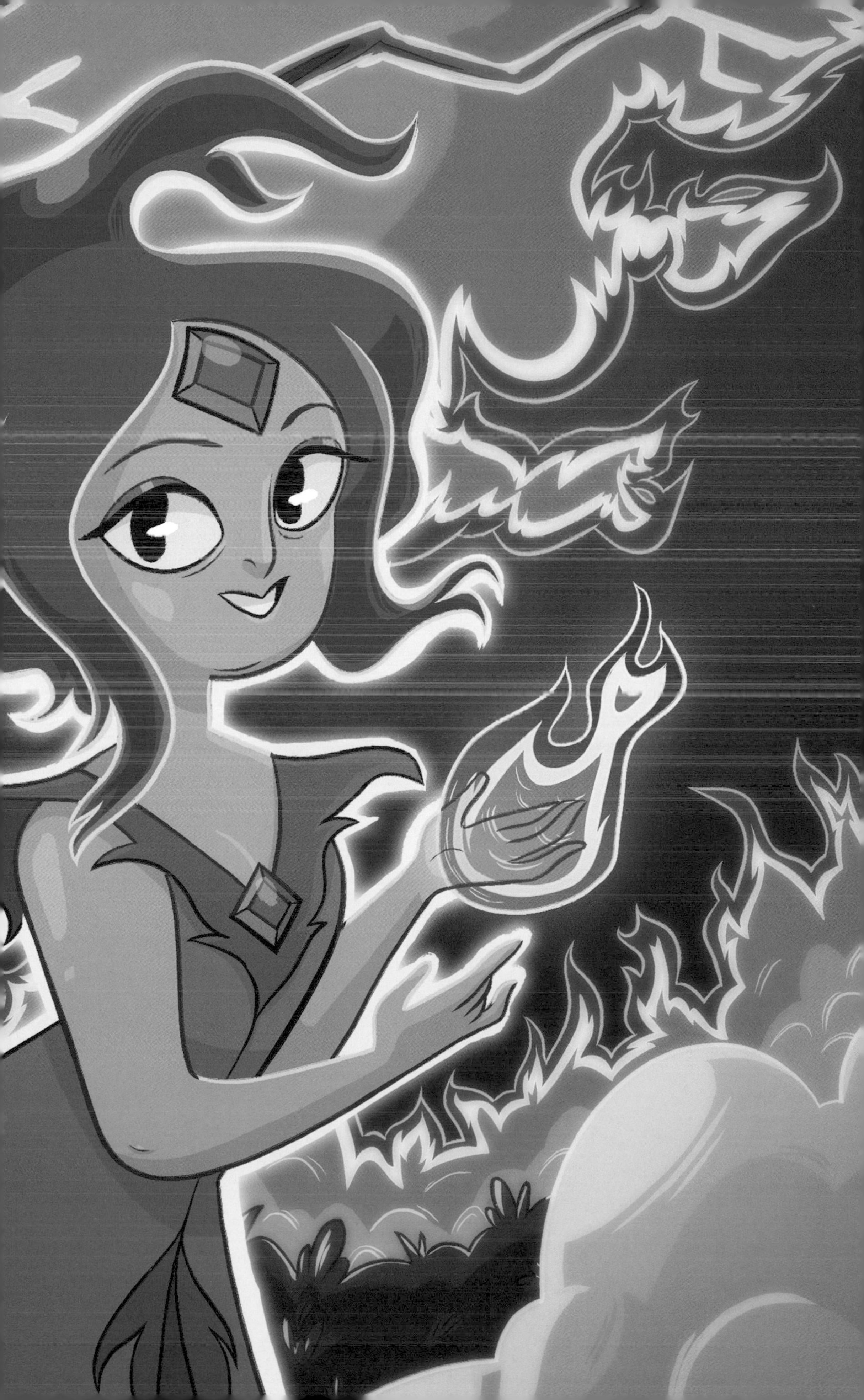

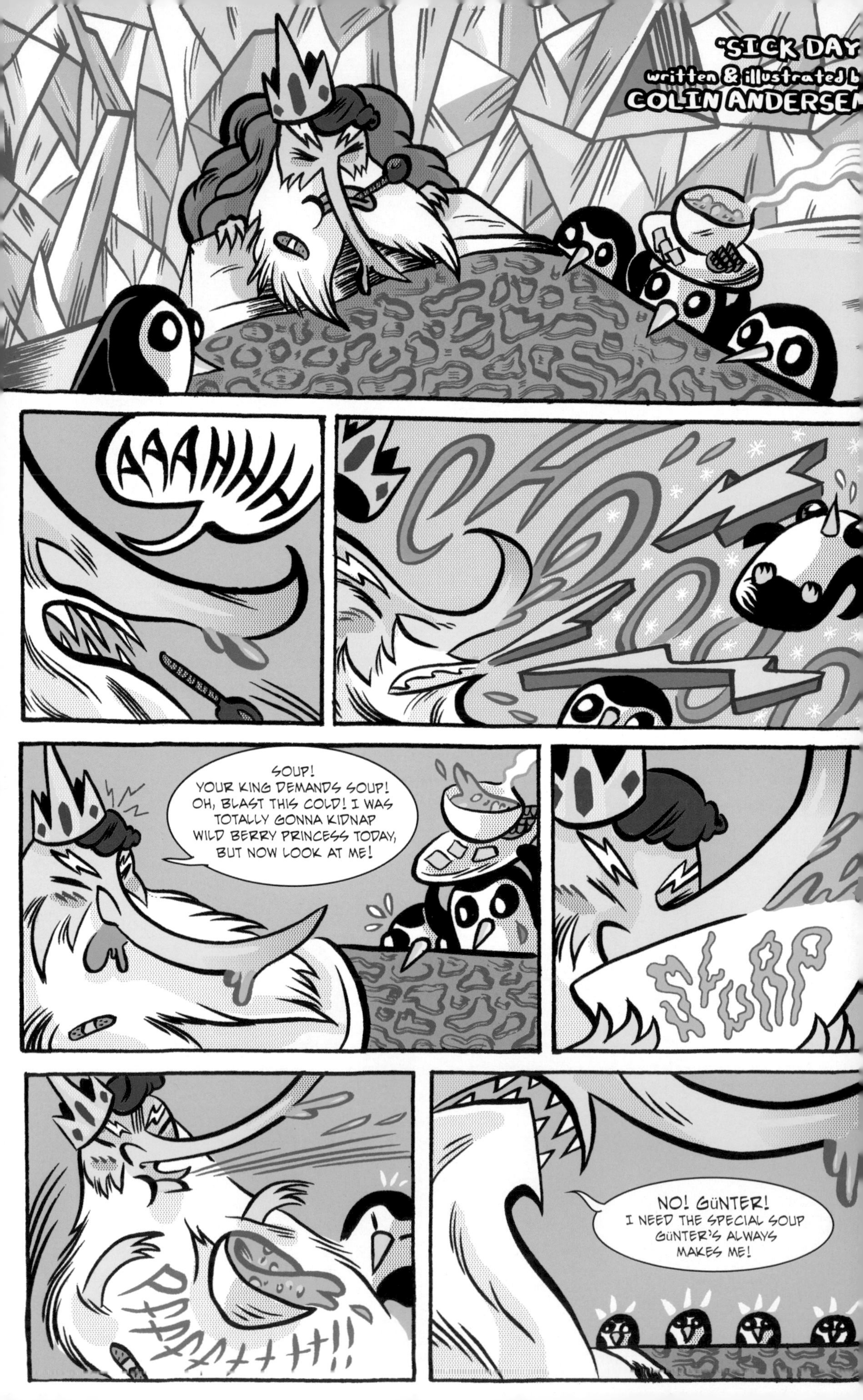
"SICK DAY
written & illustrated b
COLIN ANDERSE
AAAHHH
SOUP! YOUR KING DEMANDS SOUP! OH, BLAST THIS COLD! I WAS TOTALLY GONNA KIDNAP WILD BERRY PRINCESS TODAY, BUT NOW LOOK AT ME!
SLURP
PFFFTTTT!!
NO! GÜNTER! I NEED THE SPECIAL SOUP GÜNTER'S ALWAYS MAKES ME!

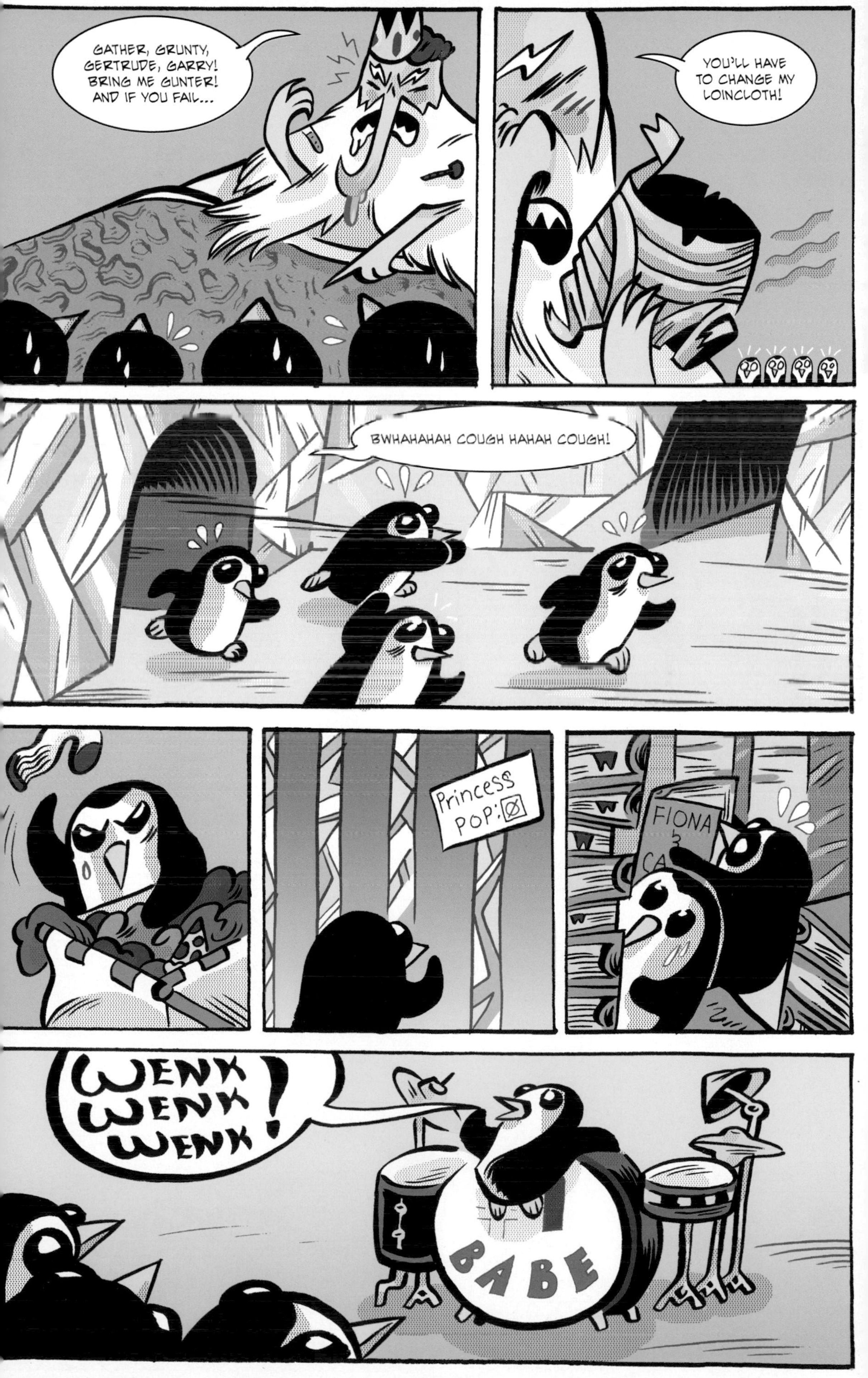
GATHER, GRUNTY, GERTRUDE, GARRY! BRING ME GUNTER! AND IF YOU FAIL...
YOU'LL HAVE TO CHANGE MY LOINCLOTH!
BWHAHAHAH COUGH HAHAH COUGH!
Princess POP: Ø
FIONA 3 CA
WENK WENK WENK!
BABE

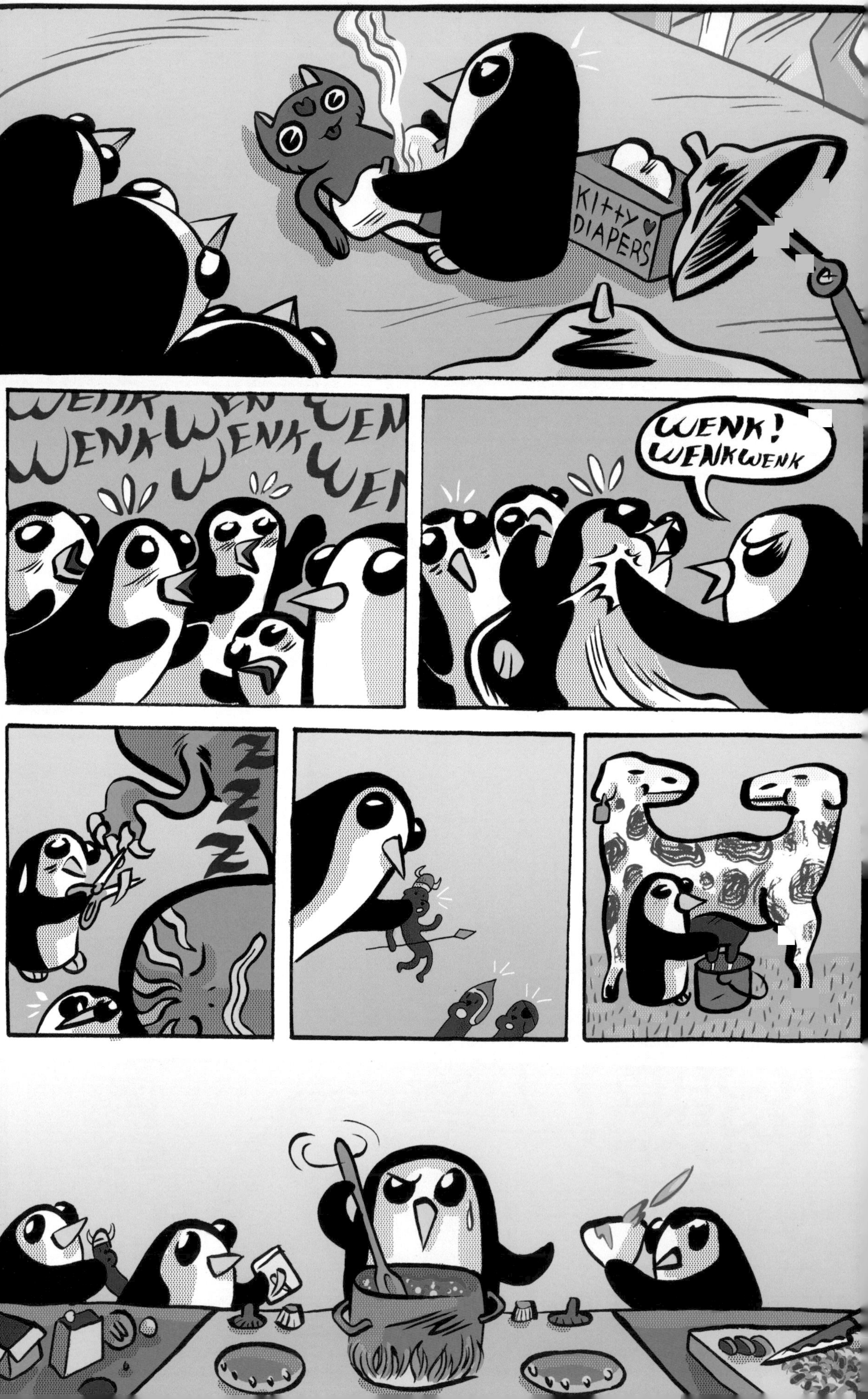

Kitty ♥ DIAPERS
WENK WENK
WENK! WENKWENK
Z Z Z

It's about time Gunter!

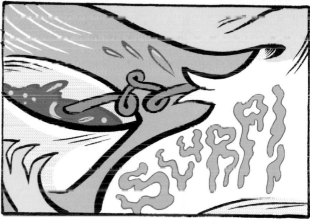

SWURP

Thanks Gunts. You know just how to take care of me

PAtPAt

AH

CH'HOO

Glob darnit Gunther! It's too cold! Make me another one!

END

FLOWERS FOR PAULTICORE

ISSUE FORTY EIGHT SUBSCRIPTION COVER
DAVID RYAN ROBINSON

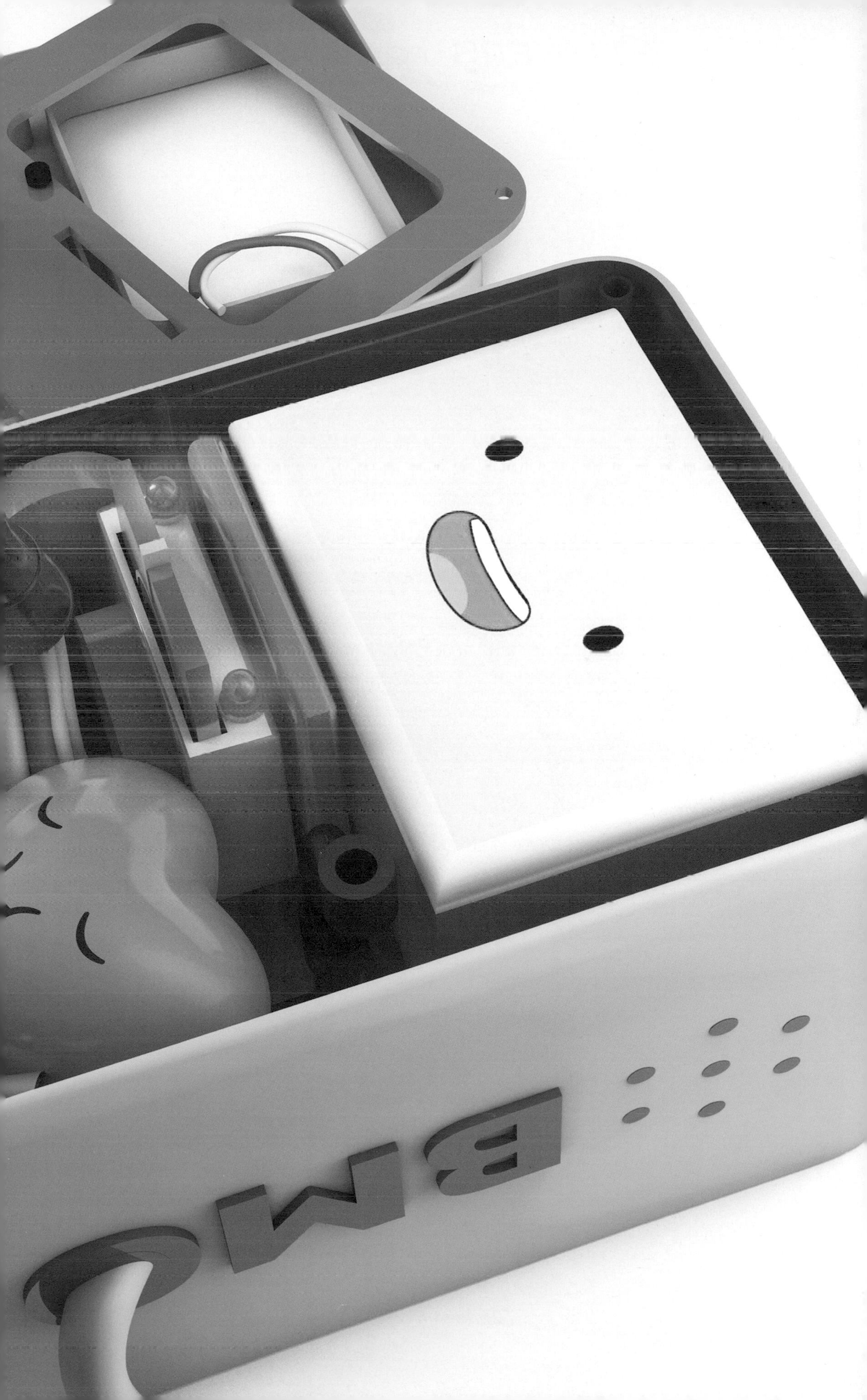

FINN AND JAKE IN

FLOWERS FOR PAULTICORE

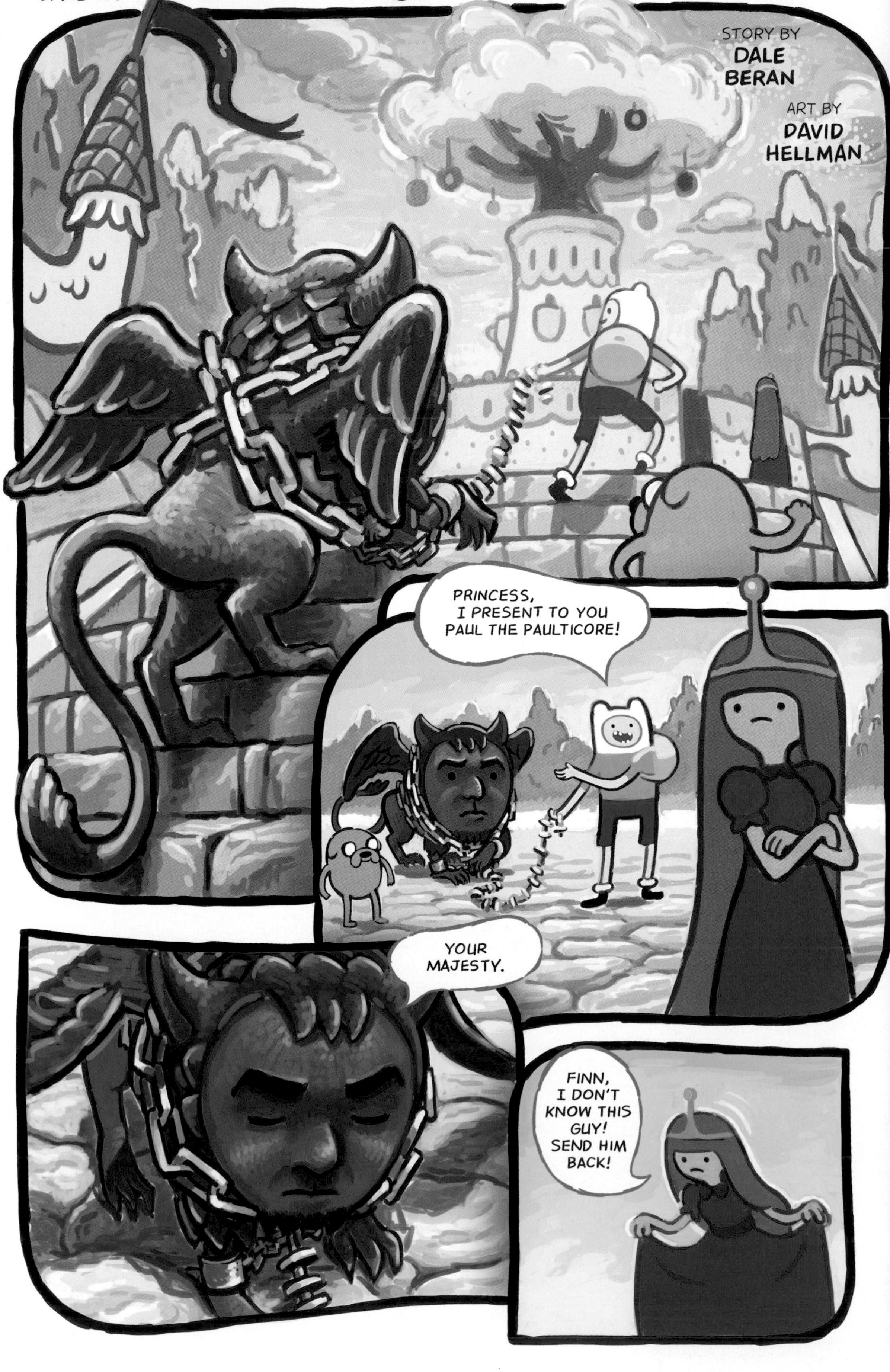
STORY BY
DALE BERAN
ART BY
DAVID HELLMAN
PRINCESS, I PRESENT TO YOU PAUL THE PAULTICORE!
YOUR MAJESTY.
FINN, I DON'T KNOW THIS GUY! SEND HIM BACK!

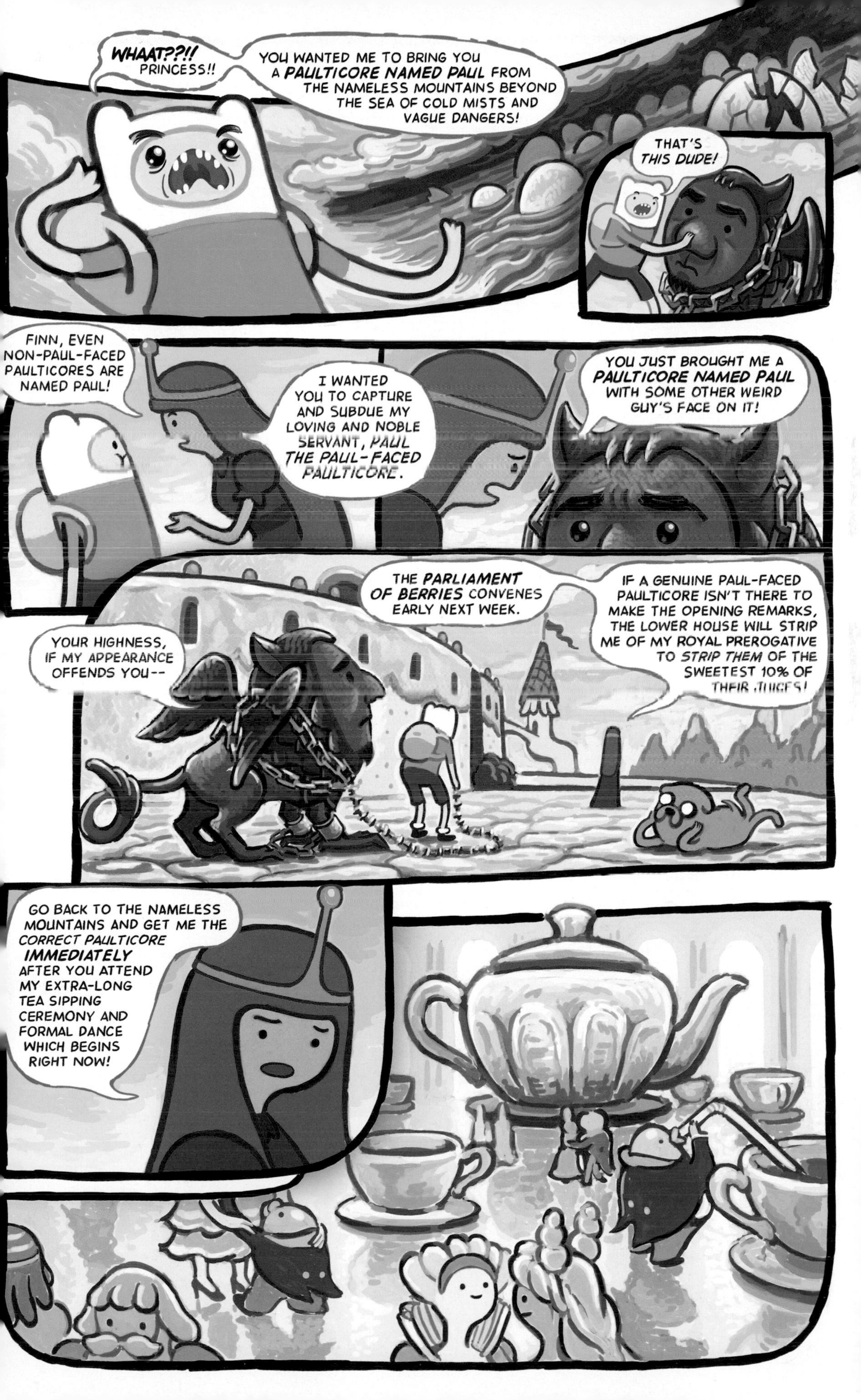

WHAAT??!! PRINCESS!!
YOU WANTED ME TO BRING YOU A PAULTICORE NAMED PAUL FROM THE NAMELESS MOUNTAINS BEYOND THE SEA OF COLD MISTS AND VAGUE DANGERS!
THAT'S THIS DUDE!
FINN, EVEN NON-PAUL-FACED PAULTICORES ARE NAMED PAUL!
I WANTED YOU TO CAPTURE AND SUBDUE MY LOVING AND NOBLE SERVANT, PAUL THE PAUL-FACED PAULTICORE.
YOU JUST BROUGHT ME A PAULTICORE NAMED PAUL WITH SOME OTHER WEIRD GUY'S FACE ON IT!
THE PARLIAMENT OF BERRIES CONVENES EARLY NEXT WEEK.
IF A GENUINE PAUL-FACED PAULTICORE ISN'T THERE TO MAKE THE OPENING REMARKS, THE LOWER HOUSE WILL STRIP ME OF MY ROYAL PREROGATIVE TO STRIP THEM OF THE SWEETEST 10% OF THEIR JUICES!
YOUR HIGHNESS, IF MY APPEARANCE OFFENDS YOU--
GO BACK TO THE NAMELESS MOUNTAINS AND GET ME THE CORRECT PAULTICORE IMMEDIATELY AFTER YOU ATTEND MY EXTRA-LONG TEA SIPPING CEREMONY AND FORMAL DANCE WHICH BEGINS RIGHT NOW!

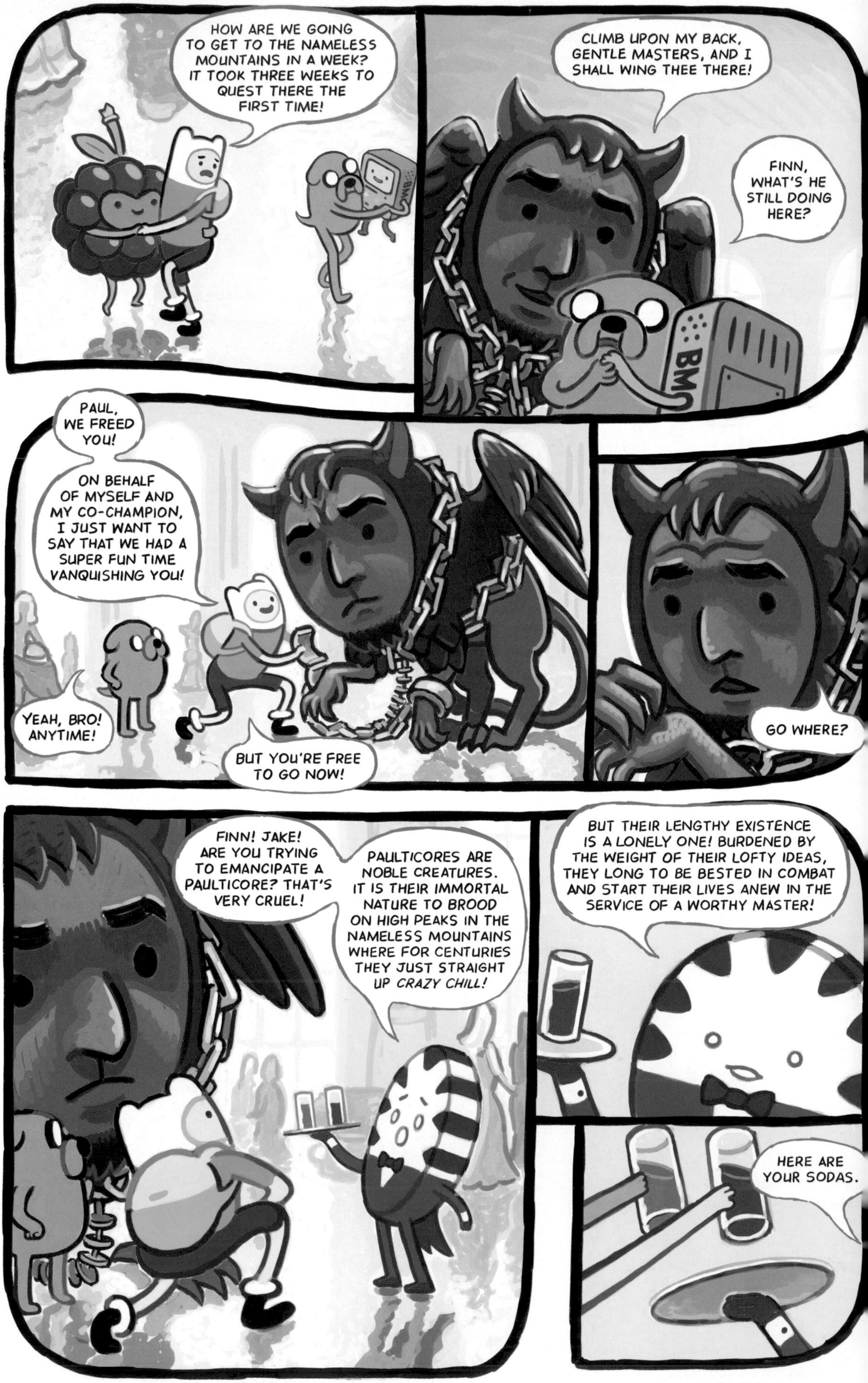
HOW ARE WE GOING TO GET TO THE NAMELESS MOUNTAINS IN A WEEK? IT TOOK THREE WEEKS TO QUEST THERE THE FIRST TIME!
CLIMB UPON MY BACK, GENTLE MASTERS, AND I SHALL WING THEE THERE!
FINN, WHAT'S HE STILL DOING HERE?
PAUL, WE FREED YOU!
ON BEHALF OF MYSELF AND MY CO-CHAMPION, I JUST WANT TO SAY THAT WE HAD A SUPER FUN TIME VANQUISHING YOU!
YEAH, BRO! ANYTIME!
BUT YOU'RE FREE TO GO NOW!
GO WHERE?
FINN! JAKE! ARE YOU TRYING TO EMANCIPATE A PAULTICORE? THAT'S VERY CRUEL!
PAULTICORES ARE NOBLE CREATURES. IT IS THEIR IMMORTAL NATURE TO BROOD ON HIGH PEAKS IN THE NAMELESS MOUNTAINS WHERE FOR CENTURIES THEY JUST STRAIGHT UP *CRAZY CHILL!*
BUT THEIR LENGTHY EXISTENCE IS A LONELY ONE! BURDENED BY THE WEIGHT OF THEIR LOFTY IDEAS, THEY LONG TO BE BESTED IN COMBAT AND START THEIR LIVES ANEW IN THE SERVICE OF A WORTHY MASTER!
HERE ARE YOUR SODAS.

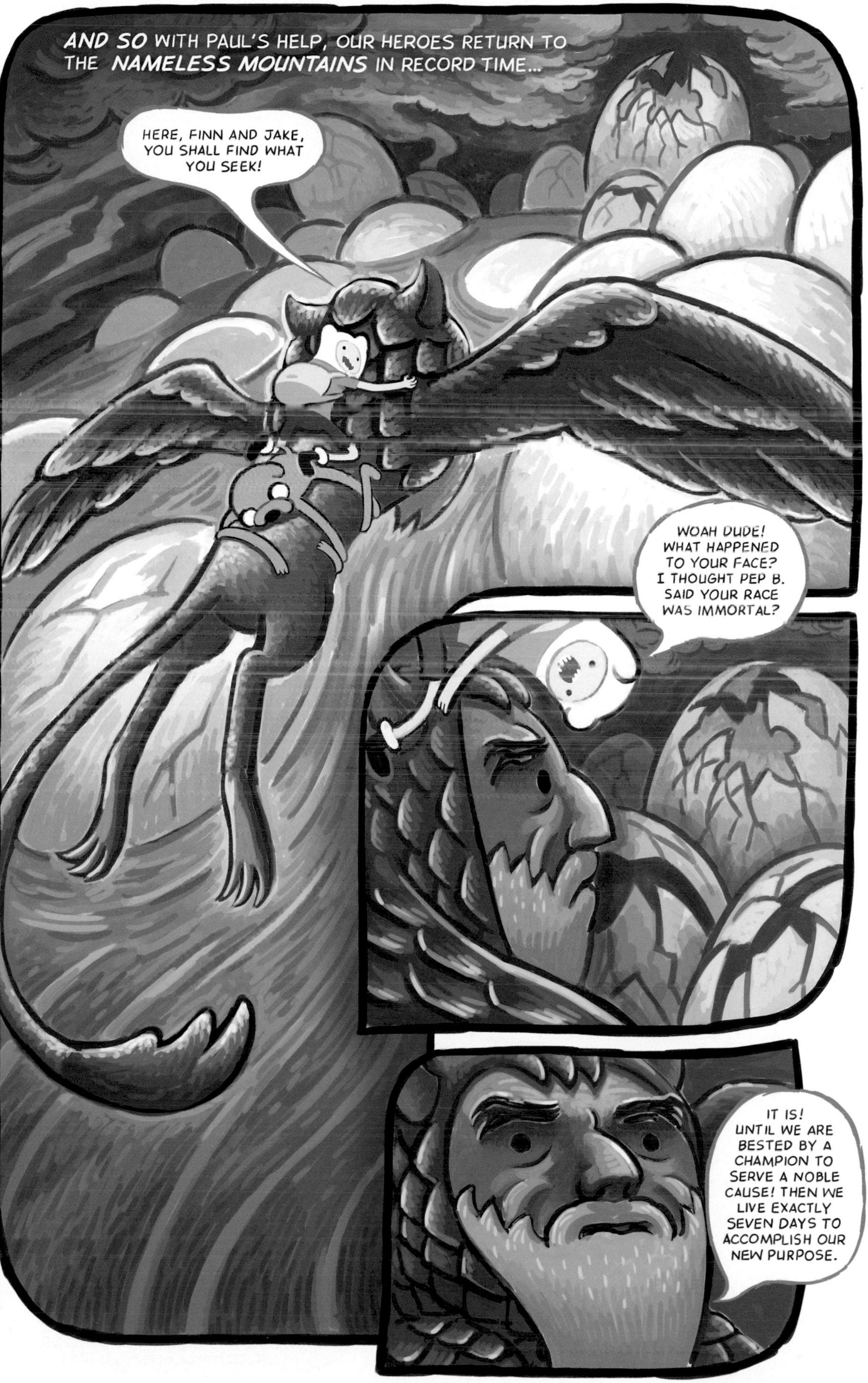
AND SO WITH PAUL'S HELP, OUR HEROES RETURN TO THE NAMELESS MOUNTAINS IN RECORD TIME...
HERE, FINN AND JAKE, YOU SHALL FIND WHAT YOU SEEK!
WOAH DUDE! WHAT HAPPENED TO YOUR FACE? I THOUGHT PEP B. SAID YOUR RACE WAS IMMORTAL?
IT IS! UNTIL WE ARE BESTED BY A CHAMPION TO SERVE A NOBLE CAUSE! THEN WE LIVE EXACTLY SEVEN DAYS TO ACCOMPLISH OUR NEW PURPOSE.

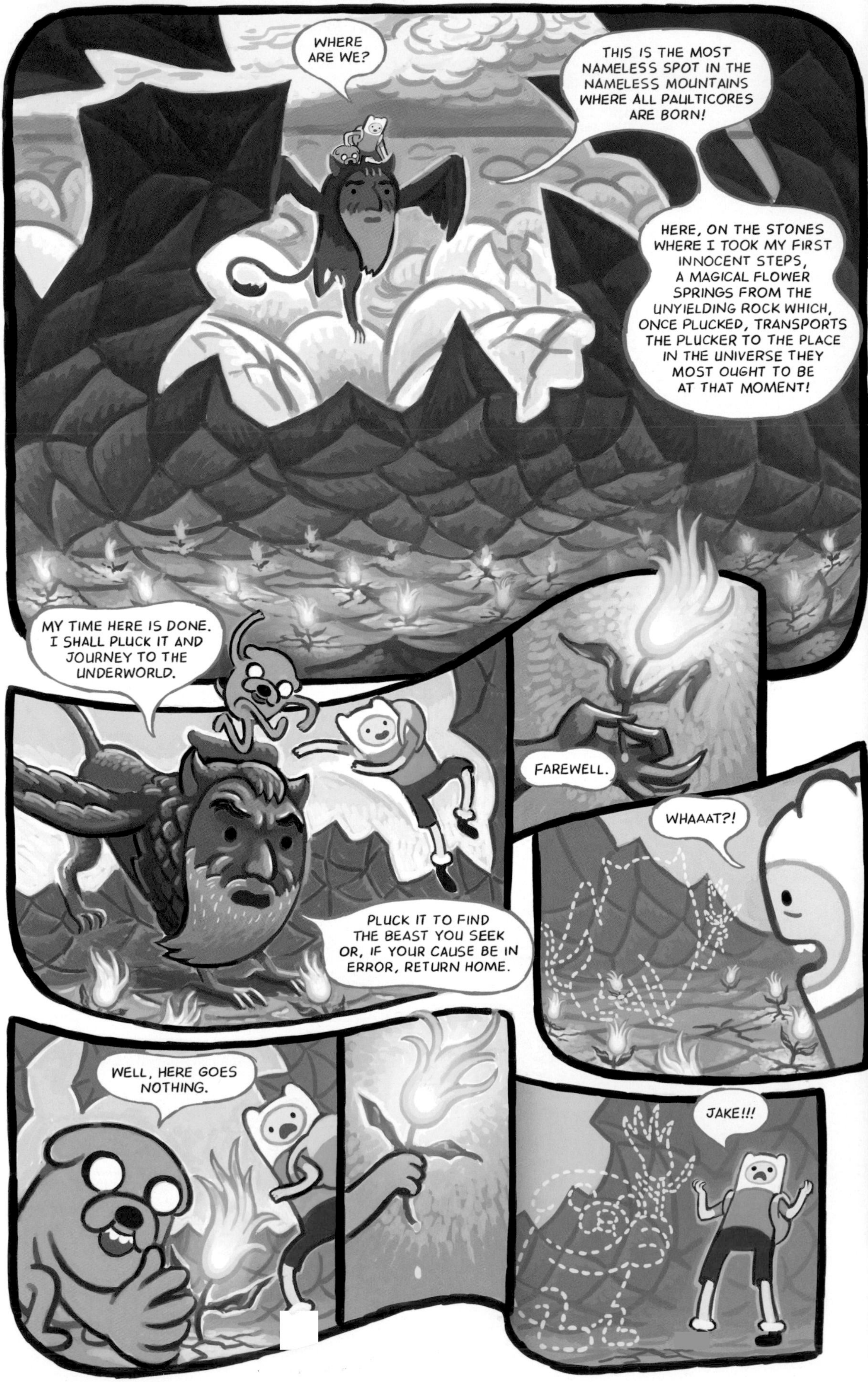
WHERE ARE WE?
THIS IS THE MOST NAMELESS SPOT IN THE NAMELESS MOUNTAINS WHERE ALL PAULTICORES ARE BORN!
HERE, ON THE STONES WHERE I TOOK MY FIRST INNOCENT STEPS, A MAGICAL FLOWER SPRINGS FROM THE UNYIELDING ROCK WHICH, ONCE PLUCKED, TRANSPORTS THE PLUCKER TO THE PLACE IN THE UNIVERSE THEY MOST OUGHT TO BE AT THAT MOMENT!
MY TIME HERE IS DONE. I SHALL PLUCK IT AND JOURNEY TO THE UNDERWORLD.
PLUCK IT TO FIND THE BEAST YOU SEEK OR, IF YOUR CAUSE BE IN ERROR, RETURN HOME.
FAREWELL.
WHAAAT?!
WELL, HERE GOES NOTHING.
JAKE!!!

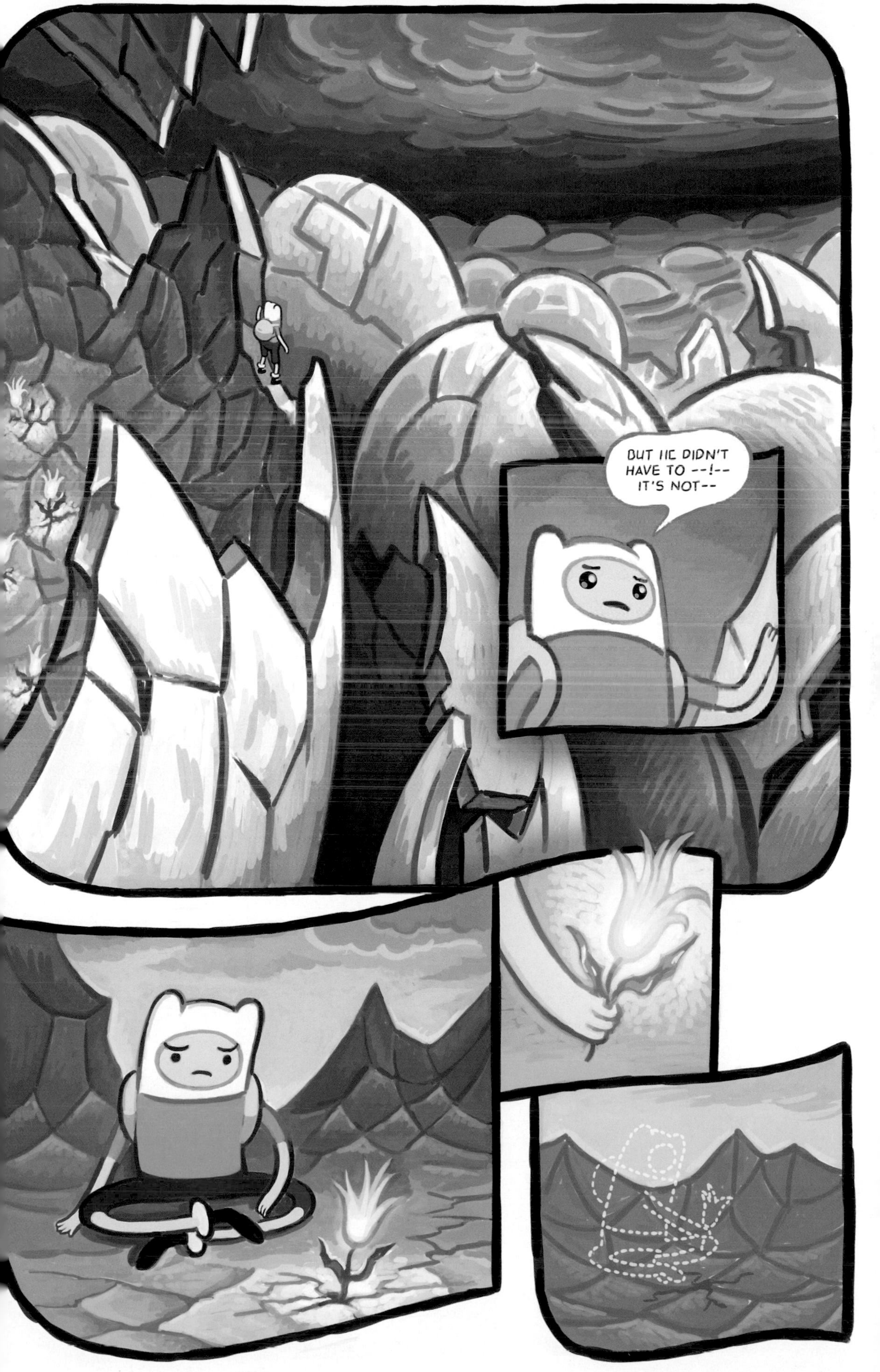
BUT HE DIDN'T HAVE TO --!-- IT'S NOT--

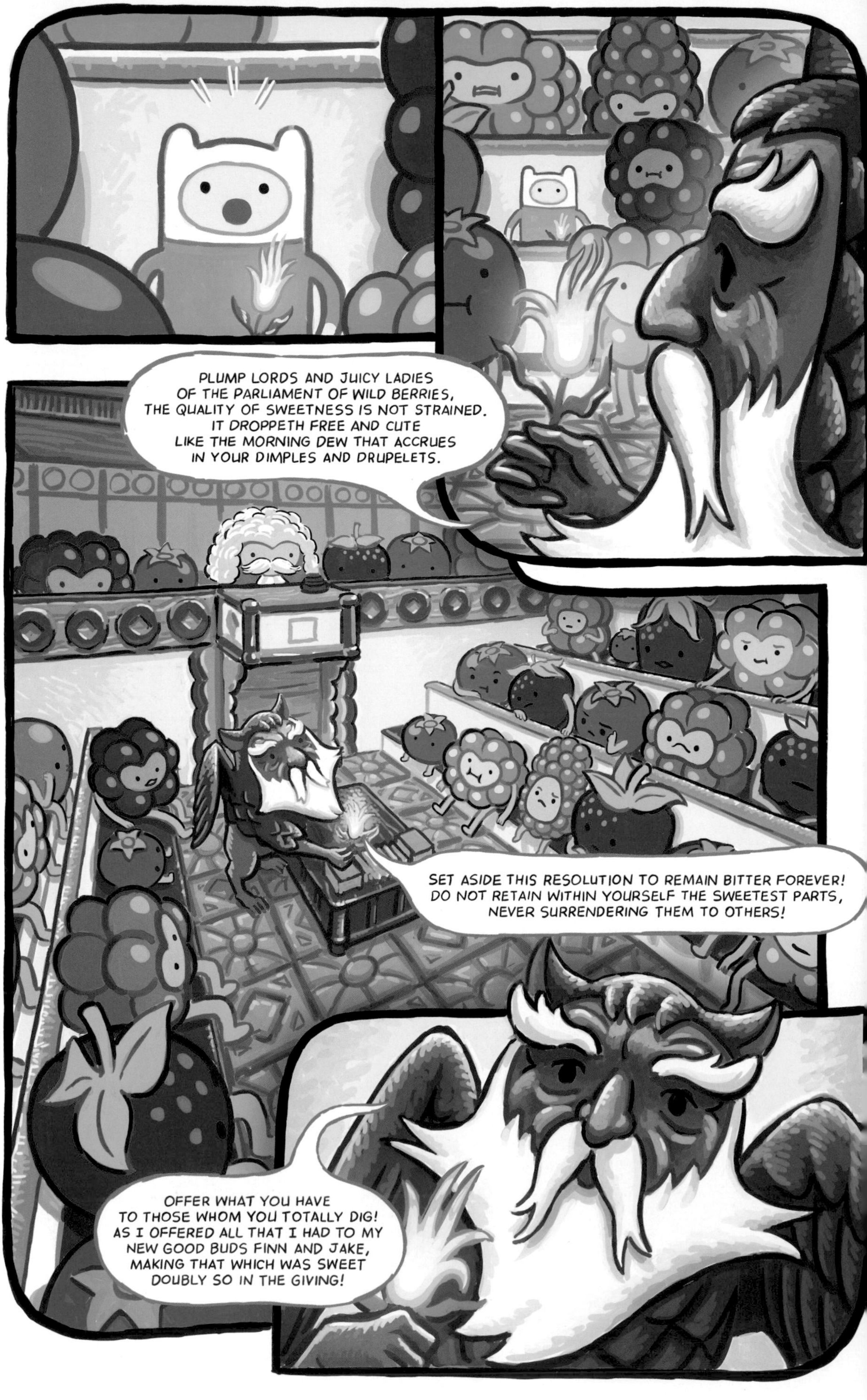
PLUMP LORDS AND JUICY LADIES OF THE PARLIAMENT OF WILD BERRIES, THE QUALITY OF SWEETNESS IS NOT STRAINED. IT DROPPETH FREE AND CUTE LIKE THE MORNING DEW THAT ACCRUES IN YOUR DIMPLES AND DRUPELETS.
SET ASIDE THIS RESOLUTION TO REMAIN BITTER FOREVER! DO NOT RETAIN WITHIN YOURSELF THE SWEETEST PARTS, NEVER SURRENDERING THEM TO OTHERS!
OFFER WHAT YOU HAVE TO THOSE WHOM YOU TOTALLY DIG! AS I OFFERED ALL THAT I HAD TO MY NEW GOOD BUDS FINN AND JAKE, MAKING THAT WHICH WAS SWEET DOUBLY SO IN THE GIVING!

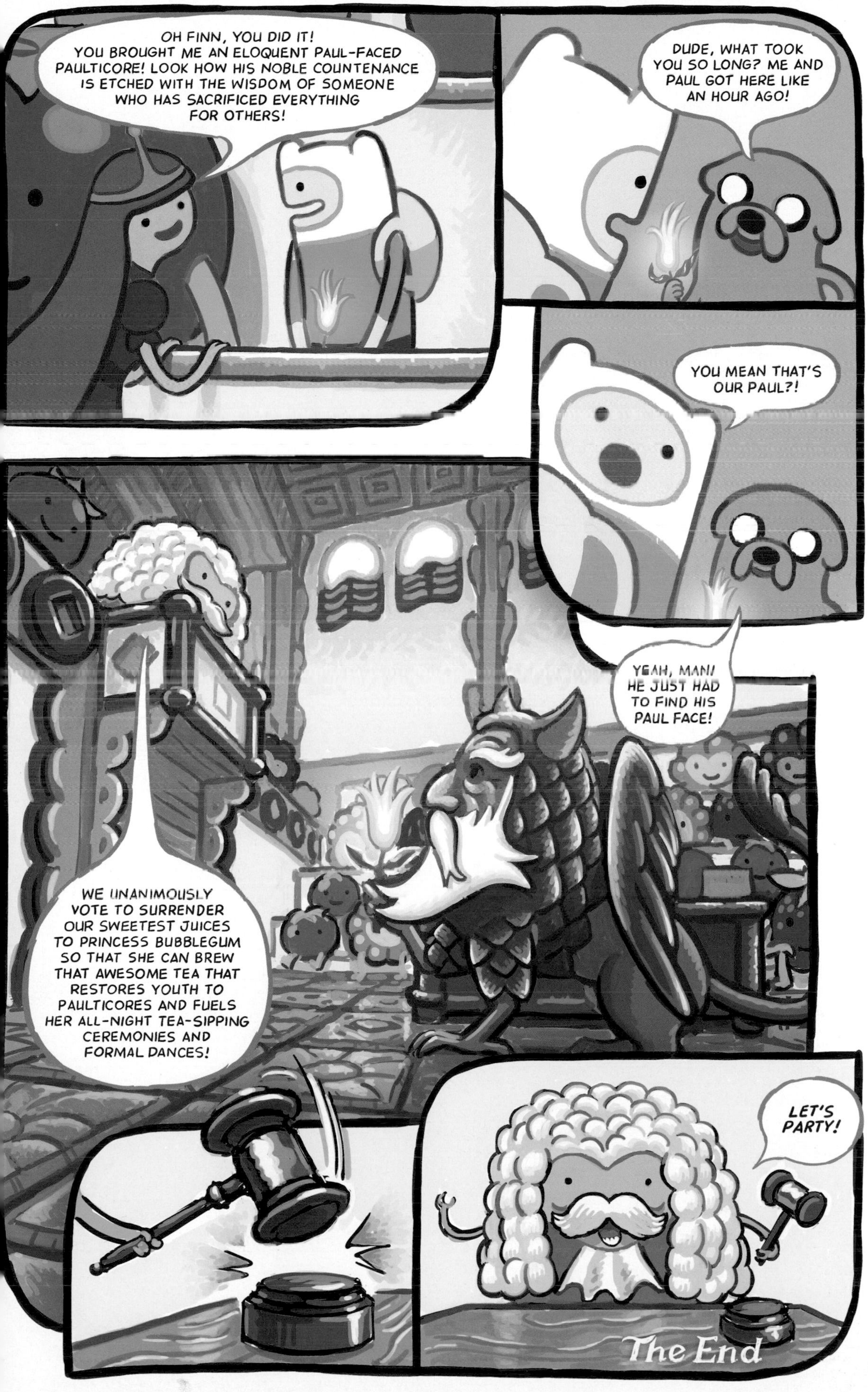
OH FINN, YOU DID IT! YOU BROUGHT ME AN ELOQUENT PAUL-FACED PAULTICORE! LOOK HOW HIS NOBLE COUNTENANCE IS ETCHED WITH THE WISDOM OF SOMEONE WHO HAS SACRIFICED EVERYTHING FOR OTHERS!
DUDE, WHAT TOOK YOU SO LONG? ME AND PAUL GOT HERE LIKE AN HOUR AGO!
YOU MEAN THAT'S OUR PAUL?!
YEAH, MAN! HE JUST HAD TO FIND HIS PAUL FACE!
WE UNANIMOUSLY VOTE TO SURRENDER OUR SWEETEST JUICES TO PRINCESS BUBBLEGUM SO THAT SHE CAN BREW THAT AWESOME TEA THAT RESTORES YOUTH TO PAULTICORES AND FUELS HER ALL-NIGHT TEA-SIPPING CEREMONIES AND FORMAL DANCES!
LET'S PARTY!
The End

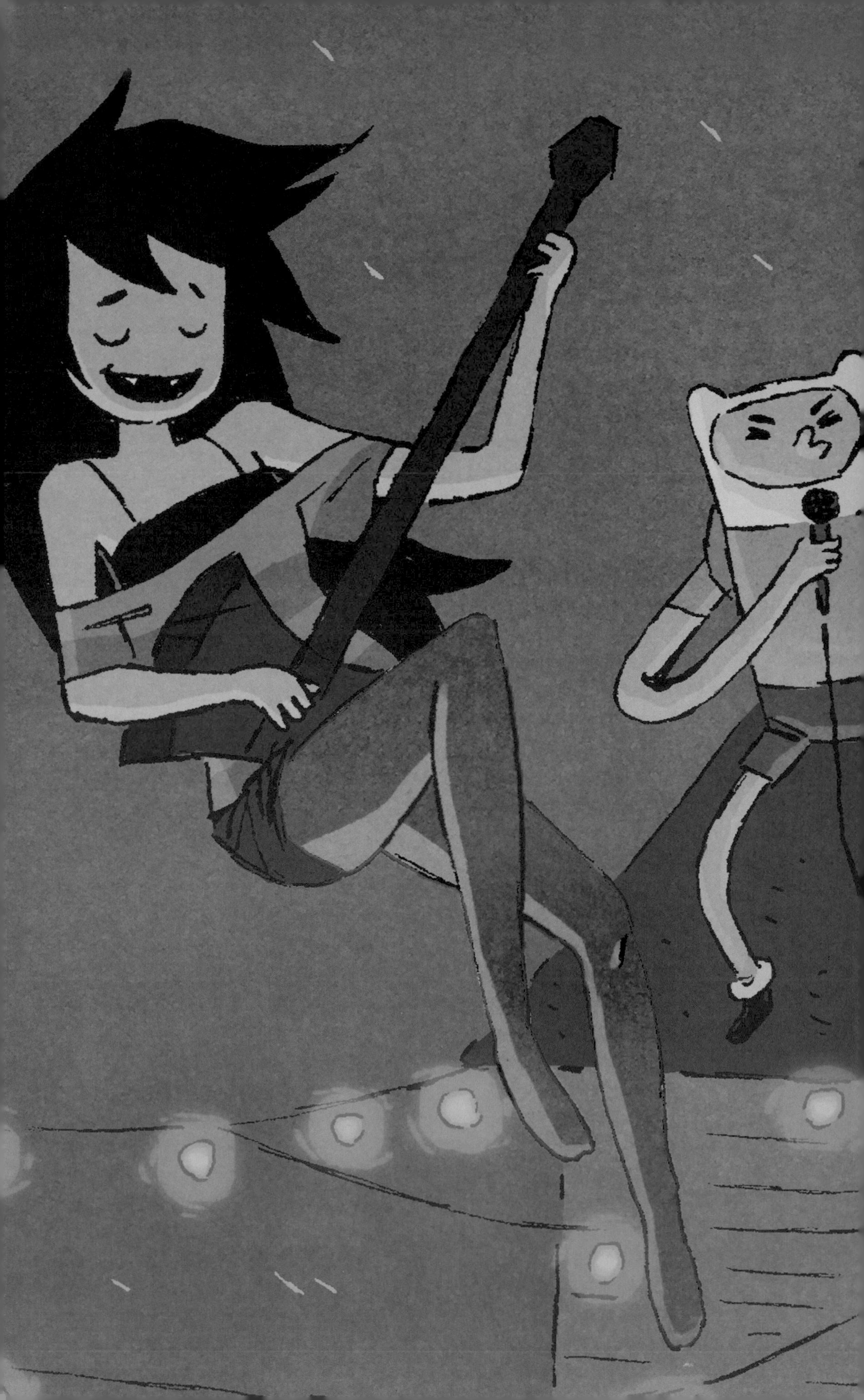

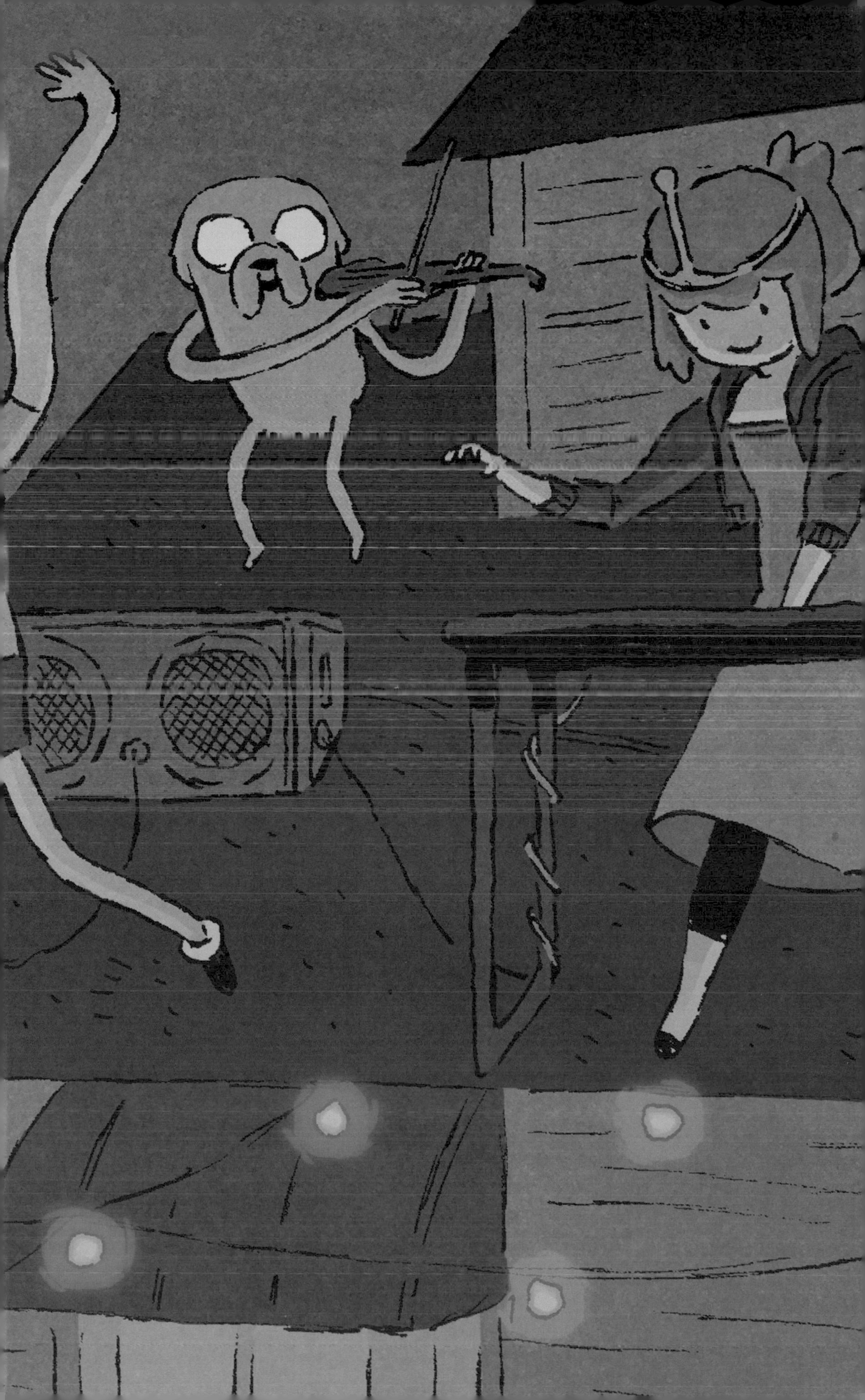

DISCOVER
EXPLOSIVE NEW WORLDS

Adventure Time
Pendleton Ward and Others
Volume 1
ISBN: 978-1-60886-280-1 | $14.99 US
Volume 2
ISBN: 978-1-60886-323-5 | $14.99 US
Adventure Time: Islands
ISBN: 978-1-60886-972-5 | $9.99 US

The Amazing World of Gumball
Ben Bocquelet and Others
Volume 1
ISBN: 978-1-60886-488-1 | $14.99 US
Volume 2
ISBN: 978-1-60886-793-6 | $14.99 US

Brave Chef Brianna
Sam Sykes, Selina Espiritu
ISBN: 978-1-68415-050-2 | $14.99 US

Mega Princess
Kelly Thompson, Brianne Drouhard
ISBN: 978-1-68415-007-6 | $14.99 US

The Not-So Secret Society
Matthew Daley, Arlene Daley,
Wook Jin Clark
ISBN: 978-1-60886-997-8 | $9.99 US

Over the Garden Wall
Patrick McHale, Jim Campbell
and Others
Volume 1
ISBN: 978-1-60886-940-4 | $14.99 US
Volume 2
ISBN: 978-1-68415-006-9 | $14.99 US

Steven Universe
Rebecca Sugar and Others
Volume 1
ISBN: 978-1-60886-706-6 | $14.99 US
Volume 2
ISBN: 978-1-60886-796-7 | $14.99 US

Steven Universe & The Crystal Gems
ISBN: 978-1-60886-921-3 | $14.99 US

Steven Universe: Too Cool for School
ISBN: 978-1-60886-771-4 | $14.99 US

AVAILABLE AT YOUR LOCAL COMICS SHOP AND BOOKSTORE
To find a comics shop in your area, call 1-888-266-4226
WWW.**BOOM-STUDIOS**.COM